Mistletoe
Magic

Books by Fern Michaels

Fearless
Spirit of the Season
Deep Harbor
Fate & Fortune
Sweet Vengeance
Holly and Ivy
Fancy Dancer
No Safe Secret
Wishes for Christmas
About Face
Perfect Match
A Family Affair
Forget Me Not
The Blossom Sisters
Balancing Act
Tuesday's Child
Betrayal
Southern Comfort
To Taste the Wine
Sins of the Flesh
Sins of Omission
Return to Sender
Mr. and Miss Anonymous
Up Close and Personal
Fool Me Once
Picture Perfect
The Future Scrolls
Kentucky Sunrise
Kentucky Heat
Kentucky Rich
Plain Jane
Charming Lily
What You Wish For
The Guest List
Listen to Your Heart

Celebration
Yesterday
Finders Keepers
Annie's Rainbow
Sara's Song
Vegas Sunrise
Vegas Heat
Vegas Rich
Whitefire
Wish List
Dear Emily
Christmas at Timberwoods

The Sisterhood Novels:

Crash and Burn
Point Blank
In Plain Sight
Eyes Only
Kiss and Tell
Blindsided
Gotcha!
Home Free
Déjà Vu
Cross Roads
Game Over
Deadly Deals
Vanishing Act
Razor Sharp
Under the Radar
Final Justice
Collateral Damage
Fast Track
Hokus Pokus
Hide and Seek

Books by Fern Michaels (Continued)

Free Fall
Lethal Justice
Sweet Revenge
The Jury
Vendetta
Payback
Weekend Warriors

The Men of the Sisterhood Novels:

High Stakes
Fast and Loose
Double Down

The Godmothers Series:

Getaway (E-Novella Exclusive)
Spirited Away (E-Novella Exclusive)
Hideaway (E-Novella Exclusive)
Classified
Breaking News
Deadline
Late Edition
Exclusive
The Scoop

E-Book Exclusives:

Desperate Measures
Seasons of Her Life

To Have and to Hold
Serendipity
Captive Innocence
Captive Embraces
Captive Passions
Captive Secrets
Captive Splendors
Cinders to Satin
For All Their Lives
Texas Heat
Texas Rich
Texas Fury
Texas Sunrise

Anthologies:

Winter Wishes
The Most Wonderful Time
When the Snow Falls
Secret Santa
A Winter Wonderland
I'll Be Home for Christmas
Making Spirits Bright
Holiday Magic
Snow Angels
Silver Bells
Comfort and Joy
Sugar and Spice
Let It Snow
A Gift of Joy
Five Golden Rings
Deck the Halls
Jingle All the Way

Published by Kensington Publishing Corp.

FERN MICHAELS

Mistletoe Magic

ZEBRA BOOKS
Kensington Publishing Corp.
www.kensingtonbooks.com

ZEBRA BOOKS are published by

Kensington Publishing Corp.
119 West 40th Street
New York, NY 10018

All Kensington titles, imprints, and distributed lines are available at special quantity discounts for bulk purchases for sales promotion, premiums, fund-raising, educational, or institutional use.

Special book excerpts or customized printings can also be created to fit specific needs. For details, write or phone the office of the Kensington Sales Manager: Attn.: Sales Department. Kensington Publishing Corp., 119 West 40th Street, New York, NY 10018. Phone: 1-800-221-2647.

Zebra and the Z logo Reg. U.S. Pat. & TM Off.

First Zebra Books Trade Paperback Printing: November 2017
First Zebra Books Mass-Market Paperback Printing: December 2020
ISBN-13: 978-1-4201-4852-7
ISBN-10: 1-4201-4852-4

ISBN-13: 978-1-4201-4683-7 (eBook)
ISBN-10: 1-4201-4683-1 (eBook)

10 9 8 7 6 5 4 3 2 1

Printed in the United States of America

Contents

Making Spirits Bright

Chapter 1

Placerville, Colorado
November 2011

Melanie McLaughlin positioned her cursor on the send icon, double-clicked, and waited for the window telling her that her mail had been sent to pop up. She signed off her e-mail account, then moved her mouse to exit the complicated graphics program she'd helped design last year. It was her biggest job to date, and she was happy to be finished. She didn't want to work during the upcoming Christmas season. Fortunately, she was her own boss, so she made the rules. She just wanted to enjoy the holidays without any professional commitments, no last-minute all-night projects to finish. She'd worked diligently through the Thanksgiving holiday to make sure her schedule was completely cleared until after the new year.

She'd promised Stephanie Marshall, her best friend, that she'd watch her girls, Amanda and Ashley, today, so that Stephanie and her fiancé, Edward Patrick Joseph O'Brien, "Patrick" to his friends, could spend Black Friday Christmas shopping. She thought it very courageous of the couple to tackle the crowds. Melanie had promised the girls she would take them skiing at Maximum Glide, then they would come back to her condo, where they would spend the afternoon learning to knit.

Melanie had been an avid knitter since junior high, long before it was fashionable. Both girls were eager to learn, telling her they wanted to learn to knit so they could give their mother handmade Christmas gifts. Melanie smiled, remembering the first scarf she'd made for her own mother. Uneven stitches and a horrid fluorescent orange; her mother had been delighted with her gift. She'd kept the scarf packed in a shoe box in the back of her closet all these years. For safekeeping, her mother'd said. Personally, Melanie thought her mother kept it out of sight to prevent temporary blindness to those unfortunate few who'd been forced to *admire* her handiwork. At the time, Melanie had reasoned the color would stand out on the slopes, her mother easily spotted in case of an emergency.

She'd made sure to purchase plenty of red and green yarn for the girls' first project, a pot holder. No way would she subject Stephanie to such a horrific color as her mother's!

She pushed the POWER button to turn off her computer. For the entire month of December and what was left of November, she vowed not to turn it back on unless it was a dire emergency. That didn't mean she couldn't check her e-mail. She'd just do it from her cell phone.

Melanie rolled her chair away from the desk and almost ran over Odie, her three-year-old boxer. "Hey, bud, don't sneak up on me like that. You're liable to give me a heart attack."

"Woof, woof!" Odie stood up on all four paws, his shiny brown eyes beseeching her not to leave him behind.

She gave him a quick scratch between the ears. "You're a lucky boy today. I promised Candy Lee I'd let her dog-sit, so there." Candy Lee, a high school student who worked part-time at The Snow Zone ski shop was a die-hard animal lover. Melanie brought Odie to the store whenever she knew Candy Lee was working. Today would be crazy busy, but Melanie knew there were three staff members on loan from their ski-lift positions to assist Candy Lee since both Stephanie and Patrick had taken the day off.

An ear-piercing meow directed her attention to her newly adopted cat, Clovis. He had a rich butterscotch coat and giant jade-colored eyes, which were staring at her to demand her attention. Another ear-splitting meow. She reached down and scooped up the giant ball of fur. "I guess this means you want to come, too?" Another meow, and two quick slaps from his bushy tail, and Melanie knew she couldn't leave Clovis alone.

Weighing in at twenty-seven pounds when she'd spied him at the local animal shelter, he'd caught her attention two months ago when, on a whim, she decided Odie needed a pal. Though her intent was to adopt another dog, Clovis had glowered at her from his cage as she'd walked through the shelter. She'd heard his manlike meow, and decided a cat would be a perfect companion for Odie, who was docile and lived for belly rubs and the occasional bit of rare steak. A cat would be perfect given the boxer's disposition.

When she'd taken the husky feline out of his cage,

he'd licked her face just like a dog. He'd captured her heart on the spot. The dog and cat had taken to each other like jelly to peanut butter.

She rubbed her nose against Clovis's before placing him on top of her desk. "Let me load up the ski equipment, guys," Melanie said, sure both animals understood her.

Odie dropped down on his haunches, and Clovis perched upright as though saying, "Okay, but speed it up."

She made fast work of getting her skis, poles, boots, and helmet from the front closet. She grabbed a tote that held her ski pants and all the miscellaneous gear one needed when skiing. She peered inside the bag just to make sure she had a full bottle of sunscreen. The morning sun blazed like a giant lemon in the powder blue sky. Given that and the blustering winds, sun- and windburn was a sure thing without proper protection.

That day, Melanie was thankful her condo had its own private garage. The temps were supposed to be in the low teens. Her Lincoln Navigator took forever to warm up when left outside. After stuffing her equipment in the back, she tossed her tote on the front passenger seat.

She made three trips to the condo and back to the Navigator before she had all her supplies. Since she was bringing Odie and Clovis to The Snow Zone, she'd brought their beds just in case Candy Lee needed them out of the way. Odie didn't like being shifted to the small office at the back of the store. Melanie was sure he understood the difference between the rows of sweaters and ski coats and the actual ski equipment. She'd often commented to Stephanie that if she were ever in a pinch, Odie was sure to be a great assistant. Neither animal liked being relegated to the back office, yet they seemed to make the best of their situation. Both animals got along famously. So far, they'd remained in the office without any signs of mass destruction.

Once they were all secured properly in their seats, Melanie made the short drive to Stephanie's little ranch house in Placerville. She grinned at the memory of last year's Christmas. She had purchased the little ranch home for Stephanie and the girls. She'd placed the deed and the rest of the paperwork that goes along with purchasing a house in a plain envelope as though its contents were unknown to her. Stephanie still told anyone who would listen what a grand gesture Melanie had performed.

Melanie had inherited millions when her grandmother died. Her parents had bought real estate when the market was hopping, before she was born, and they, too, weren't lacking in the financial department. This made their lives and that of many others better. Her mother always told her you get back what you give, tenfold, and it wasn't necessarily a monetary return. Melanie tried to practice on a daily basis what her mother preached. So far, she'd never been disappointed.

Melanie had come to love Stephanie like the sister she'd always dreamed of having. Adding her two adorable daughters, Ashley and Amanda, they completed the rest of the family she didn't have. Settling the three of them into a home of their own was the least she could do given all they'd been through. Married to an abusive husband, Stephanie had found Hope House for her and the girls. The secret shelter was for battered women and their families. Melanie's mother had long been a financial supporter of Hope House. It was there that Melanie found Stephanie and her girls. Grace Landry, the founder and a therapist, had taken the family of three under her wing and given them their first real chance for a normal life. The little garage apartment Grace had secured for them was owned by Melanie's parents. Melanie lived right down the road. And, as they say, the rest is history.

Melanie adjusted the heater controls on the dash, then stretched her arm over the seat to reach for a large blanket, which she placed over Odie and Clovis. Both readjusted their positions, allowing the blanket to drape comfortably around them.

She smiled from ear to ear as she engaged the four-wheel drive and skillfully maneuvered the steep winding road leading to Stephanie's. Careful not to slide off the side of the mountain, Melanie safely pulled into Stephanie's freshly shoveled driveway ten minutes later.

Patrick. It was his new mission in life to take care of Stephanie's every need, no matter how great or small. And the girls had him so tightly wrapped around their little fingers, their wish was his command even before they asked. Patrick of all men. A confirmed bachelor, he'd always intended to remain single. And then Stephanie Marshall entered the picture. Though they'd had a few rough patches, anyone who saw them together knew they were madly in love.

One evening after Stephanie had invited them all over for dinner, making her specialty, three-cheese manicotti and her famous homemade garlic-knot rolls, Melanie, Grace, and her husband, Max Jorgenson, who brought their new baby daughter Ella, listened intently as Patrick told them about Shannon, his niece. She had died of an extremely rare blood disorder on the day she was supposed to graduate from high school. Suddenly, Melanie had understood his fear of getting close to Stephanie and the girls too soon. He was afraid of being hurt all over again.

But Patrick, being a truly decent guy, had taken another look at Stephanie and her girls. And just as his best bud Max Jorgenson, famous Olympic Gold Medalist skier, had proposed to Grace, Patrick asked Stephanie to marry him. On New Year's Day, they were planning to take their vows at the top of the slopes and, together, as man and wife, they'd ski down Gracie's Way, and at the bottom of the run, all would celebrate the much-anticipated union of the couple.

Melanie hopped out of the Navigator, stomping her tan colored Uggs on the cleared pavement. "You two sit tight. I'll be right back," she called out to her menagerie. She hurried up the short steps to the front porch, where she grabbed the doorknob, only to have it slip from her grasp before she even had a chance to twist it.

"Auntie M, Auntie M, are you really taking us skiing today? Are we still gonna go back to your house and learn how to . . ."

"Shhh, Amanda. We're not supposed to tell, remember?" Ashley chastised her little sister.

Stephanie chose that moment to join them at the front door. "Seems like I almost overheard a secret."

Amanda and Ashley looked away, not meeting their

mother's stern look. Melanie broke in before the girls revealed their afternoon plans. "I'm teaching the girls a new skill. We're just not telling what it is," Melanie said.

"Good. I don't know what I'd do if you were to . . . to . . . do something like you did last year."

They all broke out in laughter, even the girls. Melanie tossed her long blond braid over her shoulder. "I don't think I'll be able to top that gift, at least not for a while. At the rate you're all going, I'll be a hundred and six before you stop ragging me about that."

"It is the best, Mel. Have you seen the bathroom since I painted? Patrick installed granite counters, and it's just absolutely to die for, not that it wasn't in the first place, but this just feels so . . . elegant. Come on and have a look-see."

"As much as I would love to, Odie and Clovis are waiting in the Navigator. They're staying with Candy Lee while the girls and I ski. I hope that's not a problem."

"Of course not. Candy Lee says Odie directs the customers to the ski equipment. Tell Candy Lee if Odie keeps this up, her job might be in danger."

"Mom!" Amanda shouted. "She needs this job. She's saving up for college."

Stephanie took her younger daughter in her arms. "Oh, sweetie, we're teasing. Candy Lee has a job forever if she wants."

Melanie knew the girls were a bit on the sensitive side. They'd seen so much violence from their father that, oftentimes, when the girls thought they or someone else was being wrongly disciplined or spoken to in a harsh manner, they spoke up for themselves and others. Melanie knew Stephanie was pleased with this, but didn't want them to take every word she said quite so literally.

"I would bet my last nickel Candy Lee gets that soccer scholarship she's applying for. She's a straight-A student and a killer soccer player," Melanie stated.

"How come you know all this, Auntie M?"

Melanie observed Stephanie as she lowered herself by her daughters and placed a hand on each of their pink-and-purple padded ski jackets. "It's not always polite to ask questions about situations that don't concern us. I'm sure Candy Lee will manage to get to college, so let's leave it at that. Now, Clovis and Odie are probably freezing their fur off in the Navigator. You two grab your bags, and I'll take care of your skis and poles." Stephanie looked at Melanie. "Keeping up with them wears me out sometimes, but it's the best worn-out you'll ever experience."

Melanie squinted her eyes and scrunched up her nose. "As Mom keeps reminding me, I don't have a man in my life, no children, and I just don't see either one happening anytime in the near future. At the rate I'm going, I'll be lucky to adopt another animal from the shelter, so I'll just take your word even though the time I spend with the girls is the best ever." She teared up at the thought of not having the two little sprites in her life. She was content to remain Auntie M.

For now.

With Odie and Clovis relegated to the rear cargo area and both girls safely ensconced in their seat belts, Melanie glanced in her rearview mirror one last time, making sure they all were where they should be. She recalled the last time she'd taken the girls skiing. They'd wound up lost in a snowstorm and had delivered a litter of pups. Now she could smile at the memory. Grateful that Stephanie still allowed her within pitching distance of the girls, she shrugged her thoughts aside, focusing on their plans for the day.

Black Friday was usually one of Maximum Glide's busiest days. Melanie dreaded the crowds, the long lines at the chairlifts, but spending the day with the girls was worth the hassle. Both girls were excellent skiers. Max, Grace's husband, had taught the girls how to ski properly. Black diamond runs were easy for both, but Melanie wasn't that comfortable with them, so they'd tackle the blue runs.

She steered the Navigator carefully down the narrow road, mindful of the wet slushy conditions. Growing up in Colorado had its advantages. She'd learned to drive in foul weather at an early age, and while she wasn't excited at the prospect of driving up the mountain in such bad conditions, she was quite confident in her ability to do so safely. Snow chains and four-wheel-drive vehicles had nothing on her.

"Auntie M," Ashley called from the backseat. "Do you think you'll ever get married?"

Melanie almost lost control of the Navigator. She cleared her throat, needing the extra seconds to come up with an answer appropriate for an eleven-year-old. "I'm sure that someday I will." *Lame, Melanie, lame,* she thought as she glanced in her rearview mirror. Ashley wasn't buying it; Melanie could tell by the look on her face.

"That's not an answer! You sound just like Mom. 'Maybe' and 'someday' aren't real answers," Ashley stated in that clear and concise matter-of-fact way eleven-year-olds have.

Melanie chuckled. Ashley was right. "Truthfully, I don't know when or if I'll ever get married because I haven't dated anyone long enough to fall in love, so marriage hasn't been my number one priority."

"What's a priority?" Amanda asked.

"It means something that is very important, right Auntie M?" Ashley replied.

"Yes, that's exactly what it means. And right now my top *priority* is to arrive safely at The Snow Zone so we can drop Clovis and Odie off. I need to focus my attention on the road. It's incredibly slick."

Again, Melanie glanced in her rearview mirror. Ashley rolled her eyes.

"That means we're not supposed to ask any more questions about Aunt Melanie's personal life."

"Why?" Amanda asked.

With her engagement to Patrick, Stephanie talked about marriage constantly. It seemed the girls had acquired an avid interest in the topic as well.

Melanie wanted to tell the girls it was okay with her to ask such questions, just not while she was driving on an icy road, but this was Stephanie's rule, and she would respect that.

"You ask too many questions," Ashley informed her little sister. "Doesn't she?"

Melanie peeped in her rearview mirror again. "It's okay, Ash. All little girls like to ask questions."

"Mom says Amanda talks too much, but I would really like to know if you plan on getting married sometime in the future, because Krissy Haygood—she's a girl in my class—all she talks about is her big sister getting married this summer. She's the maid of honor and said it was highly unusual for someone her age to act as maid of honor, and, well, I sort of thought if you were to get married, or think about it, maybe I could . . . you know, be your maid of honor."

For once, Melanie was at a loss for words. She never remembered having such desires or thoughts when she was eleven, but times were different, kids matured earlier nowadays. She took a deep breath, fearing she was about to put her foot in her mouth, but decided if she did get married, there would be absolutely no reason that Ashley couldn't act as her maid of honor.

"When I get married, I promise to ask you to be my maid of honor."

Chapter 2

Melanie wrapped a thick towel around her wet hair, swooped her old worn-out yellow terry-cloth robe off the hook on the back of the bathroom door, slipped her arms inside, then secured the belt around her waist. She hurried to the kitchen just in time to hear the microwave's bell ding.

After spending the morning skiing, and the afternoon instructing the girls how to make a slip knot to cast on, Melanie was pleasantly worn out. Too tired to make a proper dinner, she'd popped in a microwave meal while she showered. Clovis and Odie were curled together beneath the kitchen table, waiting. She smiled at the sight.

"I know you two had more than your share of treats today, so what is it?" Melanie asked as she removed her lasagna from the microwave, placing the black plastic container on a dinner plate.

Odie yawned, and Clovis gave her his "don't-mess-with-me" look. Sure that Clovis had been an emperor in another life, Melanie turned around and gave the feline a quick bow. She did a double take when Clovis nodded his furry head, then reclined against Odie's belly. *He really does think he's an emperor.*

I am definitely spending too much time alone.

This reminded her of Ashley's earlier question. Would she ever marry? Have children of her own? She certainly didn't have any prospects, but that was her own doing. Since she'd started working from her home, she'd devoted most of her spare time to caring for her pets and to Stephanie's little family. She loved the excitement on the girls' faces when she surprised them with a visit or an unexpected treat. She often wished for a family, a child of her own, but knew until she met the man of her dreams, it was not to be. She was still young, still had enough time to pick and choose the right man. Thing was, the man supply had grown very slim since college. Most of the guys she'd met and dated in college were married with families of their own, and those who weren't already taken were not her type. Whatever that was.

So, she thought as she grabbed a can of soda from the refrigerator, *what exactly* is *my type?*

Tall, dark, and handsome? No.

Sensitive and shy? No.

Alpha male? Definitely a no.

She took a drink of soda. After several seconds' contemplation, Melanie decided she didn't have a type. She'd dated winners, a few losers, but none that knocked her socks off or made her feel like "he's the one." Nope. *Nada.* So, that left room for all those guys out there who were just waiting to beat her door down. Zero in that department, too.

For a young, well-to-do woman, she wasn't doing all that well. Yes, she had a condo to die for here in Placerville, another in Telluride that she kept rented for most of the ski season, and she was considering buying a house with a big yard, a white picket fence, the whole nine yards. She'd put that big purchase off, telling herself she didn't need that much space. Her condo in Placerville was perfect for her. She scanned the kitchen. While not as large as her condo's kitchen in Telluride, it was decent. Large enough for a table for six, an oak butcher-block island in its center, Sub-Zero refrigerator, a top-of-the-line Wolf stove and oven, all stainless steel. She'd softened the sterile look with cheery yellow accent pieces: canisters, local pottery, yellow and red Fiestaware, accentuated by cherry red place mats and matching curtains she'd had custom-made.

She'd chosen pale pinks and cream for the master bedroom, and a neutral gray and maroon for the guest bedroom. Both bathrooms had Jacuzzi tubs and walk-in showers large enough for two. The living room needed some color; she'd just never gotten around to finishing the decorating. Two beige sofas with a matching love seat and two overstuffed chairs filled the room. A fireplace on the main wall had been used only once since she'd bought the place, but Melanie told herself it was too much of a hassle, since she spent most of her time in the third bedroom she used for her office. She had a gas fireplace there, and, when needed, all she had to do was flick a switch and boom, within minutes, the room was as toasty as a wood fire. She did miss the smell of wood smoke, but figured the lack of a mess was worth the sacrifice.

She finished her lasagna, rinsed the plate, and placed it next to the others in the dishwasher. Sometimes it took her more than a week to fill the dishwasher. *Sad,* she thought as she removed the box of Cascade from beneath the sink. She either needed to cook more, have company over more often, or acquire a big family. There it goes again! Why couldn't she stop thinking about a family of her own? Was she spending too much time with Amanda and Ashley? Was she subconsciously envious of Stephanie? Growing up an only child, she'd longed for a brother or sister. Melanie had been a change-of-life baby, much wanted, her mother always added, and she knew that to be true, but she had also known that the chances of her acquiring a sibling were slim to none.

She wondered why her parents hadn't adopted another child. They were certainly financially able, they'd both been in good health and still were. Maybe it was a blood-is-thicker-than-water kinda thing. No, no! Her parents weren't like that. They would have welcomed another child. Maybe they'd never considered it. Whatever, she told herself, it didn't matter now as she was a grown woman. She knew that her parents were counting on her to provide them with a houseful of grandchildren to spoil someday. She hoped they weren't holding their breaths.

Rolling her eyes at the path her thoughts were traveling, Melanie grabbed a damp cloth, swiped it over the countertops, then washed and refilled Odie's and Clovis's water dishes. She folded the dishcloth in half, placed it on the counter, and grabbed another soda from the refrigerator.

Odie emitted a low growl, which was followed by a

junglelike meow from Clovis. "Come on, you two, it's time to call it a day." She said this every night to the pair of mismatched animals. Like clockwork, they wiggled out from under the kitchen table and followed her to her office.

She'd promised herself she wasn't going to work the rest of the holiday season, said she wasn't going to turn her computer on until the year had ended, but she hadn't voiced the promise out loud, so that was okay. As long as she hadn't verbalized the commitment to anyone else, she wasn't really worried about being accountable to anyone for breaking her promise, something she normally wouldn't do. Without another thought, Melanie went to her desk, clicked on the lamp, then hit the ON button to her high-end Titanus computer. A slight hum from the machine was the only sound in the room. Odie and Clovis had found their favorite spot by the fireplace. There wasn't anything or anyone to prevent her from doing what she was about to do.

She logged on to the Internet, typed Google into her browser, then typed three words and hit SEARCH.

Adoption in Colorado.

Her heart raced, and her stomach fluttered as though a thousand butterflies were dancing inside her. So many Web sites appeared, Melanie was sure she'd misspelled something. She typed the words a second time, this time watching her hands as they moved across her keyboard.

A-d-o-p-t-i-o-n-I-n–C-o-l-o-r-a-d-o. She hit the SEARCH icon.

Again, hundreds and hundreds of Web sites appeared on her screen.

"Okayyy, I can do this," she said out loud.

Melanie clicked on the first blue hyperlink at the top of

her screen. She scanned the Web site, knew she didn't want to travel across the globe to China, and clicked on the second link. She perused the contents, then moved on to the next site.

After two hours of reading about Colorado's many adoption agencies, Melanie leaned back in her chair and twisted her stiff neck from left to right, her mind wondering at all the possibilities she'd just examined.

Is it possible?

She thought of all the tabloids she'd scanned while in line at the supermarket. It seemed just about every superstar in Hollywood was adopting a child. Many of them were single. If they could do this, why couldn't she? She was financially able to provide for a child, and she certainly had lots of love to give. Her parents would be surprised at first, but Melanie knew that once they got used to the idea, they would be as thrilled as she was beginning to feel.

Yes! She could do this! She *would* do this. First thing tomorrow morning, she was going to call World Adoption Agency in Denver, a local orphanage. Out of all the Web sites, this one held the most appeal. Children of every age, every race, some with health issues, some with emotional troubles, resided at the state-funded home. Yes, this would offer her a wide selection of children from around the world. Sex or age didn't matter to her. Melanie sensed she would know exactly which child she would adopt when the time came.

Chapter 3

At one minute past eight, Melanie dialed the number for World Adoption Agency. They opened at 8:00 A.M. according to their Web site and were open on Saturdays. It was meant to be, she figured, because it was Saturday, and she had absolutely nothing planned.

She wasn't going to waste another minute worrying about the timing of her phone call. Her mother always told her the early bird catches the worm. She'd been unable to sleep last night as thoughts of adopting a child filled her brain. Finally, around four in the morning, she'd given up all hope of sleeping, took a long, hot shower, and dressed in her old denim jeans and her favorite University of Colorado sweatshirt. She'd taken Odie for a short walk throughout the complex.

Impatient now that she'd decided to act on what she

thought of as her newly budding motherly instinct, she didn't bother with the greenway behind the condos. Odie knew something was awry when she rushed him through his morning routine. He barked as though he were asking what did she think she was doing, then dropped his head to his chest.

"I promise we'll take an extra-long walk later," she told him. That had seemed to cheer the boxer up.

Back inside, Melanie made bacon and eggs for breakfast, giving half to Clovis and Odie. After she cleaned up, she stripped the sheets from her bed, tossed them in the washing machine, and mopped the kitchen floor. When she couldn't find anything else to distract her, she'd taken Amanda and Ashley's knitting needles from the baskets she'd given them. She removed several knots, rewound yarn, then tucked the beginner's instruction booklets neatly beside the balls of red and green yarn. On the verge of climbing the walls, Melanie brewed another pot of coffee and sat at the kitchen table watching as the hands on the clock turned more slowly than they ever had. Or so it seemed.

Just what I need—more caffeine. As if I'm not wound up enough.

And now that she had made the call, all she heard on the other end of the phone was an answering machine asking her to please leave her name and number, and they would return her call as soon as it was convenient. How dare they do this to her!

Melanie wanted to scream. This was ridiculous. There are hundreds of children just waiting for a home, and she's told to wait! Maybe she'd picked the wrong agency. If she owned such a business, if one even wanted to call an orphanage a business, she would make sure she never missed an opportunity to place a child. Deciding she would search for another agency, Melanie practically ran to her office.

The ringing telephone stopped her dead in her tracks.

The kitchen or the office? She was in the middle. The kitchen. She raced the few feet back to the kitchen, and grabbed the phone. Exhaling, she spoke into the receiver. "Hello?"

A heavily accented voice said, "I am returning your phone call."

Without asking, Melanie knew this was the adoption agency.

"Uh, yes, I called. I wanted to . . . I was thinking of adopting—"

"Madam, that is why most people call us."

Madam?

"Oh, well, of course." Now that she had the agency on the phone, she was suddenly at a loss for words.

"Miss," the woman with the accent said. "I am a very busy woman. You called the agency, I am to assume that there was a reason."

It took Melanie a second to recover. "Yes, I would like to know what the procedure is for adopting a child."

There, she'd said it; she couldn't take it back now!

Melanie heard the woman's sharp intake of breath. "This is not the way we practice. You must schedule an appointment with the office first. If we decide to consider your application, then you will be given the proper instructions."

Melanie visualized the woman on the phone. Tall, stern, with waist-length hair pulled back in a tight bun. She thought of the children in her care. She decided to act quickly.

"Then I would like to make an appointment as soon as possible."

Another deep sigh, then the fluttering of paper. Melanie wondered if the woman was actually looking at an old-fashioned appointment book. Had computers not made their way to the adoption agency?

"You are in luck," the woman said. "We have an opening in the morning on Monday. Nine o'clock sharp. We do not tolerate tardiness."

Melanie's eyes practically bulged out of their sockets. She couldn't believe the way the woman spoke to her. She wasn't a two-year-old. She wanted to tell her that, but bit her tongue. Now wasn't the time to be a smart aleck. Briefly, she had the passing thought—if she was so punctual, why didn't she answer the phone at *eight o'clock sharp*?

"Of course not. I will be there promptly at nine."

"Of course you will," the woman admonished. "I will need some information from you first."

Melanie was on the phone for the next few minutes, giving the woman, who hadn't bothered to give her name, all the pertinent information one would need to run for president of the United States. When she hung up, it took a couple of minutes for Melanie to reacquaint herself with her surroundings. She was home in Placerville, in her kitchen. Images of prison camps kept flashing before her eyes. Those poor children!

The woman reminded her of a female version of Scrooge. Wired from too much caffeine, Melanie decided it was a good time to take Odie for that promised extra-long walk. The cold morning air would clear her head, plus she could burn off all her excess energy.

"Odie, let's go take that walk I promised you," she said as she grabbed her jacket from the front closet and removed his leash from a hook on the back of the front door. Upon hearing his name, Odie came running from his spot underneath the kitchen table before sliding to a stop in order for her to attach the leash to his collar. When all was in order, he jumped in circles, practically dragging her out the front door. Clovis remained perched on the windowsill in the living room, his nose in the air, apparently content to watch.

Melanie pushed the door aside and was greeted by an icy gust of frosty air. She drew in a sharp breath. It was much colder than yesterday. Even colder than it had been a few hours ago. Single-digit temperatures were predicted for the day's high.

The condo's greenway provided twelve miles of biking trails and hiking paths to satisfy all of the residents living at Pine Ridge Condominiums. As Melanie carefully wound her way down the main trail, she saw that the picnic tables were covered with a thin sheet of ice, and the dog pond that Odie loved to visit in the summer months was completely frozen over.

Once inside the off-leash area, Melanie unhooked Odie's leash, and he ran freely. Often they would see coyotes and the occasional fox, and Odie would go berserk upon catching their scent. Apparently the cold weather hadn't kept the wild animals away from the area, because Odie had his nose to the frozen ground, sniffing ninety miles a minute.

Melanie allowed Odie a few more minutes to do his business before calling to him. "Okay, bud, let's take that walk I promised." The dog would've been content to stay in the off-leash area, but Melanie knew from experience that if she let him stay too long, it would take forever to guide him back to the hiking path.

Several inches of thick-crusted snow flanked the path leading to her preferred route. Expertly, Melanie and Odie ascended the icy mound leading to her favorite trail, where in the fall one could view a pumpkin farm along the hillside. Spring green vines dotted the mountain in late summer, after which the hillside became infused with varying shades of orange in the fall. It never failed to take her breath away. Even in the stark bareness of late fall, Melanie could appreciate the Colorado beauty. Tall pines scented the chilled air, and she detected a faint hint of wood smoke. Briefly, she had a flash of herself running through the pumpkin fields with two small children at her side.

Two?

Not wanting to get her hopes up, she'd tried to close her mind to this morning's earlier conversation with the woman from the adoption agency. The possibility of one child more than excited her, but two? She allowed herself to imagine her life with two children. If the opportunity arose, she wouldn't deny herself or the children. She'd taken care of Amanda and Ashley quite well if you excluded their getting lost on the mountain last year. The image cut off further thought. What if the woman from the adoption agency asked for a reference? What if Stephanie told the woman that she wasn't ready for a child of her own? What if . . . what if . . . what if? Melanie knew her life would be closely scrutinized, she'd learned that much on her Web search.

Could one innocent mistake ruin her future chances at adoption?

Resigned that she might have to give up her dream of adopting a child, Melanie led Odie toward the condo. Maybe she'd just call and cancel Monday's appointment.

Maybe.

No!

Melanie was not a quitter.

She'd cross that bridge Monday morning. Nine o'clock sharp.

Chapter 4

Melanie spent most of Sunday morning scrubbing her condo from top to bottom. With two animals in the house, she was constantly vacuuming and dusting. She planned to spend the day curled up with a book and a pot of tea. It was minus three, too cold to venture outdoors. She wanted to get to bed early. Rather than drive six hours to Denver the next morning, she'd hired a private jet to fly her there. She was meeting the pilot and copilot at 6:00 A.M. She'd arranged for a rental car to make the drive from the airport to the adoption agency. She'd scheduled her return flight for two forty-five, so she would be home by early evening.

She phoned her mother asking if she could stop over around lunchtime to let Odie out. As always, her mother was glad to help. When she'd asked why she was flying to Denver, Melanie had clammed up. She didn't want to tell anyone what her plans were just yet, but she didn't want to lie to her mother, so she explained that she was taking a personal day to do something she'd been planning on for a while. A generic answer, but it was all she could come up with. Her mother didn't pry, and, for that, she was glad.

Melanie located her briefcase in her office, then added most of the important documents she would need to prove she was who she said she was and a dozen other papers she might need. She added her passport, just in case. She wanted to be prepared. It wasn't like they were going to look at her bank statement, and say, "Pick a child." No, the adoption process was much more detailed than even she could imagine.

Mandatory legal criteria had to be met, plus each individual agency had its own criteria as well. Melanie was amazed at the amount of paperwork required, but something as important as adopting a child *should* take a lot of paperwork. Once her application was accepted, *if* it was accepted, then the lengthy process would begin. She wasn't in a mad rush, but she knew in her heart that it was right for her. Felt it in her bones. Patience was required, and she was a very patient woman. Melanie knew one of the first requirements would be a home study, and if she was lucky enough, she would be able to bring a child home, where she would then be allowed to help the child make the transition from the orphanage to the new home.

Odie and Clovis had positioned themselves beneath the kitchen table. Melanie removed the teakettle from the stovetop, filled it with tap water, then placed it back on the burner. She took three chamomile tea bags from a bright yellow canister on the counter and dropped them in the small china teapot given to her by her grandmother when she was a little girl. In order to keep the tea warm, Melanie placed a cosy, one she had knitted years ago, around the teapot.

Maybe when Amanda and Ashley finished their pot holders, she would teach them how to make tea cosies. She knew that Stephanie loved to drink tea and would appreciate such a gift from her girls.

Melanie's tea ritual was old-fashioned, but she loved it. Her grandmother had taught her the proper way to steep loose leaf tea, how to pour properly, and also how to hold a delicate teacup. Though she didn't practice this all the time, whenever she had company, or the occasion called for it, she returned to the ways taught by her grandmother. The kettle whistled, and Melanie filled the delicate china pot with boiling water. She placed the teapot along with a bright red mug on a tray and carried them into the living room. Odie and Clovis followed.

As soon as she settled herself on the sofa with her tea and favorite author, the telephone rang.

"Why did I know this would happen the minute I got comfortable?" Melanie asked her boon companions. As usual, Odie and Clovis answered her question by trailing behind her as she returned to the kitchen to answer the telephone.

"Hello," she said into the receiver.

"Oh good, you're there," Stephanie said.

Melanie smiled upon hearing her friend's voice. "What's up?"

"I wasn't sure I'd find you at home," Stephanie explained.

Melanie leaned against the island in the center of the kitchen. "Where else would I be?" She looked at the clock and realized she was usually in church at this time. Because of bad weather, Melanie had decided to stay home today. She said this to Stephanie.

"Same here. Patrick and I both took the weekend off. We wanted to take the girls skiing again, but it's really too cold. You're never going to believe who's coming to visit this afternoon."

"Why don't you tell me?" Melanie teased.

"Grace and Max are bringing baby Ella. The girls are so excited."

"Cool," Melanie said without much emotion. She'd just seen Grace, Max, and Ella a couple of weeks ago.

"Bryce is coming with them. Apparently, he's taking a month off from teaching, and he's planning to spend his time helping Grace and Max at Hope House," Stephanie said.

Melanie knew where this was leading. She had met Bryce, Grace's younger brother, a few times. He was a professor of history at the University of Colorado in Boulder. He was a couple of years older than she, and very easy on the eyes. With his raven black hair, and sea green eyes identical to his older sister's, Bryce Landry personified hunkiness if there was such a thing. If she'd met him without knowing his academic background, never in a million years would she have pegged him for a history professor. He looked more like the ski bums that hung out at the ski resorts. Melanie knew he was an avid skier; he'd been a big fan of Max's when he won the Olympic gold medal. Grace told Melanie how excited Bryce had been when he discovered his older sister was dating such a legend in the ski world.

"That's nice," was the only comment Melanie could come up with. She must sound like an idiot, she thought, as she eyed her pot of tea in the living room.

"I'm having an impromptu Christmas party this afternoon. Do you think you can make it? I know it's short notice," Stephanie added.

Melanie didn't really have any plans other than reading and getting ready for tomorrow's flight to Denver. Why not? Stephanie lived right down the road from her; it wasn't like she had to travel on I-70, which was treacherous during the winter months. It would take her mind off the adoption and help pass the time.

"Sounds like fun. What can I bring?" Melanie asked, looking around the kitchen for something to bring, a store-bought pie, anything that didn't require cooking or baking. Seeing nothing, she remembered she had a frozen black forest cake in the freezer, courtesy of a happy client.

"You don't have to bring anything, just yourself," Stephanie assured her.

Melanie would bring the cake anyway; she could not eat the entire chocolate concoction herself. It would take hours of skiing to burn off the calories. "I'd love to see the girls. What time are the festivities?"

"Anytime after noon," Stephanie said. "The girls are bursting with energy at the mere thought of a Christmas party," Stephanie continued. "We've never hosted a Christmas party, so I figured the earlier, the better. Amanda is already mixing the ingredients for sugar cookies. If the kitchen's a disaster when you get here, you'll know why."

Just thinking of the visual, Melanie grinned. Stephanie was very neat and tidy, yet when it came to Amanda and Ashley, she was more than willing to allow whatever made them happy. Both girls loved to tinker in the kitchen, just like their mother. In time, they would learn how to clean up as they worked.

"Okay, I'll see you in a few," Melanie said, and hung up the phone. She gazed longingly at her now-cooled pot of tea and the new book she'd been dying to sink her teeth into. There was always another day to do nothing but lounge around and read.

But maybe not, she thought as she scooped up the tray carefully and placed the treasured old teapot and her mug in the sink.

If she were lucky, soon she'd be too busy to lounge around. Hopefully, by this time next year, she'd have a family of her own to take care of.

She crossed her fingers and said a quick prayer.

A child of her own. *Could life get any better?* she thought as she raced through the condo like a kid at Christmas.

Chapter 5

Cars and four-wheel-drive vehicles were filling the driveway as Melanie parked her Navigator on the street at the edge of the snow-and-ice-covered lawn. Balancing a plastic-covered cake container in one hand and her purse and car keys in the other, she lifted an Ugg-booted foot to close the car door.

The small sidewalk leading to the front porch steps had been cleared of all snow and ice, courtesy of Patrick. Before Melanie had a chance to figure out how to press the doorbell, Ashley opened the front door.

"Auntie M, you came! Ella is here and so are her mom and dad," she said excitedly, as Melanie stepped inside the warm, festively decorated house.

Melanie laid her purse on an antique bench, careful to keep a tight grip on the cake container. She stooped down to Ashley's eye level and gave her a one-armed hug. "Of course I did. I wouldn't miss your Christmas party for all the money in the world," Melanie said. Ashley grabbed her free hand and led her to the kitchen, where Stephanie was standing in front of the sink.

"Look, Mom, Auntie M brought a cake."

Stephanie rinsed her hands off, and dried them with a paper towel. She took the cake container out of Melanie's hands and placed it on the counter next to three other cakes.

"Should've kept it, huh?" Melanie said as she spied the desserts.

Stephanie leaned in for a quick hug, then stood back, grinning at her friend. "Nah, Patrick's here. He'll take care of whatever leftovers we have," Stephanie assured her. "Bryce has been asking about you."

Blushing, Melanie shook her head. "He's just being polite, Steph." She wished everyone would stop trying to throw her and Bryce in one another's path. She'd met him more than once, and, yes, he was attractive, and, yes, she liked him, but she had a feeling Bryce wasn't into the "healthy, outdoor type" such as her. No, he probably preferred tall, skinny blondes with little or no brains. He was just too good-looking, she kept thinking. Men like him didn't date women with brains. She looked at her faded jeans and snow-covered Uggs. Definitely a Colorado kind of girl. It didn't matter that she wore a Stella McCartney sweater, or that her blond hair was really *her* blond hair. Guys like Bryce went for the glamour girls.

"Melanie, how are you? It's been too long," Bryce Landry said as he entered the kitchen.

Melanie's heart did a double beat when she felt him come up behind her. She took a deep breath. She could actually smell him. He smelled like winter. Pine and something else she couldn't identify. She felt her face turning ten shades of red. Thankful he couldn't read her mind, she turned to face him, and said, "Thanks, it's nice to see you, too, Bryce. You're right, it's been too long." She cringed at her words. What if he thought she'd been fantasizing about him?

Melanie couldn't help but admire Bryce's good looks. He certainly wore them well, she'd give him that. Dressed in a black turtleneck sweater and black jeans, his ebony hair hanging over his ears and down the back of his neck, he was extremely sexy, certainly not the look of a history professor, or at least any that she'd had in college. He stepped away from her as though he just realized he'd been standing in her personal space a bit too long. He had both hands out in front of him, fingertips upward, palms splayed up and out, as though he were trying to physically push himself away from her.

Melanie felt his gaze. She glanced at him before turning back to Stephanie. She could still feel his eyes boring a hole into her back. Without thinking, she whirled around and turned to face him.

"Is there something else?" The words were out of her mouth before she had a chance to stop them.

Bryce smiled at her. "Yes, actually there is. I want a piece of that cake you brought. I didn't know you were a baker. Thought it might be nice to sample the wares."

Melanie felt sucker punched, right in the middle of her stomach. Was he implying what she *thought* he was implying?

Sample the wares . . .

Apparently he caught his faux pas. He nodded at the row of cake dishes on the countertop. "There are four cakes to choose from. I wanted to try yours first."

Before Melanie or Bryce could put their feet into their mouths again, Stephanie removed a saucer from the cabinet and a fork from the drawer and handed them to Bryce. "Try them all."

He took the saucer, fork, and a cake knife Stephanie held out for him. He sliced into the black forest cake, hefting a giant slice onto his plate. Digging his fork into the chocolate confection, he crammed his mouth full. Melanie couldn't take her eyes off his mouth. Why hadn't she noticed before how sexy his mouth was? A full upper lip, and the lower, slightly thinner. And that one front tooth, it was slightly crooked. Mesmerized, she stared at him while he devoured the cake.

Stephanie cleared her throat so loudly it startled Melanie. She took a deep breath and started coughing, which then turned into choking. She bent over gasping for air. Taking as deep a breath as her coughing would allow, she inhaled and exhaled a few times before getting her throat to open up again. Drooling like a thirsty dog, Melanie wiped her mouth with the sleeve of her Stella McCartney sweater. Stephanie handed her a glass of water.

"I must confess, I don't always have this effect on women," Bryce said.

Melanie looked at him over the rim of her glass. Before she could stop herself, she tossed the rest of the water in Bryce's face.

"Oh my gosh, I'm so sorry! I don't know—"

Bryce lifted his clingy black sweater over the top of his head, revealing a most perfect six-pack. He slung the garment over his shoulder, a grin the size of the moon on his handsome face.

"I'm not going to ask why you did that because I know you're going to tell me."

Mortified, humiliated, and *ashamed* didn't begin to describe what she was feeling. "I don't know what . . . I am so *sorry*! I have no clue why . . ." There wasn't anything she could say to defend her action. She was as baffled as the next person.

Stephanie passed Bryce a wad of paper towels. He mopped up the remaining drops of water on his face.

I should have stayed at home with my book and my teapot, Melanie thought. Appalled by her actions, she tried to come up with an explanation, but couldn't. Maybe it was just one of those knee-jerk reactions, something in her subconscious. Whatever it was, she'd never been quite as embarrassed as she was now. Shaking her head from side to side, Melanie looked at the floor, then her gaze traveled up a pair of heavily muscled black-clad legs. When her eyes came to rest on his flat abs, she looked up quickly and focused her gaze on Bryce's sculpted face. "I'm sorry. I have no idea why I did that." Lame, she knew, but she had no other explanation to offer.

Bryce tossed the crumpled paper towels in the garbage can, then slipped the black sweater back over his head. Melanie could see the darker spots where the water had soaked the wool. On the positive side, at least no one but Stephanie had witnessed her act of stupidity.

"Stop apologizing," Bryce said with a sly grin. "It was only water. I'm just lucky it wasn't coffee."

Melanie focused on her surroundings, because she had a fear that if she didn't, she might do or say something else out of character: oak cabinets. Dark brown granite countertops, flour scattered all over the top. Cream-colored curtain above the bronze sink. Stove. Refrigerator. Dishwasher. Cake containers on the countertop. A burning smell.

Okay, she was focused. Now if she could keep her hand under control, she'd survive until she could safely come up with an excuse to leave! Fire, the place was on fire!

"Something's on fire," Bryce said casually as though he were talking about the weather.

"Oh my gosh! The cookies!" Stephanie grabbed two oven mitts, and yanked the oven door open. Gray smoke billowed out in one giant puff. She carefully pulled a baking sheet topped with little black mounds of what must've been meant to be cookies out of the oven. Stephanie dumped the ruined cookies in the sink. "I can't believe I forgot the cookies! I promised the girls they could decorate them." Stephanie shook her head and began scrubbing the burnt mess off the baking sheet.

"It's my fault, Steph. I'm sorry. I'm going to visit the girls and Ella, then go home. I can't seem to do anything right these days," Melanie said, irritated at herself. If she hadn't tossed that water at Bryce, the cookies wouldn't have burnt.

"Oh stop it, you two," Bryce said. "It's cookies. I say let the girls start a new batch. Let's air the place out first." He leaned over the sink and raised the window. A small gust of icy-cold air filled the room.

Bryce grabbed a kitchen towel, fanning the smoke toward the window. Melanie grabbed a place mat off the small table and followed Bryce's moves. Stephanie backed away from the sink, allowing them the room they needed to fan the smoke toward the window.

Melanie hoped this scene wasn't indicative of her future. If so, her hopes of adopting would surely go up in smoke.

Chapter 6

The early-morning air was bone-chillingly cold. Melanie parked her Lincoln Navigator inside the hangar and followed the airport attendant to the small jet waiting on the tarmac. Holding her documents against her chest, she climbed the small steps leading inside the plane.

She was seated and buckled in when the copilot offered her a cup of coffee from a thermos.

"Thanks, I needed this." He handed her a Styrofoam cup full of the steaming-hot brew. She breathed in the aromatic scent, loving the smell of it. She had overslept and hadn't had enough time to make a pot of coffee or much of anything else. She'd grabbed her makeup kit and a bright red sweater to put on later in addition to the jeans she'd barely had time to slip into. Grateful she'd showered and washed her hair the night before, she hoped she wasn't going to be judged on her appearance. Because if that was the case, she could forget about adopting a child.

If she couldn't dress herself, why would anyone think her capable of dressing a child? Or anything associated with a child. Maybe the whole idea was a pipe dream and nothing more.

No, it was not a pipe dream. She was ready for this, knew in her heart this was the correct path for her. If the agency didn't approve her application, she would just accept that now was not the time for her to make a life-changing decision.

Melanie felt the pressure as the jet lifted off the tarmac. Takeoff was her favorite part of flying, giving her an instant rush. Once they had reached their assigned altitude, she relaxed. The flight was only one hour, just enough time to ponder last night's dinner with Bryce. She still couldn't believe she had gone to dinner with him, let alone made plans for a second date. Yesterday was just full of surprises.

She still had no clue why she had tossed a glass of water in his face. That would have to remain a mystery for a while yet. Once they'd cleared the kitchen of all the smoke and mess, she had helped the girls make a second batch of cookies, the slice-and-bake kind, but they'd had fun in spite of the smoky start.

She'd had a great visit with Max and Grace. Baby Ella was just starting to walk, and seeing the little girl convinced her even more that she was making the right decision. They'd spent the remainder of the afternoon laughing, talking, and sharing their plans for the upcoming holiday. When Melanie was reminded that Bryce was going to be hanging around until after the first of the year, she couldn't help but feel a little bit excited. After she'd gotten over her initial bout of mortification, courtesy of Bryce's easy-going manner, she'd relaxed. They'd talked about everything from the ski conditions to their preference for dark or light turkey meat.

Melanie couldn't believe she'd never taken the time to learn much more than superficial things about Grace's younger brother. They'd been around one another long enough to get to know each other, but Melanie had made the assumption that he was not interested in her or anything she had to say, so she'd kept her distance.

Now, here she was about to make a drastic change to her life, and all she could think about was their upcoming date, midmorning tomorrow. They'd planned a day of skiing, and both decided if they weren't too tired, they'd try out that new Italian restaurant everyone was raving about.

Melanie grinned. Life was good, and if she had anything to say about it—and she did—it was about to get even better.

The plane landed as scheduled, and her rental car was parked where it should be. She'd asked that the car be equipped with a GPS. She recalled the woman from the adoption agency's words: *Nine o'clock sharp.* So far, everything was going according to plan.

She programmed the GPS with the adoption agency's address. While she waited for the information to reach some satellite in space, she checked her hastily applied makeup in the rearview mirror, tucked a few loose strands of hair back into her topknot. She'd changed into her red sweater before getting inside her rental car. Yes, things were going just the way she wanted them to. Smooth as silk.

It was already 7:30 A.M., and the traffic was bumper to bumper on Denver's I-70. Miles of red taillights stretched out on the road before her. At this rate, she'd be lucky to make her nine o'clock appointment. Slowly, she crept down the heavily trafficked highway. Twenty minutes later, she looked again at the bright green digital clock on the dashboard, then back at the GPS stuck to the windshield. According to the directions, she would arrive at World Adoption Agency in fifty-seven minutes. Somehow this didn't seem possible with all the traffic, but she knew the GPS also tracked your speed, so she would trust the gizmo to do what it was supposed to do.

In her peripheral vision, Melanie saw where several of Denver's large businesses had decorated their office buildings with elaborate displays of colored lights, giant blow-up Santa Clauses, snowmen, and the usual array of decorations. If she'd had more time, she would have taken the exit to get a closer look at some of the outrageous decorations, but she would do that another time. At the moment, she had more important things to do. If she were lucky, this time next year she would have a child of her own to take to view the elaborate Christmas decorations.

Briefly, she wondered what Bryce would say about her plans. She shook her head; it didn't matter what he or anyone else thought. She'd made a decision, and she would do her part to see that her plans came to fruition.

The traffic started moving faster, and thirty minutes later, the electronic female voice told her that her exit was one mile on the right.

Butterflies danced in her stomach as she weaved her way through the back streets that led to the adoption agency. The female voice told her she had arrived. She didn't know what she had been expecting, but she knew she hadn't expected what she was seeing. She pulled into the asphalt parking lot and turned the engine off, wondering if she'd been given the wrong address.

A flat-roofed brick building, which at one time might have been an old school building or a county government facility, was surrounded by a tall wire fence. There were no swings in the side yard, no merry-go-rounds, no type of equipment that would indicate children lived here. Her heart sank. This picture certainly did not match the one she saw on the Internet. Thinking it was possible the Web site designers had gone a bit overboard when they'd created the Web site, in hopes of luring potential parents, Melanie walked down a cracked sidewalk that led to a steel door with faded black and gold letters that read OF-FICE. She looked at her watch. She was a few minutes early. Not knowing if she should knock on the door or simply step inside, Melanie went with her gut and opened the door.

Melanie stepped inside to a dimly lit reception area. A grayish green metal desk, clear of the usual clutter, with a sturdy wooden chair tucked beneath it stood in the center of the room. Behind the desk on the wall facing her were several tall gray metal filing cabinets. She looked to her left and right in hopes of finding another desk, maybe a desk with a computer on it, but saw nothing except for a few small wooden chairs pushed up against the wall. It was obvious the chairs were for children, not guests.

As Melanie was about to wander down the long hallway to her left, she heard the *click-clack* of heels coming from the opposite end of the hall. She remained in place, smoothed any imaginary wrinkles from her jeans, and took a deep breath. It was now or never. Exhaling as she'd been taught in her yoga class, she let her breath out slowly. She watched the tall figure make her way down the dark hallway toward the front reception area.

Where were all the children? she wondered. Surely they were up and about by now. But then she realized that they had probably already left for school.

In the same nasally accented voice she'd heard on the phone, the tall figure called out as she made her way over to the desk. "You must be Mrs. McLaughlin."

She was the exact image that her voice and manner projected over the telephone. Sturdily built, steel gray hair pulled back in a bun so tight her eyes were pulled upward. She wore a brown wool suit, thick stockings, and ugly black shoes with large square heels. It was the sort of outfit that brought to mind a warden in a medium-security prison for women. "Well, are you going to answer me or not?" she asked.

"Yes, I'm she . . . I am Melanie McLaughlin."

"Follow me," the still-unnamed woman said.

Melanie did as instructed. She traveled the length of the dark hallway, the woman's broad back blocking her view of what lay beyond. At the end of the hall was a small office, this one a bit more personal. There was a wooden desk with a banker's lamp placed to her right. And two matching chairs, both of which might have been light blue at one time but were now as gray as the rest of the surroundings, were placed on the opposite side of the desk.

The woman walked around and slid her chair from beneath the desk. She sat down, rifled through a stack of papers on her desk, then gave Melanie a nod, indicating she should sit.

"You have all of your paperwork in order?" the

woman said flatly, her voice displaying not the slightest bit of emotion. Melanie was beginning to regret her choice of adoption agencies. This woman was simply rude—not having bothered even to introduce herself.

She placed the file folder of papers she'd brought, along with her passport, on the desk. "I think so. I brought along a few extra things." The woman stared at her as though she could see right through her. "Just in case," Melanie added in a small voice.

"You think? If you're not sure you've brought the required documents, how is one to assume you're capable of caring for a child?" The woman, whose name she still didn't know, reminded her of the assistant principal in the movie *Uncle Buck.* John Candy in his role as Uncle Buck had told the hateful old woman to take a quarter and pay a rat to gnaw the giant wart off her face. Though the discourteous woman across from Melanie lacked the giant wart, she might as well have been that character come to life. Just thinking about the comedic scene made Melanie smile.

"You think this is funny?" the woman asked, her voice rising in anger.

Melanie wasn't going to allow herself to be treated this way one second longer. "Not that it's any of your concern, *madam,* but I was smiling at a memory that has absolutely nothing to do with my paperwork."

There, now, if the headmistress, or whatever this harridan was called, asked her to leave, Melanie would just take it as a sign that this wasn't the right agency for her.

"This isn't the place for silly thoughts, Mrs. McLaughlin. World Adoption Agency requires our prospective parents to be serious and mature. If you feel you cannot meet these requirements, please don't waste any more of my time than you have already."

Melanie was minute by minute becoming more convinced that this shrew had come directly from central casting, an exact replica of the much-hated character in the *Uncle Buck* movie. But having traveled all the way to Denver, Melanie decided that she might as well play out what was rapidly turning into a farce to the end, no matter how rude and bossy the woman was.

Practically biting her tongue, Melanie said politely, "Of course not, *Mrs. . . .*" Maybe before she left, she'd at least know the woman's name.

"Olga Krause," the woman said.

Surprised at her name, Melanie almost fell out of the sagging chair. She hoped this wasn't some kind of joke, some new adoption-based reality television show. Because if it was, she wasn't laughing. This was too unreal to be real. This was starting to sound crazy.

"Mrs. Krause," Melanie said as *maturely* as she could, "I am more than ready to start whatever proceedings are required by this agency. You asked me to bring those documents." She nodded toward the manila folder in Mrs. Krause's hand. "And I did. If there is anything more I need to bring, I assume you will inform me. I've never attempted to adopt a child before. I'm not practiced in this procedure, but will be once we get through this initial screening."

Melanie waited while Mrs. Krause went through the paperwork. She glanced around the small room, looking for a picture, a knickknack, anything that would show some personality, but she observed nothing that would indicate the room was someone's personal space. She decided that the faded blue chairs were as personal as it was going to get. She waited for another few minutes.

"I'm going to need to make copies of your documents. I will be right back." Mrs. Krause inched away from her desk.

"Those are your copies. I have the originals here if you need to see them," Melanie added, thinking *anything to speed up the procedure.*

She'd yet to hear one sound that would indicate there were children present.

"Well, that was very thoughtful of you, I must say." Mrs. Krause slid her chair closer to the desk. She stacked the papers until the edges were perfectly aligned.

Shocked at the positive words, Melanie remained silent, fearful that if she said anything, it would disrupt Mrs. Krause's train of thought.

After several uncomfortable minutes, the woman spoke up. "Your paperwork appears to be in order. Before we can proceed, we must first run a criminal background check. Once those results are in, and if they are in order, we will proceed to step two."

Melanie wanted to roll her eyes, but refrained. Images of needy children kept flashing in front of her. However, she didn't want to stay in the room any longer than necessary, so she spoke up. "And may I ask what step two consists of?"

"I can tell by your question you did not fully read through the information provided on our Web site."

And here we go again, Melanie thought, as she waited for Mrs. Olga Krause to enlighten her.

"Each agency has certain criteria that must be met as you know since you read all of the fine print." Mrs.

Krause paused, her wicked brown eyes staring at Melanie as though she'd committed a crime. "Since this agency receives state funds, we require a private meeting with your husband before we can schedule an interview with both of you together as a couple."

Melanie felt like she'd just been slammed with the old proverbial ton of bricks.

A husband.

Olga Krause was absolutely correct. She had missed *that* part of the fine print.

Chapter 7

Melanie inserted her key in the front door and hurried to unlock it. Odie was reclining against the door. Melanie slowly pushed the door inward, letting the dog know it was safe to move.

She let the boxer jump up and lick her face. Clovis rubbed against her leg. *The best part of owning pets*, Melanie thought. Returning home. They were always glad to see you no matter what kind of mood you were in. And she was in a very, *very* rotten mood. She'd stewed on the drive back to the airport, stewed on the short flight to Placerville, and continued stewing on the drive home.

"Give me a second, Odie, and we'll make a quick trip outside." She kicked off her black leather boots and replaced them with the Uggs she always kept by the front door. She hung her purse on the knob next to Odie's leash. "Clovis, you wait right here." She rubbed the cat's head before snapping Odie's leash to his collar.

Being late afternoon, it was almost dark. Melanie didn't like this part of late fall, *but it is what it is*, she thought as she led Odie to the greenway. A walk in the frigid air would do her good. Clear her mind a bit.

Shivering, Melanie led Odie to the off-leash area. She unhooked him. "Three minutes, bud, and that's it. Too cold for animals and humans," she muttered to herself.

While she waited for the dog to make his rounds, she revisited the scene at the adoption agency. Mrs. Krause—*Miss* Krause, she'd informed her as Melanie was leaving—told her not to expect a phone call from the agency unless her background check came back clean. She'd treated her like a criminal, but Melanie knew it wasn't personal. The old woman was a spinster, probably treated all prospective parents the same way. Still, she didn't see how she could've missed such vital information on the Web site. She was going to reread every bit of fine print. Twice.

"Okay, Odie, your three minutes are up." Like the obedient animal he was, he came out of the off-leash area, stopping in front of her when she held the leash out.

It had to be at least twenty below, she thought, as she jogged back to the condo. No one in their right mind should be out in this weather. At the moment, however, she wasn't in her right mind. She felt like a total and complete idiot. Of course she had forgotten to mention to Miss Krause that there wouldn't be a need for her to run that background check since she didn't have a husband. But something had stopped her from revealing that important bit of info to the old woman. Why? She didn't know, but went with her gut instinct and simply said good-bye before racing out to her rental car. Once inside, she'd almost had a panic attack! *How could I have missed such vital information?*

Inside, Odie shook off the wet snow before resuming his position beneath the kitchen table. Clovis jumped on the countertop in search of his evening meal. Melanie removed a can of cat food from the pantry, flipped off the aluminum lid, and dumped the stinky contents in Clovis's bowl before placing the bowl on the kitty mat by the back door. Odie dragged himself out from under the table, apparently remembering it was dinnertime. Melanie scooped a large portion of kibble into his bowl. "Okay, you two. Now let's see what the human is going to have for dinner."

She opened the refrigerator, but didn't see anything that appealed to her. Not that she was hungry. She grabbed an apple out of the bowl in the center island. She wanted to cool down, to wait a bit before she went back to the agency's Web site, but she couldn't.

Inside her office, Melanie munched on her apple while she waited for her computer to boot up. Did it always take this long? A few seconds later, she heard the familiar hum. She clicked onto the Internet and found the agency's Web site. She read all the fine print, then read through it a second time. And a third time, just to make sure she wasn't losing it. Nowhere did it say one had to be married to petition for an adoption. She clicked on all the pages a fourth time, went through all the links one by one, and still didn't see anything stating that only married couples could adopt.

That Miss Krause was a true old bat, she thought as she clicked through the pages. Spiteful. Maybe she had an unhappy life and wanted to make those around her as miserable as she was. Knowing all hope wasn't lost, if push came to shove, she would have the law on her side since there was absolutely nothing saying a potential parent had to be married. Miss Krause was mistaken, there was no other explanation.

Stay hopeful, that's what she would do. If this agency didn't work out, she'd simply find one that would. Single parents adopted children all the time. Maybe Miss Krause was new to the job. "Nah, I doubt it," she said out loud. The poor old woman was probably childless, with no family to speak of. Melanie did a mental three-sixty.

That could be me, thirty years down the road.

Chapter 8

The sun shone like a brilliant goldenrod. Though the temperatures were in the mid-teens, Melanie wasn't the least bit cold. She wore the latest in outdoor wear, her favorite top-of-the-line Spyder Gear, which promised to keep its wearer warm in temperatures much colder than that day's.

She'd dropped Odie and Clovis off at The Snow Zone, knowing Stephanie was there by herself. Candy Lee was out of town with her parents, so Melanie knew that the animals would keep Stephanie company. Not that she'd have much time for them, because the store was jam-packed with customers when she'd dropped the pair off, but Melanie knew having Odie around was an added comfort for Stephanie.

She'd agreed to meet Bryce at the chairlifts at ten o'clock. She glanced at her weatherproof wristwatch. Ten of. She'd left early, allowing herself the extra time needed to drop the animals off. She put her skis and poles on the metal rack alongside dozens of others. In all the years she'd been skiing, she'd never had anything taken. Ski bums were good people. Skiing was not a poor man or woman's sport. The equipment was extremely expensive, the price of the lift tickets outrageous. The food in the lodge was quadruple the normal rate. But it was a sport that one either liked or not.

Melanie loved to ski, loved the freedom, and, more than anything, loved being outdoors. Her work kept her rooted to her desk, so when she had the opportunity to get away from it all, she took it.

She supposed you could call today a date. Sort of. Not a traditional date, where the guy knocked on your door with flowers, walked you to the car, and held the door open. In all honesty, Melanie couldn't recall ever having a date like that, but the fantasy was nice. No, she and Bryce had agreed to meet right here at the chairlift. She paid her way, he paid his. She liked it better that way because she didn't feel the slightest bit obligated to "pay back" in a manner she wasn't comfortable with.

Even though it was still early by ski-bum standards, the lift lines were longer than normal. While she waited, she observed the beginners at the bunny hill. People of all ages dressed in every color of the rainbow were either wedging, or, as the instructors taught the little ones, "pizza-ing" down the small hill. Those who were better balanced positioned their skis side by side and "french-fried" their way up and down the mini slope. The unlucky ones lay sprawled on the snow, struggling to bring themselves upright, so they could try one more time to make it down without falling.

"I remember those days well," Bryce said. He'd come up beside her without her noticing. He tapped her on the nose. "Earth to Melanie." Wearing his skis, he couldn't get much closer to her without tripping over them.

Melanie whirled around. "Hi, Bryce. You sneaked up on me, no fair! I don't have my skis on yet. Give me a second," she said, then raced over to the racks, where she removed her skis and poles and placed them flat on the ground. She clicked each boot into the proper position and adjusted her gloves before poling back to the chair-lift.

"Okay, now I'm fair game," Melanie said as she slid into place beside him.

"Blue or black?" Bryce asked as they poled their way to the front of the line.

Melanie raised her eyebrows. "A daredevil now, are we? I never would've guessed. Let's start with a blue run, then we'll see how things progress. I'm not as young as I used to be," she said teasingly.

Bryce laughed, showing that one crooked tooth. *Sexy as ever,* Melanie thought as she laughed with him. Why hadn't she noticed that before? *Doesn't matter,* she thought, as they stood waiting for the chair to tap the back of their knees. *I'm here now.*

In one giant swing, they were airborne. Bryce lowered the protective railing before sliding closer to her. "I'm scared."

Both burst out laughing. "A college professor, and you can't come up with a better pickup line than that?"

He inched closer, so close in fact that she could smell his minty breath. Melanie was glad they had on their heavy outerwear. She did not want to see those flat six-pack abs, or his well-muscled chest, not even a hint at what he looked like under all that down. At least not yet.

"I thought we were past that," Bryce teased.

The lift stopped midway up the mountain. They were dangling on the topside of a mountain, and neither seemed to notice. The gears ground, then they resumed the climb.

"You did, huh?" Melanie replied.

"Yeah, I did," Bryce said, "so let me see what I can come up with." Bryce placed his index finger on his cheek as though he were in deep thought. "How about a little Shakespeare?"

He cleared his throat, then began,

Shall I compare thee to a summer's day?
Thou art more lovely and more temperate:
Rough winds do shake the darling buds of May,
And summer's lease hath all too short a date:
Sometime too hot the eye of heaven shines,
And often is his gold complexion dimm'd;
And every fair from fair sometime declines,
By chance or nature's changing course untrimm'd;
But thy eternal summer shall not fade
Nor lose possession of that fair thou owest;
Nor shall Death brag thou wander'st in his shade,
When in eternal lines to time thou growest:
So long as men can breathe or eyes can see,
So long lives this and this gives life to thee.

"How's that?" he asked when he'd finished.

"If you don't hurry up and raise the bar, we're gonna be in trouble," Melanie said as they came within a few feet of their drop-off point.

Bryce slid across the seat, checked to make sure their skis and poles were out of the way, then raised the bar. They inched as close to the edge of the seat as possible, raising their ski tips. As soon as they could feel the heavily packed snow beneath them, they shoved off the lift and skied to an area where they wouldn't be in the way of the other skiers and snowboarders. Skiing had its rules.

Both adjusted their goggles and helmets. Bryce pointed to an easy blue run. Melanie nodded, then shoved off. The run was packed with people, and Melanie had to use every ounce of her skill to maneuver between them without tripping over the fallen skier or snowboarder. She whizzed through a group of students, then heard a loud thump behind her. She slowed down to look behind her, but all she saw was a flash of royal blue as Bryce practically flew past her.

"So he wants to play rough. I'll show him rough." Melanie leaned down and forward, increasing her speed. Seeing that the bowl ahead was scattered with skiers of every skill, Melanie made a quick decision, turning left on the trail, which would lead her to a shortcut. Not many knew about it, but this was an emergency. Kind of. She laughed. Yes, it was off the map, but no way was Mr. Landry going to beat her to the bottom. She flew down the hill, slowing down when she saw a fallen skier. He or she—one could never tell, bundled up in all the clothing—gave her the thumbs-up sign to indicate there was no injury, so she used her poles to regain speed.

Passing through the tall evergreens, Melanie was suddenly grateful to be alive. She inhaled the familiar pine scent mixed with a touch of wood smoke; this was life in Colorado at its finest. Seeing that she was almost at her destination, she leaned forward, legs practically touching one another as she soared to the bottom of the mountain. Hurrying to get back in the lift line before Bryce, Melanie hit a patch of ice. Before she knew what happened, Bryce Landry was helping her get back on her feet.

"Hey, just because I recited you a love poem doesn't mean I expect you to fall at my feet," Bryce said, his verdant gaze full of mischief.

Melanie removed her goggles and helmet. "If I had a glass of water right now, I'd toss it squarely in your face." She looked at him and gave him a genuine ear-to-ear smile. Again, for the second time, she was thrilled that she and this hunk of burning love were friends.

And who knew, maybe it would turn into something more. Today, for some reason, she believed that anything was possible.

Chapter 9

Melanie and Bryce stopped once for a quick lunch before heading back to the slopes. She was tired, but in a good way. They were on the chairlift again, and this time she slid closer to him. "For the record, I liked your poem."

"It wasn't original, but I could write you one if you like," Bryce said, nudging his helmet to hers.

"Okay," she murmured. "I like."

"Good. I was hoping you'd say that."

"Really?" She leaned back in order to see his face, or at least the part that wasn't covered by his helmet. She saw nothing but honesty reflecting back at her.

"Yes. Really. Because that means you'll have dinner with me tonight even though you're probably going to be too tired. I'll need some more inspiration."

Melanie shook her head. "Okay—you left me at the last hill. I'm not getting something here."

"The more time I spend with you, the more inspiration I'll have for the poem I'm going to write."

"I see," Melanie said. "I thought you were a history professor."

"I am, but I'm also a lover of words."

Just then, they reached the top of the mountain, preventing her from responding. Again, they flew down the trails, this time side by side, as though they'd practiced it a dozen times.

This time, when they reached the bottom of the mountain, Bryce removed his helmet and goggles, kicked his skis aside, and wrapped his arms around her bulky jacket. Without giving her a chance to remove her helmet, Bryce dipped his head forward, slightly tilting it to the side, and touched his lips to hers. She leaned back and closed her eyes, savoring the warmth from his mouth.

It was the best kiss she'd ever had.

They stood silently for a few minutes, kissing one another. Little nips, light smacks, nibbles. Suddenly sensing a presence, Melanie gently pushed him away. "We have an audience." She gestured to a little girl no more than five or six years old, staring at her. The child couldn't seem to take her eyes off them. Melanie removed her helmet and shook out the long braid she'd wound up on top of her head. She lowered herself to the child's level. Before she could ask a question, the little girl screamed, "You're not my mommy!"

Melanie turned when she heard a shrill cry coming from behind.

"Penelope! There you are! I told you to meet me in the lunchroom with your instructor. Where is your instructor?" the woman asked, cupping a hand across her forehead in search of the missing instructor.

The woman, who was obviously Penelope's mother, wore ski attire identical to Melanie's. Red-and-black Spyder jacket and black pants with red stripes running down the leg. No wonder the little girl had mistaken Melanie for her mother.

Melanie stood up as Penelope slid into her harried mother, attaching herself to her mother's legs. "I had to pee, and that man said I had to wait till it was time to eat. I hate skiing, Mommy. I want to go home now!" The little girl started to wail, her cries attracting the attention of the other skiers at the base of the mountain.

"Don't ever leave your instructor, do you understand?" the mother admonished. "We discussed this before."

Melanie wanted to intervene on poor little Penelope's behalf, but it really wasn't her place. She stood next to Bryce while the little girl pitched a fit that could have earned her an Oscar nomination.

When the mother realized they were being watched by a large crowd, she grabbed the child by the hand. "She doesn't like to ski," she said to those gathered around. Without another word, she pulled Penelope alongside her and headed for the main lodge. The little girl continued to cry.

"Poor kid," Bryce said. "If she doesn't like to ski, she shouldn't be forced. That can be dangerous. Grace never cared that much for skiing as a kid, and Mom and Dad never forced it on either of us."

Surprised that Bryce would even comment on the child, let alone have an opinion about the mother's treatment, Melanie gave a mental high five. This guy was turning out to be much more than she'd hoped for. He was not just another pretty face.

"It's part of the Colorado heritage," Bryce said. "If you live here and don't like to ski, you're not right in the head. Speaking of which, I have had enough skiing for one day. I'm pooped."

Bryce fastened the binders of his skis together and tucked them under one arm along with his poles. Melanie followed suit, suddenly glad she wasn't parked in the spillover lot.

They walked to the parking lot in silence, the crunching of their heavy boots on clumps of brown snow on the asphalt the only sound.

"So, are we still on for dinner? Grace and Max say that new Italian restaurant downtown is to die for."

Melanie wanted to appear as if she were considering his question even though they both knew the answer. "Odie and Clovis are with Stephanie, so I have to go to The Snow Zone before I go home."

"Okayyy," Bryce said. "I'm assuming they're your pets," he stated flatly.

Maybe strike one. "You don't like animals?" Melanie said. They reached her Navigator, and she removed her keys from her pocket, opened the hatch, and put her ski gear inside. She sighed with relief when she removed her heavy ski boots. Stepping into her Uggs, she smiled as Bryce watched her. "So, you didn't answer my question. Do you like animals or not?"

"I have three dogs, so I guess you could call that a yes."

Scratch strike one. Another mental high five.

"Really? You never mentioned them." Melanie felt so comfortable with Bryce, more so than she had with any guy she'd known for such a short length of time. After the water incident, she'd relaxed, letting down her defenses.

Whatever will be, will be. She closed the hatch and twirled her keys around, smiling. "So, what breed?"

Bryce chuckled. "Mutts, all of 'em. I volunteer at an animal shelter in Boulder every Saturday. When we can't find a home for any of the strays, I take them in. So for now, I just have the three. In the future, who knows?"

She couldn't believe someone hadn't snatched this guy already. He was just about perfect. Figuring she was on a roll, she asked, "What about children?"

He switched his skis to his other shoulder. "What about them?"

She laughed, shaking her head from side to side. "Do you like children?" There!

"Of course I like children. Ella is the best niece in the world, as I'm sure you've heard. Grace and Max are lucky. I hope to have a houseful of my own someday."

Standing in the parking lot, Melanie started to feel the cold. At least that's what she thought she was feeling. The more Bryce talked, the more she wanted him. And not just as a date.

"What about you, do you want children?" Bryce asked, all traces of his earlier humor gone. He leaned his skis against her Navigator, careful not to scratch the paint.

They were having a serious talk. In the parking lot at Maximum Glide. *Okay, I can handle this.*

Should she tell him about Miss Krause, and her desire to adopt a child? Would he want to take her to that little Italian restaurant if she had a child? She knew about Stephanie and Patrick's beginnings, and Patrick's fear of loss where kids were concerned because of his niece. Patrick hadn't been too keen on kids at first because of this fear. But Bryce wasn't Patrick, and she wasn't Stephanie.

Melanie took a deep breath, the icy air burning her lungs. "Yes, I do, I've always wanted children. Being an only child, I always swore I would have at least four, but I'd settle for one or two. You know, being practical. I don't want to be another Octo-Mom. Fourteen might be tough to handle." She laughed. "Look, I would love to continue this discussion, but I'm freezing. My toes are numb."

"Why didn't you say something? Here." Bryce took her keys from her hand, unlocked the driver's side door, and hauled himself into the driver's seat. He adjusted the heater controls on the dash, then led Melanie to the passenger side, where he opened the door for her, just like in her fantasy.

"Let's go get Odie and Clovis, then you can drop me off at my car. We can finish this discussion at dinner."

Chapter 10

Max and Grace were right. Giorgio's served the best chicken marsala she'd ever tasted. Bryce had chosen the linguine and clam sauce. Both ordered caesar salads with their meal. The waiter brought a basket of homemade garlic bread that smelled divine. For a solid hour they did nothing but eat. When Bryce asked the waiter for a second bottle of wine, Melanie knew it was time to call it a night.

"I'm afraid I'm already a little bit tipsy," she said. "Any more, and I won't be able to drive safely. I can't remember the last time I ate so much."

He nodded his acquiescence. "How about dessert? Are you sure you don't want any tiramisu?" Bryce asked. "Grace said it was the best she'd ever had."

Melanie doubted she could take so much as a sip of water without exploding. "Nothing for me, thanks."

She had picked Odie and Clovis up from The Snow Zone and driven home happier than she could ever remember. After she'd taken care of the animals' needs, she'd soaked her aching muscles in the hot tub, washed and dried her hair, and even attempted to apply her makeup with a professional hand. She had agreed to meet Bryce at the restaurant because it was easier for both of them.

Now that the temperatures were dropping quickly, Melanie knew from experience that the back roads would ice over in a matter of hours. Back roads were always the last to be cleared. She didn't want Bryce driving off the side of the mountain. If one didn't know the road by the back of one's hand, it could happen, *had happened.* More than once.

Ever the gentleman, Bryce took care of the check even though Melanie offered to pay her share. "Real men don't accept money from their dates. Or at least this is what my father taught me before he passed away. And I always listened to my father; his advice hasn't failed me yet."

Melanie didn't say it out loud, but she gave Bryce another mental high five. One to his father, too. The man just kept getting better and better. Surely there was something wrong with this guy, something she'd find out when she got to know him better. But then again, maybe not. Nice guys still existed, they were just extremely hard to find these days. Not that she'd spent much time looking.

After Bryce settled up with the waiter, he walked her outside to her Navigator. "I don't want the evening to end," he said. "It's been . . . let's just say it's been one of the best days I've had in a while. A very long while."

Melanie wanted to dissect his words, take them apart

one by one, searching for a hidden meaning, but now wasn't the time. She'd leave those thoughts for later. She wanted to be one hundred percent in the moment when she was with Bryce. She was falling in love with him. She'd never felt so alive, so excited to be with a man. That was love, or at least the beginning of the falling part. In spite of the chilling temperatures, she felt a warm glow flowing through her, like a brilliant ray of sunshine. Yep, this was love, had to be.

"I feel the same way, but as you know, I've got a couple of guys waiting for me at home, so I'd better head back."

Without the bulky ski coats between them, Bryce captured her small waist, then pulled her as close to him as their winter dress would allow. He kissed the sensitive part of her ear, then trailed light butterfly kisses down the side of her neck, along her jawline, before touching her mouth with his. No longer on public display, Bryce covered her mouth hungrily. Melanie accepted his kiss and allowed herself to feel the passion. His tongue teased hers, and she teased back. He tasted of red wine and mint. He pulled away for a nanosecond, then his lips recaptured hers, but this time they were more demanding.

If they weren't in the middle of the parking lot, Melanie knew this would lead to something much more intimate. And she wanted that, but not yet. She stepped out of his arms, a hand touching her lips. She smiled, suddenly feeling shy like a schoolgirl.

"Hmm, that was nice," she said with a grin.

"That's it, just nice?" He wrapped his arms around her neck and touched his cold nose to hers. "How about that? It's the way Eskimos kiss."

"I'm not going to feed your ego, Mr. Landry. I think

you enjoyed that kiss as much as I did, and that's all I'm going to say."

"Okay, I admit it. I was fishing."

Sighing contentedly, Melanie said, "You know what they say about men who fish?"

He cradled her head against his chest. "No, but I'm sure you're about to tell me."

"I just made that up. I have no clue what they say about men who fish."

He gave a hearty laugh. "You don't play fair. What if I said, 'men who fish are excellent lovers,' would you agree with that?"

Oh boy, she thought. "I've never slept with a fisherman, so I wouldn't know."

"Fair enough." A streetlamp provided just enough light for him to see her clearly. "What about a college professor?" He looked at her, and the double meaning of his words was very obvious.

She fought the urge to rip his clothes off, right there in the middle of the parking lot, but the cold and the fear of getting arrested prevented her from taking action. This certainly wasn't the time or the place.

Taking a deep breath, and letting it out as slowly as humanly possible, Melanie spoke, her voice soft, seductive. "I'll put that on my bucket list." And without another word between them, Melanie unlocked the door and got inside the Navigator. She cranked the engine over and was about to turn the heater on when she saw Bryce tapping on her window. She hit the POWER button to roll the window down halfway. "What? It's cold out there!" she said, even though she didn't care how cold it was. Bryce didn't want to leave her any more than she wanted to leave him.

He looked down at his ice-covered boots, then back at her. "This might sound . . . well, never mind how it sounds. I'm asking anyway. I planned on taking a trip to Las Vegas next weekend. Believe it or not, I've never been there. Would you like to come along? I've got two tickets to see Cher."

That was the last thing she had expected to hear from him. Vegas, of all places. And why did he have two tickets? Had some other woman canceled at the last minute? Was she just a convenient stand-in?

Before she could stop herself, the words flew out of her mouth. Sort of like the water incident.

He threw back his head and let out a great peal of laughter. "Actually, Mom was going to go with me but had to cancel at the last minute."

His mother? This guy was good. Really good.

"I planned to decorate my Christmas tree this weekend." She did, but also, what if the adoption agency called and she was out of town.

She'd given Miss Krause her cell number.

"Okay," he said. "I can see where decorating your Christmas tree would take precedence over a trip to Vegas." He turned away from the window, heading toward his Jeep.

Melanie rolled the driver's side window down as far as it would go. "Bryce," she called out to him, and he turned around. He appeared to be amused, not angry as she'd thought. "Do you want to come over and help me decorate my tree tomorrow? I need to do this before the weekend. I'm going to Vegas with a friend."

He stared at her, then burst out laughing. "I knew you would see things my way."

"Careful, a girl can change her mind in a split second. How's noon sound? It's about an hour's walk from the condo. I have all the equipment." She watched him and tried to suppress a giggle.

"You cut down your own tree?" he asked, apparently amused by this.

"Every year as far back as I can remember. You game or not?" She put her foot on the brake, shifted into reverse slowly, and eased the SUV out of her parking space. Bryce walked slowly along the side of her vehicle.

"Rest assured, I am game. I'll see you at noon."

Melanie smiled and punched the accelerator a bit too hard, fishtailed, and caught herself just in the nick of time, before pulling out of Giorgio's parking lot. She looked in her rearview mirror. Bryce stood in the middle of the asphalt lot smiling from ear to ear.

Merry Christmas to me, she thought as she drove home to her condo.

Chapter 11

Melanie wanted to tell someone about her and Bryce's evening but saw it was almost midnight. Too late to call Stephanie, too late to call her mother. If Mimi were still alive, she would've called her no matter how late. She'd had an extraordinary relationship with her grandmother and knew that Mimi was looking down on her from the heavens above. Melanie smiled at the image. Mimi would've told her to pack her best undies and bring her most expensive perfume.

And that's just what she did after taking Odie out for an extra midnight potty break. Inside, she was too wired to even think about going to sleep. The animals sensed there was something different about her. They hopped on top of her bed and watched her as she went from closet to chest of drawers to luggage, their heads moving in perfect unison.

"Mom will take you two for the weekend. Dad might even grill you two a steak, but don't tell him I know he does this, or I'm sure it'll stop. Now, what's left to pack?" She spoke to Odie and Clovis like they were people. She swore sometimes they could understand her.

She checked the contents of her luggage once more, making sure she had double of everything. Just in case. A slinky black dress, a slinky black sheer blouse, a slinky pair of formfitting black slacks. Black bikini undies with a matching bra. Yep, this would do for a weekend. She would wear her black leather boots on the flight, so she didn't have to pack an extra pair of shoes. Seeing there was nothing left to do, she closed the luggage again, placing it on the floor next to her bed.

She couldn't believe how her life had changed in just a matter of a few days. What a fantastic Christmas season. Now all she had to do was wait for Miss Krause's phone call confirming that her background check was clear, which she knew to be a fact since she'd never had so much as a speeding ticket. Then she could honestly say that her life was close to perfect. Well, if you didn't add that one teeny little element about marriage, then her life would be as close to perfect as it was ever going to get.

Odie yawned, reminding her of the late hour. Too keyed up to sleep, she retrieved her novel from the living room, then washed her face and brushed her teeth. She stripped down to her undies, slid into her favorite pair of sweats, and an old T-shirt from her high school days. Once she'd gently moved Odie and Clovis to their side of the bed, she opened her book and began to read about the latest saga in the vampire world. Within minutes, she was sound asleep.

* * *

Bryce finally gave up. In bed tossing and turning for the past two hours, he couldn't have stayed still if his life depended on it. Shoving the heavy covers aside, he decided to get up and go downstairs in search of a snack. Grace always had some type of baked goods just waiting to be sliced into. Thankful there were no residents staying at Hope House, he didn't bother putting on a shirt.

Downstairs in the kitchen, he poured himself a glass of milk, then spied a plate of brownies sitting next to the stove. He grabbed a saucer from the cabinet, stacked three large brownies on top of one another, and headed back upstairs.

It was going to be a long night, he thought as he entered the guest room. Switching on the lamp next to the bed, he placed the glass of milk and plate of brownies on the night table. Grace usually had a stack of novels tucked inside a drawer. He opened the drawer on the night table and was not disappointed. James Patterson's, Vince Flynn's, and Harlan Coben's latests were neatly lined up side by side. Grace must've known he wouldn't be able to sleep, because those were three of his favorite authors. He hadn't read any of the three novels, either. He picked up Vince Flynn's newest. He read the jacket copy, read the dedication, then the prologue. When he realized he'd read the prologue but hadn't a clue what he'd read, he closed the book.

Normally, after a day on the slopes like the one he'd had today, he would've crashed hours ago. Instead, he felt renewed, like he'd just run an easy marathon and won. It was Melanie. He couldn't stop thinking about her. He'd met her casually a few times, thought she was a knockout, but for some reason hadn't pursued her. When she'd tossed that cup of water in his face, well, it'd been an opening for him. Not having a clue why she'd acted in such a manner, he was glad she had. Of course, he wouldn't tell her that.

He couldn't believe she'd accepted his invitation to spend the weekend with him in Vegas. It almost seemed too easy, but he wasn't going to question his good fortune. Tomorrow, he would help her chop down a Christmas tree; heck, he might even chop one down for his room. Then they'd go back to her place and decorate. He'd never been inside her condo and found himself suddenly curious about her. Did she prefer the right or the left side of the bed? Tea or coffee? Sugar or cream or both? Such inconsequential things. But he found he wanted to know all about her. He wanted to feel her next to him when he woke up in the morning. He wanted to wrap himself around her, wanted to make love to her until they were both pleasantly exhausted. And he would, as soon as he felt the time was right.

He wasn't the man-about-town a lot of women thought he was. Not that Melanie had implied this to him, but he knew what his so-called reputation was on campus, and somehow he knew it would follow him for the rest of his life. If only he'd had such luck in high school. Gangly and tall, with crooked teeth and the beginnings of acne, he didn't seem to appeal to any one particular girl. He'd dated in high school and had his first serious relationship in his second year of college. He'd thought Diana was the love of his life until he caught her sleeping with his dorm mate. In his bed. A life lesson, Grace had said, and she was right.

Since Diana, he'd dated a few women, even slept with a few that he thought he cared about, but he'd never felt such instant attraction for any woman, nothing like what he was feeling for Melanie. Until now, he'd never believed in love at first sight, or rather, at first splash. He suddenly realized he'd never believed in it because he hadn't experienced it. And now? He looked around the bare but quaint bedroom. Pine chest of drawers, two twin beds with the night table separating them. Max's magazine covers framed and hung neatly on the wall opposite the beds. Everything looked the exact same way it had the last time he'd slept in this room.

The only difference: now he was seeing it through the eyes of a man in total, absolute love.

Love. He'd fallen head over heels. Big-time.

Chapter 12

"I can't believe you've spent your entire life in the fine state of Colorado and never chopped down your own Christmas tree. It's practically unheard of," Melanie joked, as they trudged through ankle-deep snow. The day was bitter cold, but at least the sun was out. A perfect day to cut down a tree.

"Yeah? Well I know something else that's unheard of," Bryce said.

Winded, Melanie stopped to catch her breath. "What's that?"

Bryce dropped the canvas bag of tools on the snow-crusted ground next to his sturdy boots. "This." He wound his hand around her loose hair, something he'd been wanting to do all day. With his free arm secured firmly around her waist, Bryce kissed her with all the pent-up emotions he'd spent the past forty-eight hours confronting—kissed her because he wanted to and because he could. Her response matched his. Both were eager to take their passion one step further, but Bryce wanted to wait until the timing was right. Or that's what his brain kept telling him. Another part of him said, forget timing, but that part would have to wait. He drew away from her but kept both arms wrapped around her waist. "You taste like chocolate." He licked his lips, teasing her.

She grinned the grin of the cat that ate the canary. "Think it has anything to do with that cup of hot cocoa I drank before we left?"

He nibbled at the tender spot where her shoulder met her neck. "Mmm, I've never done this," she muttered between kisses, "while searching for the perfect tree."

"There's a first time for everything," Bryce whispered, sending chills down her spine.

Melanie nodded in agreement. "This isn't the place . . . it's too cold." She visibly shivered. "Let's go find my Christmas tree before I turn into an icicle. I don't remember it ever being this cold, do you?" She moved away from him and grabbed the bag of tools by his feet. He took them from her, and she let him. He was a true gentleman, and she found that she liked that about him. Kind of an old-fashioned sort of guy. Women's libbers would not approve, that's for sure. She laughed out loud.

"What?" he asked. "Tell me what you're laughing at."

Melanie plodded along, content to have Bryce by her side. "It might not be funny to you. But I can see you're not going to let me brush it aside. Actually, I was thinking how nice it is to be with a man who has manners. You know, you're sort of old-fashioned. I like that about you. Not something a modern woman admits to these days."

She glanced at him, surprised at the tenderness in his expression.

"I guess I should say thanks. And you're right, I am a bit old-fashioned. My dad was adamant when it came to treating women with respect. He always treated Mom and Grace like they were a queen and a princess. I just followed in his footsteps. Are you telling me you dated a bunch of ill-mannered slobs?"

They came to a clearing, one Melanie was quite familiar with. Tall pine trees flanked the clearing, their pungent odor refreshing. Even though cutting one's own Christmas tree down in Colorado without a permit was illegal, Melanie's parents had owned this particular piece of property for at least twenty years. Her father always replanted what they took. It was kind of like their own personal Christmas tree farm.

Spinning around hoping to catch a glimpse of just the right tree, Melanie watched Bryce watching her. "Hey, you're not looking. You have to spin around like this." She twirled around, both hands splayed out at shoulder level. "When I was little, I would use this method, and whatever tree my right hand pointed to, that's the one we would chop down. Didn't matter the shape or size, Dad can work miracles with a pair of clippers, so . . . well, that's what I did—actually, still do. Look." She pointed to a small blue spruce about fifty feet away from where they were standing. "What do you think?"

Melanie watched Bryce closely as he came up next to her. He didn't touch her, he simply looked at her, his forest green eyes shining as bright as the sunlight that filtered through the massive pines. "I think I'm falling in love with you, that's what I think."

A soft gasp escaped from her lips, her breath caught in her lungs, then she exhaled.

"I think I am, too. Falling in love."

There. She'd said what she'd never imagined she would say to a man she'd practically just met.

Bryce wrapped his arms around her, pulling her down on the snow-laden ground. "Ever make a snow angel?"

Chapter 13

Olga Krause normally wasn't one for theatrics, but that day she would make an exception. It was, after all, the time of year one showed goodwill to one's fellow man. Besides, she really didn't have a say in the matter.

"I want you to know this is highly unusual," she said to the police officer and to Carla Albright, a social worker she'd known since coming to work at the orphanage twenty-seven years ago. "Come inside; you'll let out all the warm air the state has to pay for." Olga Krause opened the back door for the pair. Highly out of line, they were.

"I know it is unusual, that's why we're here," Carla stated matter-of-factly.

The policeman, who couldn't have been a day over thirty, held a small infant carrier by its sturdy plastic handle, while in his other hand, he gripped the hand of a little boy. The child's face was red, his bright blue eyes cloudy and puffy, as if he'd been throwing a temper tantrum. Miss Krause peered inside the carrier. Practically a newborn. And she did not accept newborns under any conditions. Or she wouldn't if given the choice. They cried constantly and were never satisfied. Fortunately, the state agency rarely saw a newborn. It seemed adoptive parents wanted them. She did not understand why. Why would one willingly want a baby? She had eleven children at the agency ranging in age from nine to fourteen. Not that she liked them, but they were much easier to manage than infants. Babies required constant attention.

"Follow me," Olga Krause said to the two unwelcome visitors. "Let's go to my office."

They followed her down the dark hallway.

"You would think the state would spring for some lights," Carla said to Olga's back. "It's as dark as a cellar in this place. And it's too quiet. Where are all the children?"

When they reached the office, Olga Krause turned the desk lamp on. She nodded toward two old blue-gray chairs. "Sit."

The small boy hiccupped, then stuck his thumb in his mouth. "Take your thumb out of your mouth right now, young man. You'll have an overbite, and the state will be responsible for the bill."

Carla Albright practically flew out of her chair. "How dare you speak to a child that way! He's only three years old, and he just lost both of his parents in a terrible car accident! Why do you care what the state has to pay for? It certainly doesn't come out of your paycheck."

Carla reached for the little guy's hand. She gathered him in her arms and sat down, holding him tightly in her lap. She dabbed at his eyes with the sleeve of her blouse. "Officer Rogers, please sit down. You're making me nervous."

"Yes, ma'am," he said. At least six-foot-three, Officer Rogers looked like an oversized child in the small chair. Careful so as not to wake the little girl resting peacefully inside, he balanced the carrier on his lap.

"Now, tell me exactly why you're here," Olga Krause demanded. "It's after eight o'clock. We normally don't allow visitors at this ungodly hour." She crossed her arms over her more-than-ample bosom, waiting for an answer.

"You need to retire, Olga. You're too old for this job," Carla said through clenched teeth.

"How dare you tell me what I can and cannot do! Now, get on with it before I ask you both to leave. Explain." She directed her hateful gaze at the little boy and his infant sister.

"Every state agency except yours has reached its maximum occupancy. It's Christmas, Olga. Where is the Christmas tree the state allocates its tax dollars for?" Carla smoothed the little boy's damp hair. "I'm serious. Olga. Something is not right here. I'm sure you have an explanation, but before you say another word, hear me out. Officer Rogers, would you mind taking Sam—that's his name, by the way—to the restroom, wipe his little face off, and see if he needs to potty. It's my understanding he has been trained for quite some time now," Carla said.

"Uh, sure . . . but," Officer Rogers looked at the baby in his lap.

"I'll take her." Carla gently helped Sam off her lap, then took the infant carrier from Officer Rogers. Sam looked like he was getting ready to cry again. Carla was so sad for the two children, she was tempted to take them home herself, but it was against state policy. If something didn't change soon, she would have to risk the state's wrath.

"Where are the children?" Carla demanded as soon as they were alone. "And don't you dare tell me they're sleeping, because no one puts a child to bed this early anymore, unless they're sick. And where is the Christmas tree? I'm not going to ask you again." Had she not had the infant seat in her lap, Carla would've reached across the desk and smacked Olga Krause right upside her homely face. Thank goodness for the baby, she thought as she fought to control herself. No wonder World Adoption Agency never ran at capacity. Who in their right mind would send a child to this . . . this *prison camp*?

"The children are in bed. I don't know if they are asleep; if they aren't, they should be. Bedtime is seven thirty, prompt. No exceptions. I have used the funds allocated for a tree for another purpose, which is none of your concern. Now, what is it you expect me to do with these two . . . kids?" Olga Krause gestured toward the baby as though she were garbage.

Carla was a calm woman. Never married, she'd devoted her life to finding homes for children who needed them. At sixty, she wasn't quite ready to call it quits, but after this experience, she wasn't so sure. Olga was in her midseventies and as mean as a belly-crawling snake. Carla prayed she never became as bitter and hateful as the woman sitting across from her. The state should have fired her years ago. Why they hadn't remained a mystery.

Forcing herself to bite her tongue, Carla spoke between gritted teeth. "Two days ago, these 'kids,' as you so eloquently call them, were made wards of the state when their parents were killed in a car crash on I-70. It was on the news—I'm sure that if you watched the news, you would have heard about the pileup. Eight cars were involved. Sadly, Sam and Lily, she's three months old, in case you're interested, were left without any family. Both parents were adopted and had no family to speak of. They were young and apparently they hadn't made . . . arrangements for their children, which is the worst injustice in the world. Now, does that answer your questions?"

"You want to leave them here? I am not equipped for an infant, I'll have you know. We don't have a crib, and certainly there are no baby bottles to be found. I'm sure one of our sister agencies is much more equipped than I." Olga Krause drummed her fingertips on the desk.

"Trust me, if I had a choice, we wouldn't be here. There is nowhere else, Olga. You have to take them. Unless you've a family willing to foster them on such short notice. My fosters are full, especially during the holidays. Poor little things," Carla said.

Olga cleared her throat. "Well, I have a young couple who might take them in, but I can't say for sure until I speak with them. The woman was just here; we haven't even completed her background check, though I'm sure she passed. I haven't counseled her or her husband. Never mind, they're not qualified. Forget I brought this up."

"No. Let's call them. I'll see to it that their paperwork

is expedited. Give me the information before I do something I'm not proud of." Carla made a mental note to check on the other children before she left. This was worse than she'd imagined.

Olga removed the single file from her desk drawer. She hadn't placed a child in over twenty years. With luck, that was about to change.

Chapter 14

With a slight screech, the plane touched down at Las Vegas's McCarran International Airport at precisely 1:40, just as scheduled.

Melanie and Bryce were seated in first class and had been given the royal treatment, courtesy of Caesars Palace and Bryce's checkbook. When he'd originally booked the trip, he'd had his mother's creature comforts in mind. Now he was glad he'd sprung for the extras. Melanie looked like a kid at Christmas when he'd picked her up this morning. She'd brought a small Louis Vuitton carry-on and nothing else. A woman with taste, he thought as he'd watched her at the airport in Denver. A true class act.

"What?" Melanie asked him while they waited for the cabin doors to open. "You've got this funny look on your face."

Bryce placed his hand on her cheek. "It's just the look of a guy head over heels in love, that's all." All the corny, lovey-dovey stuff he'd made fun of in his younger days wasn't corny anymore.

"Oh."

"Yeah, *oh.*"

Melanie giggled. "Sorry. You just looked funny to me. Guess I've never seen what a guy in love looks like."

A flight attendant's voice came over the intercom, telling them they were allowed to unfasten their seat belts but should remain seated.

"I know it's crazy, but I've never felt this way. Ever," Bryce said. He'd told her about Diana, and she'd told a few stories of her own. Both were on equal footing in the romance department.

Another flight attendant told Melanie and Bryce their limousine was waiting on the tarmac.

"Top of the line, Bryce, top of the line."

"Only the best." He grinned.

Since they were going to be in Vegas for just two nights, both had brought only carry-on luggage so they wouldn't have to wait at the baggage claim. Bryce carried both pieces of luggage in one hand.

In a cordoned-off private section on the tarmac, a sleek white Lincoln Town Car limousine waited for their arrival. Inside the limo, they found a chilled bottle of Cristal with two crystal goblets. With expert skill, Bryce removed the cork. He filled each goblet, the creamy white foam overflowing. "Let's make a toast."

Melanie nodded, holding her flute aloft. "Cheers." Bryce touched her glass with his. "To the future."

"To the future," she repeated.

If anyone would have asked Melanie a week ago what she would be doing a week later, she certainly could not have told them she would be drinking champagne while riding in a limousine with a man she was madly in love with. She still hadn't told Stephanie or her mother and dad about her blossoming relationship with Bryce because it was still so new to her. They hadn't even slept together. Melanie was a patient woman, and she knew for a fact that Bryce was a patient man. They'd had more than one opportunity to throw all caution to the winds, yet they hadn't.

Lost in her daydreams and expensive champagne, Melanie reclined into the soft leather seat, suddenly too tired even to think about anything romantic, let alone act on it. She closed her eyes. She was almost asleep when her cell phone rang. Fumbling through her purse, by the time she located her phone, whoever was calling had hung up. She didn't recognize the number, so she assumed it was a new client. She wasn't even going to think about work until after New Year's.

She and Bryce were on the same page in that department for sure.

"Anyone I know?" Bryce asked as she put her cell phone back in her purse.

"I don't recognize the number, so it's probably just a new client."

"Spoken like a woman of means," Bryce teased.

She winked at him. Though she hadn't gone into avid detail about her finances, she had told Bryce that her grandmother had made her a very wealthy young woman.

He told her that was fine with him, but he wasn't interested in her money.

When they arrived at Caesars Palace, a uniformed attendant actually rolled out the red carpet for them as they entered through a private entrance reserved for VIP guests only. He took their luggage and followed them at a discreet distance. Melanie felt like a movie star.

"A girl could get used to this kind of treatment," Melanie whispered.

"I have no clue where I'm going," Bryce remarked. The young man with their luggage revealed a small card in his hand. "If you will follow me," he said politely.

Bryce and Melanie stepped aside, allowing him to take the lead. Roman elements with a contemporary style made the elegance at Caesars Palace stunning. Everywhere one looked, there was marble, sculpted statues, and chandeliers that glistened like diamonds.

A replica of Michelangelo's statue of David stood eighteen feet high in the center of the grand lobby, adding a more imperial atmosphere. Melanie had only been to Las Vegas once, with a group of girlfriends right after she turned twenty-one. They'd spent most of their time lounging by the pool drinking wildly mysterious-looking cocktails. (That's probably why she didn't remember the trip that well.) So in a way, Las Vegas was as new to her as it was to Bryce.

The young man used the card to open the door to their room. They were staying in the Palace Tower Deluxe suite. After their luggage was put away inside a closet, Bryce gave the guy a wad of cash, then closed and locked the door behind him.

"This is awesome," Melanie said as she gazed around the room.

Decorated in brown, gold, and several shades of cream, the suite boasted a living room complete with sofa and contemporary end tables with exquisite lamps atop each one. A small dining area close to the balcony gave one a bird's-eye view of the famous Las Vegas Strip.

"So, what to do first?"

Melanie laughed. "Now that's a loaded question if ever I heard one. This hotel is humongous. It'll take days to see everything. It's a shame we only have two. I don't remember much about my last trip here. I guess I wasn't old enough to appreciate the concept."

She walked over to the sliding doors that led out to the small balcony and stepped outside. The December air was dry and cool, similar to that at home, but not nearly as cold. She had forgotten to pack a bathing suit, but somehow she doubted she would have time to visit the various swimming pools at the luxurious hotel.

"Let's go to the casino while you decide what you want to do first. Remember, this is my first time here."

"Okay. Let's go."

If anyone were to see them together, odds were good they would pass as a happily married young couple on their honeymoon. Certainly not a man and woman who, until last week, barely knew the other existed.

They spent the next six hours in the casino, Bryce at the blackjack tables while Melanie tried her hand at the roulette wheel. Deciding too much thinking was required, Melanie had wandered over to the slot machines, content to lose her winnings. She'd draped her purse shotgun style across her shoulder. Reaching inside to grab another twenty-dollar bill out of her wallet, she spied her cell phone. Flicking it open to check her missed call list, she saw that the same telephone number she'd seen in the limousine had called her numerous times. Highly unusual. Melanie felt a tinge of alarm. For someone to make so many phone calls, it must be something important. She clicked on the number and pushed the SEND button.

What she heard sent shivers down her spine.

"I've been looking all over for you," Bryce said. "I was starting to think you ran out on me. Hey, are you okay? You don't look so good. Melanie?" The sudden change in his tone brought her back to reality.

Not knowing what to do, or say, Melanie opted for the truth. At the bar over lattes, she told him about her desire to adopt a child. She explained that her reason for not telling him was that their relationship was too new, too fresh. Tears pooled in her eyes when she said, "I think I should just go home."

"Why would you even think such a thing? So, you want children, you're willing to adopt, become a single parent. What's not to like about that? Hell, I admire you even more than I did already." He blotted her tears with the tip of his finger.

"Really?" she asked, surprised at how easily he accepted her choice. He really was the most perfect man alive. Almost. They still hadn't slept together, but that didn't matter. When the time was right, she knew it would be worth waiting for.

"Yes, really. Now dry those tears, because we've got tickets to see Cher. You still up for that?" he asked, a wicked grin revealing his sexy white teeth.

When did I start thinking of teeth as sexy?
"Of course I am, but, Bryce, there's more."
"I'm listening."

Five hours later, they were on a flight to Denver. Only this time, as man and wife.

And what happens in Vegas stays in Vegas. They still hadn't slept together.

Chapter 15

Melanie looked at the fake, cheap, metallic gold ring on her finger. Then she looked at the fake cheap metallic gold ring on Bryce's finger. Then she looked at the marriage certificate printed on cheap, plain white paper. Then she looked at Bryce, who was still in a state of semi-shock.

They were married. Husband and wife. Till death do them part. The old ball and chain. She had married Bryce Landry. She was Melanie *Landry* now. She had to admit, she liked the sound of her new name.

Unlike the flight to Vegas, they were unable to purchase first-class tickets on such short notice, so the only seats available to them were those in coach at the very back of the plane. By the restrooms. The stench was atrocious.

Melanie had barely uttered a word since she'd confessed to Bryce that, even though she had been told by the horrible woman at the adoption agency that she wouldn't be able to adopt a child unless she was married, she'd gone ahead and had her application processed anyway. She said that she knew it was selfish and foolish of her.

She was flabbergasted when he told her there was no time like the present, that he would've married her anyway. He said it was his destiny.

"I told Ashley when I got married she could be my maid of honor."

Bryce took her hand in his. "Let's worry about one problem at a time. We can always have another wedding. Now, tell me again what this woman Carla said."

Melanie's eyes flushed with unshed tears. "It's like something right out of a novel. Apparently there was an eight-car pileup on I-70, nothing new there. A couple in their early thirties died at the crash scene. Carla said there were no relatives, no foster parents available. So I guess the next step was World Adoption Agency.

"According to Carla, Olga Krause has been stealing the state practically blind. She believes Olga is hoarding away money for when she retires. There are eleven other children in need of a home. Those poor little kids; I should've known something was wrong. And to think that old bat was in charge of all those innocents! She reminded me of Scrooge—I remember thinking that at the time. She just had a mean look about her. I hate to judge, but I hope that woman is prosecuted to the fullest extent of the law. Let her live the remainder of her life behind bars. Carla said the children were malnourished and frightened. Oh, Bryce, what in the world have I gotten myself into? And you, too."

Bryce squeezed her hand because, for once, he really

didn't know what to say. The only thought that kept beating against his skull was the fact that he'd married Melanie. They'd been dating for less than one week, and he'd married her. What he couldn't get past was the fact that he'd never felt such pure and complete happiness. Yes, it had been a crazy thing to do when Melanie told him she wouldn't be able to adopt a child unless she was married. Like the gentleman he was, he'd quickly made arrangements for a Vegas-style wedding, and now they were on their way home to Denver. Melanie had called her parents, telling them she was returning sooner than planned and that she would pick up Odie and Clovis as soon as she could. She had neglected to mention she was coming home a married woman.

Bryce had a feeling this Christmas was going to be unlike any other. Past and present.

"We'll work things out. I have lots of friends in Boulder." What he didn't say was that he wasn't sure if any of them would be willing to take in thirteen children.

Less than twenty-four hours after leaving Denver International Airport, they'd returned to Placerville. Seated in the rear seats of the private jet Melanie had engaged, they were the last ones to exit the plane. Neither spoke while they waited for the other passengers to retrieve their book bags, diaper bags, and the like from the storage compartment.

Bryce would've been happier seeing Cher, but Melanie and the thirteen kids were much more important. Being in academia, he was around young adults most of the time. Of course, he was beyond thrilled to be Ella's uncle, but would he pass muster as a parent if it came to that? He could only hope. Now more than ever, he wanted to be the stand-up kind of man his father would've been proud of.

After they had gotten to Denver, Carla had explained that there was no prohibition on single-parent adoptions in Colorado—that Olga must have deliberately misled Melanie on that score, because anytime a child left the orphanage, the funds available for Olga to embezzle decreased. But neither Melanie nor Bryce had the least regret about the solution Bryce had come up with for Melanie's adoption woes. Married they were and married they would remain. Till death do them part.

With a renewed sense of purpose, Bryce vowed those thirteen children were going to have the best Christmas ever.

He would make sure each and every child found a home, and, maybe, if he was lucky, each and every one of them would have a home before Christmas.

Epilogue

One week later . . .

Melanie quietly closed the door to the spare bedroom, careful not to shut it all the way, just in case Sam or Lily needed her during the night. This was their second night together, her first night as a legally certified foster parent. Carla had expedited her application given the circumstances. Normally, she would be required to take parenting classes and undergo an extensive background check, but her circumstances were anything but normal.

Bryce and her parents were waiting for her in the living room. She'd invited them over to thank them for their help locating temporary homes for the other eleven kids. It hadn't been easy, but they'd managed.

World Adoption Agency had been permanently closed. Olga Krause had dozens of charges filed against her. She'd been jailed, then released on her own recognizance. It would take years before her case was heard in court. Melanie rather hoped that the old woman would die first, saving the taxpayers money. Melanie knew that was callous, but she didn't care. The children in her care had suffered greatly on her watch, and who knew what kind of psychological problems they would endure in the future? Her mother always told her that children were most resilient. She hoped this was true.

And now it was time for her and Bryce to tell her family they were married. They'd decided to wait until all the hoopla died down, since the story of the orphanage had made headlines.

She took a seat next to her husband, still amazed at the changes in her life in such a short span of time. Bryce kept reminding her, saying over and over that you only live once. She agreed with him.

"Melanie, you've been dancing around all night. I know you're happy you have Sam and Lily—your father and I adore them already but something is bothering you. Am I right?" her mother asked with the sweetest smile. She was the best mother in the world. Melanie loved her so much at that moment, she had to close her eyes for a few seconds to compose herself. She was truly the luckiest woman alive.

"You're not sick, are you, kiddo?" her dad asked. "If you are, we'll get you the best doctors in the world."

"Dad, you're such a riot. No, I am not sick. At least, I don't think I am." She turned to Bryce. "Do I look sick to you?"

"You look beautiful, Melanie," Bryce said, his voice laced with love. And longing.

"Mom, Dad." She paused. "There is no other way to say it, so I'm just going to say it: Bryce and I got married in Vegas."

There.

She looked at her parents, waiting for their reaction. When they said nothing, she repeated herself.

"Bryce and I are married, and we're going to adopt Sam and Lily."

Her parents looked at one another, then at Bryce, and back at her. They high-fived each other. Then came the congratulations.

"Wonderful news! I knew something was up." Her parents hugged her; her dad shook Bryce's hand so long that she was sure it would fall off. That old guy thing. Mother and daughter hugged each other, tears puddling in their eyes.

"I couldn't have handpicked a better man for you, Melanie dear. Now, why didn't I see this coming?" her mother whispered loud enough for the others to hear.

Bryce laughed. "We didn't see it coming, either, but it's the best decision I've ever made."

Melanie kissed her husband on the cheek.

"So you're both okay with this? You're not going to have me committed?"

They all burst out laughing.

Bryce nuzzled her neck, whispering in her ear, "If I don't have you tonight, they'll commit *me*."

"Patience, Bryce. Patience," she whispered back.

Then Melanie giggled like a kid at Christmas. Right now at that precise moment, her world was absolutely perfect.

Merry Christmas, world!

Mister Christmas

Prologue

"You can't be serious?" Claire said, though deep down inside she knew he was as serious as the disease with which he claimed to have been recently diagnosed. "Christmas is one week away. I promised my brother I'd spend the holidays in Colorado with the family this year." Claire O'Brien paused as she listened to Donald Flynn's litany of reasons why it was imperative she come to Ireland, first thing in the morning. Lastly, he explained to her that it was a matter of life and death, that his disease was fast-moving, and there wasn't much time left, though she didn't believe him. She'd just spoken to him last week and he hadn't even hinted he was ill, let alone about to meet his Maker. "I'm ill, Claire. Can I count on you?"

She'd said of course.

No, he had something up his sleeve. She was far from naive. Living in the land of glitz and glamour had wizened her real quick-like to the ways of the rich and famous. Claire O'Brien was used to all sorts of people. Demanding. Spoiled. Rude. Whiny. But this? She wasn't sure what to call it. A plea maybe? She'd met Donald Flynn four years ago, when she was introduced to him at a party given for the firm's newest partner, Lucas Palmer. According to managing partner Brock Ettinger, Donald had been completely taken with her and had requested that all of his financial dealings be turned over exclusively to her.

And now he was dying, or so he says. "Bull. He's up to something."

Requesting her presence immediately, and she detested flying. Donald certainly didn't sound ill, or fearful. Just his usual commanding self. Though Claire had to admit, she truly liked the old guy even if he was a bit demanding at times.

As she calculated the necessary changes to her schedule, she realized that she would be lucky to catch a flight by midnight. Hopefully, some airline would have an international flight available on such short notice. Though she hated the thought, as much as she wanted to spend the holidays with her family, a part of her was almost relieved knowing she had a good reason to bow out, albeit with her usual excuse. Of course, the flying part wasn't good, but it is what it is.

Work, her usual excuse. And always valid.

Her family was used to it by now. Ever since her niece Shannon died from a rare blood disorder, something called thrombocytopenia, she no longer enjoyed her family visits. There was always that little something that seemed to be missing when they were together. Of course, it was Shannon. Her jolly bantering whenever they were together. As the firstborn grandchild, Shannon had been the life of the party, the link in the chain that bound them together, the one who made sure that they all had wrapped gifts under the tree exclusively from her. If someone felt the least bit cranky, Shannon had always made it her job to cheer them up. Shannon had always been the life of the party since day one, when she'd wrapped the entire O'Brien family around her tiny, pink finger. So if she was completely honest with herself, and she tried to be most of the time, she was actually grateful for Donald's request. Before she had a chance to change her mind, she scrolled through her BlackBerry for Patrick's phone number.

"Hey, sis," Patrick answered, not bothering with hello.

Caller ID, Claire thought. Sometimes a good thing. Sometimes not so good. The personal etiquette of phone calls no longer existed in today's high-tech-oriented world.

"Hey, yourself," she replied, knowing she was stalling. She couldn't just blurt it out. "So, how's the family?"

Lame, Claire, lame.

"Why do you want to know?" Patrick asked.

Darn! He was onto her already. She could hear the telltale indications of an inquisition in his voice.

She might as well get it over with. "You know how much I want to spend the holidays with you guys, right?" She paused, waiting for him to agree with her.

"No, but I suppose you're about to tell me?" he shot back.

"Patrick Edward O'Brien! Stop being such a shit. This is hard enough as it is. Look, I just received a call from a major client. He's near death and has requested my presence. You know, the will and all." At least she guessed it was about his will, but Patrick didn't need to know that. She held her breath as she waited for him to reply.

"Really, Claire?"

"Of course, really! I wouldn't lie about something so important. I am ashamed of you, Patrick. You ought to know me better than that by now."

She heard his chuckle and knew she'd gotten through the worst of the conversation. "What I know is you're an attorney who, it just so happens, has a way with words. So, seriously, little sister, is your client really at death's door?"

Attorney-client privilege prevented her from explaining further. "That's what I'm told. You know I can't go into details about my clients. I really wanted to see you guys, but this is my bread and butter. If I don't hustle my rear over to Ireland, I could be out of a job."

Claire heard his sharp intake of breath. "Ireland? Did I hear you correctly?"

She couldn't help smiling. Coming from a big Irish family that had never had the opportunity to travel across the pond, she had expected precisely this reaction. "Yes, as a matter of fact, you did."

"Then I say go for it even though Stephanie and the girls are really looking forward to your visit. Stephanie has a secret, but you'll just have to wait to hear what it is."

"Stop it! I hate it when you do that," Claire said, truly meaning it. Patrick had a way of saying things that irked her to no end—or rather a way of not saying them. "Spit it out."

"No can do. You'll just have to wait until your next visit."

"I'll call Stephanie myself. I am sure she won't make me come all the way to Colorado just to hear a little secret. And for the record, I do not know what that saintly woman and those two precious girls see in you."

More chuckling across the phone lines. "They adore me, what can I say? Of course, the feelings are mutual. Seriously, Claire, can't you reschedule this trip until after the holidays? We were really looking forward to seeing you this year. I know it's hard since Shannon's death, but the rest of us seem to manage to get through the holidays."

To be sure, he was right. It had been over five years since her niece's untimely death. Claire remembered all too well the utter shock she'd felt upon hearing the news. Even worse, she'd died on the day she was due to graduate from high school. She'd be out of college now had she lived. Claire's eyes teared up just thinking of the loss that Colleen and Mark, her sister and brother-in-law, must feel. Seeing how they'd suffered, Claire avoided committed relationships like the plague. Of course, Patrick had as well, but then he'd met Stephanie, a young woman with two daughters. They'd married three years ago and had yet to have children of their own.

Children of their own!

"Stephanie's pregnant!" she blurted out. "Patrick? Is this the secret you're not telling me?"

More laughter. "Hey, I'm not saying another word. When you get your client's affairs in order, come home and find out for yourself."

"That is so not fair!" Claire said, sounding as though she were still in high school. "I'm going to call her myself as soon as I hang up."

"She's been sworn to secrecy, just so you know. And Stephanie is my wife; her loyalties lie with me." More cackling across the lines.

If she thought he could see her, she would roll her eyes and stick her tongue out like she did when they were kids; but they were adults, and she would do the adult thing.

"You are an asshole, Patrick O'Brien." There, now that was the *adult* way to handle her older brother.

"Some may agree with you, but don't count my wife as one of them," Patrick cautioned her. "She's loyal to the end."

"Yes, Stephanie's a gem. She had to be to marry you. So, you won't give an inch?" Claire waited, hoping he'd cave, but her brother was as stubborn as she was. An Irish trait the entire O'Brien family shared.

"Not even a centimeter," he said.

"Then what am I supposed to tell the girls, and the rest of the gang?" Since she had planned on spending Christmas with the family, she had all their gifts wrapped and stuffed inside three extra suitcases in preparation for her flight to Colorado. Now, she'd have to mail them, and most likely, at this late date, they wouldn't arrive until after Christmas.

"The truth, just like you told me. You have a wealthy client who just happens to be dying. How convenient for you," Patrick said a bit smartly.

Damn!

"Look, this isn't funny. I have three giant suitcases stuffed with presents for the entire family. I had every intention of spending the holidays in Colorado. I miss my family. Plus, I am long overdue for a vacation."

"Look, I understand. Really I do, it's just the rest of the gang. It's just difficult for them to understand why you always seem to be too busy to spend time with them, especially the kids," Patrick said, then added, "And us."

Claire wanted to choke Patrick but couldn't. Did he really believe this was her choice? Surely he remembered how terrified she was of flying? Thoughts of spending hours in the air, with nothing but miles of water between her and land, almost caused her to refuse to make the trip. But unless she was prepared to lose Donald as a client, she really didn't have a choice. Damn Patrick for making this harder than it already was.

"I'll make you a promise. The second my work is finished, I'll fly straight to Denver from Ireland. Deal?" she asked.

"You've got yourself a deal. For now, I won't tell the others you're traipsing across the pond. Is that a deal?"

Unsure of how long Donald would need her to remain in Ireland, though clearly it couldn't be more than a couple of days, she readily agreed to delaying news of her trip to Ireland to the rest of the family. "It's a done deal."

Pressing the END button on the phone, Claire could only hope to keep her promise. It was that magical time of year, a time to enjoy and to cherish those whom she loved so dearly. If she broke her promise, Patrick would taunt her for the rest of her life.

Decision made, she quickly dialed the number for the travel agency the firm used. Twenty minutes later, she had a reservation to leave for Ireland in four hours.

Chapter 1

By the time she arrived in New York City, Claire was beyond exhausted and just a wee bit tipsy. She'd been so nervous on the flight from Los Angeles, she'd had one too many glasses of wine in hopes of calming her nerves. It hadn't helped.

After going through Customs, with a two-hour wait before her flight to Dublin, Claire found a vacant spot at one of the many bars at JFK. Knowing she would regret it, she hoisted herself up on the barstool and, in doing so, managed to get her shoe caught on the footrest at the bar, where she proceeded to lose her four-inch heel. Horrified because she did not have access to another pair of shoes—in her carry-on she'd packed only a book and a travel pillow for her trip—Claire crammed her foot in the shoe where the spiked heel dangled from the sole.

"What'll you have?" a twentysomething good-looking bartender asked her as she adjusted herself on the barstool.

"Uh, something that'll wake me up."

"Coffee?"

"No, I meant something that will make me sleepy."

"Long flight?" the bartender asked.

"Yep," Claire said somewhat woozily, then hiccupped. "Just came from LA, and now I'm headed to Ireland."

"I'll fix you up then. I know the perfect drink. Once you're on board, I promise you will sleep like a baby."

"I'll have that then," Claire said, not really caring what it was as long as it knocked her out. She did not like to fly. Period. It was not natural. If humans were meant to fly, they would have been born with wings.

Two minutes later, he placed a cocktail napkin in front of her, topping it off with a tall glass filled with amber liquid and a slice of lemon. Claire immediately took a sip. "This is good. Tastes like sweet tea." She downed the glass easily, then moved it aside, motioning to the bartender for another. He laughed, shook his head, and again placed another one of the tasty drinks in front of her. "This is really good," she said after she took another drink.

"It will help you sleep," the bartender commented as he wiped the bar down. "Just don't drink too many, or I can't promise you'll find your seat on the plane."

Claire finished the last of her drink, suddenly feeling beyond woozy. Her words came out fuzzy and slurred when she spoke. "How much ya need?" she asked as she fumbled inside her purse for her wallet.

"Forty bucks should cover you," he said.

Even in her state of inebriation, she thought the price outrageous. She smacked a fifty-dollar bill beside her empty glasses, then said, "Merry Christmas," but to her it sounded more like *Meruhkissmus.*

"Happy Holidays," the bartender called over his shoulder as he made his way over to his next customer.

"Yeah, sure," Claire mumbled as she exited the bar. Quickly scanning her surroundings for the ladies' room, she spotted it across from a Best Buy mini kiosk.

Limping through the throngs of travelers, Claire joined a long line of women waiting for their chance in the ladies' room. Too-bright fluorescent lighting along with her consumption of too much alcohol, made the room begin to swirl. Leaning against the wall, Claire closed her eyes, praying that the sudden urge to throw up would pass.

An elderly woman tapped her on her shoulder. "Honey, it's your turn."

Claire opened her eyes just in time to see an open stall waiting just for her. She waved at the kindly woman before she skip-hobbled the short distance. Dropping her purse and duffel on the floor, not caring that the germs of the world were probably seeping inside, she dropped to her knees, wrapped both arms around the base of the commode as though she were locked in a passionate embrace, and proceeded to purge herself of the alcohol she'd just downed.

Amid the sounds of running water, the whisper of air hand dryers, the clinking of the metal locks on the stall doors, and a lowered whisper from a harried mom, Claire had a brief moment of lucidity when she heard the same woman whispering harshly to her daughter that the woman in the next stall, *her,* was a very bad example. Claire gritted her teeth and squeezed her eyes into gator-like slits as another wave of nausea forced her to lean over the toilet once again. However this time, she neglected to hold her shiny black hair behind her. Not only did she now have vomit in her hair, but the automatic flush chose that moment to do its thing, and giant drops of toilet water splattered her in the face.

Claire came to the conclusion she was more than a bit tipsy: She was drunk, smashed, inebriated, highly intoxicated, whatever. She should know better, she thought, as she grabbed on to the giant plastic container that held an equally giant roll of tissue and struggled to steady herself. "Shit," she muttered when the plastic surrounding the tissue fell off, landing in the toilet. More water splashed her navy skirt. Bits of vomit clinging inside the bowl flew out of the water, creating tiny polka dots on her skirt.

Still woozy from the alcohol, Claire acknowledged that she was still drunk. She hadn't been so drunk since she'd passed the bar exam, and she knew that a killer hangover loomed in her near future. Taking a deep breath, she carefully eased into a standing position, heedful as she tried to balance herself on one four-inch heel, the other heel dangling from its sole, all while carefully stretching her arm to her side so she could retrieve her purse and duffel bag.

Forcing herself to appear normal, Claire managed to unlock the stall door and tumble to the sinks. The sight of herself in the mirror almost made her throw up again. Chunks of something she didn't want to put a word to clung to the ends of her hair. The makeup she'd applied so carefully in California was smeared across her face. Her mascara had run, leaving her with two raccoon eyes. The lipstick that promised to keep her lips plump and full for twelve hours made her look more like a clown. And she had always hated clowns, thought them beyond creepy.

She took another quick look in the mirror. If she weren't so pathetic, she would have laughed. Her main concern was getting to her gate. Anything more in the way of hygiene and cosmetic repairs could wait until she was safely aboard the plane. She did rinse out her mouth and rake a shaky hand through her hair. Turning around, she almost fell flat on her face before she remembered her high heel was broken. Catching herself, she stopped and removed both shoes, stuffing them in her canvas bag. Maybe she'd find a pair of slippers in one of the shops.

Taking a deep breath, Claire reunited with the throngs of travelers, ignoring the stares of the few who caught a good look at her appearance and her lack of shoes. Holding her head as high as she could without making herself dizzy, she walked what felt like ten miles before locating Gate 27. Spying one of the usual shops that sold everything from earplugs to blankets, Claire, still a bit woozy, but not nearly as drunk as she had been an hour ago, entered the shop and searched for a slipper, a flip-flop, anything to put on her feet. She perused the mini aisles and saw nothing that remotely resembled footwear of any kind. Seeing that the cashier was watching her every move, Claire took advantage of it. "Do you sell slippers of any kind? Shoes?"

The older man was dark-skinned and extremely attractive. He nodded, then motioned to the wall at the very back of the store. Claire followed his instructions and saw several pairs of children's slippers before locating the footwear for adults. "Oh." She almost said *shit* again but thought better of it as there were small children in the store. Realizing this was it, all or nothing, she grabbed a pair of Betty Boop slippers in a size seven. At the register, she paid for them, had the gentleman remove the tags, then slipped them on her feet. Warm, she thought with a smile. She hadn't realized how cold her feet were. She'd been too nauseated to pay much attention to anything else.

Slowly, she made her way back to her gate. No sooner had she sat down, preparing to relax for a bit before she boarded yet another long flight, this time across the Atlantic, was she surprised to hear the airline attendant telling those in first class to begin boarding. Taking extra care to appear steady on her feet, Claire slung her duffel over one shoulder while clutching her purse to her chest. She did not like flying. Not one little bit. Even first class.

Donald Flynn had better be on his deathbed.

She plucked her boarding pass from her purse and gave it to the attendant, then stumbled backwards.

"Are you all right, miss?" the attendant asked.

Yes, she was fine, still a bit intoxicated, but she wasn't going to mention this. "Yes, just a bit of jet lag," Claire answered, taking her boarding pass and tucking it in the side pocket of her purse.

Walking down the Jetway, Claire wanted to turn around and catch the next flight back to Los Angeles. As she stepped from the Jetway onto the Boeing 767, she mentally erased the image of sandy beaches and sunshine. She was on her way to Ireland, her ancestral homeland. A trickle of excitement inched down her spine as she located her seat. Her mother and father would've come with her had she invited them. Now, sitting here all alone, she was sorry that she hadn't invited them; but this was a business trip. She wouldn't have had enough time to spend with them. Maybe she would give them a trip to Ireland for their wedding anniversary.

With her thoughts all over the place, Claire's fear of

flying took a backseat as she attempted to cram her duffel beneath the seat in front of her. Once that task was accomplished, she removed her compact from her purse. She peeped in the mirror and didn't recognize herself. That bartender surely added ten times the amount of liquor called for in whatever it was she'd drunk. Still feeling slightly woozy, she was ticked at herself for acting so irresponsibly. She rarely had a drink, and now here she was flying to another country, letting a strange guy fix her a drink without even asking what was in it. Feeling the need to right herself some way, she took a packet of wet wipes from her purse and cleaned the smeared makeup from her face. Then she ran another wipe along the length of her hair to remove the horrid smell, along with little chunks of—she didn't even want to go there. Before she changed her mind, she hit the CALL button. Within seconds, a perky blond flight attendant hovered over her. "Ma'am?"

Ma'am? Claire thought, feeling old and dirty beside the perfectly groomed young woman.

"Ma'am? Is there something I can get you before we prepare to take off?"

"Uh, yes. Would it be possible to get a wet cloth and a cup of strong coffee?"

Chalk white teeth smiled down at her. "Absolutely. Would you like cream and sugar?"

"No, black is fine, thanks."

Minutes later, the perky flight attendant delivered a warm cloth along with a steaming cup of coffee. Claire thanked her, placed the coffee on the side table, then ran the warm cloth across her face and neck and the strands of her hair. She practically downed the hot coffee in one gulp and felt a bit better physically. Still slightly nervous, she leaned against the headrest and closed her eyes. She forced her mind to another place—her happy place, she called it. Rainbows, lots of sunshine, and warm, sandy beaches with cool blue water lapping against a creamy shore. She'd found this simple exercise quite useful when she had to fly. If only she hadn't added alcohol to the mix, she might've enjoyed the hours of forced relaxation, but she'd acted impulsively, and now her method wasn't quite as effective.

Claire continued to lean back against the headrest as more passengers made their way down the narrow aisles. Since it was a night flight, she figured all would be quiet, and she would use the time for some much-needed rest. No more had the thought flickered across her mind than she heard an infant's high-pitched cry. She sat up in her seat and turned around. A pretty redheaded woman, probably in her mid-thirties, held the baby next to her chest and bounced the child up and down as she tried to put a bag in the overhead bin with one hand. A flight attendant saw her attempt and finished the task for her. The woman and crying child sat in the aisle seat beside Claire, which meant if she had to get up to go to the restroom during the long flight, she'd have to disturb the mother and child. On an impulse, Claire turned to the woman. "Do you want to trade seats? I wouldn't want to bother you"—she nodded toward the crying infant—"if I have to go to the restroom."

"Aye, that would be helpful," she said in a thick Irish accent. "I like the window seat. I can"—she pronounced *can* like *kin*—"lean me head against the window an' have a rest if this little bairn allows me."

Claire grinned. "Boy or girl?" she asked as she removed her duffel from beneath the seat.

"This wee one's a lad, and a mighty hungry one, I might add."

With quick precision, the young woman eased out of her seat, her grip on the baby firm, yet she still continued to bounce him up and down to soothe his now-soft cries. Claire stepped into the aisle while the woman adjusted herself in the window seat.

Relieved, Claire sat down, fastened her seat belt, suddenly glad for the young woman's company. At least she wasn't seated next to some old man who wanted to tell her his entire life history and that of his ancestors. She'd been through that scenario more than once.

"I'm Claire O'Brien," she said.

"I'm Kelly, and this is Patrick, but we've taken to calling him Paddy, an' I think it's gonna stick."

"My brother is named Patrick, though most of his friends call him Eddie."

"Must be the name no one wants to own up ta," Kelly observed as she removed a blue plastic baby bottle from her bag. "This one is hungry, an' I can't put off feedin' him any longer. I wanted to wait till we were airborne, but he's gonna start wailin' again if'n I don't."

Claire adored Kelly's accent and couldn't wait to hear the rest of Ireland's folk speak the brogue she'd wanted to hear for most of her life. She'd mimicked the accent many times, but she never sounded quite the way a true Irishman would.

"Poor little guy," Claire said for lack of anything better. She didn't have children, and though she'd been around her nieces and nephews plenty of times when they were toddlers, not too much as infants. She was as unschooled in the care of an infant as much as little Paddy himself.

"This is his first flight, and my first time flyin' with a babe. My mum tells me their ears hurt, and I should make sure he's feedin' until we reach altitude."

Again, Claire was completely out of her element and didn't know what to say, so she said the first thing that popped into her head as she observed the white liquid in the light blue bottle. "Looks like he'll be finished before we even take off."

"Aye, that's what I was afraid of," Kelly said suddenly, no longer the confident mother she appeared to be.

"I can help," Claire spurted out of the blue.

"You've experience with babes?" Kelly asked, her eyes brightening with hope.

She swallowed, then licked her lips. "Not really, but I can learn."

Kelly laughed, the sound almost magical. "He's just eight weeks. Not sure I'm even qualified to offer suggestions, but I'll manage."

The mere thought of the responsibility of caring for a child instantly sobered her up. She thought of her sister Colleen, and how she must have felt losing Shannon. And Megan, her other sister, had three sons. How *did* they manage to care for a family and do all the other things required? Claire had spent her entire adult life pursuing her career, climbing up the ladder in hopes of making partner in a prestigious law firm. Now, though she was within a year of achieving that goal at Arleo, Hayes and Ring, she thought it insignificant compared to her sisters' accomplishments. Raising a family wasn't in the cards for her. She'd be up a creek without a paddle if she were Kelly.

"If you need to stretch your legs, or use the restroom, I'll be happy to hold him." *Yes,* Claire thought, *I can do that.* She'd held babies before.

"And I might just let ya," Kelly replied. "I didn't want to travel alone so soon after having the babe, but me gran passed away, and I had to come to New York for the services."

"I'm sorry. My sister lost her oldest daughter a few years ago. It's still hard for her. Really, for all of us. Especially during the holidays. Shannon was always the bright light of the family. She was the first grandchild."

Kelly adjusted the now-sleeping Paddy to her other shoulder. "Oh that's terrible. I'm very sad for yer sister. I would die if somethin' were to happen to my babe here."

With the effects of the alcohol practically gone, Claire was glad when the captain announced they were taxiing to the runway and were third in line for takeoff. She didn't want to think about Shannon, or anything sad. Having Kelly and Paddy next to her would keep her occupied for the flight.

But deep down inside, seeing them together forced her to think of her future and just how empty it was.

Chapter 2

As soon as she was through Customs, Claire saw a beret-wearing older man holding a sign with her name on it. This must be the driver Donald had promised. Not wanting to keep him waiting, she hurried to greet him. "I'm Claire O'Brien. I'm waiting for my luggage."

The old guy was red-cheeked with white tufts of hair peeking out from the side of his plaid beret. "Not a problem, Missy. Take as long as ya need. I'll be here to help ya," he said, then added, "By the way, me name is Martin. My friends call me Marty." His smile was as genuine as the accent with which he spoke.

Claire couldn't help but laugh at the old guy. A friendly twinkle in his eye, and a happy grin, she liked him instantly. "Marty, then. Give me a few minutes, and we can be on our way. I don't want to keep Mr. Flynn waiting. Will we be going to the hospital first?" she asked before checking the board to see which carousel her baggage was on.

The old man looked as though she'd knocked him upside the head. "Why in the world would you think Flynn was in the hospital?"

He truly looked perplexed. "I was told by the man himself that he'd been diagnosed with a deadly disease and it was only a matter of time before he"—she didn't want to say died to this old man because he appeared to be in a state of semi-shock—"well, he said there wasn't a lot of time left and asked that I come to Ireland immediately."

"That old coot, I knew he had something up his sleeve."

Claire stared at him. "What do you mean?"

"I'll let Mr. Flynn explain himself to ya," he replied.

Clearheaded now after a few hours of sleep and several cups of hot coffee, Claire was her old self again, yet she wondered if she'd somehow misunderstood Donald's words. No, she thought to herself, she had not. Something wasn't right, but until she met with the man face-to-face, there wasn't a thing she could do but wait and hear him out. Maybe Martin, *Marty* hadn't been told of his employer's imminent death.

She saw her flight number and the designated carousel on the board, and, lucky for her, it was just two rows down. Within a couple minutes, she spied her luggage, yanked it off the conveyer belt, then returned to follow Martin to the car.

Outside, the weather was cold and damp, the skies a slate gray. Claire shivered as she removed her jacket from her duffel bag and slipped it on while Marty took care of her luggage.

Though he was older, Marty hefted her luggage in the

vehicle's trunk as though it were light as a feather. Maybe he looked older than he actually was, Claire thought. She laughed when she saw *Marty* slide into the driver's seat as it appeared completely foreign to her. "I don't think I could ever drive a car like this," she said as soon as she was settled in the backseat.

"Aye, it's what I'm used to, don't know nothin' else, Miss Claire. I've never traveled across the pond to America, and don't mean to be rude, but I ain't never wanted to. I love ma country."

"A man should be proud of his country. There is certainly no shame in that. My ancestors are of Irish descent, yet I'm the first one in my family to have the opportunity to travel to Ireland. I can't wait to see the countryside, all the shades of green."

"Aye, there's about forty of 'em, maybe more. It's a grand old place to be," he said as he maneuvered his way out of the line of traffic. "If you want to see the countryside, I'll drive as slow as I can. Though it's cold, and we'll see fog all over, it's still unlike any beauty ya've ever seen, lass."

Claire wrapped her arms around her waist, unused to the biting cold. "Is it always this cold this time of year?" she asked.

"Aye, and it'll get colder, too. Am used to it, though, as are most Irish. That's why we spend sa much time in the pubs. A tall Guinness or a hot whiskey warms the soul."

After her experience with alcohol yesterday, there was no way she was going to imbibe any form of booze while in Ireland. After all, she was here on business. At least that's what she'd been led to believe. She now suspected Donald Flynn had called her across the pond for reasons that had nothing to do with his supposed imminent death. And if he'd called her away from her family at Christmas unnecessarily, she would show him her Irish side. She grinned at the thought, but still, if Donald hadn't been truthful, she wasn't going to let him get away with it, wealthy client or not.

Chapter 3

Once they were out of the city, Claire took the time to view Ireland's great beauty. Though it was foggy, she was still able to view the green farmland, some of it filled with dairy cows, others dotted with sheep, some shaved and others waiting for their turn at the shears. She'd get the family some good wool socks while she was here, she thought, as they passed yet another farm. Colorado winters were brutal.

Man-made stone walls separated areas of each farm they passed. Often, in the middle of a lavish field of green, there stood more of the man-made stone fences, with a small bit of what once might have been a small cottage, or possibly a church. Ancient cemeteries, some she knew were hundreds and hundreds of years old, dotted the countryside, with the occasional Celtic cross. Claire knew a bit of the cross's history, but in her mind now she summed it up as a cross surrounded by a ring. When and if the opportunity presented itself, Claire would return to Ireland, maybe even bring her family along, and together they could explore their homeland together as a family. Powerscourt Gardens, the Blarney Castle, and the Cliffs of Moher were just a few of the places she wanted to visit when time permitted.

"So how long will ya be here?"

Good question. If Donald Flynn wasn't dying, she might leave tomorrow, but she wasn't going to tell this to Flynn's employee. "I'm not sure at this point. I promised my family I'd be home for Christmas." And she would do her best to keep that promise.

"Aye, you don't want to be away from the wee ones, especially this time of year."

"No, I don't have children. I live in California, one of my brothers and his wife and children live in Colorado. My brother manages a ski lodge there, and I was planning to spend Christmas with them this year, or at least I was until Mr. Flynn called."

"Got that stiff-headed nephew on his back for something. Won't tell me what it's all about, but I can tell ya, Quinn Connor ain't a happy man."

Quinn Connor? She'd heard his name before but couldn't recall where at the moment.

"I'm sure Mr. Flynn will keep me informed if there is a situation," she said though now she didn't believe anything Mr. Flynn had said. If he were truly on his deathbed, would his nephew be on his back? And if he were dying, what kind of man was this nephew? Heartless? She would avoid any preconceived notions just yet. She would wait and see for herself.

"Aye, I hope so, miss, I sure hope so."

For the next hour, they traveled in silence. Claire strained to see as much of the countryside as possible through the fog, which had gotten even heavier since they left the airport in Dublin.

Breaking the silence, Claire asked, "How far to Glendalough?"

Marty glanced at his watch. "Another half hour. With this fog movin' in, I'm not wantin' to drive too fast."

"No, of course not. I just assumed it was a short distance from the airport." The roads were so small, she couldn't believe two vehicles could drive either way without scraping against one another. Twice they'd had to practically take to the ditch when a tour bus zoomed down the road as though they were on the freeway. She didn't want to drive in Ireland, or at least not this trip.

"You just sit back an' relax, lassie, so when we arrive at the Flynn estate, you'll be all rested up, ready for whatever it is that old Donald's got up his sleeve."

Relax, right. She wouldn't be able to relax until she had a hot shower, a good night's rest, and at least one pot of coffee. She felt crummy because she hadn't showered in almost twenty-four hours. And how could she forget her upchucking episode at JFK? Once she'd settled in for the long flight, she spent a bit of time in the airplane's restroom. She managed to stick her hair under the meager stream of water, which she had to hand pump, then used the hand soap to wash the vomit completely out of her hair. She had managed to clean herself up a bit more with the baby wipes Kelly gave her. She'd added a bit of lipstick and combed her hair before they landed. Lucky for her, the Betty Boop slippers were an item much desired by Kelly. When they landed she'd actually offered to buy them from her. When Claire explained her broken-heel situation, Kelly whipped a pair of gently worn black leather ballet flats from Paddy's diaper bag and offered them to her. She'd gladly accepted them, giving the Betty Boop slippers to Kelly. They'd exchanged phone numbers, and again Claire made another promise to visit her before she returned to the States. She'd made lots of promises, *commitments,* and she hoped she would be able to keep them.

The soft lull of the engine and the narrow winding roads forced her to recline against the plush headrest. Her eyes were gritty from being awake so many hours. Closing them for a few minutes, she fell into a deep and troubled sleep.

"No!" she shouted in her dream, only to realize she'd screamed aloud.

"Nightmares?" Marty asked.

Claire took a deep breath, trying to clear the cobwebs from her head. She never remembered her dreams, but whatever this one was, she must've been frightened and running because her heart continued to pound even after she came fully awake. "No, not that I remember. I'm just overly tired."

"We're turning down the road leading to the estate now. You might want to have a look as we round the corner. The Flynn place is a sight ta behold, especially with the fog hoverin' above."

Claire nodded. "I'm sure it is," was all she could come up with.

Marty was right. As soon as they went around a sharp curve, she saw the Flynn estate. The mountains behind the estate were stunning. Claire drew in her breath as they made the final round, where she had a bird's-eye view of the Flynn *estate* . . . This was not an *estate*!

"Good heavens! This is a castle," Claire exclaimed.

"Aye it is, lassie. Been in the Flynn family since the 1700s, though it's been modernized several times."

For a minute, Claire was truly awestruck. A castle. Why didn't she know this about her client? Why hadn't she been made aware of his . . . living arrangements? She was quite aware of his financial status, knew he was one of Ireland's wealthiest men. But a castle? No, she truly hadn't a clue.

"Wait till ya see it tonight when it's all lit up. It's all decorated for Christmas. People from all across Ireland drive by to have a look. Mr. Flynn even opens the gates so they can get a close-up. Old Flynn's a good fella, just a bit ornery at times."

She stared at the *castle*. She had actually been *summoned* to a *castle*. A week before Christmas. It reminded her of one of those cheesy Lifetime movies she loved to watch. No, this was real. She couldn't wait to hear what Mr. Flynn had to say. It was becoming more and more obvious that he wasn't dying. Marty didn't have a clue, and when he'd called her, he'd sounded just fine. No, there was something more going on at the Flynn estate, rather *castle,* and she planned to find out exactly what as soon as she entered. *I won't be the least bit surprised if there's a moat,* she thought, as they reached the end of the winding lane leading to the front of the castle.

Chapter 4

Even though it was the dead of winter, the grounds were a lush, deep forest green, with shrubs in so many shades of green, she couldn't count them. And the flowers she couldn't even begin to identify; she'd never seen anything like them in America, anywhere. "How do the flowers survive in the winter?" she asked, finding it odd.

"Some only grow in the winter," Marty said. "The fall is our best time for color, though. It's a mighty sight to b'hold."

Claire couldn't begin to imagine just how beautiful the grounds were in the fall. Mesmerized by the site of the castle, the mountains in the background, the complete and total enormity of this place Mr. Flynn called home, she couldn't wait to see the inside.

There was a circular drive at the side of the castle, and Claire knew full well that this hadn't been here in the

1700s, but it appeared as though it had. The stones were an exact match to those on the castle, the small garage-like area where Marty parked the car was also an exact match to the rest of the castle's stone. Claire wondered if this had been a carriage house of sorts back in its day.

Marty opened her door and took her by the hand, help-ing her out of the car. "Tilly will be wantin' to feed ya as soon as ya walk through the doors. She's Mr. Flynn's chef, and she's a fine one, too. But if you don't wanna eat any o' that fancy stuff she puts out, she makes a mighty fine Irish stew. I saw Quinn's motorcycle. He must've ar-rived while I fetched you from the airport, but don't pay him no mind either."

Claire laughed. "Does this mean I'm to ignore every-one but Mr. Flynn?" she asked, her tone light and teasing.

Marty chuckled. "I'll let ya decide that for yourself. Now let's get inside outta this cold. Me old bones are aching from the chill."

Claire couldn't agree with his proposal more.

The door they used led them to the kitchen. Claire didn't have a clue what the aroma that she smelled was, but all she knew right then and there was that she had to have whatever it was, and it was absolutely heavenly. She en-tered a kitchen that reminded her of something they used on *Iron Chef,* a popular TV show in America that aired weekly on the Food Network. She stared at all of the chrome appliances; pots and pans of every shape and size hung from a giant rack from the ceiling. A bay window that faced the sunshine, when there was sunshine, Claire imagined, held dozens of colorful pots filled with aro-matic herbs. Rosemary, thyme, and cilantro were just a few that she recognized. She wasn't much of a cook but did appreciate a well-stocked kitchen. From the looks of it, Mr. Flynn had it all in the food department.

"Told you it was pretty nice in here," Marty said.

Claire smiled. "You did, you just didn't say how pretty it was." She walked around the kitchen amazed that she was actually inside of a castle. In all the fairy-tale books she'd ever read, castles did not have kitchens that looked like this, but she supposed that could be part of *her* fairy tale.

Claire had to remind herself that she was not in Ireland, in this castle, to admire the kitchen and call up fairy tales from her childhood. She was here as an attorney, a financial advisor to one of Ireland's wealthiest men, who just so happened to be at death's door, or so he had said. Not wanting to waste another minute, Claire spoke up. "So where is Mr. Flynn? I really need to see him." About that time, a tiny little Asian lady appeared from around the corner. Claire thought she couldn't have been much over four feet tall and *might* weigh eighty pounds, and that only soaking wet. Her jet-black hair was cut as though a bowl had been placed around the circumference for a guide. Her bangs, or at least what there were of them, were cut so short, they barely covered her forehead. Tiny, almond-shaped eyes focused on hers, then a grin as big as the castle lit up the little woman's face. *This must be Tilly,* Claire thought.

"Mr. Flynn was right," Tilly exclaimed to no one in particular. "You are perfect for that one. And you are tall like him, too." The little woman spoke as if Claire were in another room and not there to observe and listen as the diminutive woman stared at Claire as though she were an object to be admired.

"Tilly," Marty admonished the little woman. "You're here to make sure Miss Claire has a nice hot meal waiting for her as soon as she's had a chance to clean up."

Claire would've sworn Marty was giving Tilly the evil eye. She observed the two of them together, and that is when it clicked.

Donald Flynn was not sick; nor was he dying. He was probably looming above them somewhere in this giant castle, looking down at the scene below him, laughing. Claire clinched her hands in a fist, completely ticked off.

Tilly chose that moment to acknowledge that Claire was actually in the room with them.

"You want dinner now? Or do you want to wait for the men?" Tilly asked.

Claire actually had to close her eyes for a couple of seconds. Then she opened them again just to make sure she wasn't living in some fantasy fairy tale of a dream. She looked around the kitchen. No, this was very real, too real. Could it be possible that they still lived by the rules of etiquette from another century? Possibly the seventeenth century? No, that was too much.

"So, which you want?" Tilly asked again.

Marty cleared his throat, shook his head, walked across the kitchen, and placed a caring hand on Claire's shoulder. "Tilly sometimes forgets her manners, thinks she's back in China, where women are ruled by their men."

That explains it, Claire thought. She mentally forgave the little woman her faux pas.

"And isn't that as it should be?" said a deep male voice.

Claire directed her gaze in the direction from where the words came. She blinked once, then twice, and yet again, sure what she viewed was just another part of this fantasy world that she had stepped into when her feet touched the green grass of Ireland. Because, nowhere in her world, and her world was quite the fantasy land living in Los Angeles, California, did men look like the one that bracketed the doorway with lanky yet muscular arms, extending from an equally broad chest that led to a narrow, but not too narrow, waistline. He wore faded black denim that looked as though it choked the muscular legs encased inside and clung in other places that it shouldn't. Claire felt her cheeks flame as she stared just below the man's belt. Quickly raising her eyes to his chest, she saw that it clung too tightly to a worn-out black T-shirt. When she was able to take her eyes away from his massive chest, she swallowed quickly, then turned her eyes away.

"So you're that attorney who flew all night long to get here before Donald kicks the bucket?"

Claire took a few seconds to gather herself. She had to remember she was a professional woman used to dealing with men of all kinds. "I'm Claire O'Brien," she stated firmly, confidently. "And you are?" She let her words hang in the air.

The man chose to fully show himself. He walked across the giant kitchen as though he belonged there. *It would be funny,* Claire thought, *if a man's life wasn't hanging in the balance.* Well, she didn't really know that, not yet. She reminded herself that she was about to find out. She looked at Marty and Tilly, who watched the two of them as though they were both animals about to pounce on their prey.

"I guess he doesn't speak. Possibly you're a younger version of Liam Neeson, maybe a stand-in?" Claire couldn't help but notice the strong resemblance between the two.

And she would never admit it to the man who stood before her, but he was much better-looking than Liam Neeson, and certainly much younger. Raw power and a keen intelligence emanated from him, despite his good looks.

The guy had the audacity to laugh, loudly. "I hear it all the time, but no, that isn't my chosen profession. Like you, I'm an attorney."

It was then that Claire remembered Quinn Connor and where she'd met him. "We've met before," she said, using her best attorney voice. Firm, commanding, and no-nonsense.

All six-foot-four of him walked across the room, stopping a couple of feet in front of her. He held out his hand to her. "I'm sure I would have remembered," he said with barely a trace of an Irish accent.

Claire was sure he was speaking the truth. It had been during her last year of law school, and though their introduction was only a brief one, she'd never forgotten him. And looking at him now, she realized he had only gotten better with age. Like a fine wine, maturity had only made him sexier, more appealing to the opposite sex. Now the question was, did she remind him of that long-ago meeting or should she let it go? Deciding on the latter, she spoke. "You're probably right; I must've mistaken you for someone else."

If he suddenly remembered their chance meeting, she would simply use time and age as an excuse. Though something told her, by the glint in his eye, that he knew exactly when they'd met, and where. Los Angeles, a cocktail party when, fresh out of law school, the firm at which she had begun her career, Visco, Walsh and Mack, opened a second office in a new high-rise they'd built. The managing partner had invited attorneys from across the globe, and a few of the clerks who were in their last year of law school and had been offered associate positions in the firm, Claire being one of them. Quinn Connor was the legal golden boy that day, as was mentioned numerous times throughout the evening. He had garnered a perfect score on the bar exam. She remembered watching him throughout the evening, smiling at him. The few times his eye had caught hers across the room, he really hadn't paid much attention to her, and for some reason, even now, she remembered feeling rejected by him. She wasn't the girl she'd been back then. Now she was a powerful professional woman who could hold her own against men like Quinn Connor.

Chapter 5

Claire took immediate control of the situation before it got even more out of hand. "It's been a long twenty-four hours. If Mr. Flynn is well enough to see me, I'd like to freshen up a bit before I make my appearance." Claire turned to Marty and Tilly, who watched her and Quinn as though they were a circus sideshow act.

Quinn laughed, then replied, "You do appear to be a bit rough around the edges; you look like you could use a shower and a hot meal."

Knowing he was trying to get under her skin, she lifted her chin, meeting his sexy gaze straight on. "And you, Mr. Connor, look as though a trip to a clothing store might be in order. Or is this the mode of dress attorneys affect when they're in Ireland?"

Suddenly, Marty stepped between the two. "Quinn,

leave this young lady alone; she ain't used to your warped sense of humor. Right, Ms. Claire?"

Marty was wrong. She liked a good sparring partner now and then. It broke up the monotony when things got boring.

"I get his sense of humor," Claire remarked, then stepped away from Quinn's penetrating stare. Apparently he wasn't aware of the fact that she had five brothers whose sense of humor was most likely more warped than Quinn Connor's.

"I like a woman who understands a sense of humor. Actually, it's one of the main requirements for all the women I date," Quinn said teasingly.

Claire didn't believe that for a minute. With a man who looked like Quinn Connor, he needed a matching beauty, a bit of competition in the looks department. While Claire wasn't a great beauty, by any means, she'd been told on more than one occasion that she was quite attractive. She supposed when she put on makeup and did her hair, she wasn't too hard on the male eye. At five-foot-seven, with long, shiny black hair and clear blue eyes, Claire had turned a few heads in her day.

"I don't know what that is I'm smelling, but I'm dying to taste it. Tilly, Marty tells me you're the best chef in all of Ireland." Claire watched the little woman squirm under her praise.

Tilly chuckled, her little almond eyes twinkling like the lights on a Christmas tree. "I wasn't sure what you would like, being from America and all, so I made entrées for you to choose from. I wasn't sure if you are one of those vegans or a vegetarian, whatever they call them over there, so I made a little bit of everything. I've made a cheese platter. You might like to get started on that. Ireland has some of the finest cheeses in the world. Ardrahan, has a rich nutty taste, and then there's Corleggy, a pasteurized goat cheese I get from County Cavan, some of the best in Ireland. And, lastly, I have Durrus, a creamy, fruity cheese. Of course, we have an array of breads, scones, and biscuits. I didn't know if you were one of those girls who watched their figure all the time, but apparently it looks like you don't have to, so you might want to try my potato, cabbage, and onion soup with my hearty brown bread. Made just this morning when I heard you were coming. Donald insisted I make a traditional Irish stew for you. It's good beef, lamb, lots of potatoes, and a few secret ingredients I'll never reveal. So, if you're hungry," Tilly finished.

If she weren't hungry before, she certainly was by then. She wanted a taste of everything. "I don't know when I've been offered such a variety of foods to choose from. Would it be rude of me to want to try a bit of everything?" Claire asked, grinning. Just that moment, her stomach chose to make its state of hunger known to all who were within a few feet of her. She couldn't remember when she'd had her last meal, only that she'd had way too much alcohol in her system during the past twenty-four hours and not near enough food.

"I think you probably just made Tilly the happiest woman in the world," Marty said.

"And me, too. I just hate to eat alone," Quinn teased, then actually had the nerve to look Claire straight in the eye and wink at her. "Do you mind if I join you?"

Claire thought it a little late for him to ask for permission, but she didn't see any reason to deny him. "Not at all."

Tilly scurried about the kitchen, filling platters with cheeses and bread, ladled the thick, hearty soup into bowls, and brought these to the table, a giant wooden structure that Claire would bet was hundreds of years old and had been in the Flynn family forever.

"I'll let you two get started with the soup and cheese; then, if you're still hungry, I'll serve you both up a dish of my Irish stew. Marty, why don't you make a pot of tea for these two while I get their plates ready."

"Would it be possible for me to clean up a bit before I sit down to eat?" Claire asked, dying to remove her wrinkled skirt and Kelly's too-tight black ballet slippers.

"I'm sorry, Miss Claire," Marty said. "Donald told me where to put you."

He spoke of her as though she were a thing, something to be placed wherever he desired. Again, Claire thought, as soon as she saw Mr. Donald Flynn, she was going to give him a piece of her mind, American-style.

"If you wouldn't mind taking me there, I'd love to clean up before I eat," Claire stated firmly, letting them all know how she felt about Mr. Donald Flynn's *putting* her anywhere.

Tilly called over her shoulder as she prepared their plates of food. "Marty doesn't always remember his manners, Miss Claire. You follow him upstairs, and when you come back, I'll have your meal waiting for you." Tilly happily bustled around the kitchen, in her element. Claire couldn't help smiling as she watched her.

"I'll be right down," she said as she made her way up the winding staircase. "This is some place," she said to Marty's back. "Not sure I'd want to live in a place this size."

What she assumed were oil paintings of the Flynn dynasty decorated the stairway. Polished sconces that Claire would swear were pure gold lit up the staircase, bright red velvet ribbons hanging from them. "This way," Marty said, directing her down a narrow hall, where a giant spruce decorated with tiny white lights and angels met them.

"The tree is spectacular!"

"Donald likes his trees; there's one in just about every room."

"Must be a lot of work, but the fun kind. I always put up a tree, a small one, but it brings back memories," Claire said, then thought of Shannon, and that wasn't on her good-memory list.

He opened the door and stepped aside so Claire could enter. Delighted, she spun around the room, again thinking she had stepped right into a fairy tale. "This is gorgeous!" A set of tall windows provided a perfect view of the massive estate's gardens. It looked like a park, not someone's backyard, Claire thought as she gazed out at the beauty. This was definitely not a backyard, at least the kind she was used to. She reminded herself not to be taken in by all of this. Donald Flynn had taken her away from her family, and at Christmastime, too. Short of a real diagnosis of terminal illness, he'd best have a darn good explanation.

"There's the bath, and Tilly assured me there's all the stuff in there you'll need. Russell brought your bags up." Claire saw her luggage placed discreetly at the foot of the giant canopied bed. She wondered who Russell was and what his position was around the castle but wasn't going to ask as it really wasn't her concern. "I'll be downstairs shortly," she said to Marty, who was waiting by the open door. "Tell Tilly I'm starving."

Marty laughed, then closed the door. Finally alone,

Claire opened her luggage and removed a change of clothes. She almost screamed with delight when she saw the giant claw-foot tub. A separate glass area enclosed the shower opposite the tub. She turned on the tap and quickly shed her clothes, leaving them in a heap on the floor. Standing under the hot shower, she groaned. "Oh, this is wonderful," she said out loud. She leaned back so that the warm water ran down her face. She could stay here for hours she thought, but later, after she learned why she was here, she planned to spend some time in that claw-foot tub before heading back to the States. Quickly, she found a bottle of lilac-scented shampoo. She washed her hair, rinsing away all traces of the muck from yesterday. A bottle of bath gel, along with a mesh sponge, was sitting on another shower shelf. Squirting the floral-scented wash into the sponge, Claire washed as fast as she could, then stood under the shower for a full minute before stepping out. Though she didn't want to keep Tilly waiting, she couldn't help but smile at the thought of keeping Quinn Connor waiting. She toweled off, slipped into the black leggings and a bright red sweater that hung just below her rear end. Thankful for her own shoes, she slid into her favorite black Uggs. Raking a comb through her freshly washed hair, she piled it in a topknot, secured it with a clip, and, as an afterthought, spritzed her favorite jasmine perfume on her neck.

Racing down the stairs, the enticing aroma from the kitchen made her stomach growl once again. With some food in her stomach, she would feel almost human again.

Though when she saw Donald Flynn himself seated at the head of the table, she almost fainted.

"I see you finally arrived," Donald said as he helped himself to a slice of bread.

Anger fueled Claire across the room to the table where she stood next to Donald Flynn. "It's barely been twenty-four hours since you demanded that I come to your deathbed, and from what I can see right now, you are the picture of health. Do you mind telling me what this is all about?"

Donald Flynn didn't bother to stand up as most gentlemen would. No, he continued to spread cheese on his bread carefully as though he hadn't a care in the world. "Claire O'Brien. You're as beautiful as I remember."

Hunger overriding her anger, though only for a second, Claire sat in the chair across from Donald. "Look, I didn't come all the way across the damned Atlantic Ocean to listen to compliments. You told me you were dying, that it was a matter of life and death. I rearranged my holiday to come here. Now, don't you think it's about time you tell me why I'm really here?" Claire no longer cared about manners. She reached across the table for a slice of bread and dipped it into her hot soup. If she hadn't been so ticked right now, she would have sighed with pleasure, as the soup was to die for. Marty was right. Tilly was an excellent chef.

"Brock Ettinger assured me you had no plans for the holidays. He said you rarely traveled out of California. Knowing your Irish heritage, I just assumed you would be happy to have a chance at a vacation, especially in Ireland, and at my expense."

For a moment, Claire was at a loss for words. "Brock told you this?" She was fuming. Maybe it was time to step out on her own, walk away from corporate law and the good-old-boy system since they thought they could control her life.

"Oh come on, Claire, do tell me that this is the best

offer you've had all year long. Working for a man like Brock Ettinger can't be all that exciting," Donald said between bites.

"I'm sorry I can't keep quiet any longer," Quinn said, his voice laced with anger. "Tell her the truth. Donald, tell her why you've really asked her to come to Ireland."

Claire felt as though she had been completely and utterly duped. That, she supposed, was because she *had* been completely and utterly duped. She was so mad, she wanted to toss her bowl of hot soup in Donald Flynn's face, but, frankly, the soup was too good to waste on such a sneaky old man. "Yes, why don't you tell me why so I can explain to my family why I had to back out of my Christmas plans?" Now she felt guilty when she remembered the relief she'd felt when she'd explained to Patrick that she wouldn't be spending the holiday week with him and Stephanie. As soon as she finished eating, she planned to call the airlines and book a return trip home.

Donald Flynn placed his napkin in his lap, then lay his spoon next to his soup bowl. "Okay, I admit I wasn't completely honest. Though we're all going to die someday, that part was true. You see how large this estate is, and this is just a small portion of all that I have. I have no children, and, of course, no grandchildren, not even a great-niece or -nephew." Donald stared at Quinn. "He's my only living blood relative. I want to leave everything I own to him, but he refuses to be named as my beneficiary."

Claire took another sip of her soup, pulled off a chunk of bread, and washed it down with tea. "And what does this have to do with me?"

"You're an O'Brien. Let me see if I have this right, and correct me if I'm wrong. Don't you have five brothers and two sisters? There's Colleen, who married her high-school sweetheart, Mark Cunningham, they had two daughters, Shannon Margaret and Abigail Caitlin. Sadly, Shannon Margaret passed away several years ago. There's Megan, who's married to Nathan, and they have three sons. I believe their names are Joseph, Ryan, and Eric. Your parents, Eileen and Joseph, are still alive, and they've retired to Florida. And that still leaves Connor, Aidan, Ronan, and Michael."

"You're forgetting Patrick," she couldn't help but add. "Five brothers, two sisters."

"Yes, I forgot about Patrick. Isn't he the one that married Stephanie, who has two little girls named Ashley and Amanda."

Claire now knew the true meaning of feeling violated. How dare he go behind her back and bring her family into something that they weren't even aware of. She wasn't even aware of where this was going!

Quinn spoke again. "Uncle Donald here seems to think you and I, and of course your large family, would be the perfect occupants for this . . . *house* he claims to love so much."

Stupefied, Claire's jaw dropped to her chin and back. She was truly at a loss for words. Was it possible Donald Flynn was suffering from Alzheimer's? What person in their right mind would concoct such an insane plot? And why?

This was too much. "Look, I don't know why you've picked me to be your, I don't even know what you've picked me to be, but this much I do know, I want no part of this scheme. And if I find out that Brock had anything to do with this"—Claire paused, trying to come up with a plausible statement—"I'll quit the minute I see him. He can shove the firm up his ass!"

Quinn laughed. "You've got moxie, I see. I like that. Now, let me fill you in. Uncle Donald seems to think when he dies, this great castle will go to the great country of Ireland and be made into a tourist trap. So, since I'm his only living blood relative, who just so happens to be single living in California, as do you, my dear old uncle's plotting an arranged relationship, at least that's what I assume. Am I right?" Quinn asked his uncle.

Donald actually had the audacity to laugh. "You have to admit it's not a bad idea. You're both Irish, you both come from good families, not to mention you're both quite good-looking, can you imagine what beautiful children you would have together?"

Claire felt her face turned fifty shades of red. Even Quinn appeared stunned.

During this entire exchange of words, Marty and Tilly kept themselves busy washing pots and pans and banging them whenever they felt they shouldn't be privy to certain parts of the conversation.

"I'm sorry, Claire," Quinn said. "I suspected he had something like this up his sleeve when he demanded that I be here today. I returned to Ireland for the holidays, thinking I would ride my bike along the coast. Maybe take a day trip to see the Cliffs of Moher, the usual touristy stuff. I planned to kiss that Blarney Stone, too. Even though I was born here, I've spent most of my life in the States. My parents lived in America. We only spent a short period in Dublin before my father's job, he was a pilot for Aer Lingus, took him to New York. Mom loved the city, all the hustle and bustle. Me, on the other hand, once my parents died—my father was Uncle Donald's younger brother—I think I forgot to add that in here somewhere, but once they were gone, I moved out West. And now, you pull something like this." Quinn was mad, Claire could tell, but he was also hurt that his uncle had used him like this. Claire barely knew Quinn, but she saw the hurt in his eyes, heard it in his words. "Dad wouldn't have wanted this."

"Don't you think I know that? Your father didn't want this castle, didn't want all the responsibility that goes along with the family wealth. All he ever wanted to do was fly airplanes. He could have cared less about our family's fortune. Once he was out of college, he got away before our father insisted he join the family business. I, being the older of the two, didn't have a choice." Donald stopped talking and, for a minute, actually seemed ashamed of himself. "The farms, the dairies have been in the family too long to just let them go to a stranger."

"I'm a stranger, Donald. You don't really know me. All you know of me is my professional life, you know nothing of my personal life. No, forget that. Apparently, you made it your business to find out all about my family. I don't appreciate it, either. It's almost vulgar to think all the while I was looking after your finances, you were scoping out my family tree hoping to preserve your precious family castle and your fortune, which, by the way, is enough for hundreds of families. Has it ever occurred to you to use all these millions for something other than acquiring more?"

Claire held out her hand. "Don't answer that. Look, Quinn, I'm going upstairs and make a few phone calls. If you could offer me a ride back to Dublin, I'd appreciate it." With that said, she stood, took her dishes to the kitchen, where Marty and Tilly were nowhere to be found. She rinsed her bowl, spoon, and cup, then put them inside the industrial-sized dishwasher, wondering why he needed such a large dishwasher in the first place since the castle was hardly occupied.

On her way back upstairs, she passed several beautifully decorated Christmas trees that hadn't been lit up before. Reds, greens, gold, and silver sparkled throughout the parts of the castle, but Claire no longer felt any pleasure at being in her homeland. All she wanted to do now was pack her bags. No, she didn't even have to do that as she hadn't bothered to unpack. The gods were smiling on her, she thought as she entered her guest room. Digging through her purse for the cell phone that she'd never bothered to turn on since landing in Dublin, she turned it back on and saw that she had five voice mails, all from a number she didn't recognize. As she was about to listen to her voice mail, she heard a light knock on her door. Tossing her phone on the bed, she walked across the room and leaned against the door. "Yes?" she asked, unsure who was there. And if it was Donald Flynn, he could stand there and knock all night long before she would open the door.

"Claire, it's Quinn."

As soon as she heard his voice, she opened the door.

"Okay if I come in?" he asked.

Quinn Connor wasn't the ogre his uncle was, that she was sure of. "Sure," she said, and stepped aside.

"I knew he'd put you in this room. It has the best view of the back of the estate, plus the mountains. I've spent a night or two in this room myself."

Claire wondered if he'd been alone, but it wasn't her business, and right now, it was unimportant.

"Yes, it's beautiful, and I'm sorry, but I can't stay here. I was about to call the airlines to see if there's another flight available tonight. I promised my family I would be home in time for Christmas, and from the looks of it, I'm going to be able to keep my promise."

"Look, I want to apologize for my uncle's behavior." Quinn walked across the room and stared out the window. "For the past year, he's been obsessed with keeping the property in the family."

"Apparently. I was about to check my voice mail when you knocked. Mind if I check it now? I saw several calls from a number I don't recognize. I hope it's not bad news." Claire took her phone from the bed.

"They're from me," Quinn said. "As soon as I got wind of Donald's plan, I tried calling you, but you were already on your way. I'm sorry you had to travel so far for nothing."

Claire smiled suddenly, liking this guy a wee bit more than she had an hour ago. "Thanks, that was good of you, but I had the phone off, and to be truthful"—Claire felt the urge to spill the beans—"I got a bit tipsy on the flight from LA to New York. When I arrived at JFK, I was a total mess. I had two drinks, and I swear they tasted like sweet tea. I drank them too fast or something, I don't know, but by the time I left the bar, I was so drunk I couldn't walk. Well, no I couldn't walk because I'd managed to break the heel on my shoe, so I limped through the airport and purchased a nice comfortable pair of Betty Boop slippers, but this was after I spent a while hugging the porcelain god." Claire laughed. "I am terrified of flying."

Instead of laughing like she expected, Quinn took a deep breath, then blew it out, all the while clenching and unclenching his fists. "It's just like him to do this. Did he know you weren't fond of flying?"

Claire saw where he was going. "No, it's not something I talk about. In my line of work, I have to travel, and it's something I've learned to live with. I usually do a few relaxation techniques, and they actually work quite well. I think all the alcohol in my system just amplified my fear. Though I did have a very pleasant seat mate. I promised I'd try to visit before I left." Claire hated to make promises and not keep them, but she would call Kelly and send her a brand-new pair of Kate Spade ballet flats as soon as she returned to the States.

Curious, Quinn asked, "I take it you liked his company?"

"Actually, he was quite pleasant when he wasn't crying," Claire said.

"Crying?" Quinn asked.

"Yes. His name was Patrick, too. Though he prefers to go by Paddy. I thought the name was cute. It suited him."

"Paddy, huh?"

"I'm sure when he's older, he will grow out of the name, but until then it suits him just fine. I'm just sorry I won't be able to tell him good-bye, he was quite the guy."

Quinn stepped away from the window and sat on the edge of the bed. "So this Paddy, do you think he's someone you could have a relationship with?"

Claire couldn't help herself any longer. She laughed out loud, then sat on the bed with Quinn. "Yes, I think I could have a relationship with him. As I said, he was quite the guy. But he's too young for me. I'm sure his mother, who traded her shoes for my Betty Boop slippers, would agree. I think he was about eight weeks old. It was his first flight, too."

He turned to face her. "You mean Paddy was a baby?"

"He was, and he had a set of lungs on him, too. Kelly, that's his mother, had to fly to New York to attend her grandmother's funeral. We hit it off, and I am truly sorry I won't get to tell her good-bye in person though I would like to call her before I leave." She glanced at the clock on the bedside table. "I suppose it's not too late to call, but I want to call the airlines first. I do not want to spend the night in this place." Claire realized she spoke a bit too harshly. "I'm sorry, I know this is your family home, or castle, but I can't help it. Your uncle took unfair advantage of me. And you, too."

"I don't want the place, trust me. It's beautiful, and grand, but it's not a home. No one lives in a castle anymore. I've told Donald for years he should turn the place over to the country, it's an historical landmark, but he refuses to let go. I think his dad made him swear on his life he'd keep the castle in the family forever, but times aren't like they were then."

"True, but I can appreciate Donald's desire to preserve his heritage."

"I can, too, but it's more than that with him. He's obsessed. He rarely talks of anything else. You don't see that side of him. I've been more than concerned. Thank God for Marty and Tilly. They know what's going on, and we stay in contact almost daily since the change in him."

"I'm sure I know this, but right now it escapes me. How old is Donald?" Claire asked.

Quinn appeared to do a quick mental calculation. "He's turning eighty, get this, on New Year's Day."

"Wow, he's in good shape for his age, at least physically. I'm not so sure about his mental status," Claire said, then regretted it. It wasn't her place to make a medical judgment. She was an attorney. She'd best leave the medical diagnosis to the pros.

"Yes, he is, but he's been declining the past couple of years. Repeats himself. Marty says he's forever losing things, then blames him or Tilly for hiding whatever it is he's claimed to have lost." Quinn truly hated this, but it was what it was. "I guess it's inevitable. We're all getting older, and I don't know about you, but it sure beats the alternative."

Before she realized what she was doing, she reached for his hand. His glance slipped to their entwined hands, and when he looked at her and smiled, Claire knew then and there that she was toast. About to pull her hand away, he placed his other hand on top of hers. "Don't pull away, Claire."

She didn't want to. But this would never work. She lived in California. He lived in . . . California!

What was she thinking? She smiled at him and continued to hold his hand. Wanting to stay this way for as long as possible, she knew she couldn't. "I don't think I can call the airlines without the use of my hands."

Before letting go, he took both of her hands, wrapped them in his, then before releasing them, he placed a light kiss on the palm of her hand. Her heart jolted, and her pulse pounded as though she'd just run a marathon. She took a deep breath but said nothing, as words weren't necessary.

"You finish getting your things together, and I'll call

the airlines," Quinn said, his voice husky, seductive. "If that's okay?" he added.

Claire nodded, not sure she could speak. Her emotions were all over the place. Here she was prepared to dislike this handsome, intelligent Irishman, and all she could think of at the moment was the feel of his lips when he'd lightly kissed her palm. She looked at her hand, amazed that it still tingled from his lips, and his touch.

Before she lost total control of herself, she went to the bathroom and grabbed her dirty skirt, blouse, and under-clothes off the floor. She hadn't used her toiletries, so there wasn't anything else to pack. She rearranged a few items in her luggage and found a plastic Target bag to put her dirty clothes in. A trick she'd learned years ago. She tied the bag into a secure knot, then tucked it beneath the shoes Kelly had so graciously traded for those silly slip-pers. Claire saw that the shoes were cheap and worn, which made her feel twice as bad for taking them. Maybe it was the only extra pair of shoes she owned. Claire hadn't paid too much attention to Kelly's feet, but she believed she'd had on sneakers. Yes, she would send her a brand-spanking-new pair of Kate Spades, along with a pair of warm Uggs. And a pair for Paddy. Ireland winters being as cold as Marty said, she was sure the mother and baby could use a warm pair of boots. She already knew Kelly wore a size seven, and between all her nieces and neph-ews, her sisters surely could advise her on a close size for baby Paddy. That settled in her mind, she listened to Quinn as he spoke on his cell phone. When she saw him reach for his wallet to remove a credit card, she practi-cally leaped across the bed. "No! I have a return ticket," she whispered loudly.

He smiled and brushed her hand away, then grabbed it and planted a wet kiss on her index finger. Jolts of desire shot through her, settling in the middle of her body. She wanted to yank her hand away but didn't. She liked his lips, liked his kisses, no matter how slight. She smiled at him and leaned up and planted a kiss on his chin. He was too tall for her, and that was nice. She liked tall men. And she was liking Quinn Connor more by the minute.

Chapter 6

Claire turned away, suddenly embarrassed. She was thirty-four years old and couldn't ever remember being so instantly physically attracted to a man. Her insides danced like Mexican jumping beans when he blew her a kiss while he continued to speak on the phone. "Yes, we'll make sure to arrive on time. Thanks," he said before clicking off.

"We're all set," he told her before pulling her into his arms. He wrapped his hands around her shoulders, and the gesture seemed familiar and comfortable. Claire lifted both arms and placed them around his neck. Before either of them could stop, Quinn's lips gently covered her mouth. Slowly, he teased her mouth with the tip of his tongue, then he traced the soft fullness of her lips with his own. Desire burned inside her, and when he pulled away and stared into her eyes, her entire being was filled with a longing unlike any she'd ever known. It was more than physical, and she knew he felt it, too, from the sensuous light that passed between them. His gaze was tender yet smoldered with passion. He took a deep, shaky breath before pulling her completely against him. When she felt his hardness, a ripple of pure lust shot through her. She wanted Quinn Connor badly. And she wanted him now. Right here in his uncle's guest room.

"Are you thinking what I'm thinking?" he whispered against her ear.

"Probably," she answered.

Lightly, he fingered a loose tendril of hair on her cheek. "If you want to make the next flight out, we have to leave now."

She touched his thick hair, wanting to plant her hands in it, wrap her fingers around the long hair at his nape, but resisted. Now wasn't the time, and maybe there would never be another time, but for now Claire cherished these few moments with this man, whom she'd thought of as an adversary only a short time ago.

"Let's get out of here before I forget I'm a gentleman," he said, then kissed her again, only this time on her cheek. Still, Claire felt hot with wanting. It would be a miracle if she didn't jump his bones on the way to the airport.

Quinn carried her luggage, while she strapped her duffel over one shoulder and her purse on the other.

"I need to tell Marty and Tilly good-bye," she said as they walked down the long hallway. Part of her felt a moment's sadness knowing she was leaving Ireland behind without really having seen all that she'd longed to see, but she made a promise to herself; she would come back, and when she did, she would bring the entire O'Brien family with her.

Marty and Tilly must have possessed a sixth sense because both waited at the bottom of the staircase. "I didn't think ya'd stay the night, an' I'm sure sorry 'bout Mr. Flynn. I don't think he's in his right mind," Marty said. Claire could see that it hurt the older man to speak such words about a man whom he admired and respected. There was probably some history between the two, Claire guessed.

On impulse, she gave Marty a quick hug and kissed his ruddy cheek. Tilly lingered behind him, though Claire saw the bag she tried to hide behind her small frame. When she saw Claire looking at the bag, she stepped forward and held it out to her. "This is for your trip. It's cheeses, and breads, with a fresh batch of cranberry orange scones. I put a slab of butter in a plastic bowl, and a knife, too, but it's one of those plastic kind. I didn't want you to get in any trouble with the airlines. I see how they take stuff away from people now. It's a shame what the world has come to."

Claire stooped down and gave Tilly a tight hug. "Thank you so much, Tilly. I'm sorry I can't stay and try another of your tasty dishes, but I'll appreciate this"—she held up the bag—"on the flight home." Before she knew it, tears filled her eyes. She sniffed, then Tilly handed her a wad of tissues. "Thanks, Tilly. Would you mind if I stayed in touch with the both of you?" Claire had only known the couple for a few short hours, but she felt as though she'd known them forever.

"We'd like that," Marty said, then removed a slip of paper from his pocket. "That's our snail-mail address, and our e-mail addresses. If you want, friend us on Facebook, and we can stay in touch that way, too."

"I'd like that," Claire said.

"We better get on the road if we want to make it to the airport in time. Keep in touch with me, and if you need me here, just say the word." Quinn shook Marty's hand, then he practically lifted Tilly off the ground when he hugged her.

Dark outside, the night air damp and bitterly cold, Claire suddenly remembered Quinn rode a motorcycle. "Do you have a car?" she asked as they walked to the side of the castle where Marty had parked earlier.

"No," he said.

They were really going to ride a motorcycle to the airport? In this frigid night air? She'd be an iceberg by the time they arrived in Dublin! Or die of pneumonia!

They walked to a modern building, that looked as if it were recently built. It didn't have the stones like the area where Marty parked. Quinn removed a set of keys from a box, then unlocked the door. He flipped a light on, before Claire stepped inside. When she did, what she saw almost took her breath away. It did take her breath away.

"You said you didn't have a car."

"I don't. I have *several* cars. I had this building constructed last year when I was here. Donald had a fit, but he loves these cars as much as I do. He kept them in a specialty garage in Dublin and never drove them. I finally convinced him the cars would be useless in a few years if he didn't drive them. So, take your pick." Quinn gestured to an array of vehicles.

"Should I ask which you prefer?"

"I like them all," he said as he walked her through the rows of cars.

"How many?" she asked.

"Fifteen here, and three more in Dublin undergoing repairs."

"So, you're telling me you have eighteen cars? Here in Ireland?"

Quinn threw back his head and laughed. "I am."

She could only nod. "So, you pick. I know absolutely nothing about cars other than they get me from point A to point B."

"Stick with me, and I promise to teach you a thing or two," Quinn said. Claire caught the double entendre.

"The roads might get icy. I think we'd better take the Range Rover. It has four-wheel drive, too."

"Wait! I can't leave yet. I have to call Kelly," Claire suddenly remembered.

"Okay, but you do know you can call her from the car? We've got cell towers here in Ireland, too," Quinn teased as he unlocked a black Range Rover. He took her luggage and duffel bag and placed them in the back of the car, along with Tilly's doggie bag.

Unlocking the passenger door, he helped Claire climb inside. Once they were settled and their seat belts fastened, Quinn pressed a button, and an automatic door opened. "Nice," Claire said.

"Yes, building this was one of the best things I've done for myself in years," Quinn said as he backed out of the garage.

Claire supposed it was if you were a car buff but didn't voice her thoughts.

"I'll call Kelly now, if you don't mind."

Quinn handed her his cell phone. "Use mine. It's local."

"Sure," Claire said as she searched through her purse

for the paper with Kelly's number and address. As soon as she found it, she punched in the number.

" 'Ello?"

"Hi, Kelly, it's Claire. From the plane," she added, just in case Kelly had forgotten she'd given out her phone number.

"Oh, Claire, it's mighty fine ta hear ya voice. I was hopin' you'd call."

She couldn't help but smile hearing her heavily accented voice. "It's hard to believe, but I'm on my way to the airport now. My business . . . only took a couple of hours." And she wasn't even bothering to spend the night? Claire realized how crazy she must sound. It'd been close to thirty-two hours since she'd slept in a bed.

"Aye, that was fast, I must say. Are ya sure ya can't stay? Paddy would love to see ya again."

Claire heard the laughter in her voice. "And I would like to see Paddy as well, but I have to rush home. I promised to spend Christmas with my family."

Though Claire had spent several hours with Kelly, she suddenly realized that all she knew about her was that her grandmother had passed away, and she had a newborn son. Come to think of it, Claire hadn't heard her mention the baby's father. She'd spoken of her mother, but never mentioned a husband, if she had a career or anything remotely personal.

"That's nice ya know. Family and Christmas. I was gonna decorate a tree this year, but aye, they're so expensive. Paddy's too wee to know about Christmas just yet," Kelly said, her voice sounding far away and sad.

What the heck was wrong with her? Was Claire so self-centered that she couldn't assess a situation that wasn't connected to her or her legal life? Yes, she was, she thought, as Kelly told her about Paddy's first giggle.

"I would've loved to hear that. I'm coming back to Ireland, though I'm not sure when. I'll make sure to come for a visit. Stay in touch, okay?" Claire said. Kelly promised she would. When Claire punched the END button, she felt sad. Seeing the scrap of paper with Kelly's address, she read it to Quinn. "Are you familiar with the area?"

Quinn looked in the rearview mirror, adjusted it before answering. "It's Dublin's worst possible area. Drugs, prostitutes, murders. You name it, it happens there."

"I can't leave without seeing her, Quinn. She's a young woman, and I think she's in need of a friend and maybe some financial help." Claire really didn't know what to do.

"You'll miss your flight, you do realize that?"

"Yes, yes I do. Never mind. Let's just get to the airport. I'll figure out a way to help Kelly and Paddy."

"I have an idea," he said, a grin showing his white teeth in the darkened car.

"Let's hear it."

"How would you like to play Santa Claus?"

"Well for starters, I would need a sleigh, along with eight reindeer, about a hundred extra pounds, a white beard, and a red suit, but I'm game. I'm all ears."

"It'll take a bit of work, but I think I can make sure that Kelly and Paddy have a Merry Christmas."

"Go on," Claire prompted.

For the next half hour Quinn explained what he would do as soon as they arrived in the States. It took Claire a minute or two before his words registered. "What do you mean, when *we* arrive in the States?"

"I'm going home, too. A bit earlier than planned, but with such a sexy traveling companion, I couldn't resist."

Claire was at a loss for words. "But . . . why? You have all those cars, and your uncle is here. He's not well, Quinn. Someone needs to keep an eye on him."

"Marty and Tilly are highly qualified. Not only is Tilly an amazing chef, when she lived in China, she was also a doctor—an internist, I think."

"You're not joking, are you?"

"I wouldn't joke about that."

Claire realized she hardly knew Quinn Connor, yet she knew she could trust him, knew he was a man of his word. Plus, he was a really good kisser, and beyond good-looking. And an attorney, too. She couldn't have handpicked a more suitable match for herself, but she'd keep those thoughts to herself. At least for now. When Colleen and Megan heard about him, the matchmaking would never end. She'd keep him a secret for a while.

"Does Donald know this?"

"I think he has an idea, but as long as she prepares gourmet meals, he doesn't really give too much thought to anything else she does. Or Marty. Though Marty's been working for my uncle since I was a boy, so there's a story there. And they're really good friends even though Marty works for him. He's very well-off, and doesn't need to work, but he seems to believe Donald couldn't get along without him."

"Then Marty and Donald must be about the same age," Claire stated.

"Marty's in his early seventies. And Tilly just turned sixty-seven. She made sure to remind me that I missed her birthday this year."

"She hardly looks a day over fifty."

"She's a very intelligent woman. She's never told anyone why she left China, but it can't be good. Whatever her reason, I'm glad we have her. And so is Marty. They've been more than friends for a number of years."

"I guessed as much. They make a cute couple."

Quinn reached across the bucket seat and placed his hand on her upper thigh. "I know someone else who would make a cute couple, too."

Claire grinned.

"Who would that be?"

"That's for me to know and you to find out," Quinn said, then squeezed her thigh, sending shocks of desire through her.

And Claire would find out.

Chapter 7

They arrived at JFK on time. Claire had never been so happy to get off an airplane in her entire life. The return flight home was much longer, and they'd had seats in coach by the toilets. Between the passengers' coming and going, not to mention the smell that seeped out every time the door opened, Claire never slept a wink. By now it'd been close to forty-eight hours since she'd had any real sleep. Her eyes were gritty, her teeth felt like she hadn't brushed them since they'd come in, and on top of everything else, she felt like she was coming down with a cold.

Once they passed through Customs and retrieved their luggage, Quinn made a phone call. Twenty minutes later, they were picked up in a black Lincoln and whisked off to a private airport.

"Where are we going?" she asked, though truly she didn't care. As long as it was away from that terrible smell.

"I thought you wanted to spend the holidays with your family," Quinn said. "I am making it my personal mission to see that you arrive safely. I've chartered a private jet to take you to Colorado."

"Tell me you're kidding."

"I would, but I'm not."

"I don't know what to say, other than thank you." Claire was too tired to think straight. All she wanted to do was sleep. If Quinn wanted to hire a private jet to take her home, it was fine with her. As long as she could sleep, and the plane didn't smell like urine, she was good. She didn't even think about being afraid. And she hadn't been afraid on the return flight from Ireland. Quinn had entertained her, they'd watched two movies, shared the goodies Tilly sent, and talked about everything and nothing. By the time they landed on American soil, Claire felt as though she'd known him her entire life. Quinn told her about his law practice. He was a defense lawyer but devoted much of his time to the down and out. She wanted to ask him how he managed to earn a living, but she knew he'd inherited half of his father's fortune when he'd died. Quinn Connor was a very rich man but Claire didn't care. She liked him, maybe a bit more than liked, but again, she would keep those thoughts to herself. For now, she was content to let him take charge of her life even if it was only for a few hours.

"You don't mind if I come along for the ride?" he asked, as they climbed aboard the luxurious Beechcraft Super King Air B200.

"Not at all, but I can't promise to keep my eyes open

much longer," Claire said, then immediately yawned. "I am tired."

Quinn helped her get settled in her seat, showed her all the fancy buttons, and as soon as they were at a safe altitude, he explained to her how her seat reclined. He removed a soft pillow from the overhead bin, along with an equally soft blanket that smelled like Downy fabric softener. "You sure know how to make a girl happy."

He sat in the seat facing her. "You ain't seen nothing yet."

It wasn't long after takeoff that Claire fell into a sound, restful sleep. When she awoke, she was surprised to learn she'd been asleep for almost five hours. Her eyes didn't feel gritty, but her mouth felt horrible. Quinn was sipping a cup of coffee and reading *The Wall Street Journal.* He must have sensed her watching him because he tore his gaze from the paper, and when he looked at her, Claire truly felt her heart skip a beat. She smiled at him.

"Have a nice nap?"

"Beyond. That coffee smells luscious."

"I knew you'd want a cup, so I made sure to save some for you." Quinn had to stoop as he walked to the small galley at the back of the aircraft, but when he returned with a cup of strong black coffee in a real china cup, Claire felt as though she'd died and gone to heaven. She sipped the hot brew, relishing every drop. When she finished, Quinn poured her a second cup, this time bringing her a wrapped blueberry muffin and a paper plate with a knife and fork. "Sorry about the paper plate. Jack forgot to pack the good china plates."

"Hey, this is the most luxurious plane I've ever seen. And you know what?" she asked as she opened the cellophane-wrapped muffin. "I'm not even remotely nervous, or afraid.

If I could travel in a plane like this, I don't think I'd be nearly as fearful. Is that crazy or what?" she asked, then took a bite of her muffin.

"Not at all. Now do you want to hear about Kelly and Paddy's surprise? While you were sleeping, I made a few phone calls. It seems that Kelly's husband died in a motorcycle crash right after she learned she was pregnant. Her mother barely gets by, but Kelly didn't have much choice after her husband died, so she moved in with her. It's public housing, which isn't so bad, but the area is Dublin's worst. Apparently, Kelly works as a full-time housekeeper for a well-to-do family. They bought her and Paddy's tickets to New York."

"How do you know all this?"

"First, and foremost, I am an attorney with contacts across the globe. Secondly, I have access to the Internet and a telephone. Now does that answer your question?"

He grinned, and once again, Claire felt her heart skip a beat or two. "Has anyone ever told you what an amazing man you are?" She couldn't help it. This guy was almost too good to be true. And like him, she, too, had her contacts. As soon as she was able, she just might have a look-see into his past, just to make sure there wasn't anything . . . what, she thought? Bad? A juvenile record? An unwanted child? No, she would not do this. She trusted him, and she trusted her gut instinct as well. Quinn Connor was the man she thought he was. Decent, giving, and kind. Not to mention good-looking, brilliant, and, yes, she might as well add rich to his long list of growing attributes. And he was an excellent kisser. If his skills in the bedroom were anything like the rest of him, then Claire knew making love with Quinn Connor would be life-changing.

"Claire?"

She jerked herself out of her reverie. "Sorry, I was fantasizing."

"About me? Us?" he asked, all traces of humor gone.

Claire wasn't sure how to answer him. Did she tell him the truth? Or was she willing to be just another woman in a string of many? Someone to toy with until he grew tired of her? Was all of his kindness and concern for others nothing but an act? No, no, no! She had to stop second-guessing herself. She had feelings for this man. Real feelings that had nothing to do with his looks, his financial status, or the number of cars he owned. She just clicked with him, pure and simple.

"Claire, did I say something to upset you?" Again, he was serious.

She shook her head. "No, I'm just not sure why the sudden change of mood. One minute you're teasing me, and when I tell you I am fantasizing, you're suddenly serious. Did I say something to upset you?"

"No, you didn't. So tell me what you're thinking? Please," he added, a trace of his earlier humor in his words.

"I'm thirty-four years old, Quinn, not some young cutesy girl that you can discard as soon as you tire of me." There, she'd said it. Now all she had to do was wait for him to explain that he really liked her, and yes they were going to enjoy one another, but that's as far as he was willing to go.

What the hell happened to her? The Claire that needed no one. The Claire that was self-reliant and independent? The woman who vowed to remain footloose and fancy-free? She didn't know. Maybe she'd left that woman behind when she'd crossed the Atlantic. Whatever it was, she wasn't Super Claire anymore and didn't want to be.

More than anything, Claire O'Brien wanted to be loved. And she would accept nothing less. And that was the old dynamic Claire talking. She grinned.

"Want to tell me what's so funny because right now, I don't seem to see the humor in what you just said. And for the record, Claire, I'm almost forty years old. I am not looking for some 'young cutesy girl' to have a fling with. I thought we had something. Was I mistaken? Am I moving too fast? Tell me, I want to know."

The old stubborn Claire was up and running, putting her foot in her mouth. The new, softer Claire was glowing inside just knowing that Quinn might have more than lust on his mind.

"I was fantasizing about sleeping with you, when you asked why I was grinning. Then I decided that you're way too handsome, way too accomplished, and way too rich to want . . ."

"—what?"

"A relationship." There, it was out. She barely knew the man, and she wanted a commitment from him. Sort of.

"Do you think I make a habit of traipsing across the globe to help damsels in distress? Is that the kind of man you want to be with?"

"No and yes," Claire replied.

"I suppose I have to ask if that was answered in the order in which the questions were asked?"

Claire smiled, she couldn't help it. She needed to learn to stop putting words in the mouths of everyone she came in contact with. It was truly a bad habit, one she wanted to rid herself of, but it wasn't going to be easy.

"Now you're laughing at me," Quinn commented, but he, too, had a slight grin on his face and a twinkle in his eyes.

"I would never laugh at you, Quinn, but I promise I will laugh *with* you."

"I like that answer. And let me say something before we land, because something tells me it might be a while before we're alone again. But before I say anything else, I just want you to know that Kelly and Paddy, and, of course, her mother now have a brand-new home, courtesy of Flynn Financial. That's the name of my private company. And Kelly will no longer be cleaning other people's homes to earn a living. A little bird told me she's always wanted to go to school to become a nurse, and, of course, I made sure that this will happen. I did save that for Christmas Day, though. I thought the house was enough for now. And Paddy. He'll never have to worry about a college education because that's been taken care of, too."

Claire was truly at a loss for words. And here she thought sending Kate Spade shoes and Uggs was a grand gesture. A house? An education for Kelly *and* Paddy? No, she didn't even want to try to top that. Stunned that he'd managed to accomplish all this while she slept, and aboard an airplane! If ever there was a true Santa Claus, it was Quinn Connor.

"You know what? From now on, I think I'm going to call you *Mister Christmas*."

Chapter 8

When they arrived in Denver, Claire called Patrick as soon as they were on their way to the city. "Bet you don't know where I'm at?" she asked as soon as Patrick picked up the phone.

"Now, let me guess. Kissing the Blarney Stone? Having a Guinness? No, scratch that, you wouldn't like that. Too strong for a wimpy kid like you. Let me see, maybe you're about to jump off the Cliffs of Moher?"

She laughed. "Wrong on all accounts." She placed her hand over the phone. Whispering to Quinn, she said, "He thinks I'm still in Ireland."

"What did you say?"

"Oh for crying out loud, Patrick, I'm back in the States. As a matter of fact, I'm about to head out to I-70 tomorrow. Wanna give me a road update?"

She heard her brother laughing. "Seriously? You've

been to Ireland and back in two days? I take it the place wasn't up to your standards?"

"It's beautiful there, but I had to leave. I'll explain it to you when I see you. Tomorrow. I'm spending the night in a hotel tonight. I've hardly slept since I last spoke with you. Make sure to tell Stephanie and the girls that I'll see them tomorrow, okay? And the rest of the gang, too. They'll all be there, right?"

"Yep."

"Good, because I'm bringing a guest along. Someone special that I want to introduce to my family. Okay, I'm about to lose what's left of my battery. See you tomorrow." Claire clicked END, then turned her phone off before it rang again. Knowing her brother, he was probably calling the rest of the gang right about now. Since there were so many, Claire knew it would take at least half an hour for the news to spread throughout the O'Brien family. Once the news was out that she was bringing someone for them to meet, her cell phone would never stop ringing. She explained all this to Quinn. "And that's why I won't turn my phone on until we arrive."

"And you say they're in Telluride?" Quinn asked as he exited off the interstate.

"Yes. Where are we going?" She assumed they would stop at a motel along the way, share some private time together, maybe she'd jump his bones, but apparently he had other plans. He drove down Sheridan Boulevard and pulled into a McDonald's. "I have a confession to make. I'm addicted to Big Macs. I treat myself once a week, no more, but it's been almost two weeks since I've had one. Do you mind?"

She busted out laughing. "I learn something new about you by the minute. And for the record, I like a fish sandwich from Mickey D's myself now and then. Minus the cheese, though. A large fry, extra ketchup, and a large Dr Pepper."

"Now that we have that out of the way, let's go inside. I'm starving."

Claire was tired to the bone but in a good way. She'd slept on the plane, and it'd been a good, deep sleep, but she still longed for a bed, a hot bath, and a steaming mug of Earl Grey tea. But for now, she planned to enjoy every minute of her time alone with Quinn.

Inside, they placed their orders. As soon as the food was ready, they sat by the window overlooking the parking lot. It wasn't much of a scene outside. It had snowed in Denver two days ago, but now the sun had melted it, and it was nothing more than brown slush. Cars with rust from the salt on the roads were parked haphazardly throughout the lot. Snowdrifts were banked against the curb. A few kids jumped around in the play area, and Christmas tunes could be heard from hidden speakers. A fake tree decorated with empty french fry boxes and the paper boxes they now used in place of the styrofoam ones for the variety of sandwiches they carried hung from the tree. Cookies and the tiny toys that came inside the kids' meals were strung across the branches. It wasn't much of a tree, Claire thought, but it was quite appropriate for McDonald's.

Silent for a change, they were both focused on eating when Claire suddenly had an epiphany. "This is the first time we've been out to dinner together."

Quinn raised his eyebrows in surprise. "I believe you're right. Now my Big Mac cravings will be even more meaningful. And I'm serious, Claire. This isn't a joke, or small talk. You've become very special to me, and I hope you feel the same about me."

Claire's heart did another dance, the rumba, from the way it was beating out of control. "I do, Quinn. It's just a bit unexpected, that's all."

"Why? You never planned to fall in love?"

More rumba dancing in her chest. "I'd always hoped to, I just never met the right person. Trust me, I tried; it just didn't happen for me."

"And this means?"

"That it's happening for me. Hard and fast." *Crap! I didn't say that, did I?*

"And it will be the first time. After that, it's slow and easy, all the way."

Good grief, Quinn was verbally seducing her in McDonald's! She almost choked on her french fries. She felt her face turn red, glad the few customers in the place weren't mind readers. "If you keep talking to me like that, I will not be responsible for my actions," Claire stated, then dipped a fry in her pile of ketchup.

"I'll hold you to that." He wiped his mouth with a paper napkin, then stuffed it inside his empty Big Mac box. "You told your brother you were staying in a hotel tonight. Did you have a particular place in mind?"

More rumba from the dancers in her chest. "Not really. I usually stay with my family when I'm here, and they're in the mountains. Except for Colleen and Mark. They live in Washington State, but they'll be here. They're the ones who lost a daughter, my niece, Shannon. They're always sad during the holidays, but it's to be expected. We all are in our own way, but we try to make each other happy. I really should warn you, though. They're a great group of people, but my sisters are incredibly nosy, and my five brothers, well, they take protecting their sisters seriously. Mom and Dad, they're the best. You'll like them."

"They raised you, so how could I not?"

"If I didn't know better, I would think you were trying to butter me up." Claire ate the last of her french fries. She neatly wrapped her empty boxes together, then added Quinn's pile to her own. She watched him as she did this. Togetherness.

"Actually, there is something I want you to know. It's nothing major, but I should have told you."

Here goes the bomb, she thought. "What's that?" She wanted to appear calm, as though nothing he might tell her could affect her, but she knew better, and so did he. They'd moved fast and furious, but whatever it was, it was very real for both of them.

"That Beechcraft belongs to me."

"What?"

"The airplane. It's mine."

"That's it?"

"I'm afraid so," he said, a smile in his eyes and a grin the size of the moon on his handsome face.

"Somehow, I think I can live with that."

"How would you feel about flying to Telluride rather than us driving? I don't want to force you to do something you're not comfortable doing, but you did say you weren't afraid."

"Oh. I don't have a problem, as long as you're with me," Claire said.

"Then let's fly. We can surprise your family."

Claire had never been excited about flying in an airplane. Ever. Until now. She was sure it had something to do with the man and not the plane.

Chapter 9

They all agreed to meet at The Snow Zone at ten o'clock. Claire's entire family plus a few extras had all accepted her invitation when she asked them to come skiing last night. Part of her was beyond excited for her family to meet Quinn, and another part of her was afraid they wouldn't like him. She hadn't told them about his wealth, and she certainly hadn't mentioned they flew to Telluride on his private jet.

On the slopes, everyone was having a good time. Claire assumed Quinn could ski since he knew how to do most everything else, and he hadn't said otherwise. The downside: He'd insisted they have separate hotel rooms when they arrived yesterday. She'd told him about Max's owning the resort. Though she'd fantasized about spending the night in Quinn's arms, it would wait. And they both decided it wouldn't look good if someone were to catch them sleeping in the same hotel room. Claire had thought it old-fashioned and courtly. She hadn't met a man quite like Quinn, and she didn't want to take a chance on anything. If he wanted to wait a while before they took their relationship to the next level, she was perfectly fine with it, however much her hormones said otherwise.

So here she was, all decked out in the latest ski fashions, courtesy of Stephanie and Patrick. When she realized she was planning a ski meet with no gear, they'd opened up the shop after hours and let her choose whatever she wanted and insisted it was on the house. She seemed to be getting a lot of things on the house lately.

But now here she was. Almost ten o'clock, and there was no sign of Quinn or her family members. Had she said ten o'clock? And they were all supposed to be here at The Snow Zone. She went inside, expecting to see Stephanie but saw a young girl working the register. She must be Candy Lee. Amanda and Ashley talked nonstop about her whenever she spoke with them on the phone.

Bing Crosby billowed throughout the ski shop. The scent of warm chocolate filled the air. A giant Douglas fir was decorated with mini skis, tiny scarves, and hats. Red and green lights twinkled on the tree. Claire took a deep breath, inhaling the scent of fresh pine. This was almost too perfect, she thought as she walked up and down the aisles. All the jackets and ski pants were perfectly stacked in neat piles. Mittens, hats, and the usual ski supplies filled up the shelves next to the register. Claire knew the office was in the back of the store. But it wasn't much larger than a closet, so there was no way everyone could fit in the office. And why would they be in there in the first place? There was no reason for any of them to hide.

She'd simply got the time mixed up. She was a few days shy of her normal sleep pattern, plus the high altitudes. She'd spend her time looking at all the goodies the place had to offer. Briefly, she thought of purchasing a few gifts while she was here, but no one would appreciate them since they all had their own gear, and it was always top-of-the-line. She wished she could send for those three suitcases packed with gifts, but she'd have to wait and send them when she returned to California.

The thought actually depressed her. For the first time in her legal career, she wasn't excited about her work. While she would always practice law—it was in her blood—she didn't want to go back to work for Brock Ettinger. He'd betrayed her when he'd given out her personal information to Donald Flynn. There was no way she would work for a man like him anymore, not the new Claire.

As she poked around the shop, she suddenly realized that Quinn's last name was different than his uncle's. Shouldn't they share the same last name if his father was Donald's brother? She really hadn't thought that much about it until now. She was sure there was a reasonable explanation for the difference in their names. Checking her watch, she saw that it was already ten thirty. Taking her cell phone from her pocket, she called Patrick since he seemed to be the one who always answered his cell.

"What's up, Claire?"

"Aren't we supposed to be meeting this morning? I thought I said ten o'clock."

Silence. Unusual for her brother. "Patrick."

"Uh, yeah, you did."

"Then where is everyone? I'm usually the one who's

late." Claire felt the first stirring of fear. Something wasn't right, she could feel it in her gut. It couldn't be good if her entire family was missing.

"I take it you haven't seen the news."

She'd slept in, not bothering with the television. "Patrick, if you don't tell me what's going on right now, I'm going to kick your ass. You're scaring me."

His intake of breath sounded raspy as though he were congested, or maybe he'd been . . . crying? "Okay, some whack job is in the main dining hall right now. Look around you."

She did. The lifts weren't running. The usual array of skiers who dotted the mountainside were gone. As a matter of fact, the only person she'd seen since she'd been up was Candy Lee. "Hold on, Patrick." Claire went to the girl, who sat behind the register reading Suzanne Collins's latest. "Aren't you Candy Lee?"

The girl looked up from her book. "Yes, sorry I just get so involved when I'm reading. Is there something I can help you with?" she asked.

"Where is everybody?"

Candy Lee glanced out the front of the store. "Wow, no one is out there today. I wonder what gives?"

"Patrick, you better tell me what's up. There is absolutely no one on the slopes, the lifts aren't moving, and the only person I've come in contact with since I got up at nine thirty is Candy Lee. I want to know what's going on, and I want to know right now! If you guys are playing some kind of silly prank, then just quit it because I don't like this. I have a very bad feeling."

"We were supposed to meet at ten, you're right. Candy Lee was late getting to work. Stephanie and the girls called and said for me to have everyone meet in the main dining hall. I'm still at the house, Claire. The rest of the family is in that dining hall, and there is a man in there. He has a gun. No one has been hurt, but you need to stay inside. The police have the place surrounded. It's on the news. Tell Candy to turn the TV on. Go on, do it now."

Claire's hands shook uncontrollably. "Turn the TV on now!" she screamed.

Candy Lee practically jumped off the barstool she was sitting on. "Jeez, give me a sec." She found the remote and clicked the portable television set on. The scene on the monitor instantly became familiar. Candy Lee placed her hands over her mouth, her book dropping to the floor.

"This is here! What's happening? Oh my gosh!" Candy's eyes filled with tears.

Claire looked at the screen and saw several police cars with their lights flashing yet the sirens were off. It was eerily silent. Her hands continued to shake, but she knew she had to get control of herself. She and Candy were the only two, as far as she knew, who were free right now. Though the anchorwoman's mouth moved, Claire couldn't hear what she was saying. "Turn the volume up."

Candy did as instructed.

"Patrick, are you still there?"

"I'm here, I'm listening. Hang on."

Claire listened to the anchorwoman, who stood in front of the main dining hall at Maximum Glide.

"Jeb Norris was fired from his job last night at this exclusive ski resort. Manager and operator Patrick O'Brien caught Jeb Norris with cocaine and other drugs though we cannot confirm what they were at this point. All we know now is that when the resort opened this morning, Norris entered the main dining hall, where he had worked in the kitchen. He was armed with an automatic

weapon, and we're still unclear as to the model at this time, but we do know the dining hall was full when Norris began firing his weapon. We have no information on the injured at this point, and we're not clear if there are any injured, but we want to make it very clear, Jeb Norris has fired at least six shots inside the main dining hall. A negotiator is arriving now."

"Oh my God." Claire was stunned. Here, in Telluride, at this small but luxurious ski resort. "What happened, Patrick? Why did you fire this guy?"

"First Max has a zero drug policy. If you're caught with anything, you're history. No second chances. Last night, when I went to the kitchen to meet with the night manager, I saw Jeb acting strange, like he was trying to cover something up. He was using the table we use to roll out our bread dough to snort coke. He had a mirror and two lines of coke all nice and straight, ready to go right up his nose. When I asked him what he was doing, he looked at me and said, 'What the F do you think I'm doing?' I fired him on the spot and slapped the damned mirror where he'd laid his drugs, the coke went flying, the mirror broke. I told him he had two minutes to get off the property before I called the police. He left, and now it seems he's returned. God, I could kick myself for not calling the cops when I had the opportunity. If something happens to those people in there, and most of them are our family, it's all my fault. Stephanie and the girls are inside. Mom, Dad. Mark and Colleen, their boys. You and I are the only two, besides Candy Lee, who aren't in the building. Quinn is there, too, you know that, right?"

Claire could only shake her head. "I assumed he was when I didn't find him at The Snow Zone. Of all days for Candy Lee to be late for work." Claire lowered her voice when she said the last words. It wasn't her fault, but had she arrived at work on time, maybe her family wouldn't be trapped inside with that madman. "Have you heard anything from anyone inside? They all have cell phones. Has anyone tried to contact you?"

"No, and I thought they would at least try, but we don't know what that crazy bastard's likely to do. He may have taken their cell phones. Most likely that's what's happened. I just bought Amanda and Ashley cell phones to be used in an emergency. Stephanie and I both told them if they ever found themselves in trouble and couldn't call, we made sure they know how to send a text message. I've checked my phone repeatedly, and there's nothing." Patrick sounded defeated, as if the very life had been sucked right out of him. Claire understood, as she felt the same way. Though she was new to this love thing, that didn't make it any easier.

"So we wait? Isn't there something you can do? A back door the cops can use to slip inside? Something that kook in there isn't aware of?"

"Not that I know of. Give me a minute, let me think."

Claire watched the anchorwoman, but she simply repeated what she'd just said minutes ago. There was nothing new to report. She hoped and prayed that was a good sign.

How could such a perfectly good plan go awry? Claire was having a tough time comprehending the sheer insanity of the situation, the odds of something like this happening here, in Telluride. Candy Lee shook with sobs, and Claire wanted to comfort her, but she was afraid to put her phone down for fear she'd lose her connection with Patrick. She knew he could talk, text, and answer incoming calls on his iPhone. She hated her old outdated

BlackBerry just then and wished she'd purchased something new when it was all the rage. What a stupid thought to have at a time like this. Though she'd heard somewhere that when people were under extreme stress, their thoughts tended to be a bit haywire. She totally understood that now.

"Claire, are you still there?"

"I'm here."

"I think there might be a way for the police to get inside without Jeb's knowing."

"Then hang up and call them now! Hurry!"

"I'm going to put you on hold, don't hang up, okay?"

"I won't," Claire said, her eyes focused on the TV. Something was happening. The anchorwoman kept messing with her earpiece like she was having trouble hearing something, or someone. She turned around to look behind her. Claire and Candy Lee both stared at the scene unfolding live on the air.

"Oh my Gawd, that's him!" Candy Lee said, pointing at the television set. "That's that insane psycho, Jeb Norris!"

Captivated by the scenario Claire almost had a heart attack when she saw her mother and father being held at gunpoint out in the parking lot by the madman! The anchorwoman raced to get as close to the scene as the police would allow.

Jeb Norris couldn't have been a day over twenty if that. He was medium height but much too thin. Claire saw the signs of drug abuse all over his face. The sunken cheeks, dark circles under his eyes, the manic way he stared into the camera. "Listen up!"

They did. The television, while live, was totally silent.

"These two are gonna be the first to go. I'm startin' with the oldest ones first."

Claire watched in horror as her father was shoved to the ground. Her mother tried to help him up, and when she did, the madman slapped her hard, sending her flying to the ground, her back slamming against the icy pavement. Tears fell from Claire's eyes. She could not watch her parents die. Someone had to do something, and from what she could see, no one was doing a damned thing. She laid her phone on the countertop. "Stay on the line. If Patrick comes back on the phone, tell him I'm going for help. I can't just sit here and watch my parents die on live television!"

Before Claire had a chance to reconsider, she flew out the door. She didn't know what she would do, but she had to at least try. She raced around to the parking lot, where the fired ex-employee had her parents. Several police cars surrounded the area.

"Ma'am, get down!" a police officer called out to her. "This is a hostage situation. Stay where you are!"

Claire dropped down on the wet, icy pavement. "Do not move!" came another voice.

She wasn't going anywhere, and now she realized the folly of her impulsiveness. She had to try, she told herself as she lay on the cold concrete. She couldn't live with herself if something were to happen to her parents.

"Claire." A loud whisper came from an area beneath the steps that led to the back door of Snow Zone. She turned to find Patrick huddled under the stairs. "What the frig are you doing out here? I told you to stay inside! Damn it, Claire, you don't always have to be the one in control of things. You're going to get us both killed lying out here in the middle of the parking lot where that nut job can see you!"

Tears fell from her eyes. He was right. She had always wanted to be in control. Of everything. Why, she didn't know, and now it didn't matter. She should've listened to her brother.

"Try to slide over toward me, okay?"

She nodded, then carefully moved her body like an inchworm until she was just a few feet away from the back entrance. Jeb Norris was still standing in the middle of the main hall parking area, and from what she could hear, her parents were still on the ground, unharmed at this point.

A loud voice, which sounded like it was coming through a megaphone, filled the air. The negotiator, Claire guessed.

"Jeb, if you give up now, you can walk away from this. You haven't injured anyone yet. There is no need for you to keep the other hostages inside. Let them go, and you and I will talk."

Claire breathed a massive sigh of relief; and then she prayed, something she hadn't done in a very long time. She tried to catch Patrick's eye. She did and saw that he'd heard what she had. No one was injured at this point. Thank God. But who knew what this drugged-out crazy kid would do before all was said and done.

"I want to talk to that son of a bitch Patrick O'Brien. This is between me and him! This is all his fault!"

"Listen, son," the negotiator said. "This isn't anyone's fault. From what I've been told, you've got a bad cocaine habit. I can get you some help, but in order for me to help you, you have to help me out. You can start helping both of us by letting all the hostages go."

Claire strained to hear, but nothing was being said.

"How do I know you won't try to shoot me?" Jeb Norris said. Claire knew this was a good sign. He was beginning to ask for help in his own sick way.

"I am a man of my word. If I tell you I will see that you get help for your addiction, then that's exactly what I will do. But you have to help me, too, remember? You can help us both right this very minute, Jeb. All you have to do is let all those innocent people leave. They've done nothing to you, right?"

Claire and Patrick waited for him to respond.

"I don't trust you," Jeb called out.

"Jeb, listen to me. I am all you have right now. I'm the man that's keeping you alive. As soon as I give up on you, they will, too. We have professionally trained sharpshooters. They can take you out right now if I give the order, but I'm not going to do that because I know you've got problems, and I know that you need help. Take it while I can still offer it, Jeb. I'm just doing my job, you understand? I don't want to see anyone hurt. I don't think you do, either. It's Christmas. You know that there are kids inside that dining hall right now, don't you? Kids who still believe in Santa Claus? Kids whose lives you'll be responsible for ruining if you don't let them go home to their mothers and fathers. Where's your mother, Jeb? Think she's watching this on TV right now? I bet she is, and I bet she's crying her heart out. What do you think?"

"My mom ain't got nothing to do with this! You leave her out of this, you hear me?" Jeb's voice was trembling now.

"I'm running out of patience, Jeb. Seriously. My boss tells me I've got ten minutes, after that . . . well, remember what I said about those sharpshooters. They can take you out in a split second. And I think some of them want to. They've got kids, and they don't like to see little children frightened or threatened in any way. You think about that, Jeb? Okay, I want you to think about it."

A loud crashing noise, then the sound of crying as Jeb Norris dropped to his knees. Before he had a chance to make the slightest move, he was handcuffed and lifted off the ground, then escorted to a cruiser.

The next hour was pure pandemonium. Claire rushed to her parents' side. They were unharmed, thank God. One by one, the police officers escorted the remaining hostages out of the dining hall. When Claire saw Quinn, she ran toward him and threw herself in his arms. "I was so afraid for you," she said, as they walked arm in arm to the temporary tents the police had set up. There were twenty-three people who'd almost lost their lives. It was going to be a very long day for all of them.

Chapter 10

The night before Christmas Eve . . .

Claire lost count of the cookies after the twenty-third dozen. Her entire family was gathered at Hope House, a shelter for battered women where Max Jorgenson, his wife Grace, and their daughter Bella held their annual cookie bake-off.

This was the first time Claire had attended, and she knew without a doubt that she would return next year. She was having so much fun, no wonder Tilly had chosen to be a chef over her career as a medical doctor. Donald Flynn, the old coot, was getting his way in spite of all the trouble he'd created last week when he demanded Claire come to Ireland where he supposedly lay on his deathbed. Though she wanted to stay angry at him, she couldn't. He would be eighty years old in a matter of days. Claire and Quinn were waiting until then to tell him they were a couple now. With every passing minute, she knew she'd made the right decision when she let Quinn Connor into her life, and into her heart. Connor was his mother's maiden name, she'd discovered. She hadn't wanted Quinn to be burdened with the Flynn name and had chosen to use her maiden name instead. While "Flynn" was close to "Trump" in Ireland, here in the States, it was just another Irish name.

"Can we call you Uncle Quinn yet?" Amanda asked.

"I'd be delighted if you did," he replied.

"So you're gonna marry Aunt Claire?" Ashley asked as she slopped gooey red icing on her Santa cookie.

Quinn looked at Claire. "I plan to."

"But don't you have to ask her first?" Ashley asked again.

Stephanie chose that moment to enter the kitchen, carrying another tray of cookies to the table to be decorated. Something both girls were quite good at.

"Are they being nosy?"

"No, they're just being girls," Quinn said, and winked at Claire.

There were cookies in every possible Christmas design. Angels, stars, Santas of all shapes and sizes, reindeer, Christmas trees and snowflakes set on cooling racks on the dining room table. This was the cooling station. Grace had them all set up in assembly-line fashion. The messiest job, the decorating, was done in the kitchen.

Claire's mother and dad helped to mix the batter. Once the dough was chilled, and they had lots of dough, the kids—Amanda, Ashley, and Bella, and Megan and Nathan's boys—Joseph, Ryan, and Eric—helped to roll out the dough. Abigail, Mark and Colleen's remaining daughter, supervised the young kids.

Later that evening, they would take the cookies to local nursing homes and hospitals. Claire knew there was a big surprise coming up, but she kept it to herself. She and Patrick had decided she wouldn't even hint that she knew what that surprise was.

When the adults returned from delivering the cookies, they all gathered in the formal living room, where Grace served them cookies and hot toddies, and cocoa for those who didn't wish to imbibe. Claire was definitely in the latter group. After the episode at JFK, it would be a very long time before she had another alcoholic beverage.

When the adults were settled, and the younger children put to bed for the night, they watched Bryce, Grace's brother, set up his new Apple computer. They made a big production of turning the computer on, then Bryce clicked the mouse a few times and a face appeared on the screen.

"Claire, I think you should look at this," Quinn said, seeing that she was engaged in a conversation with Melanie, Bryce's wife.

"Look at what?" she asked, then before Quinn had a chance to answer, Claire squealed with delight. "Kelly! Oh my gosh, I can't believe it!"

"Aye, these computers are quite amazing, huh? We can Skype now that Quinn gave me a computer. I can't tell ya how excited I was when he tol' me and mother we were gettin' a new place to live! And Paddy loves his new boots." Claire had just sent them three days ago, but she'd sent them overnight air, so she knew they'd receive them before Christmas.

"I'm glad he likes them. Wait until next year, he'll be walking in those boots. No, he'll be too big. I'll make sure to keep little Paddy supplied with boots, and his mom with shoes."

"Aye, the Kate Spades were ta die for! Thank ya so very much."

Claire knew Quinn had a few more surprises for Kelly. She couldn't wait to see the expression on her face. "Kelly, Quinn wants to have a peep, is that okay with you?"

She laughed. "Of course it is!"

Quinn leaned close to the microphone so Kelly could hear him. "A little birdie told me you wanted to go to school to become a nurse."

"Aye, it's always been a dream o' mine."

"Beginning in January, your tuition is paid in full at the university. And Paddy's, too, though I know it will be a while before he heads off to college, but Claire and I just wanted to make sure he had that opportunity."

Tears rolled down Kelly's face. "I don't know what ta say, except thanks to ya both; my life, me mum's life, and Paddy's life are better for knowin' ya, all of ya."

"Kelly, there is one more thing," Quinn said, his voice full of happiness. He looked at Claire, and she raised her brows. She didn't know what else he had up his sleeve, but whatever it was, she knew it would be life-changing.

Quinn Connor was a giver, a doer, and a life changer, for all those who were lucky enough to have him as a friend.

"I don't know of anything else, I have everything I could possibly want."

"When I told you the house was yours to live in as long as you want, I meant it. The deed is now in your name, and the house is yours, free and clear."

Claire looked at Quinn, then back at the computer

monitor, where she saw Kelly crying her eyes out. She blew her nose on one of Paddy's diapers, then laughed when she looked into her camera. "There's nothing ta say, Quinn, nothing left to say, except thank ya, you changed me life."

No one said a word. They were all lost in their own thoughts, their own reasons for being especially thankful on this blessed night. They'd all survived during the hostage takeover, each had their wounds, but all had a new appreciation for all that was good in their life.

The computer monitor went black, and they all clapped and congratulated Quinn on his generosity.

Patrick chose that moment to clap his hands. "Listen up, folks. I've got a bit of good news I'd like to share with you while we're all together."

This was Stephanie's clue to join her husband. "Amanda, Ashley, would you come here just for a minute. We have something we want to say, and since you're both big girls now, and don't have to go to bed for at least"—Patrick looked at his watch—"another fifteen minutes, your mom and I thought you should hear this."

Claire wanted to tell him to hurry up and share their good news, but this was special and deserving of those few extra words as it was a life-changing event for them all.

Patrick rubbed the palms of his hands together, excitement brightening his handsome face. He looked at his wife, then wrapped his arm around her shoulders. "Go on, Stephanie, tell them."

"Yeah, tell us."

"Come on, don't keep us in suspense."

"Spit it out, bro, I need to . . ."

"Okay, okay. Stephanie, the honor is yours."

She grinned, her big brown eyes shining like jewels. "Patrick and I recently learned we're going to have a baby!"

Shouts of joy, backslapping, hand clapping, and tears flowed like a fine wine. Joseph and Eileen were just as thrilled with this news as they were when Colleen had told them she was pregnant with Shannon. Though the eldest granddaughter wasn't there in body, somehow the grandparents knew she was there in spirit.

Max shook Patrick's hand. "It's about time, my friend. Grace and I were starting to worry about you."

"Bull," Patrick said.

"Watch your mouth, there are kids in this house," Grace called out, and they all laughed.

Everyone continued to offer Patrick their congratulations. Amanda and Ashley were so excited, the adults knew it would be quite some time before they settled down.

"Is it a boy or a girl?" Amanda asked.

"Yes, do you know yet, or is it too soon?" Claire asked.

"No, we haven't had the ultrasound yet. Don't we have this scheduled for next week? I plan to make a full day of it. Taking the girls with us, too."

Stephanie cleared her throat loudly, hoping to focus the attention on herself. "I hate to be the one to bring up bad news, especially tonight when we're all together as a family for the first time in a very long time, but I don't think there's going to be a more appropriate time, so please"—she paused—"hear me out."

When she saw she had everyone's undivided attention she continued, her voice quiet but strong. "When Jeb Norris held us in the dining hall the other day, I prayed for all of us. I prayed for my girls and my husband, and I also prayed for my unborn child. But as some of you know, being a mother is so much more than a name or an act. It's who I am, what I do best." She smiled when both girls took a bow. "As you can see, I've raised two hams. However, as I was saying, being a mother is the greatest joy in life, at least it has been in mine." They all knew there was time in Stephanie's life when she lived in fear for her daughters' life and her own. But those days were in the past, and nothing more but a faded memory. "When we all escaped without injury, the mother in me couldn't relax until I knew my unborn baby was safe. So, I pulled a fast one, and Patrick, please don't be upset with me for going behind your back, but I had to. I had an ultrasound the day after, and I know the sex of our child. I hope you're okay with this?" Stephanie's eyes filled with fear, but only for a moment. She was safe with Patrick and knew he would never lash out at her in anger.

"Sweetie, I could never be upset with you for wanting to protect our child." He kissed her lightly on the lips. "But I will give you a great big hickey in front of my entire family if you don't tell me, tell us if we need to paint the nursery pink or blue."

Again, all eyes were focused on the couple, and their two girls. "Maybe striped. Because you see, there seems to be one of each. So to answer your question"—Stephanie beamed—"we're having twins. A boy and a girl."

More whoops and hollers, and tears. Congratulations were said again and again.

Claire watched her brother and her sister-in-law and prayed that she and Quinn would always be as happy as they were at this exact moment.

When the excitement died down, and plans for baby showers, new baby furniture, and names dominated the conversation, Quinn grabbed Claire and whisked her outside.

"It's freezing out here! Have you lost your mind?" Claire asked, though she was teasing and thrilled to be alone with him even if it were only for a few minutes.

"I have not lost my mind, at least not yet, but I have lost my heart. To you. Donald got his wish after all, and he really didn't need to do a thing."

"Well, poor old soul, he loves his castle and his country. What more can a man want?"

Quinn gathered her in his arms, tilting her chin up so she could look into his eyes. "You, Claire. I want you."

She smiled up at him. "I'm all yours."

"No, I mean for always and forever. I want to share the rest of my life with you. Will you do me the honor of becoming my wife?"

Claire had expected anything, but not a proposal, but then she remembered who she was dealing with. "I would be honored to spend my life with you, *Mister Christmas.*"

Quinn kissed her with such passion, Claire's rumba dancer's went wild.

"I love you, Claire O'Brien."

"And I love you, Quinn Connor."

"Let's go inside and tell the rest of the family we're all going to Ireland Christmas Day."

Claire's heart swelled with love.

Life was good. Very, very good.

A Winter Wonderland

Chapter 1

Angelica Shepard tossed aside the script she'd been reading. It was beyond her skills as an actress even to begin to
get into character for a part in yet another off-*off*-Broad-
way play under financial duress, and most likely—and
this is only if she was lucky—it would have a short run,
and the reviews would be atrocious.

When she began to study acting right out of high
school, she'd given herself ten years to "make it" to the
top. Meaning, she would be able to support herself and, if
the gods smiled on her, she'd be able to quit her second
job. At eighteen, ten years had seemed like a lifetime.
Now at thirty-two, four years past her self-imposed deadline, she was still searching for the role that would cata-
pult her to stardom.

She glanced at the script, then told herself to forget it.
Something better was sure to come along.

A cup of tea would be nice right now, she decided as she walked three feet from her living room/bedroom to the small kitchen—if you could even call it a kitchen. It consisted of one small counter, four cabinets that hung above the countertop, a mini-stove, and a refrigerator. She'd made the best of the limited space, calling it home for more than ten years. It was a small studio, even by New York standards, but Angelica couldn't help feeling a wee bit of pride. Purchasing the place on her own, and in the city, was quite an accomplishment. Yes, she had to supplement her acting career with a part-time job bartending at one of New York's hottest nightspots, but without that job, she would never have been able to pay the mortgage, much less continue to pursue an acting career. Many times, Angelica had wanted to throw in the towel and just work at the club full-time, but she was determined to pursue an acting career a while longer. Maybe after six months, she would once again reevaluate her career choice.

She filled the white ceramic teakettle from the tap and placed it on top of the burner. Walking the few feet back into the living room/bedroom, she caught a glimpse of herself in the mirror above the small chest of drawers that held her entire wardrobe. She had medium-length coffee-colored hair and hazel eyes, which were just beginning to reveal the first signs of crow's-feet. Her skin was still smooth, her lips full, her teeth perfectly aligned, but she could see the beginning signs of aging. Maybe she should consider having Botox injections. Her friends swore by the stuff. But the thought of injecting botulism in her system was a bit too much.

She'd had high hopes for a part she'd auditioned for just last week. The role had called for an actress in her mid to late twenties who could sing reasonably well, dance, and, of course, act. Her agent, Al Greenberg, a kindly old guy who'd been in the business forever, had promised her he would call and tell her if she'd gotten the part. No sooner had the thought crossed her mind than her cell phone's musical ring filled the small studio apartment at the same time the teakettle began its low whistle. She grabbed her cell phone, leapt to the stove, and removed the kettle.

"Hello," she said anxiously.

"Angelica, my dear, how is my favorite client?"

She took a deep breath. "It depends on why you're calling," she said, hoping to sound light and silly rather than dark and desperate.

Al laughed before responding. "Now, now, don't hold me responsible for your moods, kiddo." He paused.

Angelica heard his intake of breath and knew then that his reason for calling was not to impart the news she'd hoped for. A heavy sigh escaped her before she spoke. "Go ahead, Al. Shoot."

"I couldn't believe it when I heard it myself. Ross called." Ross was the director and producer of the play Angelica had auditioned for. "He wants Waverly Costas for the part."

Silence.

Al did not need to explain to her what that meant. Waverly Costas was twenty-three, with beautiful ash brown hair and a body to match. The sad thing was, and Angelica couldn't help but acknowledge the fact, the younger woman was actually a gifted actress. Her stomach instantly knotted, and her eyes pooled.

Darn, dang, and double darn! She'd *really* wanted the part! Inhaling, then slowly exhaling as she'd been taught in her yoga class, Angelica chewed her bottom lip, then plunked down on the cream-colored sofa. "It's okay, Al. As you always say, it must not be the right part for me."

She heard Al's heavy sigh. "That's true. It takes time. Everyone wants to star on Broadway. You know the competition is tough, but your time will come, Angie." He used the pet name that he'd given her years ago.

"Sure, Al. You've been telling me that for how long now?" Of course, she knew exactly how long. He'd been her agent for twelve years. Yes, she'd had a number of good roles, all supporting, but never a lead.

"Ahh, come on, Angie, don't be discouraged. I hear that Johnny Jones has something in the works. It'll be the perfect role for you. Rumor is that Morgan Freeman has accepted the leading male role."

How many times had she missed out on "the perfect role"? And this one was with *Morgan Freeman*? Her favorite male actor in the world. Al knew it, too. She could just see it now. Her name beneath his on the playbill. Blotting her eyes with a corner of the dark green throw tossed on the back of the sofa, Angelica took another deep breath. "Listen, Al. We both know I'm not getting any younger. Maybe it's time to call it quits. We know youth rules the business these days. The younger, the better. I really appreciate everything you've done for me, truly I do. Maybe I'll take some time off during the holidays, rethink my career choice."

Al's robust laughter filled her ears. "I think that's an excellent idea, Angie, best I've heard all day. Why don't you head out West? I know how much you enjoy skiing. Hell, who knows, you might even meet some lucky ski bum."

Her spirits sank even further. Al sure had a way of making her feel good about herself today. "Yeah, that's what I'll do. As a matter of fact, I'll call the travel agency now. I'll get in touch when I return."

"See? That's the attitude! You have a Merry Christmas, kid, and I'll see you when you come home. Who knows what'll be waiting for you?"

"Yeah, who knows? Merry Christmas, Al." Angelica disconnected. She suddenly felt as though she were about to say a final good-bye to her dreams.

Fourteen years of hard work.

Down the drain.

Chapter 2

Dr. Parker North, trauma surgeon at Denver's Angel of Mercy Hospital for the past eight years, dropped the blood-soaked bluish-green scrubs into a disposal bin. The coppery smell of blood filled his nostrils as he removed the paper covers from his Nike cross trainers. Inside the physicians' changing room, he took from his assigned locker his favorite pair of faded Levi's and a worn-out gray T-shirt that read HARVARD MEDICAL in faded black letters, and tossed both articles of clothing on a metal chair. Catching a glimpse of himself in the mirror, he saw that his dark hair was in need of a trim. Gray half-moons rimmed his dark eyes. He couldn't remember the last time he'd had a good night's sleep, but apparently his eyes had another story to tell, looking like he'd just woken up.

He stepped inside the stall, hoping to wash away the

day's memories. Under the shower's warm, pelting spray, Dr. North mentally relived every last detail of the patient he'd spent the last three hours trying to save. Eight years old. It sickened him to think of the loss, the heartache the family felt. Seeing the young girl's parents break down had more of an effect on him than anything he had ever experienced before. Sadly, patients dying was part of the job, and Parker knew it. But seeing a perfectly healthy child die senselessly was not a part of his job that he relished. And knowing that the child's death could have been prevented, it was hard to accept. He truly sympathized with the parents, but he was also very angry. The little girl's death was the result of a total lack of parental responsibility.

Vigorously, he lathered up with the harsh antimicrobial soap the hospital provided. He scrubbed his skin until it hurt, but he knew that no matter how much he tried, he could not erase from his memory the image of the little girl's lifeless body.

She had been airlifted from Aurora, the third largest city in Colorado, just eight air miles away. Parker had been informed of her arrival minutes before the life chopper had landed in its designated area. He and his trauma team were prepared for the patient's arrival. Knowing it was a child put the team on high alert, not that an adult elicited any less of a response. They'd been informed by the paramedics that their patient had been hit by a vehicle while riding her bicycle on the street where she lived. They were also told the child had not been wearing a helmet. There were massive head injuries and severe blood loss.

Parker knew the statistics. The survival rate among children with head injuries was not good. Not at all. How could parents allow their children to ride bicycles without the proper headgear? A twenty-dollar helmet could prevent an extraordinarily large amount of traumatic brain injuries, especially in children. And donor blood could drastically improve one's chances when a significant amount was lost. This accident could've been prevented.

The swish of the trauma center's entrance doors and the thundering footsteps of the paramedics jolted him into the present. There was no time for what-ifs. He had a life to save.

Flashes of dark blue whizzed past Parker as he raced toward the gurney that held the victim. Quickly, Parker assessed the girl's visible wounds. Her left arm was almost detached from her shoulder, her right foot was shattered, the bones haphazardly resembling a set of pickup sticks. Most concerning, she did not appear to feel any pain. After a hasty examination of the still child, Parker said, "Let's get a CT scan, stat."

Within seconds, a portable computed tomography— CT unit—was quickly wheeled into the trauma unit next to the gurney. The technicians made fast work of performing the CT and getting the results to radiology.

Parker did what was required of him, but knew at this point that his efforts might not save this little girl's life. She'd lost way too much blood and was completely unresponsive. When the tech returned with the CT results, Parker's heart plunged to his feet and back. The parents needed to be told of her condition immediately.

"Where are the parents?" Dr. North barked.

"They're on their way," a nurse offered.

Dr. North nodded and probed the child's neck. "We don't have much time. Let's get this child to surgery. There is intracranial pressure." He looked at the machine, which beeped with the child's vitals. Her oxygen level was dropping. Fast.

"Let's get moving! We don't have much time." Knowing the little girl's chances were slim to none, Dr. Parker North was going to do everything within his power to see that she survived.

Two and a half hours later, he knew it was time to inform the parents of their loss.

Parker turned the water off and stood inside the shower, mindless of the cold water dripping off him as he remembered his unsuccessful efforts to save the patient. A child was dead, two parents were devastated, and his skill as a trauma neurosurgeon was not up to standards, at least not *his* standards. He should have been able to save the girl. He had tried every medical procedure he knew, but sadly, her injuries were just too severe.

Knowing it was useless to continue to mentally flagellate himself, he reached for the white towel that hung limply on a rusting steel rod.

Fifteen minutes later, he was dressed and in his rusted Ford pickup truck heading to his apartment just blocks away from the hospital. He was a trauma surgeon, and part of the job was being there when he was needed. He could make it from bed to the hospital in nine minutes flat. Faster if he ran the two traffic lights between his apartment and the hospital.

After today's loss, Parker North had decided to do something he hadn't done since he'd begun his residency. He was taking some much-needed time away from his duties as a doctor. What had happened today made him realize the true value of life and his role as a doctor in saving precious lives. He'd never suffered from the God complex that some doctors did, but at that moment he wished for any other profession than that of a doctor. Seeing the looks on the faces of the parents when he had told them he hadn't been able to save their daughter had made him cringe.

He'd wanted to be a doctor his entire life. His father had been a cardiologist, but, sadly, he'd died from a heart attack before Parker had graduated from high school. His mother was still alive and well but spent most of her time hopping from one cruise ship to another, so it was only very occasionally that he saw her. After his father's unexpected death, his mother hadn't been the same. And if he was honest with himself, he hadn't been either. His father's death had led him to this very moment in time. And right now, he did not want to be a doctor. He did not want the responsibility of holding another human being's life in his hands.

Maybe it was time to consider a career change.

Chapter 3

Angelica headed for the car-rental agency at Denver International Airport just as she had numerous times in the past. She never tired of seeing the extensive art collection as she made her way through the airport, where she'd reserved a four-wheel-drive vehicle. Sculptures, murals, and dozens of paintings rivaled those in many of New York City's museums.

She located the rental booth quickly, placing her carry-on beside her as she joined the other travelers in the lengthy line. She'd never seen the line quite so long but remembered it was the Christmas season. Like New York City during the holidays, the Colorado city was transformed into a shiny magical land of dreams and never-ending cheer. This was her first trip away from the city during the holiday season. Suddenly, she doubted her decision to leave, to ski and pretend her life was as it should be.

It could be worse, she thought, as she viewed the long lines at the other car-rental counters. She had her health, a decent amount of savings, and a home of her own. Sort of. Hers and the bank who held the mortgage. For now, Angelica figured this was as good as it was going to get. She decided she would enjoy the next two weeks and forget about her acting career and anything connected to New York. Or at least she would try.

As she waited in the ever-growing line, she observed the scene around her. Tourists from all over the world occupied every available inch of space. Some carried gigantic pieces of luggage. Others, like herself, pulled a small carry-on behind them, while some, mostly people with families, pushed fancy strollers as small children lugged mini-suitcases with their favorite superhero characters emblazoned on them. Backpacks of every shape, size, and color perched on the backs of many. Businessmen in Brooks Brothers suits carried their iPads in soft leather cases. Angelica couldn't help but smile. Technology. She hadn't upgraded to the latest and greatest in the technological field since her profession didn't require much more than a telephone, but someday she'd investigate the high-tech world and decide if the leap was worth it.

Slowly, the line inched forward. She continued to peruse her surroundings while she waited. The voices of children could be heard throughout the airport, their shouts of welcome and cries of good-bye suddenly making her homesick for the familiar sights and sounds of New York City. The scents from street-side vendors hawking roasted chestnuts, skewers of overcooked meat, and soggy hot dogs permeated the city. The acrid odor from the subway, and the exhaust from hundreds of taxis that traversed the city, were as familiar and comforting to her as a child's favorite blanket—which brought to mind the red and green afghan she'd knitted years ago and had kept in her tiny dressing room at the Forty-seventh Street Playhouse. She'd left it there after her last performance and had never gone back to retrieve it. Maybe another young actor could use it. The backstage at the theater was always too cold anyway. Her last conversation with Al let her know she was on the downside of her career. There wouldn't be time to knit backstage while waiting for her call. At her age, she'd be lucky to get an acting job in a dinner theater. The kind where the actors and actresses waited tables in between acts.

She should've gone to college. Studied literature. She'd bet the bank she wouldn't be out of a job if that were the case. The line started to move, jarring her from her negative thoughts. 'Tis the season, she thought, and forced a smile. For the next two weeks, she was not going to think about her career or lack of one.

She'd said that twice to herself already.

No, she was going to ski until she dropped, drink hot toddies by the fireplace, curl up with a good book at the end of the day. Do whatever she pleased, and all by herself.

Another wave of sadness overwhelmed her.

"Stop!" she whispered harshly. When she saw several people glance at her, she did what she knew best. She plastered a huge grin on her face and acted as though she hadn't a clue why they were staring at her.

When it was her turn at the counter, Angelica removed the required driver's license and credit card from her wallet, signed on the dotted line, and listened carefully to the agent's instructions. She'd asked for a vehicle equipped with a GPS just in case. The last thing she wanted was to get lost in the Colorado mountains. Not that she planned on leaving Maximum Glide, the ski resort where she planned to ski and sip all those hot toddies. She had splurged and rented a small cabin located midway up the mountain. She could've stayed in Telluride itself, but Angelica wanted time to reflect and come to a decision. Being isolated would force her to focus on her choice of careers.

With the keys to her rental in hand, she found the automatic doors leading to the parking garage. Instantly, they swished open, allowing the frigid wintry air into the overly warm airport for the briefest of seconds. Angelica shivered, glad that she'd worn her heavy parka. New York was cold, yes, but she thought Denver downright bone-chilling as she searched the giant lot for her vehicle's designated parking space.

After walking for what felt like a mile, Angelica spied the white Lincoln Navigator. A male attendant wearing olive khakis and a rich brown jacket greeted her, asking her to wait while he inspected the vehicle for scratches and dents. He walked around the SUV twice, then handed her a pink slip of paper attached to a clipboard. She signed the slip.

"We're supposed to get some nasty weather tonight," he said as he inspected her signature. "Be careful."

Having spent her entire adult life in New York City, she wasn't the most experienced driver in the world. Too bad there wasn't a taxi or a subway to deliver her to her destination. "Uh, what do you mean by 'nasty'?"

The young guy gave her a quick once-over. "Blizzard nasty. The Interstate closes in bad weather. If you're heading to the mountains, you'd best be on your way."

Angelica thanked him. Using the key fob to unlock the

hatch, she placed her luggage in the back before sliding into the driver's seat.

Knowing she had several hours of driving ahead of her, it suddenly occurred to her that it would be very late by the time she reached her cabin. As she adjusted her seat belt and rearview mirror she remembered that she had to program the GPS. She located the Post-it note crumpled inside her denim bag that had the address on it. It took several minutes for her to become at ease with the GPS before she tapped the address on the touch screen. When she saw the travel time and mileage displayed on the flat screen and realized she had a six-and-a-half-hour road trip ahead of her, she became weak in the knees.

"Darn, what was I thinking?" she asked out loud.

"I wasn't," she answered herself as she drove out of the underground parking lot.

Realizing it was too late to rectify her mistake, she looked at the time. Just after four thirty. She'd be lucky to make it to her rental cabin by midnight. If the car-rental attendant was right, and the weather took a nosedive, she was in trouble. Big-time. She didn't know her way around Colorado and wasn't as well traveled as one would expect for a woman her age. Living in New York City, she had everything one could possibly need without benefit of an automobile. There was no need to learn how to navigate through a blizzard. That's what taxis and subways were for. And if those were not available in a really bad snowstorm, then one just stayed home.

As she piloted her way through the congested roads around the airport, she focused on the task of driving, paying close attention to the animated female voice coming from the GPS. She should have booked a flight directly to Telluride and saved herself the aggravation of the long drive. She'd been in such a rush to leave after her phone call with Al, she hadn't really cared where she was headed as long as it was away from New York. Now that she had calmed down a bit, she saw the stupidity of her actions. The drive was going to take longer than the flight had.

An hour later, Angelica was cruising along on Colorado's I-70. So far, so good. Traffic wasn't too bad, and she found a radio station that played nothing but Christmas music. The weather was holding its own, too.

Maybe the trip wasn't going to be so bad after all.

Chapter 4

Dr. Parker North hated leaving at the last minute, but he felt that he had no other choice. He needed time away, time to reflect on his future as a medical professional. When his father died, he'd decided to become a doctor, a trauma surgeon. He wanted to see and heal up close. Never once had he questioned his choice of careers. It was in his blood. Both his father and grandfather had been doctors. But, for the first time in his life, he wondered if he'd made the right decision. Losing that little girl had left its mark on him. She should be alive now. But she wasn't because he hadn't been able to save her.

Briefly, he thought that her parents should be charged with neglect. If they'd used their brains, this would never have happened. Parents should always provide helmets for their kids. In his profession, he saw head injuries daily. Seeing the devastation, the regret, the sorrow on the faces of the little girl's parents, he knew they had to know they were responsible for their child's death. Quite the burden, he thought. If only they'd been more aware.

He could "if only" all day. It would get him nowhere.

Parker couldn't put it off any longer. He'd taken an indeterminate leave of absence. He wasn't going to sit around his apartment and mope. He'd hear the ambulances anyway; he lived that close to the hospital. No, he had to leave, go somewhere to relax, clear his head, and decide if he wanted to continue practicing medicine. So, he was about to do what he'd promised an old college buddy he would do years ago.

Parker North was going to call Max Jorgenson and take him up on his offer to spend some time at Maximum Glide, his ski resort in Telluride, Colorado. Then he remembered Leon, his ten-year-old black and white tuxedo cat. He'd have to bring him along or hire someone to sit for him. It was too late to find someone, so that decision was made. Leon, who absolutely hated riding in his truck, was going on vacation with him. He knew that Max had dogs, was an avid animal lover, so he wasn't worried about Leon being unwelcome.

Once Parker had made up his mind, there was no stopping him. He found his ancient suitcase stuck in the front closet, along with his old skis and boots. He examined them and decided he could always replace them once he tested them on the slopes. It'd been almost twenty years since he'd skied, and he was a native.

He yanked jeans and sweatshirts from his single dresser, warm wool socks, and several T-shirts. In the bathroom, he stuffed his shaving gear and toothbrush in a Ziploc bag. He found Leon's carrier, grabbed several cans of cat food, then, since Leon was an indoor cat, he emptied the litter box, rinsed it out, and tucked a thirty-pound sack of litter next to the front door so he wouldn't forget.

Once he finished, he checked his e-mail, responded to a few that were important, then figured he might as well make the call to Max.

He'd met Max when they were both students at the University of Colorado in Boulder. Max had gone on to achieve Olympic fame, winning several gold medals. The last Parker had heard, he'd married, and his wife, a police officer, had been shot and killed in the line of duty. That'd been three or four years ago. Hopefully Max had healed and moved on, but Parker knew it couldn't have been easy.

He himself had been involved in a serious relationship while attending Harvard. Jacqueline Bersch. A knockout. Tiny, with large brown eyes and chocolate hair, she had a smile that would've made Scrooge grin. He'd fallen for her hard and fast. They'd been inseparable through medical school and during their residency. After graduation they'd both accepted positions in Denver. Dr. Jac, as he'd referred to her, went into private practice a year after they returned to Denver. Sadly, she'd fallen for her partner, Dr. Jonathan Flaherty. She broke Parker's heart, and he hadn't been in a serious relationship since. Too much effort anyway.

He flipped through the contact list on his cell phone, found Max's number, and hit Send.

Max answered on the third ring. "I hope my caller ID is working," he said. "It says that this call is from Parker North, but I know that can't be right."

Parker grinned. "It's working just fine, my friend. I called to see if that offer still stands."

Max chuckled. "I thought you had forgotten. It's been what—ten, fifteen years?"

"I don't think it's been that long," Parker answered, then did a quick mental count. Close to fifteen. Where had the years gone? It seemed like yesterday he and Max had shared a dorm and spent many late nights kicking up their heels and suffering for it the next day. The memory made him grin. "It's been a while. Hey, I heard about your wife. It's probably too late, but for what it's worth, I'm sorry."

"Thanks. It was a tough time in my life. I remarried a few years ago. I have a daughter now. Her name is Ella. She's two. Life is good right now."

At the mention of a child, Parker clammed up. It took him a couple of seconds to get his bearings.

"Congratulations, Max. I've let too much time pass. I've missed a lot of life. I just took a leave of absence, which is my reason for calling. Would it be too forward of me to think that offer you made me after you purchased that big resort still stands?"

"Hell no, it wouldn't be too forward. Just give me a time and date, and I'll make sure you're taken care of. I'd like to get you on the slopes again, my friend, and I'd like you to meet Grace and Ella."

Parker wasn't up for kids just then, but he wasn't going to tell that to Max after all these years. He'd perfected avoidance after Jac dumped him. There was no avoiding the occasional bumping into one another as they both spent most of their days and some nights at Angel of Mercy. "Actually, I'm leaving now. I need to relax a bit, take some time for myself. I haven't taken any time off since I started practicing. And I'm bringing Leon, my cat—that is if it's okay with you." He could not bring himself to explain the real reason why he needed a break.

"You know what they say about all work and no play," Max said, then added, "It's crazy busy this time of year, but I'll hook you up. I'll reserve one of my best condos for you. You're more than welcome to bring Leon; hell, you know I love dogs and cats."

"Yep, just me and the fur ball. You sure this is a good time? I don't want to mess up anyone's holiday plans."

"Anytime is good, Parker. We always leave a few condos vacant. Just in case, you know, the president or the secretary of state decides at the last minute to come for some time on the slopes. I can't wait to introduce you to Grace and Ella. I'll tell Grace to set an extra plate for dinner tomorrow night. She can cook better than anyone, and her mother cooks, too. And she's the sweetest old gal you'd ever want to meet. The mother, of course. Grace is definitely not old."

Parker couldn't help but smile. Max had it bad for his wife *and* mother-in-law. He was happy for him. "I'll look forward to meeting them both," he said.

"I promise you won't be disappointed," Max said. "When you arrive, just come to the main building, you can't miss it. You'll see the signs that lead to the registration office. I'll have everything set up for you. Drive safe. The forecast is calling for massive amounts of snow once you're on the continental divide side."

"I'm leaving now. If the weather gets too bad, I'll call you and drive in tomorrow morning. Max, I really do appreciate this, especially since it's last minute. I owe you, big-time."

Max chuckled. "Not to worry. It's my pleasure. Now get your ass on the road before that storm hits."

"I'll see you tomorrow." Parker was about to hang up when he realized he had no clue where Max lived. "Where can I find that dinner you promised?"

"I'll pick you up tomorrow evening around seven," Max said.

"Good, then I'm out of here. And, Max, thanks for this. I really need to get the hell out of Dodge for a while."

After hanging up, Parker looked around at his apartment to make sure everything was as it should be. There were no plants to water, no mail to hold, as he had most of his bills paid electronically now. No one in the complex would miss him, that's for sure. He did set the automatic timer, so his single lamp in the living room would come on for three hours every evening, but that was it. He took one last glance around, then locked the door behind him.

It took twenty minutes to force Leon into the carrier. Another ten for him to stop howling. "Look, it'll be nice for both of us. We need a change of pace, and you, my friend, are coming along no matter what, so give it up and get over it." He placed all of Leon's necessities in the back of the old Ford, then tossed the skis and boots in the back, too. He placed his suitcase on the passenger's side, below Leon's carrier.

After programming the radio station to his favorite rock station, he checked his gas gauge, then pulled out of his assigned parking space. He'd devoted his entire life to medicine and hadn't bothered with much of a personal life since Jac. It was a sad testimony for a man nearing forty years of age.

As he turned onto the street, Parker focused on nothing but his driving. The last thing he needed was to wind up at Angel of Mercy as a patient. Hearing a favorite tune on the radio, he cranked up the volume and headed north. Fortunately, Leon didn't seem to mind the loud music.

Chapter 5

Angelica checked the bright blue numbers on the dashboard and saw it was 11:36. She'd accomplished her goal by arriving at her cabin before midnight. The snow hadn't been as heavy as predicted, and she'd only stopped once for gas and coffee. She'd listened to Christmas music, singing along to several songs she'd known since childhood and focusing her attention on arriving safely. Once she was ensconced in her cabin, then she would contemplate the real reason behind her sudden trip.

She found the registration building without too much trouble. Not only was the area well lit, but there were hundreds of colorful Christmas lights strung throughout the small ski village. Tall pines were decked out in sparkling white lights from top to bottom. Freshly fallen snow resting on the tree branches reminded her of a scene directly out of a Norman Rockwell painting.

A piercing night wind sent up flurries of snow through-out the parking area. Shivering, Angelica carefully made her way across the icy asphalt. The last thing she needed was to fall. She'd been there, done that, in the city more than once. With that in mind, she practically tiptoed to the office.

An engraved wooden sign indicated she should ring the doorbell when arriving after hours. Sure that midnight qualified as after hours, she placed a gloved finger on the bell and pushed. Hearing a dim buzzing from inside, An-gelica hoped she hadn't gotten anyone out of a warm bed, but if she did, she assumed this was part of their job re-quirements, and they were used to waking at odd hours. When no one answered her buzz, she pushed the lighted dial again. In seconds, she heard heavy footsteps leading toward the door. "I'm coming, I'm coming. . . . Keep your britches on," said a male voice from inside.

Britches? Angelica couldn't help but smile. She could hear little beeps coming from inside. Probably deactivat-ing an alarm. After hearing of several burglaries in her area, she had had one of her own installed in her apart-ment just last year and recognized the familiar beeps.

A bearded older man opened the door. "Come on in, you're letting the cold inside. You must be that actress from New York. Max told me you'd be coming today. He didn't mention it'd be this late."

Stepping inside the warm office, she spoke. "I'm sorry. I flew in from Denver. It was a much longer drive than I remembered. I hate to get you out of bed."

The old man, probably in his mid to late seventies, brushed a bearlike hand in the air. "Who says I was in bed? I was checkin' my Facebook page and got to talkin' to an old pal from high school."

Angelica couldn't help but grin. Seniors were certainly keeping up to date with technology these days. "I hear a lot of people say they've found old friends through the social media. I'm afraid I'm behind the rest of the world as I don't even own a computer. Just a cell phone." And an extremely old one, too, but she didn't say that.

He gazed at her, then turned, motioning for her to follow him. She'd bet anything that this old guy, when he was not behind the counter pecking away at the keyboard, dressed up as Santa. He had the requisite white hair and matching beard. Crystal-clear blue eyes sparkled behind rimless, round glasses. The belly was perfect, too. Not that she would mention that. She grinned as she imagined him all decked out in red.

Behind the counter, he clicked a few keys, then, without looking up, said, "I know, I know, I hear it all the time. And just so you know, I only dress up because Amanda and Ashley expect me to."

A mind reader, too? She had no clue who Amanda and Ashley were, but figured if he wanted her to know, he'd tell her.

"I would've never guessed," she added. "But you do look the part. The Santa at Macy's in New York City doesn't look quite as realistic."

"So they say. Now"—he stared at the monitor—"Ms. Shepard, it says here you've reserved the Gracie's Way cabin. You'll love the view."

"Uh, yes." She didn't realize the cabin had a name. "I want to spend the days skiing and the nights relaxing."

"Then you've come to the right place. Gracie's Way is smack-dab in the center of the mountain. Has its own lift, too, but I assume you already knew that." He turned his back to her.

No, I didn't, she thought, *but he doesn't need to know just how unprepared I am*. If she'd been thinking straight, she would have booked her flight directly into Telluride, but she'd had other things on her mind.

"Of course, it's just what I wanted," she said, winging it and filling the silence while the old guy removed several sheets from the printer behind him.

While he busied himself with the paperwork, Angelica took the time to view her surroundings. On the wall to her right was a giant rock fireplace. A log chose that moment to fall from the top of a large stack. Red, yellow, and orange sparks shot out like a miniature shower of fireworks. She took a deep breath, loving the heady scent of wood smoke.

A roomy dark brown sofa was placed directly across from the massive structure. A table made out of logs was covered with magazines and a few paperback novels, inviting one to sit and relax. Angelica imagined that during business hours, guests took advantage of the charming arrangement while they enjoyed the warmth from the fire. Floor-to-ceiling windows flanked the fireplace. She guessed that, during the day, the view of the mountains was out of this world. But she wasn't here to stay in the registration area and knew her view would certainly rival this one, or so the travel agent said when she'd made the booking.

The old man fanned the white sheets of paper across the counter, reminding Angelica of the snow angels she used to make in the snow when she was a kid. The memory made her grin.

"If you'll just sign here, here, and here," he said, adding, "and we'll need a credit card and your driver's license."

He turned the papers around for her signature. She scribbled her name, removed a credit card and her license from her wallet. He took them, then turned away from her. She observed him as he made copies of her identification. Soft tan khakis and a black and gold flannel shirt looked to be well worn, comfortable. On his feet were a pair of snakeskin cowboy boots. *Well, I am out West*, she thought.

He placed a single-page map in front of her. "Okay, young lady, it looks like you're all set. If you'll just follow this road"—he traced a single black line with a bright yellow highlighter pen—"all the way to this intersection, then turn right. You can't miss the cabin. The lights are on, and there's coffee fixins, but no food. You'll want to get down to the market first thing in the morning if you want eggs and milk and the like. Food sells out fast, just so you know." He nodded at the exit, his way of dismissing her.

So focused on arriving safely, she hadn't given the first thought to food. She should have bought a few basic necessities when she'd stopped for gas, but again shoulda, coulda, woulda didn't cut it.

"I'll keep that in mind," she said before stepping out into the bracing night air. She gave a half wave to the old man, then trekked back across the parking lot.

Tiny snowflakes swirled beneath the amber glow from the lights. An old beat-up pickup truck pulled into the lot, blocking further viewing of the snowflakes' late-night performance. Probably works here, she thought as she walked carefully across the lot. No one in his right mind would be out in this kind of weather unless he absolutely had to.

A loud meowlike sound startled her. As she turned

around to see where the noise was coming from, she lost her footing. Flailing about as she searched for something to hold on to in order to break her fall, she suddenly found two large hands wrapped around her waist. Stunned at the speed of her rescuer, she turned around to look and see who'd saved her from total humiliation—sort of.

Describing her rescuer as tall, dark, and handsome in no way did justice to the stranger who gently helped her to regain her footing. Stunned by the sudden turn of events, Angelica took a moment to gather herself, to recover from whatever it was she needed to recover from. Never one to be at a loss for words, she couldn't come up with a single syllable as she stared at . . . this . . . *classic Greek god* who was still holding onto her arm.

"Miss, are you all right?"

All she could manage was a slight nod as she stood there, blank, amazed, and very shaken. Finally she found her voice. "Uh, yes, I'm okay, just . . . well, I'm fine," she said, her tone almost defiant. *Why does this strange man make me feel defenseless, and totally aware that I'm a woman?* It was entirely out of character for her, but she was out of character. She was completely out of her element there in that . . . ice palace. *I should have stayed in the city.*

"If you're sure?" the man said, his voice sounding impatient.

Who is this guy? And why the attitude? Angelica wondered. Blinking rapidly to clear her vision, she turned to face her rescuer. What she saw momentarily threw her off guard again. She'd spent plenty of time around some of the sexiest men alive—she was an actress, after all, and it was part of the job. But this . . . this guy defied the rules. He didn't own a sports car if that rusted old truck was his.

His clothing didn't appear to be custom made, and Angelica couldn't forget the fact that he was there so late. More than likely, he worked at the resort and had been on his way inside the registration building when he'd rescued her.

Lucky for me.

Forcing herself to step away from him, Angelica tossed her hair over her shoulder, something she'd learned from improv, then she put her hands on her hips. If that didn't reek of confidence, she didn't know what would.

"Actually, I am more than all right. I am on vacation, and I plan to enjoy every single minute of it. It's gotten off to a bad start, but I'm sure it can only go uphill from here."

She was about to walk to her SUV when the man placed a strong hand on her forearm. She shivered, and it wasn't from the outside temperature. "You're sure you can drive? You look a bit rough."

Had she heard him right? Did he say she looked *rough*? Taking a minute to absorb his words, her first response was to tell him to kiss off and mind his own business. Her second response was to tell him to take a flying leap, but gazing at the giant mountains that surrounded her, that might not be such a good idea. Especially if the guy had issues.

Knowing she couldn't continue to stand there and stare, she found her voice. "I'm quite capable of driving, thank you very much. I was simply startled by that noise. I'm sure I heard a wild cat or something. Did you hear anything?" she asked, and gazed at his hand, which still lingered on her forearm. Apparently, he realized he was still touching her and quickly removed his hand, stuffing it in his pocket. *He appears to be uncomfortable*, Angelica thought. *Good. Let him stew for a bit. He would probably look a bit rough himself if he had just driven for almost seven hours in not so perfect conditions.*

He nodded. "It was Leon. My cat. He hates riding in the truck. Sorry he scared you. Watch your step, this ice can be treacherous," he added before proceeding to walk toward the registration building.

What does he think I am, she wondered as she watched him walk away. *A kid?*

No, she was definitely not a kid. A kid would not be looking at a man's rear view with such blatant lust.

Chapter 6

Parker pressed the doorbell and waited. He'd left the truck running, with the heater cranked up to high for Leon, but cracked the window an inch, just in case. He hated arriving at such a late hour, but it couldn't be helped. The old Ford pickup truck maxed out at fifty-five miles an hour. After stopping for gas and a quick bite, he'd taken his time, and it had gotten away from him. It had been almost midnight when he'd pulled into the deserted parking lot at Maximum Glide.

He'd only just stepped out of his truck when he'd seen the woman slip when she heard Leon's cry of misery. Lucky for them both, instinct kicked in, and he'd caught her in the nick of time. Another second and she would've smacked her head against the icy asphalt. The last thing he wanted to do on his self-imposed sabbatical was step back into the role of medical doctor. Hell, he wasn't sure if he even wanted to return to Angel of Mercy at all. Maybe he'd just enjoy being a ski bum for a while. He and Leon could hang tight on the slopes indefinitely. He wondered if they made skis for cats. Something to look into later.

Before he could pursue the thought of life without the responsibilities of being a doctor, the door opened. A heavyset man with a white beard and rosy cheeks stood to the side. "You must be Dr. North. Max said you were coming this evening. I figured you'd be late, too. The weather and such."

Parker smiled, then stepped inside out of the cold. The old man held out a hand to him. "Thanks for waiting," Parker said. "I just took my time; I guess I should have phoned ahead."

"Not to worry. I'm up. Just checked in that actress from New York City. Poor girl drove all the way from Denver."

"She must be the woman I saw in the parking lot," Parker said out loud.

"I would suspect she is. Now, I have instructions to personally drive you to your condo. Max said you would probably be arriving in a beat-up old truck that wouldn't make the climb."

Parker laughed. Figures. Max remembered everything. "Yeah, I still have the old truck, but I'm sure she can make it up the mountain. There's no need for you to bother. It's late and cold. If you'll just give me the directions, I'm sure I can find my way." He didn't add that he had an angry feline in the truck. No, he'd keep that tidbit of info to himself. As long as Max was okay with it, then that's all that mattered.

The old man, unnamed at that point, pondered his

words. "If you're sure. I'd hate for you to get lost. The weather gets mighty cold at high altitudes. You sure your truck can make it?"

No, he wasn't. He wasn't sure of anything other than that he was dead tired and wanted to lie down and forget about the day, but Parker wasn't totally without social skills. "I'm sure. She's in the best shape ever. Just had a new transmission installed last winter."

The old man nodded. "Yep, that'll make it up the mountain, no doubt. Now, if you'll just look at this." He produced a single sheet of paper. "If you follow this road"—he traced a thin white line with a yellow highlighter pen—"then turn here. The condo unit Max has reserved for you is the best. The penthouse. It's smack-dab in the middle of the mountain. You'll have access to the private ski lift. There are skis and boots of every size waiting for you. Max wasn't sure you'd have them, so he took a few guesses and had Candy Lee pick out several pairs. She works at The Snow Zone—that's the ski shop around the corner. The kid picked out the best of the best and left them next to the fireplace. There's a boot warmer inside, too. Make sure and use it. Most people don't and then don't find out until it's too late that it's lots of work puttin' on a cold boot. Boots slide right on when they're warm. Remember that."

"I will, thanks," Parker said. Somewhere in the back of his mind he knew that but was glad for the reminder.

"Well, then you'd better get goin' while you can. I'll let Max know you arrived first thing in the mornin'. He said he was coming to pick you up for supper tomorrow. I'm sure Grace and Ella will be with him, too. Probably the other girls, as well."

Parker stopped.

Other girls?

It would be just like Max to try and fix him up without giving him a chance to explain that the last thing on his mind was women. No, he'd better give the old man a message for Max. "Tell Max I'm flying solo now and prefer to keep it that way. I don't want to see any girls," he said, a bit abruptly, but he wanted the man to understand that when he relayed his message to Max, he was serious. He was there to relax and reevaluate his future, not entangle himself in a winter romance.

The old guy chuckled, hearty and warm. He shook his big head from side to side. "He didn't tell you about the girls, did he?"

"No, he neglected to tell me about the girls."

"They're Stephanie's kids. She's the manager at The Snow Zone. They usually ride up with Max and Grace when they get the chance, Ashley and Amanda. Both smart as a whip. Max'll want you to ski with them while you're here, too."

Parker felt as though he'd been poked with a pin, and all the life drained from him.

Kids? The girls were kids!

Maybe Max had changed after all.

"Sure, I guess I'm up for meeting a couple of kids," he said when he couldn't think of anything else to say. Relief flowed like oxygen throughout his veins.

"You best get started. It takes about forty-five minutes to make it up the mountain in the daylight, a little longer at night."

Parker nodded, took the sheet of paper with the map off the counter. He turned for the door, then stopped. "You never told me your name."

The older man shifted his eyes up, then down. "No, I reckon I didn't."

Suspicious, Parker waited. The man shoved his large hands inside his pants pockets. "Aww, you'll just laugh like everyone else does. The name's Nick. Nicholas Star."

For a second, Parker thought the old guy was teasing him, but when he saw the red flush creep across his face, he knew he was serious. Having a somewhat unusual name himself, Parker just nodded, then spoke. "It was nice meeting you, Mr. Star. I'll see you around."

Blue eyes sparkled, and Parker would've sworn Mr. Star's belly shook just like Clement C. Moore described in " 'Twas the Night Before Christmas."

Chapter 7

Angelica pulled off to the side of the road, allowing a semitruck to get in front of her. It had been virtually blinding her, its glowing headlights shining in her rear-view mirror. Pulling back onto the winding road, she crept up the mountain, careful to keep her speed low in case she hit a patch of ice. Though the SUV had four-wheel drive, she was not anxious to use it. No, she would take her time. It wasn't as if she had a schedule to keep. She glanced at the clock on the dash. Almost one in the morning. Smiling, Angelica mused that if she were in the city, she would be going out for breakfast with friends right now. They'd be lucky to get to bed before sunrise. She'd kept up this routine for so many years, she wondered if she would be able to adjust her internal clock. Given the time difference, it shouldn't be too hard, but again, she had no curtain call, no one to make any demands on her time. She was totally on her own, without responsibilities, for the first time in her adult life.

Grinning, she shifted the SUV into low gear. She could get used to this, but if anything, despite her chosen career, Angelica was a realist. Being an adult in and of itself was a responsibility. A couple of weeks of snow and fun was her due. She'd worked hard. At thirty-two, she wasn't about to shuck all responsibilities and give up completely. Give up her career? She might not have a choice. Youth was everything in her business, but there were other areas in her profession to explore.

She adjusted her rearview mirror and focused her attention on the road. It wasn't the time to mull over her professional life. The satellite radio station she'd been listening to since she'd left the airport turned to static. "You'd think the reception would be better at this elevation," she observed out loud. Adjusting the dial to another station, she turned up the volume, singing along as Bing Crosby crooned "White Christmas." It was her all-time favorite Christmas song.

A flash of light coming from behind made her take a glance in her rearview mirror. Whoever was behind her had the bright lights on. "Idiot," she muttered before tapping on her brakes several times in a row, hoping the driver would notice and realize that the lights were blinding her. Careful to watch the road ahead but aware of the vehicle trailing her, she slowed down. Then she realized the car was stopping when she saw the driver pull to the side of the road. Whoever it was flashed the bright lights several times.

Not wanting to, but fearing the passenger or passengers in the vehicle might be a mother with children, or someone with a health issue, Angelica did what anyone else in her position would do. She stopped, made a three-point turn, then pulled alongside the other vehicle but kept her cell phone in her hand and did not put the SUV into park. If she had to hightail it back to the registration office, at least she would be heading in the right direction. She hit the button to lower the window.

When she realized that this was the same old beat-up pickup truck she'd encountered in the parking lot, she wasn't sure if she should be happy that at least the man wasn't a total stranger to her. He *had* prevented her from smacking the asphalt and injuring herself after being startled by that noisy cat of his.

Angelica watched as he struggled to lower the driver's window. What she knew about trucks could fill a thimble, but it was enough to judge that this one was probably close to her age. *Poor guy*, she thought, *it must be all he can afford.*

"Hi," was all she could come up with when she saw his face. She was glad for the darkness.

"Yeah, hi. I'm thinking this old gal just decided to take a rest. Could you give me a lift to the office?" He smiled at her, and Angelica's heart rate quickened.

I'll take you anywhere, she thought, then mentally smacked herself.

"Sure, I'd be happy to, but I don't know if it will do you any good. That old guy in the office wasn't too thrilled when I took him away from his social networking." She smiled, hoping she'd licked all the chocolate from her teeth. She had a sweet tooth and rarely went anywhere without a few chocolate bites. Lucky for her, it didn't take much to satisfy her craving.

"I think he enjoys every minute of his job; he's just slightly embarrassed by his name," Parker informed her.

Angelica realized the old guy had never told her his name. "And what would that be?" she asked, still allowing the blistering cold air inside.

"Nicholas Star."

Laughing, she understood. "He does look somewhat like the man in red, with that white beard and big belly," she said. "Do you work here?" she asked brazenly. What else would he be doing out this early in this kind of weather?

"No, I'm here to ski for a couple of weeks," he said. "It's not getting any warmer inside this old gal, so how about I lock up, and you can drive me down the mountain? I'm sure they have one of those all-night towing services in a place like this."

Angelica was surprised that he was a guest but didn't say so to him. He'd probably scrimped and saved all year for this trip. "If you're sure that's what you want. I could drive you to wherever you're staying and bring you back in the morning." Before the words were out of her mouth, she regretted saying them. She didn't know this guy, didn't know if he was a weirdo or what, though she had to admit he appeared normal and was certainly easy on the eyes.

"That's probably a good idea. I'll just leave a note on the windshield and call Max first thing in the morning. I'm sure he wouldn't mind."

She wanted to ask who Max was, but by that time she was so cold, her teeth were chattering, and she really didn't need to know. "Okay, let me turn this vehicle around while you lock up and write your note, but hey," she called out before rolling up her window, "you didn't tell me your name."

"Oh, sure. Parker North." He nodded, gave a brief,

sexy smile, then removed his personal items from his truck, along with the whiny cat inside its carrier. "Mind taking him? He hates the cold."

"Angelica Shepard, nice to meet you, Mr. North," she said, as he walked around to the driver's side of the SUV, opened the rear door, and placed the carrier on the seat. As an extra precaution, he adjusted the seat belt so that the carrier wouldn't fall off the seat. One never knew in this kind of weather.

She settled back in her seat before turning the heat to the highest setting. It was bitterly cold that night.

Angelica suddenly remembered how snippy and rude she'd been to him after he'd referred to her as rough, but it wasn't the most flattering comment she'd ever received. It wasn't a compliment at all, she reminded herself.

She watched as he pulled the old rattletrap as far off the narrow mountain road as possible, grabbed an outdated suitcase, an ancient pair of skis and ski boots, and what must have been a litter box. He waited next to the old truck. She hit the electric button to open the hatch. He tossed his things in the back before coming around to the passenger side. Angelica hit the automatic lock, praying she wasn't making a mistake by allowing a complete stranger to accompany her on a deserted mountain road in the wee hours of the morning. If her mother were still alive, she could just imagine what she would say to her. But she *had* lived in New York City for most of her life and was a fairly good judge of character. Though he appeared to be a bit unrefined, that didn't make him a bad person.

He slid into the passenger seat and held his hands against the heater vents. "It's much colder at this high elevation," he said before turning around to check on Leon. His accent remained neutral, giving no indication about what part of the country he was from. And she wasn't going to ask either.

Angelica put the SUV in low gear and slowly retraced the short distance she'd made before turning around. "I'm staying at Gracie's Way—that's what they're calling my cabin. How about you? Does your place have a name?"

Parker North seemed to be contemplating her question. "No, I don't believe there was a name. It's the penthouse apartment at the main condos mid-mountain."

Penthouse apartment? I have totally misjudged this man. Of course, he might've won the trip. Given his mode of dress and transportation, he does not look as though he is financially equipped to foot the bill for an extravagant penthouse condo at a luxury ski resort.

Her surprise must've been obvious because Mr. North apparently felt the need to explain. "I went to college with Max Jorgenson. He owns Maximum Glide. He won several gold medals in the Olympics several years ago. He invited me for a complimentary stay, and I decided to take him up on his offer."

College? With the owner of the resort? Wow. Of course she'd heard of Max Jorgenson. Who hadn't? She had to admit, she was a wee bit impressed.

He produced the same map Mr. Nicholas Star had given her. Removing a penlight from his pocket, he shined it across the map. "According to the map, we're about four miles from our turnoff."

"Okay, I'll watch for the turn, but I don't want to drive too fast. I'm not used to driving." She felt the need to explain her reason for barely going thirty miles per hour.

"Would you feel more comfortable if I were to drive?"

he asked. "I've lived in the area most of my life, and I'm used to driving in snow and ice. Actually, I can drive in just about any condition."

Wondering why he was so experienced, it occurred to her that he probably worked on one of Colorado's road crews. He said he'd gone to college with the owner, but it didn't appear that he was as successful as his friend.

"No, but thanks, I'm fine as long as I focus my attention on my driving," she explained.

"Well, if you're sure," he said.

This insignificant conversation could go on and on. Angelica just wanted to make it to her cabin, take a long, hot bath, and spend the day on the slopes.

"Thanks, but I can handle it. I need the practice. Just relax. You look like you could use a nap."

He didn't really, but she had to say something to his remark that she looked rough.

"Thanks, I think I will do just that." He closed his eyes and leaned back against the headrest.

Angelica was more curious about her passenger now than ever. He seemed to be capable of relaxing at a moment's notice.

Fifteen minutes later, she made the turn as indicated on the map. She saw the lights from the high-rise and knew it was her passenger's destination. Not bothering to wake him just yet, she drove through the parking lot to an underground garage. She'd give him a few more minutes to rest. He certainly appeared to be sound asleep.

When she found a parking spot, she turned off the engine, which immediately awakened her passenger.

"That was fast," he said. "Thanks for the lift."

She hit the electronic switch to open the hatch. A burst of frigid air filled the vehicle.

He removed his skis and suitcase, then came around to her side of the SUV for Leon. "Again, Leon and I appreciate the ride. I really am tired and want to call it a night."

Angelica gave him her best smile. "Anytime. Maybe we'll bump into one another on the slopes."

"Just so you know, I didn't come here to make friends." A sudden chill hung on the edge of his words.

Glad of the semidarkness that hid the flush in her cheeks, she punched the electronic window, raising it as fast as she could. With nothing but glass and harsh words between them, not to mention her humiliation at his total rebuff when she mentioned meeting on the slopes, Angelica had nothing more to say. This guy was an ass. Before she changed her mind, she lowered the window once again. "For the record, I didn't either. I felt sorry for you and was just trying to be polite. I wouldn't ski with you if my life depended on it."

Before he had another chance to humiliate her, she tromped down on the accelerator, hoping the ice and snow that blew in her wake smacked him right upside the head.

Chapter 8

Angelica found the turnoff to Gracie's Way without any trouble. Just as Mr. Star had said, the lights were on, both inside and out. A warm greeting, but this only reminded her of the cold send-off she'd received from her . . . travel partner, for lack of better words. She pulled the Navigator into the long drive, still somewhat miffed over the remarks made by Mr. North.

As she unloaded the SUV, she thought about the two men she'd met in the past hour. Mr. Star and Mr. North. Made her think of the North Star. Was there any significance between the two names, some kind of divine message that someone was trying to give her? She didn't think so, but one could never be too sure.

Dragging her carry-on up the wooden steps, she found the key just where Mr. Star said it would be. Unlocking the door, she stepped inside, surprised at the cabin's luxuriousness.

A giant fireplace, an exact replica of the fireplace in the registration office, dominated the great room. A cherry red plush sofa and two forest green chairs were strategically placed. A fire crackled in the fireplace, popping embers filling the large room with inviting sounds and the enticing scent of wood burning.

As she dropped her luggage next to the fireplace, a log fell, sending blazing orange, red, and yellow embers upward. Deciding that she had better add another log so as not to lose the warmth from the fire, she found a fully stocked supply next to the hearth. She placed two large logs on top of the others, found the fire poker, and nudged the logs until she was satisfied they were positioned properly in order to continue to burn. Satisfied that the fire would burn for another hour or two, she located the kitchen around the corner from the great room.

She was shocked at its size—she could have placed her entire apartment inside and had room to spare. It had a full-size range, two ovens, and more counter space than she'd ever seen in one kitchen. She continued to explore, finding a Sub-Zero refrigerator that could hold enough food for an entire winter. Maybe that's what it was used for, she thought, as she opened it to look inside. Mr. Star, of course, was right—it was as empty as her stomach was beginning to feel. She should have prepared a bit better. She'd have to make a trip tomorrow down the mountain for supplies. She found the makings for coffee exactly where he said they would be and decided to make a small pot for herself. She wasn't ready for bed yet. Her New York habits were not going to be as easy to put aside as she'd thought.

Walking through the cabin, she saw that the walls were made from honey-colored logs, as was the staircase that led upstairs to the two bedrooms and a loft. Why she'd felt the need for so much space, she didn't know. After spending fourteen years in New York City, she had gotten used to living in minimal space. But she was *not* going to focus on what brought her to Colorado, at least not that first night. She was there to ski, think about her life, and decide if it was time for a career change. But her first night was for her to do nothing but explore her new digs for the next two weeks. Later, there would be plenty of time for deep thoughts, but not immediately.

Inside the master bedroom was a king-sized bed, also made of giant honey-colored logs. A navy and red quilt covered it. Several pillows were scattered about, making the bed as inviting as the rest of the cabin. She had a sudden flash of what Parker North would look like sprawled across the bed but quickly focused her attention on anything but him. He was a rude, overbearing jerk as far as she was concerned.

Angelica realized she'd come to that conclusion very quickly, which wasn't her usual style. She was the least judgmental person in the world, but this man had gotten under her skin, and she did not like that at all. Clearing his handsome face from her mind, she found the second bedroom. It was much smaller than the master but just as warm and inviting. It also had a bed made out of logs, with a hunter green quilt and several matching pillows. It would be a shame not to use the room, but hey, she could if she wanted. This was *her* place for two weeks, and she would sleep in each room. Between the two bedrooms was yet another surprise. A bathroom the size of her apartment had a giant glassed-in shower that looked as though it could hold at least a dozen people, and in the center of the room was a giant Jacuzzi tub that would hold at least half that many people. Plush towels hung from a warmer, bars of scented soaps and creams were artfully arranged on a dark green marble countertop flanked by two long mirrors, their frames made from branches. The outdoorsy theme dominated the cabin, and she thought it perfect.

It was exactly what she needed. Space, time, and a bit of fun on the slopes.

The smell of coffee lured her back downstairs. She searched through the cabinets, finding a bright red mug. Pouring herself a cup, she walked back into the great room, where she spied a giant box marked clearly with the words "Christmas Tree and Decorations."

She hadn't really thought of trimming a tree, figuring there would be trees all over the resort for her to enjoy, but instantly decided that setting it up and decorating it might be a fun way to spend the next couple of hours since she was wide awake.

Placing her coffee on the hearth to keep it warm, she dragged the artificial tree from the box. It was at least six feet high if her judgment was correct. It only took her a few minutes to put the tree together, as there was just a bottom, a middle, and the top, and all she had to do was insert one on top of the other. Once she had the tree together, she placed it next to the fireplace, careful that it was far enough away that there would be no fear of its catching fire. With that out of the way, she strung colorful bright twinkle lights from top to bottom, then began opening the boxes of decorations. The first box held several glass angels. She hoped that what she was doing was okay, and that the owner of the cabin didn't mind her taking the liberty of using their decorations, but they were there, and she assumed they were hers to use as well. They were delicate, and Angelica made sure to handle each carefully. The second box held more angels, but those were department-store varieties. After an hour, she had a beautifully decorated angel tree. She went to the kitchen for one last cup of coffee, bringing it to the great room, where she sat on the sofa, admiring her handiwork.

As the fireplace warmed the room, combined with the comfort of the sofa, and her general contentment with how her vacation was turning out to be much more than she'd hoped for—minus Parker North—she relaxed and fell into a deep sleep.

Chapter 9

Parker didn't bother with a walk through the condo. There would be time for that later. At the moment, all he wanted to do was take a hot shower and crawl into bed. It would be the first time since he'd been working in the trauma unit that he would not have to worry about being awakened in the middle of the night by a phone call. The thought brought a smile to his face. He might sleep until noon, but then remembered he had to call Max and make arrangements for his truck to get towed off the mountain. That old guy, Nicholas Star, would be sure to say "I told you so" when he learned that the pickup truck hadn't made it up the mountain as Parker had assured him it would.

After a hot shower, he dressed in sweats and a worn-out T-shirt, yet another from his college days. He let Leon

out of his carrier, opened a can of smelly Chicken Delight, and filled a small cup with water. Leon had it made
and didn't even know it. Maybe Parker would come back
as a cat in another life.

Right. If you believed in such garbage.

"Meow," Leon offered after he'd finished his dinner.

"Yep, I'm tired, too," Parker said absently.

The black and white ball of fluff pounced from the
floor to the countertop. "Meow, meow!"

"Hey, I said I was tired. And I don't think so," he said
as he scooped Leon from the countertop. "This should
meet your needs." Parker set Leon in the black leather re-
cliner situated next to the fireplace. "Warm and comfy.
What more could a guy ask for?"

Leon's fluffy tail flapped slowly from side to side, letting Parker know he was being dismissed. Cats, he
thought as he reached down to scratch his buddy between
the ears. Can't live with them, and he personally couldn't
imagine life without a feisty feline. Sort of like women.
Couldn't live with them, or without them. Though if he
were honest, he'd lived just fine without one. And this
brought to mind that gorgeous actress. She was sexy, easy
on the eyes.

And he was *not* going to even think about her. Not
now. Tomorrow he planned to shop for a new wardrobe in
The Snow Zone, or at least something warmer than what
he had on. He didn't think the college T-shirts were going
to cut it in the weather at Maximum Glide. He spent so
much of his time in scrubs, he'd never given too much
thought to what he wore beneath them. He'd have to at
least consider making a few purchases out of necessity.
Remembering that Mr. Star had said that someone with a

funny name, Candy something or other, had taken care of this, he'd take a look at her selection before calling it a night.

He went in search of the ski supplies the girl had delivered. Leave it to Max. He knew him well even though it had been years since they'd seen one another. Max knew that his old friend wouldn't have bothered replacing his skis or boots. *When had there been time?* he wondered, as he spied several items of heavy-duty clothing on the sofa. A red and black Spyder jacket, with matching ski pants and wool socks that promised to keep one's feet warm in subzero temperatures. Boots that weighed as much as a small child were sure to support his ankles and keep his feet warm in the iciest conditions, too. And there were several fleece shirts and a pair of mountain boots. From the looks of it, Max's employee hadn't missed a bit. Three pairs of what he knew had to be top-of-the-line skis leaned against the wall. He chuckled, as he viewed the windfall. Christmas was going to be good this year. No more holidays spent caring for people who were either ill, injured, or incapacitated by their own hand—or their parents', he couldn't help but add, as he recalled the reason he'd needed to get away in the first place. He shook his head, thankful for Max's generosity. The first full day there, he'd ski until he dropped and try to forget the real reason he was at Maximum Glide in the first place.

Satisfied that he'd be properly outfitted when he hit the slopes, he returned to the master suite, dropped his sweats and T-shirt on the floor, and crawled beneath the heavy comforter. Leon had situated himself on the pillow next to Parker's the same way he did at the apartment. So much for the soft leather chair.

It had been forever since he'd slept in the nude, and he

could not recall ever having slept on sheets as soft. The thread count must be up there in the thousands. Again, Max spared no expense when it came to his guests.

Guests. He couldn't help but remember the woman who'd given him a lift up the mountain, a total stranger. Then he'd had the audacity to tell her he wasn't out to make friends. Damn, it'd been too long since he'd been with a woman, in an intimate setting, or any setting, for that matter. If he ran into her, he would apologize, and if she didn't tell him to go to hell, he might even ask her out for a drink. It would take his mind off that little girl who wasn't going to be celebrating Christmas this year or any other, opening presents and screaming and shouting her delight.

With an even heavier heart, Parker slid farther beneath the plush bedding, willing himself to go to sleep and forget about events of the dreadful day.

Tossing and turning, Parker concluded sleep was not his friend that night. Normally, he could fall asleep instantly; given his profession, he had to catch a few winks when the opportunity arose. Now, there he was in that luxurious condo, nothing to keep him from doing whatever he wanted, and he could not force himself to fall asleep. Unwilling to lie in bed any longer, Parker found his sweats on the floor where he'd left them. He slipped them on and went to the kitchen in search of a late night, or in this case, an early morning snack.

Upon hearing his feet hit the floor, Leon stretched, arching his back into a V, then had the audacity to crawl into the warm spot Parker had just vacated.

Laughing as he found the kitchen, Parker realized Max had outdone himself yet again. The kitchen was all black and chrome; a man's kitchen, Parker thought. He found a giant refrigerator filled with so much food, he had a hard time choosing.

Between fresh meats, fruit, and a variety of cheeses, he finally settled on slicing a Granny Smith apple and a few wedges of sharp cheddar. Some gourmet he was. He poured himself a large glass of milk and took everything to the living room, where he found a giant-sized television mounted on the wall. It had to be at least sixty inches if his estimate were correct. He found a remote on the table by a long, sleek, black leather couch. While the leather was a nice touch, it wasn't him, he thought, as he sat down with his plate of food and his milk. As he munched, he surfed through hundreds of channels yet saw nothing that would grab his attention.

Without knowing or understanding why, his thoughts returned to the woman who'd driven him up the mountain to the condo. Hadn't old Nick Star, as he was now going to refer to him, said she was an actress from New York City? *What in the world is she doing out West? Or is she simply taking a vacation, like me? And alone, too.*

It surprised him that someone with her good looks would be alone. *Maybe she isn't*, he thought. *Maybe she has a lover, boyfriend, beau, however they referred to them now, coming to meet her tomorrow.* She had said she'd be on the slopes, but she really hadn't indicated if she would be skiing solo. And, of course, he'd had to put his foot in his big-ass mouth and let her know he would not welcome any new friendships. On or off the slopes. Period. So, just like everything else in his life, he'd screwed that up before he'd even had a chance to start anything.

Normally, Parker was not one to wallow in self-pity. As a doctor, he knew you couldn't allow your emotions to get the best of you, knew that there was a risk with all patients, even those with nothing more than a runny nose. It is what it is, he'd told himself. But in all his years as a trauma surgeon, he had never lost a child. This event had marred his vision of himself as a professional.

Then he reminded himself, before that day, he'd never had a child die on his table.

Never.

Chapter 10

Angelica jolted awake, disoriented. Seeing her surroundings brought it all back to her. She was in Colorado to ski. She'd fallen asleep on the sofa, her cup of coffee still sitting on the hearth, the Christmas tree lights still twinkling. She rubbed the sleep from her eyes, tossed another log in the fireplace, then went to the dream kitchen, where she made another pot of coffee.

Excitement tingled in her veins for the first time in a very long time, even more so than her first time walking on stage in a semi-big production. She'd spent so many years trying to "make it" in the theater that she hadn't focused on life's simple pleasures as much as she should have. As she waited for the coffee to brew, she peered out the kitchen window.

A clear blue sky shone on glistening ivory snow on the

mountain. Giant spruce trees, cedars, and firs of what must be every variety in the world dotted the mountain-side like individual Christmas trees, their branches full and heavy with recent snow. Snow that sparkled like diamonds instead of the brown slush she was used to. Yes, the first real snowfall in the city gave Manhattan an added purity, but once it melted, the beauty became nothing more than a hassle to get through. Angelica didn't see that where she was now. What she saw boggled the mind, the great majestic mountains serving as a protector of Mother Nature's bounty.

Not wanting to waste another minute looking out the window, she gulped her coffee down, poured a second cup, and brought it to the master bath. She would have loved to sink into the large Jacuzzi tub but knew she would appreciate it much more when her muscles ached from a day of hard skiing. She opted for the giant shower and was mildly surprised to see there were eight shower-heads, each placed at a different level, so that no part of her would be without the shower's warm spray. Ingenious, she thought as she lathered with a grassy-smelling body wash provided by someone who knew the business. All she was lacking were a few groceries. She scrubbed and washed her hair, then dried off with a warm towel from the heating rack. She could get used to this lifestyle. Afford it, no; used to it, most definitely.

From her luggage, she removed a pair of old jeans she'd had since high school, which, fortunately, still fit. She pulled a white tank top on, then topped it with a bright yellow wool sweater. Layers always worked in the city; she didn't know why they wouldn't work at the ski resort. She pulled on red wool socks, then slid her feet into her worn black Uggs. She wouldn't trade her Uggs for anything. Well, maybe a new pair, she thought as she saw that the heels were low and worn.

She piled her wet hair on top of her head, then thought better of it. The temperature was due to drop into the single digits. She found a blow-dryer in the bathroom cabinet, dried her hair, then placed it in a ponytail. It was nice not to wear a wig, or have her own hair styled in such a way that it actually hurt. No, this was perfect. Clean hair and nothing more. Again, one of the simple things in life that she'd been somewhat deprived of. Then she thought about the makeup. No wonder she was starting to see early signs of aging. She'd allowed her skin to take a brutal beating daily with stage makeup. Other than sunscreen, she was not going to put anything on her skin either. It was time to go au naturel.

Angelica finished her coffee, then turned off the pot and Christmas tree lights before heading out to her rental. Though the air was cold, it was dry, making it much more tolerable than what she was used to. She hadn't bothered to wear her gloves or hat, deciding she wouldn't need them since she would be inside the car except when she'd make a fast run inside the minimarket. She cranked the heat to max and was greeted with an icy blast of cool air. She clicked the fan off, allowing the engine to warm up before turning it on again. Just showed her lack of driving experience. Once she adjusted the heat control and her rearview mirror, she backed out of the narrow drive and steered the SUV downhill toward the main village at Maximum Glide.

Angelica drove carefully down the mountain. Though there was snow piled at least five feet high on either side of the road, salt covered the road itself, assuring her that someone was watching out for those slick patches of ice she did not want to become acquainted with.

She'd traveled approximately two miles when she almost ran off the road. Not from a patch of ice, but from what she saw. Slowing down to a crawl, she lowered the passenger window, straining to make sure she was seeing what she thought she was seeing, that her mind wasn't playing tricks on her. Squinting against the bright Colorado morning sun, Angelica checked her rearview mirror for traffic, then, seeing there wasn't any, she stopped right in the middle of the road.

"Hey," she called out to the guy she'd taken to the penthouse condo last night.

Parker North.

He stopped and turned to look at her. When he saw her, he shook his head and stepped up to the passenger side. "We've got to stop meeting like this," he said, his voice and attitude the complete opposite of last night's.

"I take it you must've had a visit from old Scrooge himself," she added, trying not to smile. She was not going to make this easy on him. He'd told her she looked *rough*, and he'd been incredibly rude to her after she'd driven him all the way to his condo.

In the early morning sun, Angelica thought him much more handsome than she had last night. His dark hair flipped up at the ends, and his eyes were a deep chocolate brown with gold flakes, making them appear as though a fire radiated from within. He wasn't tan at all, so she could safely assume he didn't spend too much time on the slopes. She guessed he did most of his work inside, though she had no clue exactly what kind of work he did and didn't really care. As he'd said last night, he really wasn't there to make friends. Well, she wasn't either. Not really. She reminded herself she was in Colorado to relax, enjoying life's simple pleasures while she debated her future as an actress.

He leaned against the door, peering inside the open window. Angelica was sure he was blushing. Or maybe he was about to have a heart attack from walking in this thin air and at such a high altitude. "Oh my gosh, are you okay? Get inside, quick!" Without further thought, she leaned across the bucket seats and opened the passenger door. "Hurry!"

He did as instructed but didn't appear to be in any kind of physical distress. "Thanks, I guess I deserved that." He hit the button to raise the window.

Angelica glanced at him. "What are you talking about?" She put the car in gear and cautiously drove down the mountain, trying to watch the road and her passenger at the same time.

"I was rude last night. I'm usually not so quick to snap a pretty girl's head off."

She slowed down, then stopped. "You're not having a heart attack?" she inquired, suddenly unsure of everything that had passed between them in the past minute.

"Why would you think I'm having a heart attack? I'm not in the best of shape, but I do work out when my job allows me to."

Angelica felt like the idiot of the month. She wasn't sure what to say but knew she needed to say something, anything, that would get her out of the hole she worked her way into. "Uh . . . your face was red. I just thought . . . the high elevation, you know, some people have trouble with it." If ever she sounded airheaded, it was then.

Parker North smiled, and when he smiled, Angelica thought a second sun chose that moment to shine exclusively for her. This guy had a smile that truly lit up the world, or at least her portion of it. He adjusted the heater's vent so that it was aimed directly at his face. "Lucky for me, I don't have any trouble. I've lived here most of my life."

Yes, he'd told her something to that effect last night, but it escaped her just now.

"I need to get my truck. I tried using my cell phone to call Max but couldn't get a signal. I figured I'd keep walking until this piece of electronic magic decided to do its thing."

She never would've thought about that; her cell phone was so old, she was sure it still used the old analog system if it still existed, but he didn't need to know this. Was he into all the new electronic gizmos? And if he was, how did he afford the stuff? You would think he would invest in a new vehicle. She knew the latest models of cell phones were quite pricey, and it hadn't been something she'd been willing to pay outrageous sums of money for because she had a phone that worked just fine, thank you very much. She did not need all the extras. She'd learned to live in a small space and on an even smaller budget all those years ago when she'd migrated from Texas to New York.

Taking a deep breath, hoping to clear the air of her idiocy, she said, "I was just on my way to the minimarket, and you're welcome to ride with me." She couldn't come up with another intelligent word. She would have sworn he was looking her over in a . . . a *seductive* way?

Maybe the high altitude was getting to *her*?

Chapter 11

Focusing her attention on the road, Angelica did her best to ignore her passenger. He was charming, witty, and sexy as hell. She didn't need his attention any more than he'd needed to make friends, but she wasn't going to tell this to him, at least not now.

"So why aren't you on the slopes?" Parker questioned. "I figured you'd be up with the chickens."

She laughed. She hadn't heard anyone use that expression since she was a kid in Texas. "My stomach is telling me it has issues to deal with. Like starvation." Suddenly, her stomach growled, and she busted out laughing. She couldn't help herself.

"I wish I would've known. I made pancakes, eggs, and sausage this morning. Had a ton of leftovers, too. Left a plate out for Leon, but he hadn't touched it when I left. He's peculiar."

Was he trying to tell her something? That he'd cooked too much or that someone had cooked for him? Or was he simply making small talk? She wasn't about to ask but hoped it wasn't the latter—yet didn't know why it would even matter to her as he was practically a stranger. But for some unknown reason, it did matter.

"Max filled the refrigerator with every kind of food imaginable. It's been a while since I cooked a meal for myself. It's harder to cook for one person than a crowd, don't you agree?"

Again, Angelica wondered if there was an underlying meaning to his question. Was he asking her in a round-about way if she was involved, or committed? Or was he simply making small talk until they reached the bottom of the mountain? It didn't matter either way, she thought as she stepped hard on the brake, finding that the road practically nosedived for a few feet before leveling out. She was no more in the market for a relationship than he was. He could be married with ten children for all she knew.

"I don't cook much. The theater usually orders take-out, so there's really no need," she explained.

"So you really are that actress from New York?"

Has he actually seen me in a play? Or maybe he recognized me as that piece of dirt in that floor-cleaning commercial currently airing!

"After you left the registration office last night, Nicholas—*Mr. Star*—told me you were an actress."

He'd answered her question, and she hadn't even had to ask. What a relief! It suddenly occurred to her that she'd felt a bit embarrassed when he'd asked her if she was an actress! Her entire career suddenly had the power to make her feel nothing but . . . *shame?* Did Meryl Streep and the late Elizabeth Taylor feel shame at their chosen careers? She doubted it. They were two of the greatest actresses of all time, in her opinion. She'd aspired for so many years to be just like them. Stage, film, television, she wanted it all, yet when a stranger asked her about her career, she found that she didn't want to discuss her profession. As though she'd been struck by a bolt of lightning, Angelica had just answered the question she'd mentally asked, but she pushed it aside. It wasn't the time to make a career choice or change. She was driving in snow and ice, and was just distracted.

"An actress with nothing to say," Parker added. "That seems a bit unusual."

"Like you, I'm not here to make friends or discuss my career." She knew that she sounded terribly juvenile, but she didn't care. She'd just had an epiphany and did not want to deal with the significance behind it, or at least not with a stranger in the car. This trip down the mountain was becoming way more than a quick trip to the market.

"I guess I deserved that," he said, turning away.

Lucky for her, she spied the turnoff for the registration building just then. She assumed that was where he wanted to be dropped off, so she found an empty spot close to the entrance and parked. Part of her felt a tiny bit of sadness and a sense of loss. She had never had these kinds of feelings about a stranger, and it bothered her. She wasn't sure if it was a good thing or not. Most likely not.

She turned to face him. "So," she said, struggling to fight her sudden confusion, "I guess you can use the phone in the office if you can't get a signal on yours." Angelica said the words quickly as she tried to still her rapidly beating heart.

Lame, lame, lame, she thought as she felt an unwanted

warmth flow through her. *This is* not *happening! What is wrong with me?*

"I'm sure of it," he agreed. Then he continued, "Are you going to be on the slopes later? Maybe we can meet at the lift."

Unexpectedly, Angelica didn't know what to say. One minute, he was telling her he wasn't there to make friends; the next, he alluded to a possible relationship with some-one—well, not really, but she wasn't going to assume anything where this man was concerned—and now, he was asking her to meet him. Confused, and surprised at his change of heart, all she could manage was a quick nod.

"I take it that's a yes," Parker stated.

Again, she'd made an idiot out of herself. "I'd planned to ski all day anyway. If we see each other at the lifts, then sure, I can ride up with you, race you downhill." She didn't want to appear too anxious, but she didn't want to brush him off, either. She kinda liked this guy she'd known for less than twenty-four hours.

What does this mean? she wondered.

Is this *love at first sight?*

Chapter 12

"Ouch! That hurt, but I see where you're going," Parker said, obviously chagrined by her comment.

Angelica offered up a mischievous grin but said not a word.

"I owe you an apology. I was tired." He held up a gloved hand. "And I know that's not an excuse for being so crabby, but I'd like to start over." He gave her his dazzling smile again, and her heart did another flip-flop.

She liked that he'd used the word *crabby.* A regular guy, not the suave sophisticated GQ type she normally dated. Angelica was getting way ahead of herself, though. First, he'd only asked her to ski with him, and she didn't really believe that qualified as a date. Second, she lived on the East Coast. What happened if she really liked the guy? No way would she commute from coast to coast for a date.

"Earth to driver," Parker said, jolting her back to the present.

Looking at him as though he had two heads, she wasn't sure if he was insulting her while trying to apologize.

A driver? Am I being oversensitive? Yes, I am. It was so unlike her to be so offended by comments that were simply *comments.* The critics had been beyond hard on her many times throughout her career. It went with the territory. *So why him and why now? Why am I so defensive with this man?*

"Apology accepted," she said before she changed her mind. It *had* been late when he'd rescued her. She could be a tiger herself when she didn't get enough sleep. Maybe Parker was telling the truth. He had fallen asleep last night in the car, after all. So maybe he *had* been overly tired. Besides, she had no real reason not to trust him. She'd met and made friends on the slopes many times before. No harm in hanging around with the guy for a few hours.

He opened the door and climbed out of the car, then smacked his gloved hand against the roof. "So I'll meet you at the private lift in a couple of hours. If you agree," he added, offering her his drop-dead killer smile.

Two hours would be more than enough time to go to the market, make breakfast, and prepare herself to spend the day skiing with a really hot guy. She smiled. "I'll be there."

Parker closed the door, winked at her through the window, then turned away and walked toward the registration office.

She gave a half wave and backed out of the parking lot onto the main road that led to the center of Maximum Glide. Angelica slowed the SUV to a crawl, searching for another parking spot, when she spied a black Hummer leaving. She whipped the Navigator into the spot before someone beat her to it. Grabbing her purse and keys, she opened the door and, once again, was greeted by bitter cold, but the kind of cold that didn't make you cringe and race back inside. After New York, where the cold was damp from the ocean, she found the sharp coolness refreshing.

The sidewalks in the village were clear of all traces of ice and slush. Angelica observed several maintenance men working hard to keep the streets and pathways clear. Briefly, she wondered if Parker was part of this crew, but he really didn't look like he spent too much time in the sun. Maybe he was a supervisor and spent his time behind a desk. It didn't really matter what his profession was. In two weeks, he would be nothing more than a memory. A pleasant one, she hoped.

She found the village market around the corner from The Snow Zone, a ski supply shop she planned to visit later. Her old ski jacket wasn't quite as warm as some of the newfangled ones she'd seen in the catalogues; it was time to replace it.

Entering the market, Angelica was greeted by the scent of fresh-baked bread, reminding her that she hadn't eaten since her last bite of chocolate yesterday. With the warm yeasty smell guiding her, she found the bakery at the back of the store. As expected, the line was long, and she could see plenty of baked goods displayed for those waiting in line. Several young women wore white coats, with their hair matted against their heads with the required hairnet. Each performed her task with a smile on her face. Angelica thought that she might like to learn how to bake someday.

As the line inched closer to the front, she made a mental list of the supplies she would need for the next two weeks. She added a bottle of wine and a nice pair of filets, thinking if the opportunity arose, she would invite Parker to her cabin for dinner.

Greeted by a friendly blonde, Angelica selected a loaf of freshly baked sourdough bread, three poppy seed bagels, four red velvet cupcakes, and a loaf of French bread. With both arms loaded, she headed to the front of the market, where she found a small shopping cart. In New York, she usually just grabbed a few things and never required a shopping cart, only buying as much as she could carry home on foot. She walked up and down the narrow aisles, picking items that she normally wouldn't even consider and placing them in her cart. Two bags of potato chips, something she never indulged in as her profession didn't encourage weight gain. A large hunk of dark chocolate because she simply could not go a day without it. She filled the cart with cans of soup, milk, eggs, and two packages of precooked bacon. In the produce section, she filled bags with apples, oranges, and grapefruit. At least some of her purchases were healthful, she observed, while waiting at the checkout counter.

Ten minutes later, she had the Navigator loaded with groceries. As she pulled out of the parking place, she glanced at the clock on the dash. She had more than an hour before it was time to meet Parker at the lift.

Angelica felt blissfully happy, totally alive.

Did this have anything to do with Parker, or was it simply the fact she was on vacation and had shucked all responsibilities for the next two weeks? It didn't matter. Whatever the reason, she was boundlessly happy, and didn't care why.

Chapter 13

Angelica found her way around the kitchen and decided she enjoyed the simple act of preparing breakfast for herself. She microwaved the bacon, scrambled eggs, and had three slices of toast. If this wasn't enough carbs and protein to see her through her ski run, then she was in big trouble. She was not going to count calories on this trip, no way, no how.

After a quick cleanup, she began the laborious task of dressing for a day on the slopes. Because her jacket was so old, she made sure to wear several layers of T-shirts and a warm sweater. She put on two pair of tights before topping them off with her old ski pants. First thing tomorrow, she would visit Snow Zone and update her ski gear.

She planned to rent skis when she'd originally made her vacation plans, but was told by the travel agent that the cabin provided skis as well. All she had to do was give them her height and weight, then visit the repair shop, where they would make sure the fit was right for her. As she shoved her foot inside the cold ski boot, she was surprised when her foot slid in comfortably without all the hassle that she usually encountered. Tromping outside in the heavy boots, she found the skis and poles inside the storage shed, just where the agent told her they would be. She should have brought them with her in the morning, when she'd made her trip to the village, but she figured she would just ski to the repair shop, where they could make any adjustments.

Kicking the toe end of her boot, then pushing down on the heel, she found that the boots fit perfectly in the ski's bindings. Same with the other foot. There was no need for a trip to the repair shop, she thought as she poled her way several yards away to the private lift.

Her skis cut through the snow, leaving tracks in her wake. She took a deep breath, reveling in the pure scent of pine and fresh powder. Her part of the mountain was still and calm, except for the soft whir from the wind that blew gently through the tops of the tall pines. She could get used to this, especially after the city.

Remembering the directions she had read that morning while eating breakfast, she found the private chairlift without any trouble. The operating instructions were easy, so no worries there. It gave her enough time to smooth her hair and add an extra layer of lip balm. As soon as she tucked the tube inside her pocket, she looked up to see Parker, all decked out in Spyder's latest red and black ski attire. He poled his way across the small expanse to the lift, then turned sharply, spraying her with snow.

Winded, but smiling, he said, "I still have it."

Angelica's heart raced at the sight of this incredibly sexy man, but she did nothing to reveal this. "You thought you'd lost it," she commented wryly.

"Never, but it has been a long time since I've skied. Work has kept me occupied, and there really hasn't been time for a vacation," he explained.

Of course, she wondered what he did for a living and why there wasn't time for a vacation, but she was not going to ask. If he wanted her to know, she guessed that he would tell her. For the moment, she was happy to be accompanying him.

"Well, we're here now. Let's take the lift to the top of the mountain," Angelica said. "Or is that too much for a first run?"

Parker gave her a look that sent a warm glow throughout her body. Yes, she was in trouble, she thought, as they poled across to the chairlift. This guy was definitely worth pursuing.

"Of course I'm up to it. I wouldn't be here if I wasn't. What about you?"

"I'm ready. It's been a couple of years, but I think I can handle a run down the mountain. Though I have to admit, I am a bit leery of this lift. I have never used this kind before." She had read the instructions just a while ago and hoped the timer was set to allow them enough time to get seated comfortably before shooting up the side of the mountain.

Angelica punched in the number of seconds required for the lift to come to life, then poled over to the entrance area with Parker by her side. In fifteen seconds, the chair, squeaking but moving at a slow pace, swung from the heavy cable, stopping when it crossed the line where they waited. As soon as the chair stopped and touched the back of their legs, they dropped down onto the icy seat, and Parker pulled the safety bar into position.

With a squeal and whine, the chairlift began its climb up to the top of the thirteen-thousand-foot mountain.

Angelica inched into a comfortable position, or as comfortable as one could be on a ski lift, carefully placing her skis on the bar provided directly below the chair. Sitting on the left side, she held her poles in her right hand over her left shoulder. Parker did the opposite. Once they were settled for the slow climb, the wind in their faces and the sun almost blinding in its intensity, Parker turned to look at her.

Glad that her face was covered by her scarf, her eyes hidden behind the amber lenses of her ski goggles, she knew she was blushing.

Damn, I am thirty-two years old! This stuff only happens in those terrific little romance novels I used to read back when I was in high school.

As was becoming the norm for her when she was with Parker, her heart beat so fast, she wondered if it would pound right out of her chest.

His words were muffled when he spoke, but she clearly understood him. "Are you nervous?"

Darn! Am I that transparent?

Shaking her head from side to side, she adjusted her scarf so she could speak. "Not at all, just cold."

Before she knew what was happening, with his free arm, he pulled her closer to him. Their heavily clothed thighs rubbed against one another, and her shoulder was hard against his. Trying to inch away was not possible as

Parker now used his free hand to tilt her chin up. Again, he surprised her when his lips lightly touched her own.

For a few seconds, again, she was at a total loss for words. When she found her voice, all she could manage was a low, "Wow!"

Chapter 14

"I'll take that as a compliment," Parker said, mere inches away from her face. He smelled like freshly washed skin and shaving cream.

She wasn't sure what to say or if she should say anything at all. She decided on not saying anything simply because she was shocked by her reaction to such a . . . chaste kiss! Mentally ticking back the clock, she realized it'd been almost a year since she'd gone out on a real date. Yes, that had to be the reason she was reacting like a lovesick teenager.

Angelica felt Parker's gaze on her. It wasn't like she could turn around and leave. Nope, she was stuck. Deciding to make the best of her situation, as there really wasn't another choice, she looked him squarely in the eye. "What do you want from me? If you're looking for a . . . cheap fling, look elsewhere. I certainly hope I haven't done anything that would make you think I was that kind of woman."

Did I actually say that? I must have sounded like an old spinster right out of the nineteenth century!

Parker laughed, and Angelica couldn't help but smile behind her scarf. Once again, she came across as an idiot.

They were more than halfway up the mountain when Parker spoke. "Trust me, a fling, cheap or otherwise, is the last thing on my mind." His voice became more serious, as though an unpleasant memory had surfaced.

Angelica wished she had kept quiet. Why couldn't she just accept that a nice, handsome man kissed her for no reason other than that he wanted to? Did there have to be an answer for every move a man made toward her? Yes, yes, and yes, she told herself. It was probably the reason why she'd had so many dates, most of them disastrous in one way or another.

She pulled her goggles on top of her head, then wiped her eyes. The air was so cold, her eyes were watering. She knew without looking in a mirror that her nose was probably as red as Rudolph's.

"Look, I shouldn't have said that. I do that a lot," she said as a way of explaining herself.

Parker still looked serious, all traces of that fantastically sexy smile gone. "No, I shouldn't have kissed you. I don't know what came over me. Look, I don't normally do that either. Hell, I can't remember the last time I kissed a woman. It's been too long. I'm sorry," he said.

Wanting to ask him to explain further, she stopped herself before she put her foot in her mouth again. "Hey, it was just a kiss. As long as you don't expect anything else, then we're okay. And if it makes you feel any better, it's been a long time since I went out on a date myself. I work odd hours. Broadway being Broadway and all." She didn't dare tell him that, in point of fact, she worked off-*off* Broadway. She'd already gotten the impression he thought her profession was unprofessional.

And why did I just tell him I haven't had a date in a long time? What is wrong with me? Surely, I must be oxygen deprived!

The cable whined, then came to a complete stop. Knowing this was a private lift, it seemed odd, but Angelica was sure the lift was used by other guests, too. Hanging in midair, the wind whistling through the trees, snow swirling beneath them, she couldn't have asked for a more vulnerable position to be in, but again, her heart beat double time when she looked at the man seated next to her.

"I guess someone fell," he said.

"I'm sure," she answered, then turned away. She didn't understand why she was feeling the way she was. It had never happened to her before. Ever. Zilch. *Why now?* And she didn't know squat about the man! He could be a pervert or . . . well, she was sure he was decent and upstanding. She trusted her instincts on things like that. But her reaction to him was just not normal, of that she was sure.

With a clunk and groan, the lift slowly came to life, transporting them to the top of the mountain. Feeling as though she had to fill the silence between them, Angelica spoke the first words that came to mind. "Look, I didn't mean what I just said. I mean, I haven't had a date in a while, that's true, but the other." She turned away again, feeling a tiny bit ashamed of her chosen profession. "I don't work *on* Broadway. Only once, and that was a very long time ago. I've been bartending and working in off-*off*-Broadway plays. Don't get me wrong, they're very successful in their own right, but still they *are* off Broadway."

She could actually feel Parker's gaze. It was as though he were trying to penetrate through all the layers of heavy clothing and see what lay beneath.

"You don't have to explain your choices to me," Parker said. "To each his own."

That was not the answer she was hoping for, but it was what it was, she thought, as they dangled once again in midair. "I wonder why they keep stopping," she said.

"People fall, and it takes a few minutes to get them up and out of the way. If they're inexperienced, it takes longer."

She knew all of that. It was not her first time on the slopes. Wishing she'd skied downhill to the public lift, Angelica felt very confused as a tumble of thoughts and feelings assailed her. One moment, she wanted to throw herself at this handsome man seated next to her, and in the next, she wanted to run, or rather ski away from him as fast as she could. She'd heard her friends talk, and she wasn't so unsophisticated that she did not know what was happening to her. The question was—why now? Why this man, who lived across the country? Why not one of the actors she worked with? Someone she knew and could see whenever she chose? She hadn't come halfway across the country just to fall in love with a stranger. She came to meditate on her chosen profession.

The lift returned to life, jolting her back to the present. Though they were only stopped for a couple of minutes, it had seemed much longer. She could not sit next to this man and say nothing. She felt too exposed, and somewhat puzzled at this new turn of events. But, she remembered she was an actress, and acting she could do. She only had to pretend that she was onstage and that this situation was staged just for her.

The only difference was that she did not have a script, so she did not know her partner's lines.

Chapter 15

Finally reaching the top of the mountain, Angelica couldn't wait to ski downhill, where she knew there would be hundreds of other skiers to take her mind off Parker North. Quickly, as though they did this together daily, both she and Parker moved effortlessly off the chairlift and toward the right, where they both zoomed downhill.

Angelica felt free of all negative emotions as she surged downhill, Parker at her side. When they reached the middle of the mountain, Parker skied off the trail to an area where he could rest if he so desired. She slid into the sectioned-off area but not without a little snow pluming of her own. Before she could stop herself, she quickly whipped her skis around so that she showered Parker with snow.

Blissfully happy to be alive, Angelica dropped to the

snow-covered ground, where she proceeded to laugh loudly and uncontrollably. Parker dropped down beside her. "Want to tell me what's so funny?" he asked, all traces of his earlier stuffiness gone.

Saying the first thing that came to mind, Angelica spoke. "This sounds stupid, but I can't remember being so . . . happy!" There, she'd said it, and the world hadn't swallowed her up. So what if she came off as nerdy or silly. She *was* blissfully happy to be there, glad to be alive, and more than thrilled to be sitting in a deep pile of snow with this man who'd unknowingly captured her heart.

A shadow dimmed the otherwise golden sparkle in Parker's eyes. Clearly, Angelica's words had upset him. She didn't want to do or say anything that would interfere with this moment, so she clammed up, keeping her joy to herself.

"It's good to see you so cheerful, happy. In my line of work, it's not always the outcome," Parker said as plumes of cold air spilled from his mouth.

Her heart quickened with anticipation. *Finally*, she thought, as she turned to look at him. He'd removed his goggles, and she did not like what she saw. Yes, he was the sexiest guy she'd encountered in a very long time, mostly, she thought, because he wasn't trying to be sexy like the guys she was used to. But there was such a look of loss and sadness about him that she reached out and placed a cold, gloved hand on his cheek. "Tell me. You look as though you've lost your best friend. Why so sad?"

She could see that he struggled with his thoughts, as if he was contemplating whether to reveal them or not. He shook his head, his dark hair damp from the wet snowflakes that had begun to fall. He removed his gloves and placed them on his lap. "What makes you think I'm sad?" he asked.

She hesitated a moment before answering. "You look sad, Parker. No mystery there. Are you having problems at work?" Angelica watched Parker's expression change from sad to ticked off.

"Who told you I was having problems at work? Was it Max or Grace? Because I didn't say anything to them," he said vehemently.

"Good grief, you don't have to bite my head off! And for your information, I have never so much as spoken to Max or Grace. I don't even know who they are." She stopped and backtracked. "Yes, I do know who Max Jorgenson is. Who doesn't? But Grace, no, I don't know her, and no one told me a thing about your work situation. Whatever it is you do." She mumbled the last words.

He reached for the gloves in his lap, then pushed himself up off the snow. After adjusting his goggles, he grabbed his poles and wrapped a leather band around each wrist, then skied out of the sectioned-off area straight to a trail that led to a black run.

"Hey," she shouted, but all she saw was his black and red Spyder jacket flash around the catwalk.

Wanting to catch up with him, needing to know what in the hell she'd said to send him racing off like some spastic skier, she poled out of their resting spot and across the large bowl area to the catwalk that led to some of the toughest black runs on the mountain. He must be one hell of a skier, she thought, as she approached the top of the slope. She was a decent skier, blue runs her most challenging. He must be expert, she thought, as she pushed off down the steep mountainside, traversing back and forth so as to slow her descent. There were some icy patches that could be tricky. Away in the distance, she saw his dark silhouette as he zigzagged through the unplowed snow. Hurrying to catch up with him, she used her poles to push forward, then lowered her hips and knees to a position that afforded her a bit of speed. She would be damned before she would let him beat her to the bottom of the hill.

As she careened around the moguls, she saw a lone skier in her peripheral vision. Wondering how he just so happened to appear out of the blue, she saw he was flying, and didn't seem to see she was directly in his path. As he got closer, she realized he was on a snowboard. She began to make her way to the side of the mountain even though she had the right of way. She heard him coming closer, the edge of his snowboard slicing across an icy patch.

She whipped away from the kamikaze boarder, felt herself careening as she lost her balance . . .

Then everything went black.

Parker looked up just in time to see a flurry of snow and a body as it was tossed in the air.

"Son of a bitch," he shouted as he saw the skier slam against the icy ground. Without another thought, he kicked off his skis, tossed his goggles aside, and poled his way back up the hill. Several spots were crusted over with ice, and he slipped. "Damn! I shouldn't have taken the black run, dammit!" Hurrying as best as he could given the circumstances, he gasped for air as he made his way uphill.

Out of breath, Parker managed to drop to his feet when

he reached the injured skier. And lo and behold if it wasn't his new friend, Angelica Shepard.

Knowing he shouldn't move her, yet not sure where the nearest first-aid unit was located on the mountain, he did what all skiers knew to do in such a situation. Quickly, he placed his ski poles in an X position. With any luck, someone would see them and send for help. Until help arrived, he would do what needed to be done to ensure that Angelica survived the accident.

He leaned over her and felt for a pulse. Strong and steady. Always a good sign, he thought to himself. With exaggerated carefulness, he felt her head, searching for a lump or a cut. When he found nothing, he breathed a little sigh of relief but knew there could still be spinal injuries. Not wanting to move her, he straddled her waist and so very, very gently, probed the back of her neck and spine as much as he could given the heavy ski clothes she wore.

The moment he leaned up and looked down at this striking woman, her eyes fluttered open. "What happened?" she asked in a whisper.

Parker North felt like shouting to the world but knew it wasn't the time or the place. Angelica was speaking, and that was a very good sign.

"You were hit, sweetie. It's going to be all right. I promise you," he said, vowing he would not lose this woman to a head injury. Not now. Not when he was just beginning to feel something that he hadn't felt in a very long time. Or ever.

"You're an angel, right?" Angelica said softly.

He shook his head. "I am anything but, trust me."

The sound of snowmobiles provided a much-needed reprieve. As they flew across the snow and ice, Parker could see that there were four emergency techs, two on each snowmobile. "Over here," he shouted. They jumped off the machines, carrying a backboard.

"She was knocked down by some out of control snow-boarder. I don't know where the guy wound up, but she was knocked out for at least five minutes. It took me that long to get to her," Parker explained to the medics.

They quickly shifted her onto the backboard, then carefully secured her neck and mouth with medical tape so she couldn't move.

One of the medics leaned over her and asked her a question. "Do you know what your name is?"

"Yes. Angelica."

The paramedic gave a thumbs-up sign to the others. "Do you know what today's date is?"

"No," she said.

"Okay, that's good. Now, I am going to give you a number, and each time I ask, I want you to repeat it for me. Think you can do that?"

"Sure," she muttered.

"Number eight," he said. "Now, can you tell me where you live?"

"New York."

"This is good. Now can you tell me the number I just told you?"

Angelica frowned and tried to shake her head. "I can't seem to remember. Why can't I move?" she asked, her voice a bit louder than before.

Parker watched from behind her and knew she was frightened. It was always the same. Once people knew they were injured and couldn't move certain parts of their body, they instantly freaked out. Not that he expected anything less.

"You're going to be fine, ma'am. We have your head

taped to the board as a precaution." The medics' radio came to life then. "Have a chopper ready. We need to get her to Denver, to Angel of Mercy. They've got the best neurological unit in the state."

"What?" Angelica asked. "I have a head injury?"

"We don't know. This is just a precautionary move on our part. Please, relax," the technician said.

"Wait!" Parker shouted. "Let me go down with her. She's all alone."

"Are you . . . Hey, I know who you are!" the second tech said. "You work at Angel of Mercy, right?"

Parker nodded, then placed a finger over his lips. "Shhh. Let's just get her out of here before she freezes."

Parker looked up just in time to see the helicopter swirling above them. "Where will they land?" he asked.

"We have to bring her down to the station. There is no place to land here."

"Then let's move it! Time is of the essence here!" Parker shouted as though he were right back in the trauma unit that had driven him to Maximum Glide in the first place.

Once a doctor, always a doctor.

Two of the paramedics hoisted Angelica inside what appeared to be a plastic canoe of sorts. They covered her face with plastic, then he saw her hand move slightly—another very good sign.

"Please, don't put that thing over my face," she said in an almost normal voice. "I'm a little claustrophobic."

"Of course," the tech said, then arranged the plastic so that it didn't cover her entire face. "Ma'am, we are going to take you down now. Sit tight, okay?"

In a broken voice, she replied, "It's not like I have a choice, do I?"

"That's my girl," Parker said. "We'll have you back to normal in no time."

He noted she was speaking coherently, and that was very good under the circumstances. She tried to turn her head to see him, but couldn't. "You're going for a ride, hang on," Parker said, as the two medic/skiers each grabbed an end of the boatlike plastic contraption that would carry her to safety.

Trees whizzed by, and the pure blue sky was all she could see as they hustled to get her to the hospital. Her last thought before things went black again was that she'd been saved by an angel.

Chapter 16

Angelica opened her eyes only to discover that she was in the back of an ambulance. "What happened?" The words were no sooner out of her mouth than she remembered being knocked down by that lone snowboarder she'd seen just as she'd tried to get out of his path.

"We're taking you to Angel of Mercy in Denver. You're getting the best medical care in the state," someone said to her.

"Why can't I move my neck?"

"You're secured to the backboard as a safety precaution. Once the doctor examines you, they'll decide what to do."

Angelica was not going to remain on this stupid board. Her feet were freezing off, and her hands felt like two blocks of ice. "Look, I am cold here. And what happened to my ski boots? My feet are cold."

Low voices came from behind but she couldn't make out what they were saying. "I want to know where my boots are! My toes are going to freeze off!"

"Here," someone said as he began to rub her cold feet. "Does this help?"

She could feel a slight tingling sensation in her toes. "Yes, but I still want to know where those boots are."

Laughter came from all those in the back of the ambulance.

"I don't think this is funny, not even a little bit," she said firmly and in a much louder voice than before.

"No, ma'am, it isn't funny. We're just happy to see that you're getting back to normal," the man who rubbed her feet said. "We'll be arriving at the hospital any minute now. They'll have heated blankets waiting for you."

"I don't hear a siren," Angelica said out of the blue. "Why isn't there a siren?"

"We turned it off as soon as you came around. Your vitals are good, and it appears, now mind you I am saying it *appears*, as though you have no trauma to the head, so we're simply following protocol."

It was then the vehicle came to a stop. The two rear doors opened, letting in a blast of bitterly cold air. Angelica had never been so cold in her life. Her insides shook with tremors as they removed her from the ambulance. Seconds later, she was whisked through automatic doors and, thankfully, was greeted by a gush of warm air. She smiled for the first time since she'd been plowed over.

"What is so funny?" Parker asked her.

"What are *you* doing here? If not for you, this wouldn't have happened! Go away! I don't want you near me!"

"Hey, calm down. I rode in the chopper and the ambulance because I didn't want to leave you all alone."

"You didn't seem to have a problem leaving me alone on that mountain, now, did you?" she asked, as a nurse checked her blood pressure. She wouldn't be surprised if it didn't register. She was beyond pissed at this . . . idiot who'd forced her to chase him down a trail that was meant for experts only. She would never forgive him for that. Never.

Parker took her cold, limp hand in his. "I didn't know you couldn't keep up. I thought you said you were a good skier. I thought . . . Well, it doesn't really matter what I think, does it?" he asked, more to himself than her.

Angelica jumped when the nurse placed the cold stethoscope under her clothing.

"Sorry, this is a little cold," the nurse said, apologetically.

"Tell me now," Angelica muttered between clenched teeth.

"Sorry," the nurse said.

"No, it does not matter what you think," Angelica said to Parker, "so please leave before I ask the nurse to call security." What nerve he had! It was partially his fault she was here in the first place.

"Doctor?" the nurse asked.

"You can leave now. I'll wait with her until the . . . *doctor* on call arrives," Parker said in a hushed voice.

"No, you won't! I asked you to leave. Now go away!" Angelica said as she tried to lift her head from the gurney.

"Please, don't move. You might injure yourself more," the nurse soothed. "Dr. Mahoney should be here any minute. One of our on-staff trauma doctors decided to take an indeterminate leave of absence, so we're a bit shorthanded at the moment."

Angelica would swear the nurse was upset and directing her words to Parker. "That's not my problem," she said. "Anyway, what kind of doctor takes an 'indeterminate leave of absence'?"

"That's what I would like to know," the nurse replied. "You just try to remain still and relax. We'll remove the tape and the backboard as soon as Dr. Mahoney examines you."

"I hope he gets here soon. I need to go to the ladies' room," Angelica said, feeling a bit embarrassed by the call of nature that she soon would be unable to ignore.

"Let me call a nurse's aide. They can assist you with a bedpan."

"No!" Angelica shouted. "I don't have to go that bad. I can wait." She hoped. There was no way she would allow an aide to shove a cold bedpan under her. She was already half frozen as it was.

An attractive older man, probably in his mid to late fifties, entered the room then, saving her from further conversation about her bathroom habits with the nurse.

"A ski accident, I see," he said as he punched a few keys on the computer keyboard next to the examining table where she lay freezing and pissed off.

"Yes, and it was his fault." She tried to lift her arm to point at Parker, but it, too, was strapped to the board. She could barely move her hand.

"Parker North. Hmm. Yes, a lot of things are his fault," Dr. Mahoney replied as he placed his cold hands on her neck.

"You know him?" she asked in amazement.

"Quite well, I must say. Or I thought I did," he said to her.

"Either you do or you don't." The conversation was confusing her. *Maybe I do have a brain injury, and it is just beginning to show.*

"He works here," Dr. Mahoney explained to her as he continued his examination. "Lori, let's get this tape off her. Before we release her, I want an X-ray and an MRI done just to be on the safe side. I don't think we'll find anything, but I'd rather be safe than sorry."

"Does this mean I'm okay? I can leave?" she asked.

"Provided the tests come back negative, you're free to go. You've suffered a slight concussion, nothing more as far as I can see. But I want to make sure, so we'll do an X-ray and MRI first." He turned to the computer, where he clicked a few keys, then back to her. "Is there someone we can call? I don't think you should drive or ski for a few days. You're going to be one sore cookie tomorrow, and I can assure you that you'll have a killer headache, but other than that, I think you will be just fine."

"Some vacation this has turned out to be," she said. "And no, there isn't anyone to call. I'll hire someone to drive me back to Telluride, then I'm going to catch the next flight back to New York City. I should have stayed where I belong."

"Mahoney, I can drive her back to Maximum Glide," Parker said, his voice firm and commanding.

"Yes, you can. You seem to have a lot of time on your hands now. So, there, Ms. Shepard, you won't have to worry about hiring a driver. Mr. North has offered his services. For whatever that's worth," he added.

"He's the reason I'm here in the first place. He doesn't even have a decent vehicle to drive, even if I would let him take me back to the resort. And besides, that piece-of-junk truck he has is broken down on the side of the road. I'll take my chances with a driver."

"Parker, you mean to tell me you're still driving that beat-up pickup truck?" Dr. Mahoney shook his head, then handed Angelica a piece of paper. "This is for a higher dose of ibuprofen if you need it; otherwise, you can take the over-the-counter stuff."

She just nodded while the two men gave one another the evil eye. There was a story here, but right now all she wanted was to get these bindings off and make a quick trip to the ladies' room. Whatever the two men had between them would wait.

Another nurse entered the small examination room with scissors and a bottle of something liquid. Probably alcohol.

"Now, Miss"—she looked at Angelica's arm bracelet, which had been attached sometime during her visit—"Shepard, I'll try not to pull or get your hair caught, but I can't make any promises that this won't hurt."

"Just yank it off, I really want to get to the ladies' room," she said, as the nurse began to cut through the heavy layers of tape on her neck and head.

The nurse laughed. "Sorry, I can't do that, but I'll try to make this as quick and painless as possible." She snipped, clipped, and tugged, and in under five minutes, Angelica was free from the binding tape.

Thankful that she was able to move freely, she pushed herself into a sitting position, then flopped back on the pillow. "I'm so dizzy!" she said, surprised.

"That's why you can't drive," Parker stated from his position at the foot of her bed.

"No, I'm dizzy because you had to go skiing away

from me, like that friend of yours, Max Jorgenson. If you hadn't been in such a hurry, this wouldn't have happened."

"Okay, it's my fault. Satisfied?" he asked as she tried to push herself up a second time.

Angelica knew when enough was enough, and that time had arrived. Slowly, so as not to jar her head in any way, she pushed herself up. *So far, so good*, she thought as she scooted to the edge of the examining table. From there, she swung her feet to the floor, careful to keep a firm hold on the bed.

"Dr. Mahoney said you worked here. What are you, an orderly or something?" she asked Parker when her feet found the cool tile floor.

"Something like that. Now, let me help you. The ladies' room is just down the hall."

If she hadn't been so light-headed and unsure on her feet, she would have told him flat out *NO!* But she had a concussion, and she wasn't going to risk falling flat on her face. She'd done that once already and did not want to damage anything else unnecessarily.

Parker North wrapped one arm around her waist, and with the other he held her hand firmly in his own. While he knew he wasn't one hundred percent responsible for Angelica's injuries, he did hold himself responsible for skiing off without really knowing her skills as a skier; for the rest, she could thank the jerk who didn't know how to come to a complete stop.

"So, what do you do here?" Angelica asked as she baby-stepped down the hall.

"Does it really matter?" he asked.

That made her think about her own situation. Did people always define themselves by their profession? She wasn't sure about Parker, but she knew that she'd lived her life *for* her profession. Not sure if that was good or bad, she was certain of one thing: she had *never* been this cold in her entire life. She'd pursue deeper thoughts when she was physically able. For the moment, the restroom was her goal.

Parker stopped when they reached the end of the hall. "You sure you don't need assistance? I can ask one of the nurses to go inside with you. Just in case," he said, a worried look on his handsome face.

"No, thanks. I'm fine. If you hear me fall, just call a doctor," she said before entering the restroom.

"And that would be me," he said to himself when she was out of earshot. That *was* him. Like his father and grandfather, he'd been destined to become a doctor. Why the realization came to him just then was beside the point. He was a trauma surgeon. He'd saved many lives, more than he could count. Yes, he had lost a young patient, but he knew the moment he'd laid eyes on her that it was too late. One child mattered, and he knew he would never forget her face, but he also knew that he had a job to do, and that was to save as many lives as possible for as long as he could.

The bathroom door opened, revealing a relieved-looking Angelica. "Okay, I want to see that doctor again. I need to ask him how long the tests are going to take. I don't want to spend the rest of the day lingering in the halls like an unwanted virus."

Parker laughed, deciding he'd kept her in the dark way too long even though he'd only known her for less than twenty-four hours. "It depends on how busy they are."

"And you know this because . . . ?" she interrupted.

"Because I am a doctor. A trauma neurosurgeon, and I

have asked for the same tests for patients of my own on many, many occasions."

There, it was out in the open. He was not ashamed of himself or his chosen profession. He'd worked his ass off to get to this point, and he knew, just as any other doctor knew, that there would be times when you couldn't save a patient. Those were the low times. Times he hoped he wouldn't have to experience too often, but if anything, he was a realist. Though there would be more death and sadness, he wasn't going to let that prevent him from practicing medicine.

Angelica had stopped in the middle of the hall. She stared at him as though he had three eyeballs. "Yeah right," she said before turning around and heading back in the direction she'd come from.

Parker raced to her side. Curious, he asked, "Why did you say that?"

She rolled her large brown eyes and laughed. "Come on, give me a break. First of all, if you were a doctor, you wouldn't be driving such a hunk of junk. Secondly, if you were really a doctor, you would have saved—"

"I did," he said, her reaction suddenly amusing.

She flushed, but remained silent. "You . . . it was you! The angel I thought I saw!"

"Yes, it was me. When you opened your eyes, I can't tell you how relieved I was."

Angelica wasn't so sure she didn't have a brain injury. She did remember opening her eyes and seeing a bright burst of sun, a halolike glow hovering above and behind him as he bent over her. In her state of semiconsciousness, she'd mistaken him for an angel!

"You really are the angel," she said, sounding like she'd just solved the biggest mystery on earth.

He led her back to the room. "I've been called a lot of names, but never an angel," he teased as he helped her get back up on the table before continuing. A low, buzzing noise coming from his pocket stopped him dead in his tracks.

"Now it decides to work," he said before answering the cell phone that he was going to replace as soon as possible. He was a doctor, and doctors needed to be contacted at all hours.

"Hello." He held up a hand, indicating he needed a minute. "Max, what gives?" A smile as wide as the mountain spread across his face.

"I can do that. Sure. Okay if I bring a guest? Great, I'll see you tonight. One more favor—could you send someone to check on Leon?" Parker turned to Angelica, his eyes filled with laughter. "Yeah, he's the cat I told you about." Parker spoke into the phone a few more seconds, then ended the call.

"That was Max Jorgenson—you remember him?"

Angelica rolled her eyes. "Yes, about like I recall you just said you were a doctor."

Frustrated, Parker picked up the phone and dialed a number. Less than a minute later a nurse entered the room pushing a wheelchair. "Hi, Dr. North. I thought you'd taken a leave of absence."

"I'm off for two weeks, skiing. My friend here, she needs an MRI and an X-ray, stat. Mahoney issued the order, but we're kind of in a rush. It seems I've, rather *we've*, been invited to see *Angels with Paper Wings*."

"Well, then, let's not keep this girl waiting. Come on, honey, if Dr. North asks, we jump. He's the best trauma neurosurgeon in the area. Of course, I'm sure you already knew that. We've been dying, well not literally if you know what I mean, but most of us nurses have had our eye on Dr. North for a long time. Oh, not like that, but we've been waiting for him to meet someone . . . nice, not in this profession. The hours are terrible, the money isn't that good, or at least from what I hear. Me, personally, as an RN, I do just fine, but for a man of his caliber, well you would think he'd be a—"

"Ruthie, please take Ms. Shepard down for her X-rays. And please don't annoy her with all the details of my private life."

"Oh, Ruthie, I love details," Angelica said with a wicked grin. "All the dirt and gore, too," she added, as the nurse pushed her out of the room.

"Don't you dare," Parker said, his words nothing more than an echo before he remembered there really wasn't anything in his private life worth repeating.

Epilogue

Angelica Shepard could not recall when she enjoyed a local production as much as that night's performance of *Angels with Paper Wings*. And they were high-school kids! Awed and overwhelmed with emotion, she didn't care when Parker saw the tears flow down her face like two shimmery Christmas ribbons.

The gymnasium was packed, standing room only. She could see why. These kids were better than some of the actors and actresses on Broadway! The actors returned to the small stage one last time for yet another standing ovation. Angelica clapped so hard her hands hurt, plus she was beginning to feel a slight headache just as Doctors Mahoney and North had promised. She'd taken three ibuprofen before she left the hospital just in case. All of her test results were perfectly normal, and for that she was grateful. But more than anything, she was so excited over the performance she'd just witnessed. Not because it was pure excellence, though that was part of it, but she knew what she wanted to do in her professional life. Now more than ever. Why she'd spent so many years wasting time onstage didn't matter. She'd learned her craft, had been moderately successful, and she wouldn't trade the experience for all the tea in China. However, it was time to move on. Her reason for taking this strange trip. And now, here she was, barely a day into the trip, and she'd solved her career dilemma!

"Why are you crying?" Parker asked as he thumbed the tears from her face.

"Have you ever had an epiphany?" she asked, knowing he'd just had a rude awakening in the career department himself. On the drive from the hospital to the high school, he'd told her about his doubts when he'd lost the little girl who'd been hit while riding her bicycle. Doubts that had sent him into hiding. Doubts that had led them straight to one another, she'd thought then and still did. This was not going to be easy, but they would make it work.

"I've had a few in my day. I take it this is the reason behind your tears?" he asked.

Never in her life had she ever been in such sync with another human being, and especially one of the opposite sex. "Yes and no. When I left New York, my agent had just told me that a younger actress had gotten the role I'd been dying for. If I'm honest with myself, she is the best actress for the part. Al said he'd find another part for me, but just now, here in this gymnasium filled with normal people, I realized I don't want to be onstage. I want to direct, to lead and guide and show and . . ."

She didn't get the chance to finish. Parker wrapped his arms around her and pulled her next to him. As though they'd been a couple forever, he leaned down and kissed her fully on the mouth. It took a minute for Angelica to break away. "Hey, we're at a high school! What will all these kids think? And their parents?" she asked, not really caring about anything except the moment.

"They'll think a sexy hot actress from New York City just kissed a handsome prince." He kissed her again, only this time it was deeper, more passionate. He drew in a deep breath. "Maybe this isn't the place, but I promise you, I won't forget where we left off. Now." He turned to a group of people who were waiting by the foot of the stage.

Angelica realized that they were waiting for Parker. Without another word, Parker introduced Max Jorgenson, and he, in turn, was introduced to Max Jorgenson's wife, Grace Landry, and their daughter, Ella. Not to be outdone, next came Patrick and Stephanie.

Then came the girls and Mr. Nicholas Star.

"Now, these are those girls I was tellin' you about," Nicholas said. "I think they're just about as pretty as this little actress you've hooked up with. What'd ya think?"

"They're beautiful," Parker said.

Two girls, around nine and twelve, held out their hands as though they were royalty and did this every day. "I'm Ashley, the oldest, and this is Amanda. She's three years younger than me. Are you and Dr. Parker going to get married?" the dark-haired oldest girl asked.

Normally, Angelica would've been mortified by such

a question, and coming from a child, too. Not this time. She looked at Parker before answering. "Someday, I'm sure, we'll both get married. I don't know if we will marry one another if that's what you're asking." Pure and simple. No in between the cracks.

"Ashley! I can't believe you asked Ms. Shepard such a personal question. You know better," Stephanie said to her daughter before turning to Angelica. "I'm sorry. I hope she didn't embarrass you too much. She is obsessed with weddings now. Ever since Patrick and I married, then it was Melanie and Bryce. He's Grace's younger brother. Well, I've said too much. Please, accept my apologies," Stephanie asked, then grabbed both girls by the hand and took them to a nearby corner.

"And to think I was going to catch the next flight back to New York," Angelica said, still in awe.

"You know, it is quite a leap from Colorado to New York. You have any suggestions?" Parker asked as they followed their new friends out of the gymnasium. "And there's Leon to consider. He hates flying."

"I hope you have a lot of frequent-flier miles," Angelica teased, before adding, "but if not, I kinda like this neck of the woods. And I'm sure Leon will fall madly in love with me when he gets to know me."

Parker leaned down to whisper in her ear, "Does that mean what I think it means?"

"What do you think it means?" she couldn't help but ask.

"I think it means this is the beginning of something new, maybe the best new beginning of my life. Would I be correct in my assumption?"

"Look, we hardly know one another. Plus, you owe me big-time for today's injury. But, I am willing to make you a deal," she stated before climbing back inside the limo Max had sent to the hospital.

"And what would that deal be?"

"I want free medical care for the next two weeks. If, and this is a very big *if*, you and I, well, if we are as good as we are right now . . ." She let her words trail off.

"Sweetie, you ain't seen nothing yet. This is only the beginning," Parker said before sliding in beside her.

"Something tells me this is going to be the merriest Christmas ever." Angelica finally relaxed. Her trip had started out on a sour note, but something told her this was just the beginning.

"And you have your very own personal angel to watch over you," Parker added, then kissed her.

Today was perfect, Angelica thought as she melted in his arms. Tomorrow would be even better.

Candy Canes and Cupid

Chapter 1

Hannah Ray glanced at the calendar. December already, a month and a holiday she dreaded every year. Christmas. If asked why, and she had been on numerous occasions, she would pause for the briefest of moments, as though she were truly contemplating the question, and then she would give her standard reply: "You know, I'm not really sure." Friends and colleagues would then look at her as though she were out of her mind, but it was simply the truth.

Growing up in Florida, she'd never really been bitten by the holiday bug. While she honored the religious aspects of the sacred holiday, she personally thought all the hoopla was nothing more than just one more reason for giant corporations to increase their already more-than-insanely-adequate bottom lines with even more in the way of profits, and for their CEOs to line their very deep pockets with even more money. Hannah smiled when she realized that she sounded exactly like her father, who, it just so happened, used to be one of those CEOs of a giant company. But Hannah had always assured him that he had a heart.

When he'd keeled over from a heart attack five years ago, she was shocked. Her father had always been meticulous about his diet. Red meat no more than once a week. Fish only three times, and the other days were vegetarian. An avid runner who ranked high in his class when he was nearing seventy, he'd looked at least ten years younger than most men his age. His sudden death derailed her for a while, but she knew he would want her to continue to pursue her career. After passing the bar, Hannah decided she didn't want to be confined to a courtroom. So she applied for her Florida private investigator's license, which she received without a hitch, opened an office in Naples, and one year later was so busy she had hired three full-time agents, two retired police officers as part-timers, and Camden, her best friend and personal assistant, who played a large role in running the office. Hannah didn't know what she would do without Camden's excellent organizational skills as she herself wasn't the most organized in a "paper" kind of way. Her ability to keep details clear in her head was her major talent. While Camden could locate a Post-it in a pile of a thousand, Hannah could tell you what was written on the Post-it and in what color ink.

Less than a month short of thirty-four, Hannah was pretty set in her ways, and again, she had her father to thank for that as well. Her mother had died of breast cancer when Hannah was six, leaving her father to raise her alone. With no family of his own to guide him through the waters of single parenthood, Frederick Ray did the best he could. Hannah had missed her mother after her death, but with the passage of time, and the fading memory of a six-year-old child, she was soon conversing at dinner with her father about all sorts of very adult financial and legal matters. They would discuss the law as it pertained to Ray Enterprises, a conglomerate of manufacturers that produced items ranging from high-end perfumes to plastics. When he died, her father left everything he owned to her, which enabled her to choose what she wanted to do in her professional life. While she was a voting member of the boards of directors of the various companies controlled by Ray Enterprises, she was fortunate that Albert, who had been her father's right-hand man, continued to perform in that same capacity for her, relieving her of the burden of day-to-day involvement in the affairs of those companies. Not only was he the one who acted on her behalf at board meetings, but he was like an uncle to her, and she trusted him implicitly.

Of course, Camden came in a close second. They were the same age, shared many of the same interests, and when it was time to close shop, neither she nor Camden had any trouble removing her professional hat for a night out on the town, or often a quiet meal prepared in Hannah's ultramodern kitchen. Both had taken an avid interest in cooking when they had started packing on a few extra pounds last year. Once a week, if their schedules permitted, they would take turns making dinner. Of course, dinner always included a bottle or two of wine. Comfortable with each other, they would chat about fashion, makeup, anything except work; then, as with most single females, they would discuss their current dating situations. Sadly, more often than not, neither one was having much success in that area. Not because they worked too much, and not because there wasn't quite a fine selection of available men in southwest Florida, but because both women were extremely finicky about men.

As a result, Hannah and Camden were planning to spend the upcoming holiday together, doing absolutely nothing except lounging on the beach and catching up on their favorite authors' new books. Both agreed this was the best possible decision, given that neither had close family or any reason to do anything else.

Most of her high-profile cases were coming to an end, and she hadn't planned to take on any more until after the New Year. She'd given all her employees a two-and-a-half-week paid vacation beginning December 18 and ending Monday, January 5, 2015. They were ecstatic and couldn't stop talking about her generosity. She liked her team and thought of them as friends first, then coworkers. She was not a "me boss, you employee" employer.

Her father had often told her that in business one accomplished so much more by being kind and generous to one's employees rather than bossy, demanding, and condescending. To this day, Ray Enterprises, along with H.R. Investigations, had some of the happiest employees around. And Ray Enterprises was among the top five businesses on *Fortune Magazine*'s list of the best companies to work for.

Two weeks of bliss, she thought, as she pulled up her schedule for the upcoming week. Two weeks of sun, sand, and surf, and, if she was lucky, she could delve into those books she had recently received from Amazon.

Clearing her mind, Hannah scrolled through her iPad mini. The firm had three consultations scheduled that afternoon. One was with an insurance company that suspected an injured employee collecting workman's compensation was doing so illegally. That would be a breeze to solve. She would have Ed, her number-one part-timer, do the consultation and go out on a surveillance mission, his specialty.

Next was a young woman who suspected that her husband was cheating on her. Hannah detested this part of her work and tried to distance herself from it as much as possible, but sadly, the need for it was a reality in life, and someone had to do it. Marlene would meet with the woman, as she was the expert at anything requiring a telephoto lens and being incognito, plus she was extremely nosy, always an added bonus in the private-investigation business.

The last consultation for the day she would take care of personally since the client had requested that she do so.

Last year, Hannah had been hired to keep tabs on an abusive husband when an ignorant judge had released him on his own recognizance after he had been charged with beating his wife to a pulp. Because the man happened to be from a wealthy family, several members of whom were well-known attorneys, the judge assured his wife's attorney that she would have nothing to fear from her husband and certainly not his family, even going so far as to imply that she had brought the beating on herself.

Hannah immediately contacted Grace Landry out in Colorado, told her the woman's story, and personally put Leanne on a plane to Denver. Once the abused spouse was at Hope House, Grace's shelter for battered families, Hannah breathed a sigh of relief. She'd stayed in contact with Leanne and was saddened when she learned that the woman had recently returned to Fort Myers to make an attempt to reunite with her abusive husband. And it was because of this that she had decided to pull in a few favors at Health Park Hospital. Two days ago, Leanne had been admitted to the hospital with a broken nose and a cracked pelvis. Hannah planned to confront Leanne's husband, Bruce Wells, and make a special trip to visit Leanne. This wasn't her usual modus operandi, but she was passionate about those who suffered abuse at the hands of people who were supposed to love them the most and anyone who bullied others. You might say that it was her Achilles' heel.

Stuffing her iPad in her briefcase, she grabbed her purse and raced out the door, locking it behind her, only to remember the cell phone she'd left in the master bath when she'd been blow-drying her hair. As soon as she inserted her key in the lock, she heard its familiar xylophone ringtone. "Darn," she muttered as she raced through the condo to the master suite.

She hit the green ANSWER button. "Hello?" she said, a bit winded.

"Hannah?" came a male voice.

"Yes, this is Hannah Ray. How can I help you?" She dropped her briefcase on the floor and plopped down on her vanity stool, staring at the face in the mirror. Straight blond hair, brown eyes. A regular face, she thought, nothing remarkable.

"It's Max Jorgenson."

It took a couple of seconds for Hannah to call up the image that went with the voice, but when she did, she was all smiles. Max Jorgenson. The Olympic gold-medal skier. Grace Landry's husband.

She grinned. "And to what do I owe this honor?" she asked in a teasing tone. She'd been a bit impressed when she'd met Max through Grace.

She could hear him clearing his throat. "I'm not sure you would call this an honor. It's more of a favor."

A favor? From her? Hannah hadn't a clue what Max Jorgenson wanted from her, but if he'd bothered making the phone call personally, then it must be something very urgent and important.

"Anything, Max. Just say the word."

He chuckled. "Don't say that just yet. Hear me out."

"Hey, anything for you and Grace. She really helped me out last year, and as it just so happens, I might need her services again. Same client. A sad situation, but go on. You called me. What gives?"

"I need you to come to Colorado. Mid-December if possible," Max said.

Hannah visualized all her plans for sun, sand, and surf swirling right down the drain.

In a voice she hoped didn't relay just how much she did not want to travel out West, she said, "Of course, Max. Just give me the time and place, and I will be there."

"I knew I could count on you," Max said, then gave her the details before thanking her again and clicking off.

"No sunning. No reading. No relaxing on the beach. There goes my Christmas vacation."

Chapter 2

"You know I wouldn't ask you if it wasn't important," Max said. "It's not like you to have holiday plans. I know you, old man, remember? We go back a long way."

Liam McConnell shook his head, then spoke into the phone. "Don't remind me how long, okay? I'm not getting any younger, and trust me, it shows," Liam said in a deep voice that still held traces of an Irish accent even though he'd been living in the United States since he was a young boy. "So, go on, tell me, what's so damned important? I'm all ears."

For the next fifteen minutes, Max updated Liam on the situation at Telluride. He knew for a fact that Liam McConnell was the best in the business when it came to information security. He had a bachelor's in Criminal Justice, a Harvard law degree, and had worked with the Federal Bureau of Investigation for two years before going out on his own. He was one of only a few experts on electronic-information security. Max knew that Liam could pick and choose when and where to work, but he was also sure that Liam wouldn't turn him down. He was offering his best cabin at the resort as long as he wanted and, of course, he would pay him whatever his usual fee was. Then he had an added surprise, but he wasn't going to mention that just yet. Something Grace had cooked up, and he'd agreed wholeheartedly, though that wasn't the main reason for his wanting Liam's help in finding the culprits who were trying to destroy his business.

"And you think one of your employees is hacking into your systems?" Liam asked.

"More than one," Max said.

"You do realize I am at my beach house on Sanibel Island and planned to spend December fishing and relaxing?"

"No, I didn't. If you can't do this, I understand. I just wanted the best. And you *are* the best," Max added with a lilt in his voice.

"Ah, you do know how to get to a man's heart. All right. I am yours. For two weeks. If I haven't located the source, then I'll have had a free ski vacation, and you, my friend, will be shit out of luck."

They talked more, laughed about old times, then Liam wrote down the date when he would need to fly to Colorado. After they finished their call, he had a strong suspicion his old ski buddy had something more than a job waiting for him.

Liam shook his head and reached for his iPad. Plans were made to be changed. While he disliked the idea of spending Christmas at a ski resort where hundreds of people would be filled with holiday cheer, he supposed it could be worse. In all honesty, he'd truly been looking forward to spending a few weeks at his home on Sanibel Island, but Max was a good friend. Liam counted his few close friends as priceless. If forgoing a bit of fishing meant helping his friend out, he consoled himself with the thought that he could fish anytime. With that in mind, he called Pierce, his pilot, and made arrangements to have his Learjet available for a trip to Colorado.

Liam wasn't much for holidays. Any of them. Too much money spent on silly things, in his not-so-humble opinion. He remembered a woman he'd been dating last year. She'd spent a small fortune on a fountain pen for him. He'd wanted to take it back to the store where she'd purchased it and insist she use the money for something meaningful, like a charitable organization. He had more expensive fountain pens than he could count. And to be honest, he liked BIC pens much better. The woman—he couldn't recall her name—had been deleted from his list of female contacts. The list was getting slimmer and slimmer. The women who knew him knew that he was fairly well-off. Indeed, that seemed to be the major attraction he held for them. Unfortunately, for him it was an instant turnoff.

Whatever happened to women with respect? Brains? Goals other than marrying a rich man to take care of them, to provide them with meaningless baubles and fancy cars? He was sure he'd remain a bachelor because there didn't seem to be that one special woman who couldn't get past his wealth. Or, if there was, he hadn't met her yet.

Chapter 3

December 17, 2014

Hannah was in a foul mood when her plane finally touched down at Denver International Airport. The flight had been turbulent, the man seated next to her had snored throughout the flight, and she had not been one bit happy at having to leave Leanne and her domestic situation behind. Camden had promised to keep a watch over her, but she knew that they could only do so much. Leanne had to realize that there was nothing she could do that would salvage her marriage; she had to want to make the necessary changes in her life herself. Sadly, Hannah feared that she might not be able to force herself to make those changes before it was too late.

As soon as Hannah exited the plane, she found the ladies' room, repaired her makeup, and began her search for the area where Max had a limo waiting. She liked the thought of riding through the Colorado mountains in the back of a limo. Though she disliked the cold, she had to admit that the snowcapped mountains were breathtaking.

The drive would give her a couple of hours to rest and prepare herself for the work ahead. She hoped to find Max's hackers, do what was needed, and still have time to enjoy her planned staycation at the beach. She did not like snow. She did not like to be cold. And more than anything, the thought of being at an upscale ski resort during their busiest time of year made her wish for the comfort and quiet of her beachfront condo.

"Suck it up, girl. It ain't happening, Hannah," she muttered to herself as she made her way through the crowds. She wound her way through the travelers, some loaded with tons of luggage, others with sets of skis, snowboards, and all the heavy-duty gear required to freeze in luxury. She did not understand why people would willingly place themselves in freezing temperatures and actually call it fun. But again, she was a Florida girl through and through. After a tram ride and a trip up an escalator, she spied the exit, where her limo waited. Just as Max had said.

"You must be Miss Ray?" a handsome young man with caramel-colored skin dressed in a navy blue uniform asked as he saw her approach the limousine.

She wanted to correct him. It was *Ms. Ray,* but there was no use starting out on the wrong foot when she already had one strike—the presence of cold air and gobs of snow rather than warm sunshine and a sandy beach—against her. She'd let it pass. After all, it was true. She was a *Miss. Ms.* just sounded better to her.

"I'll take that," the limo driver said, reaching for her

carry-on and opening the door for her. "Miss," he said, indicating that she should get inside.

"Yes, of course." She slid across the plush seat and inhaled the unmistakable scent of real leather. A rich man's scent, she thought as she tucked her pocketbook and briefcase on the floor next to her boot-clad feet.

Cut the attitude, Hannah. This is what it is. Work for a friend. Get over it. Do your job, then go home and enjoy the rest of your time off!

"Mr. Jorgenson said you wouldn't mind?" the driver said again.

"What? I'm sorry," she said. "Must be jet lag."

"I have another passenger to pick up. Mr. Jorgenson said you wouldn't mind sharing the limo. He has more than one client to pick up today. It's the busy season, you know?"

Hannah wanted to say, "No shit," but kept it to herself. And who was this other passenger? Another ski bum taking advantage of Max's good nature? She decided to ask. "So who are we picking up?" She tried to sound cheerful, as though she were truly grateful to have a companion for the ride.

The young man slid into the driver's seat, then hit the button that opened the window that separated the driver from the passengers. "He's a business associate, miss."

"Of course," she replied. What had she expected other than a ski bum? Max Jorgenson was a big-time resort owner, a former Olympic gold-medal winner. It only made sense that he would have associates visiting him year-round. And if they got in a few days on the slopes, all the better. If you liked that sort of thing, which she didn't.

"We just have to drive to the general aviation side of the airport; it won't take long," the driver informed her as he pulled out into a long line of traffic preparing to exit the airport.

"That's fine. I'm in no hurry at all," she lied in the sweetest voice. She was starting not to like herself very much. *Maybe I should refer to myself as Ms. Scrooge.* She smiled at the unbidden thought.

"Thanks, because we're going to be in some heavy traffic. Tomorrow evening is the beginning of Hanukkah, so we've got plenty of travelers who want to be settled in at the resort before the holiday begins at sunset. Mr. Jorgenson says this is going to be a record-breaking year."

"That's wonderful," she replied, trying hard to keep the sarcasm out of her voice. *For him.*

"I know. I'm just thrilled to be a part of it all. My kid sister, she's twelve, hopes to make it to the Olympics one day, so I'm hoping I can make a connection for her." He stopped speaking, as though he'd revealed too much. "I mean, I don't know Mr. Jorgenson well enough to ask him if he'd coach my sister or anything like that, it's just that she's very talented and needs all the breaks she can get."

Hannah wanted to add that she could almost guarantee the breaks, but they might not be the kind he was hoping for. She didn't, though. "Have you talked to Max about your sister?" she asked, trying to show some form of sincere interest.

"No! I wouldn't dream of it. At least not yet. I . . . well, I plan to play it by ear."

"Well, if you'd like, I can put in a good word for you. I'm sure Max would be more than willing to coach your sister, especially if she's as talented as you say. If not, I'm quite sure he could put you in contact with another coach." She didn't know that at all, but the poor kid seemed so excited when he talked about his sister that Hannah suddenly felt sorry for him. Trying to make it in a tough world. It was hard these days. Even more so if you didn't have the luxury of wealth and family to support you. She had no clue if that was the case now, but it was probably close enough. The kid wouldn't be driving a limo just for the fun of it. At least she didn't think so.

"You'd do that for me? I'm practically a stranger."

True, but she could tell he was decent. In her profession, the ability to size people up was absolutely necessary. And this young guy was legit. And she would make sure his sister got the training she needed, even if it meant paying for it herself. Anonymously, of course.

"Just write your name and number down, and don't forget to give it to me."

He reached inside his shirt pocket and whipped out a shiny gold business card. "This has all of Tasha's info, and mine. I'm kind of like her agent since our mom died two years ago. She used to drive her to practice every day, but I can do that now with this job. And by the way, I'm Terrence."

"It's nice to meet you, Terrence. I'm Hannah Ray." She was sorry she'd been the slightest bit snotty. This kid was trying to make something of his and his sister's lives. She'd help him and his sister. She made a mental promise to herself to arrange for Max or someone else to coach the Olympic hopeful.

Hannah might do lots of crazy things, but one thing she *never* did was break a promise. Even one she had made only to herself.

Chapter 4

"I'm not sure how long I'll be remaining here," Liam told Pierce. "You can stay if you want, or not. Up to you."

"Then I'd just as soon go home. I hate this cold weather, and you'll need someone to keep an eye on your place, right?" Pierce teased, knowing full well that he had the use of the beach house on Sanibel Island while Liam was out of town.

"Of course, and I trust you to make sure that my boat, the *Ferretti 690,* catches a few fish while she's out and about."

Liam's *Ferretti 690* was a *yacht*, but Pierce wasn't going to remind him, just in case he decided to dry-dock her while he was away.

"I think I can manage. Just give me at least a three-to-four-hour heads-up when you're ready for your return flight. I'll need to file a flight plan and prepare the Learjet."

Learjets and *Ferretti 690s.* One might be excused if one thought that Liam McConnell had been born with a silver spoon in his mouth, but that was not the case at all. Hard work and a few wise investments in his younger years had assured him that his financial future was secure. Not to mention that his security fees were right up there with the likes of Gavin de Becker, a world-renowned security specialist.

"I'll make sure to do that. Now, where is this limousine that's picking me up?" The two men waited on the tarmac next to the plane. Pierce wore the traditional dark slacks and crisp white shirt with gold wings on the sleeves of a pilot. Liam was dressed in faded jeans and a white Columbia Sportswear fishing shirt. Worn-out Sperrys, minus socks, completed his outfit. He casually held a denim jacket across his shoulder. It was cold but dry, and the sun was out. He knew the temperatures could change at the drop of a hat, but he was comfortable and didn't want to suffocate on the drive to Telluride. People out West seemed to crank the heaters in their cars up to full blast at the drop of a snowflake. It always made him a bit sick, but he'd keep that tidbit of information to himself. All the more reason to like Florida. Though the temperature and the humidity were horrendous in the summer, air-conditioning was everywhere. In fact, most places kept the air-conditioning cranked up all the way in the summer months. Liam would take that over the cold any day of the week.

He slapped Pierce on the back. "Have a safe flight home. You need me, you know where to find me."

"Will do, my friend." Pierce spied the approaching limo and motioned for it to pull up alongside the jet so he could transfer Liam's suitcase from the underbelly of the aircraft. The limo's trunk popped open, Pierce tossed the small piece of luggage inside, then shook hands with Liam. "Later."

Liam waved, then directed his attention to the limousine driver. "Mr. McConnell? I'm Terrence. Mr. Jorgenson sent me."

"Hey, I appreciate the lift. Nice to meet you." Liam shook Terrence's hand.

"Just so you know, I have another passenger. She's a business associate of Mr. Jorgenson's. She's nice." He opened the door, then closed it quickly before the cold air could slip inside.

Liam slid into the seat and saw the attractive blonde seated across from him.

Max Jorgenson, you sly devil. Let the games begin.

Chapter 5

Ever the gentleman, Liam introduced himself using only his given name. He was a bit on the paranoid side when it came to women these days.

"Nice meeting you, Liam. I'm Hannah Ray," she replied in a professional voice, emphasizing *Ray*.

A subtle dig of sorts. He liked that.

He scrutinized her as she sat across from him. Shapely legs covered in black tights and black suede boots indicated she had taste. She wore a burgundy trench coat that covered the upper half of her body. Honey-blond hair and eyes the color of a good whiskey with tiny green flecks dotted around her pupils. His vision certainly hadn't been affected by aging. Not that forty was old. Hadn't someone recently told him forty was the new thirty?

After a few awkward seconds, he acknowledged her

introduction by holding his hand out to her. "It's my pleasure."

She reached across the expanse that separated them and took his hand in hers, almost yanking it back when she felt a jolt of desire so sudden that it frightened her. Taking a deep breath, she quickly shook his hand, then pulled away. "Nice." And was he ever, she thought, as she raked her gaze over him. He had to be well over six feet tall because his long, denim-clad legs almost touched hers. Jet-black hair sprinkled with gray at the temples, and clear blue eyes; this man was a bona fide hunk. What the heck? She hadn't reacted to a member of the male persuasion like this since . . . ever!

A couple of more seconds of silence, then they both began talking at once.

"—So what brings you here?" Hannah asked.

"—I take it this isn't a vacation for you?" Liam said.

"Let's start over. Ladies first," Liam said, his wide grin revealing strikingly white teeth against a tanned face.

Hannah decided he was a ski bum. She saw that he went sockless, and this confirmed it even more. *Who lives in Colorado and went without socks in the winter?* But she told herself not to judge. He was very handsome, and he appeared to be very self-assured. Maybe he was arrogant and condescending like Richard Marchand, an asshole pharmacist she had once dated. No, she thought to herself, there just couldn't be another man like dear old Richard. Realizing that he was waiting for her to start their conversation again, she smiled. "Sorry, I was woolgathering. Long flight, and it's cold here."

He laughed. "Colorado is usually cold this time of year, no doubt about it."

"Excuse me," Terrence said, as they exited the airport. "Would either of you like something to eat before we hit I-70? I have drinks but no food, and it's a long drive: about six hours, and that's in good weather, without a lot of traffic."

"Six hours! Please tell me you're joking?" Hannah said, not caring that she sounded like a whiny brat. She had just spent almost four and a half hours on a plane, and now she had a six-hour limo ride? And apparently that was if she was lucky!

Liam removed his phone from his shirt pocket and punched in a number. "Pierce, you still at the airport? Good. Don't leave. I'm coming back. I'll explain when I get there."

"Maybe I should call Mr. Jorgenson," Terrence said as they waited at a traffic light. "He'll be upset if I arrive without his guests."

"I'm calling him now," Liam said, and scrolled through his phone until he located Max's cell number.

"Max, I'm in Denver and just realized I'm still six hours away. Pierce is still at the airport with the Learjet. Can you arrange for someone to be there in say"—he looked at his watch—"two hours tops? Good. I'll tell him. Later," he said, then clicked off.

He turned in the seat so that he was facing the front of the limo. "Terrence, Max says you can have the night off. Said for you to spend the evening having fun and to stay at the Hilton in Denver tonight. Wants you to take your time driving back tomorrow. He also said he would make sure Tasha knows you're okay."

"Well, if that's what Mr. Jorgenson wants, then his wish is totally my command." Terrence grinned. "Yours too, Mr. McConnell, Miss Ray. I hope to see you both at all the Christmas festivities. They're going to light up the mountain this year. It's gonna be a sight to behold."

Hannah knew that she must've heard Terrence correctly; she wasn't hard of hearing. Yes, she'd heard all about the holiday events, but what she'd really heard and took in was the name. *McConnell. Liam McConnell.*

Anyone and everyone in the private sector of the law-enforcement business knew of his reputation. He was the best in electronic-security assessments. Meaning hackers could not hide from this man. And if they did, he would find them. His success rate was 100 percent.

"If you'll get us back to the general aviation side ASAP, I'll be forever in your debt," Liam said to Terrence.

Terrence made an illegal U-turn, then headed back to the airport. "Right away, Mr. McConnell."

"Do you mind filling me in on the change of plans?" Hannah singsonged. "Or did you forget there is someone else to consider?" Maybe he *was* an asshole like Richard Marchand.

"I apologize. I don't see any reason to ride in this limo for six-plus hours when I have a perfectly good Learjet with an awesome pilot who, as luck would have it, hasn't left the airport yet. I think Pierce can get us to Telluride in a little over an hour." He paused, then continued, "If you'd rather not fly with me, I'll understand. I am a total stranger."

Hannah smirked. "If Max knows you, then I'm sure you're not some psycho serial killer I need to fear." She wanted to tell him she knew exactly who he was, but no way was she going to give him that satisfaction. And to think she'd felt a tiny bit of desire when he'd done nothing more than touch her hand. She needed to get a life beyond work. And maybe a little bit of romance somewhere in between.

"You do inspire confidence, Miss Ray."

"Thank you," she said, her words laced with sarcasm.

Fifteen minutes later, Terrence had arrived at the airport and pulled inside the gates that led to the private hangar area, then drove down the tarmac, where Pierce was doing his preflight check. He waved as they parked the limousine by the sleek aircraft.

Terrence hit the trunk button, but before he could race around to the back of the limo, Liam had already removed both pieces of luggage from the trunk. Hannah climbed out of the limo, stretched, and walked to where Liam stood and took her luggage by its handle. "Thanks, but I can carry this." She didn't want him thinking she was a weak, wimpy woman who needed a man to do what some considered "men's work." She was *not* one of those types at all. Independent to the core, it was something she'd learned from being raised by a single father.

"I can see that," Liam said, his words edgy, a bit sharp.

Hannah focused her eyes on his. "Look, I think we've started off on the wrong foot. I don't want to be here, and I don't know about you, but I am about to freeze to death just standing here, and I am hungry. Can we start over?" Hannah felt deflated, like she'd stepped out of her body, almost as though she were having some kind of metaphysical experience. It wasn't like her to give in so easily. *But,* she thought, *really, what am I actually giving in to?*

Liam grinned. "Must be the high altitude. It sometimes has a strange effect on people, right, Pierce?" Liam
called out, as the pilot finished his preflight check. "Remember how badly it affected the president during the
debates back in 2012?" He laughed and shook his head.

"Whatever you say, Liam. Though just so you know,
Telluride Regional Airport is one of the highest commercial airports in North America at more than nine thousand
feet above sea level. It sits atop Deep Creek Mesa, and
the view of the San Juan Mountains is totally awesome."

He adjusted his aviator glasses and continued. "You
might want to load up on water while you're out here.
Supposed to help with altitude sickness. If that kind of
thing bothers you."

It hadn't before, but he wasn't sure about their passenger. "Ms. Ray? Have you ever had any trouble with high
altitudes?" Liam asked.

She shook her head no. "Though this is only my second trip out West. Last time I was here, I didn't ski, so if
you're asking me about those altitudes up there"—she directed her eyes toward the snowcapped mountains—"I
wouldn't know, since I've never been up on one of them.
For better or worse, I am definitely not a lover of cold
weather. I am Florida born and bred. Long live the
beach."

She wanted to stomp her boots, anything to get out of
the freezing, stark cold. And she was starving. "Didn't
someone mention something about food a while ago? I
could use a bite to eat."

"I just placed an order with the airport's catering
crew," Pierce told her. "They'll have a little bit of everything on the plane." He looked up when he saw a van

heading their way. "They're here now," he said, motioning toward the catering truck.

"Great. Just what I want, more airplane food," Hannah muttered.

"This isn't the same stuff the commercial airlines serve," Pierce informed her. "Private flying does offer a few amenities that the big commercial guys don't. Good food is just one of the perks, right, Liam?"

Hannah didn't want to burst the pilot's bubble. She'd flown in more Gulfstreams and Learjets in her time than she cared to remember. She wasn't a big fan of flying any way you looked at it. It was just another form of transportation as far as she was concerned. "Then let's get on board," she said, then asked before she forgot, "Does the plane have a ladies' room?"

"It does, and it's quite modern, too. The commode even flushes in midair," Pierce said, then they all burst out laughing.

Hannah smiled. "That's good enough for me."

"About time, I'd say," Liam added. "I wasn't sure if I wanted to spend another hour in your company!" He laughed hard, then winked at her. Hannah wanted to come up with a snappy comeback but couldn't think of anything appropriate, so she gave him her sexiest smile and winked back. "Are you sure?" she couldn't help adding. Teasing him, that's what she was doing! And, by gosh, she liked it!

"Okay, you two, enough. I say let's get this bird in the air so we can all sit back and enjoy all these goodies," Pierce suggested, and nodded to the food the two caterers were carrying onboard.

Hannah and Liam said their good-byes to Terrence.

She saw Liam tuck a bit of cash in the young boy's hand and gave him a quick wave before turning toward the aircraft.

Liam brought his luggage up the short flight of steps. Hannah followed behind, dragging her carry-on inside with her. It wasn't like there wasn't enough room for a half dozen more passengers, complete with their luggage. "You have a preference where you'd like to sit?" Hannah asked Liam, while he tucked his luggage beneath a seat.

"Not at all. Sit wherever you're comfortable. This is going to be a quick flight; we'll be lucky if we have time to eat all that food Pierce ordered."

"Speaking of food, I'm ravenous. You mind if I dig into those boxes?" Hannah asked.

"Be my guest," Liam said. "It's probably a good idea to get our food. And then we can buckle up for the rest of the journey."

Inside the cabin, at the rear of the plane, was a wet bar on the left and a restroom to the right. Liam stood very close to Hannah as she tried to maneuver around in the small space so she wouldn't be practically rubbing up against him. Next to a stack of paper plates, she spied a Styrofoam container with several different types of deli meats. Another had cheeses of all sorts, and there was a variety of breads. She made fast work of slapping a few slices of turkey on some whole wheat bread, added some lettuce and a squeeze of whole-grain mustard. There were pasta salads, potato salads, and bean salads. She took a scoop of each before backing out of the cramped quarters.

"What would you like to drink?" Liam asked, stooping to peer inside a small refrigerator. "We've got soda, beer, and somewhere in here we should have bottled water." He pulled out a few cans of soda, then grabbed two bottles of water. "Water work for you?"

Hannah had just taken her first bite when Liam spoke to her. She nodded and held out her hand. Chewing and swallowing her food faster than normal, she felt a chunk of lettuce go down the wrong pipe. She started coughing and gasping, trying to force the lodged piece of lettuce either up or out. Liam dropped his sandwich onto his seat, lowered himself, and came up behind her, wrapping his arms around her sternum. Before she could understand what he was doing, the lettuce flew out of her mouth, landing smack dab in the middle of Pierce's perfectly pressed white shirt the moment he entered the cabin.

The three were quiet for a few seconds, looking from one to the other, then all three began to laugh so hard they had tears in their eyes. Hannah was embarrassed, but not so badly that she couldn't laugh at herself. When they calmed down enough to talk, Hannah was the first to speak. She opened the bottle of water, took a sip, then said, "I do believe you just saved my life, Mr. McConnell."

"I think I am going to have to agree with you this time," he said.

"What is that freaky thing that happens to the person who saves the life of another?" Pierce asked while dabbing at his shirt with a wet napkin. "I heard it somewhere as a kid; if you save someone's life, then they owe you a lifelong debt. The person who does the saving has to take responsibility for that person's life. Supposed to do anything to help you whenever you're in need, something like that."

Hannah almost choked again. "I think some kid made that up. Really, who would do something like that in this day and age?"

"Save a life or take the debt?" Liam asked.

Hannah had the grace to blush. "Thank you for saving my life, though in all honesty, I think the lettuce was about to leave on its own, but one can't say for sure. So thank you again, Liam." She liked the sound of his name on her lips. "Your debt for chivalry is paid in full."

"Hey, now wait a minute, don't I even get the chance to ask for what kind of . . . payoff I'd like?" He grinned as he scooped the sandwich from his seat.

About the time Hannah was ready to answer, Pierce pulled in the hydraulic steps and closed the aircraft's door. "You two better be buckled in and ready to roll. It's time to get this bird in the sky." He lowered himself into the cockpit. "And I mean it, too. Remember, as the pilot, I am in charge, and you *will* obey my orders."

Chapter 6

"I hope he's not threatening us," Hannah said, adjusting her seat belt.

"Nah, he just loves to fly, says the skies are his mistress. He reminds me I'm not a pilot as often as humanly possible."

They were taxiing down the runway. Liam lowered his head to his chest, mumbled something under his breath, then looked across the small aisle. "I hate takeoffs. I'd never be able to fly my own plane even if I wanted to, which I don't. That's what Pierce is for."

"So he works exclusively for you?" Hannah asked.

"Meaning is he at my beck and call twenty-four/ seven? No, not at all. He flies for Flex Jet. Several companies purchase an aircraft together and share the cost of owning it. Makes it easier for those who can't afford to have a multimillion-dollar aircraft just sitting there. So, when he's not on vacation, Pierce has to be available for them. He's staying at my house while I'm out here and will return for me when I'm ready to go home. I guess you could say we're both on vacation. Mine just happens to be a working vacation."

Hannah raised her brow in question. "Did Max Jorgenson call you around the first of the month?"

"Yes, and trust me, I am going to make him pay. Bigtime." He managed to smooth out the sandwich he had dropped on his seat when he'd helped Hannah as she was choking. He took a bite, chewing and grinning at the same time. A piece of bread clung to his lower lip, and Hannah found herself wanting to reach across the small space between them to brush it away. She had to mentally command herself to refrain from doing so. Though she wondered how he would react if she did. The thought made her smile.

"What's so funny?" he asked. He wiped the crumb from his lip.

If only he knew, she thought. "Max sent for me then, too. I wonder why the two-week wait?" Suddenly Hannah wasn't so sure Max actually had a hacker. That's what he'd said, wasn't it? And given Liam's reputation, surely he wouldn't have called him all the way to Colorado just to . . . *fix the two of us up?*

No, no, no! I'm being ridiculous. We're here to work, then return to our lives and enjoy the rest of the holiday season. Max would not go to such great lengths. She mentally removed the images of her and Liam together from her mind.

"You're not eating?"

She looked at the sandwich sitting on the napkin covering her lap. "I guess almost choking to death has taken away my appetite."

"At least have some of the potato salad; it's really good," Liam insisted as he scooped a bite between his lips.

She found her plate and fork and proceeded to eat every bite. "What can I say? I guess I was hungry, choking or not."

Pierce announced they'd reached their flying altitude, and Liam seemed more relaxed. His large frame appeared to sink into the plush seat. Hannah didn't know what to make of her reaction and scrutiny of this man. This wasn't her normal reaction at all.

"So Max sent for you, too. I understand he's experiencing a bit of in-house snooping," Liam explained. "Both electronically and the old-fashioned way. Files— the paper kind—have gone missing, some cash. I hope between the two of us, we can find the culprit. Not a good time for a thief, Christmas and all."

Hannah nodded. "That's when they crawl out of the cracks. At least in my experience." She paused. "Do you know me?" she couldn't help but ask. Hannah always believed in cutting through the flesh and going straight for the bone.

"I know *of* you. You've got quite a reputation."

"Thank you. I could say the same for you, but I'm sure you already know that," she added with a smirk.

"I've worked all over the world. It's only logical that one's success in this field is acknowledged," Liam said without a trace of arrogance.

That's true, Hannah thought.

"Do you find it odd that we both have law degrees, yet we're doing . . . undercover work?" Hannah asked. They did have a few things in common, she admitted to herself. Was this really the reason Max had sent for them? A holiday romance? No, Max wouldn't take advantage of that. Or would he? She had to admit, she didn't know him well enough to make the assumption.

Liam chuckled and ran a hand over his stubbled chin. "No, not at all. I studied criminal justice first, then got my law degree. I wasn't sure where I wanted to go, then the electronic field exploded, and it turned out that I was pretty good at it. Did a couple of years working with the FBI's Cyber Crime Unit, then decided I'd rather work alone and, as they say, the rest is history."

"Impressive," Hannah replied.

"Your résumé isn't too shabby, either," he observed.

My résumé? Has he actually checked into my background?

Hannah didn't respond.

"You've got a very good reputation, Ms. Ray. Both you and your firm. Surely you know your name is recognizable? I'm impressed," he added.

"Thank you. Yes, we're pretty well-known, at least in Florida. We don't do too much out of state, or out of the country, for that matter. I like to stay close to home."

"That's one of the reasons I decided to leave the Cyber Crime Unit. Too much travel."

"I wouldn't think there would be a need to travel as much since most of the work is electronic, via the World Wide Web."

Liam cleared his throat. "Let's just say certain clients want you on their turf. The days when I had to take such clients are gone," Liam added.

"Then why are you traveling now? Did Max threaten

you or something?" Hannah asked, though she was grinning when she asked the question.

He laughed, too. Hannah found she liked the sound, deep and throaty. *Darn, this needs to stop. Now.* She was not on her way to a ski resort to find a date, she reminded herself. She was supposed to catch a thief.

"You know Max. He didn't actually threaten me. He simply said he needed me, and here I am. We go back a long way. I'd do just about anything for him, and he knows it."

"I've only met him once, through his wife, Grace. She protected a client of mine, and sadly, that same client is in need of her services again. Whether or not she will use them is another matter entirely. Unfortunately, there isn't much one can do in cases like that. I only hope she comes to her senses and makes a decision to end her very bad marriage to an abusive jerk. Her husband is turning out to be a very dangerous man." Hannah stopped. What was she doing? Client discretion was a priority. She knew better, but in her own defense, she hadn't named any names.

"Grace is a good egg, no doubt about it. I really admire her. Plus, they've got that cute little girl now. Max adores being a husband and father; I'm so happy he's finally found his bliss."

"I suppose so," she commented lamely.

Liam reached for her paper plate, and his, then tossed them in a small plastic bag he'd removed from the pocket of the seat in front of him.

"Thanks."

"We're coming down; I can feel it. So I take it you haven't found your bliss?" Liam asked, as though he were asking her what her favorite flavor of ice cream was. Or was she just reading more into his comments and questions because she'd assumed Max had plans for the pair other than catching a thief? Most likely the latter.

Hannah peered out her window. The snow-covered mountains were breathtaking. Tall pines of all shapes and sizes looked like miniature Christmas trees placed strategically down the side of the mountain. "It's beautiful out there. Minus the cold," she said, hoping to avoid answering his question.

"Certainly different from what we're used to," he responded. "Though Florida has a beauty all its own. Especially Sanibel Island. I love it when I get to spend time there."

She smiled. "Sanibel is awesome; I love it there, too. I almost purchased a condo there, but since my offices are in Naples, I decided it would be best to stay closer to home. I love Naples, too, but it's growing too fast for my tastes."

"You realize we're practically neighbors?" Liam said. His blue eyes twinkled like sapphires.

Heat crept up her neck, settling on her face. She turned away so he couldn't see her. She was freaking blushing! Thirty-three, about to turn thirty-four, on Christmas Eve no less, something she made sure no one knew, and here she was blushing like a high-school girl with her first crush.

"Did I say something to offend you?" Liam asked sincerely.

Taking a deep breath, and hoping her flush wasn't as bad as it felt, she answered, "No, not at all. I was just . . . calculating the distance."

"By land or water?" he asked teasingly.

"Land, actually."

"It's roughly forty miles by land and around twenty-five through the Gulf."

She laughed. "Good to know."

Pierce chose that moment to come over the intercom system. "Folks, it's time to fold up your tray tables and make sure you're buckled in 'cause we're about to touch down. And Liam, I mean it. Wear the damned seat belt."

Hannah's eyes traveled to Liam's waist. "You're not buckled in! Shame on you."

"In all the excitement, I forgot."

"Right," Hannah kidded. "Seems like Pierce knows your habits quite well."

He nodded in the affirmative. "I'm hoping to get to know yours a lot better, too."

Hannah didn't know what to say, so she said nothing. Five minutes later, they were on the ground. Thank goodness, she thought, because if she'd had to come up with an answer, she wasn't sure what she would've said.

Chapter 7

Hannah said good-bye to Pierce and thanked him for saving her from a long drive. "I can't imagine why Max didn't have me fly directly to Telluride, so thanks again." She shook his hand and made her way inside the small airport. Actually, she was very suspicious of the entire setup, but she'd give Max the benefit of the doubt for now.

Liam stayed behind, apparently taking care of any last-minute plans he and Pierce had. She'd overheard them talking about Pierce's planned fishing trip, and it brought tears to her eyes. Even though her father had been a business tycoon, he never lost his love of fishing. Hannah had accompanied him on many trips, and she, too, enjoyed the sport, though she refused to keep her catch, always tossing the poor creatures back into the water. Her father respected this, and he, too, would toss whatever he caught back into its home waters. She did know he didn't practice this when it was just he and his buddies. And that was okay with her. She wasn't that unreasonable when it came to nature. She knew the fish she enjoyed so much at The Captain's Table, her favorite waterfront restaurant in Naples, didn't magically appear out of a manufacturer's deep freeze.

"Ms. Ray?" a young woman behind the counter asked.

"Yes?"

"Mr. Jorgenson has a car waiting for you and Mr. Mc-Connell. He said to tell you he was sorry he couldn't be here personally to drive you to Maximum Glide but gave directions to where each of you is staying."

Hannah saw the green-and-white plastic name tag on the woman's beige blouse. "Thank you, Mandy. I'm sure we can manage without him."

The woman looked to be in her early twenties. Black hair cut in a sleek bob, creamy skin untouched by the sun or time, she smiled, revealing a mouthful of silver braces. "He said you could, and I'm supposed to give you this." She handed Hannah a large gift box. Wrapped in shiny silver-and-gold paper with three giant bows—a red, a green, and a gold one stacked atop one another. Good grief! Was she supposed to bring a gift? She'd been such a Scrooge when it came to Christmas, she had to admit she was not up on all the latest holiday etiquette. She took the package from Mandy. "Thank you," was all she could manage to say. The box was extremely heavy, and Hannah wondered what was inside.

"Mr. Jorgenson told me that you were not to open the box until you were settled in your condo. He was very adamant about that. He even told me I'd get in all sorts of trouble if I didn't insist on emphasizing the importance of this. I hope it's okay with you?"

Poor Mandy. The young woman looked as though she was about to cry. "I promise." Hannah placed her hand in the air, with her thumb and pinkie down so that her remaining three fingers were in the correct position as she proceeded to recite the Girl Scout Law. " '*I will do my best to be* honest and fair, friendly and helpful, considerate and caring, courageous and strong, and responsible for what I say and do, *and to* respect myself and others, respect authority, use resources wisely, make the world a better place and, be a sister to every Girl Scout,' and I promise not to shake or peep in Max's box."

Mandy shrieked, "Oh my gosh! How did you know?"

Hannah nodded at the picture on the countertop. Mandy was a Girl Scout leader.

Mandy removed a tissue from the box on her desk. "I forget that's here sometimes. How cool is this?"

"Then you trust I won't open the box?" Hannah asked with a grin.

"Absolutely. From one Scout to another, I trust you wholeheartedly."

A clapping sound from the airport entrance caused both Hannah and Mandy to turn around.

"Very well said, Ms. Ray. You never mentioned you were a Girl Scout," Liam said as he strolled toward them.

"Well, it isn't exactly something that comes up in everyday conversation. Mandy has been given strict orders from Max to give me this"—she nodded at the shiny wrapped present on top of the counter—"and if I open it before I'm settled in at the condo, then not only am I in deep trouble, but she could be as well. When I saw this picture"—she indicated the silver-framed photo—"I knew that one Scout would trust another, especially if I recited the Girl Scout Law."

"I like that. A true Girl Scout."

"Mr. McConnell?" Mandy asked inquiringly.

"That would be me," he said.

"This one is for you." She reached beneath the counter and pulled out another box, only this one was larger. "Mr. Jorgenson asked that I give this to you. Same deal. You can't open it until you are all settled in at the cabin. You've got the hottest address at Maximum Glide; you know that, right? Are you two famous or something? Mr. Jorgenson has rolled out the red carpet for both of you," Mandy said, then continued, "Not that you have to be famous or anything to have the red-carpet treatment. We get a lot of famous people here. Tom Cruise, for one. But we all recognized him."

"Ah, I hate to disappoint you, but we're here to work for Mr. Jorgenson. So, no, we are not famous in the sense that you think," Liam answered for both of them.

"I'm sorry. I didn't mean to be rude, I'm just a bit on the nosy side. At least that's what everyone tells me."

Hannah spoke up. "Nosy is not a bad thing. If you ever get tired of freezing and want a change of scenery, look me up." She reached inside her purse and gave Mandy one of her business cards.

"Oh, cool! You're a private eye! And in Florida. Wait until I tell Jason, my boyfriend. He will truly be impressed. He's always after me for being so nosy. Are you for real? About looking you up and all?" Mandy asked, her eyes as wide as the moon.

"Sure, we can always use an extra set of eyes. Of course, there is training and certification required, but in my business, nosiness is considered an added bonus."

Hannah and Liam laughed together. "Yes, it is in mine, too."

"Don't tell me, you're a private eye, too," Mandy said in such an excited tone, Hannah thought the young woman was about to lose her voice entirely.

"Sort of. Now, if we could get that car Max promised, I am ready to call it a day. What with the time difference and all, I think it's nearing my bedtime." Liam winked at Hannah as he said this.

"Yes, mine, too," she added, then felt like kicking herself. Did he think she was implying something more than sleep? Surely not. He was an adult, the same as she. He acted like one, and she was acting like Mandy, a young woman starstruck by anything out of the ordinary.

"I'm sorry. I talk too much, too. Jason tells me that all the time."

Hannah silently agreed with the mysterious Jason, but she'd keep that to herself. Mandy was just young and excited.

"Here are the keys. Mr. McConnell is supposed to drive; again, this is from Mr. Jorgenson, not me," Mandy added. "I have to follow the rules."

Mandy came from behind the counter with a small bellman's rack. She placed their packages from Max on it, then Liam took his and Hannah's suitcases and placed them beside the packages. He reached for his wallet and took out a hundred-dollar bill. He placed it in Mandy's hand. "Take Jason out to dinner on me," he said, leaving the girl speechless.

"But . . . I'm not," Mandy said, then stopped. "Okay, I

will do that. Tonight. Thank you so much, Mr. McConnell. And Ms. Ray. I'm going to tell Jason what you said about nosy being a good thing, too. Now, follow me," she said, and proceeded to pull the cart through a set of automatic doors. A blast of air sent shivers through Hannah. She tightened the belt on her coat and stuffed her hands in her coat pockets before stepping out into the blistering cold. It was much colder in Telluride than it had been in Denver.

"Aren't you cold?" Hannah asked as she followed behind Mandy and Liam.

"Freezing," he shouted.

The wind was picking up, making it hard to hear and be heard. Hannah wanted sunshine and hot sand between her toes right now. She did not like being cold. Not one little bit.

Mandy led them to a bright yellow Hummer with the engine running. "This is for you to use as long as you're here," she said.

Did Mandy think they were a couple? Surely not! Had Max implied that when he'd arranged for only one vehicle?

Liam opened the passenger door. "Go on, get inside. You're freezing." For once, Hannah agreed and let him take control of loading their luggage and those mystery packages.

A minute later, he was in the driver's seat. Only she saw that he now wore the denim jacket he'd been carrying. He made a few adjustments to the seat and the mirrors, then put the vehicle into DRIVE.

"Stop!" Hannah shouted, then lowered her voice to a normal volume. "Sorry. Your seat belt. You forgot to fasten your seat belt."

He looked down. "Habit. I hate the things." He put the Hummer in PARK, then fastened his seat belt.

"Yes, but they're a lifesaver."

"You're right. Now let's get this clunker on the road," Liam said, turning to her. He gave her the sexiest smile, and her heart flip-flopped.

She was in deep trouble for sure.

"So it says here," he glanced at the sheet of paper he'd found on the dash, "that I'm to drop you off first at Forest Hills. That's the name of the condos where you'll be staying," he explained.

She wanted to say "duh" but kept it to herself. She'd already acted like a jerk more times than she cared to remember. As soon as she was settled in, she was going to call Camden and tell her about this . . . setup, if that's what it was. She was becoming more suspicious by the minute.

Liam was a good driver, even on the slick and winding road that led to Maximum Glide. There were piles of snow on both sides of the road, and Hannah was reminded of Florida and how easy it was to jump in her car and drive anywhere without worrying about icy roads and bad weather. Yes, they had hurricanes, and yes, it rained a lot in the summer months, but rarely was she in a situation where she couldn't just jump in her little red Thunderbird and go. Now, Liam was driving very slowly, never taking his eyes off the road. She didn't want to distract him, so she glanced out the window at the scenery.

The small town was decorated with strings of bright, colorful lights. Pines of all kinds were draped with giant red bows. Even the traffic lights were decorated. Giant plastic Santas in sleighs with reindeer appeared as though they were about to take flight from the rooftop of a restaurant named Snow Bunnies. Hannah couldn't help but grin as she saw yet another business decorated in shiny red and green lights that blinked "Merry Christmas!" Telluride was definitely caught up in the spirit of the season.

"Well, what do you know? Max's directions are right on the money. Looks like we've arrived at your destination, Ms. Ray."

Forest Hills.

"I'm to see you to the front desk and nothing more, as per Max's instructions," Liam said as he pulled the yellow Hummer up to the guest-entrance parking area. "No questions asked."

Hannah opened the passenger door. "And I suppose this is as per Max's instructions, too?"

"You got it," Liam replied.

Chapter 8

Liam found the turnoff to Gracie's Way without any trouble. The directions were quite clear, but frankly, he wasn't so sure he wanted to be this high on the mountain, even if this cabin was Maximum Glide's top vacation rental.

The inside lights were on just as Max said they would be, plus the entire outside of the cabin had been decorated with thousands of colorful lights. Giant pine wreaths with red ribbons tied around them were in every window.

Liam hit the garage control Max had left in the car and pulled the Hummer inside. He shut off the engine, then clicked the key fob to open the Hummer's hatch. He grabbed his luggage and the ridiculously large package and entered the cabin through the door leading to the kitchen.

He was pretty impressed when he stepped inside. The kitchen was enormous, with a giant range, two ovens, and more counter space than anyone could ever use. Liam set about exploring his new temporary digs. A Sub-Zero refrigerator was stocked with enough food for an army. Liam took out a can of Coke and guzzled it as he scoped out the kitchen. A table and chairs made of real logs seated twelve. Red and green rugs were scattered over the honey-colored wood floors. A great room off the kitchen boasted a giant fireplace across an entire wall. A fire had been started, and the smell of pine and something sweet filled the giant room. "Max doesn't do anything by halves," he said to himself as he wandered through the rooms. He followed the staircase that led upstairs to two bedrooms plus a loft. He located the master suite at the end of the hall.

Centered in the room was a giant king-size bed made of the same honey-colored logs as the walls. The bathroom had a huge, glassed-in shower. A giant Jacuzzi tub stood smack dab in the center of the bathroom. "Good old Max," he said. Heated towels and plush bath sheets were strategically placed, and pleasantly scented soaps were on the long, dark green marble countertop. Two mirrors, their frames made out of branches, made him laugh out loud. "Talk about bringing the outdoors inside. Leave it to Max. He's really into this."

Satisfied that he'd be living more than comfortably for the next couple of weeks, Liam went to the kitchen to retrieve his luggage. He was about to take advantage of that Jacuzzi.

A bellman escorted Hannah to her condo. He insisted, telling her she was listed as a top-priority client by the owner, and duty required that he obey his instructions.

More Max, she wanted to say, but didn't want to get the guy into any unnecessary trouble. He unlocked the door for her, then stepped aside, allowing her to enter first.

When she saw the view, it almost took her breath away. "Oh, wow," she said. "This is glorious."

"It's pure heaven, isn't it?" the bellman concurred.

For a few seconds, she'd forgotten she wasn't by herself in the room. "It is," she said, then handed him a twenty-dollar bill. She hoped that was enough. Her social skills were a bit rusty.

"Thank you, ma'am. If there is anything you need, my name is William. Here is my number." He handed her a card. What was this? Her personal escort/bellman?

"Thanks, but I think I have everything I need, at least for now."

"Shall I draw a bath for you before dinner?" he asked.

Hannah felt like an eighteenth-century heroine in a romance novel. What the heck. "I would like that very much, thank you, William." She'd play along with this. It wasn't like she had a man—or anyone else, for that matter—to draw her a bath at home. Well, come to think of it, she took showers at home, so there really wasn't any need.

"Indeed, ma'am. How shall I select the temperature?" He stood ramrod stiff next to the wall-to-wall windows that allowed a full view of the majestic mountainside. It truly was breathtaking. Of course, she could say this now because it was warm inside, and a fire was burning in the real-wood fireplace. The scent of something sweet lingered in the air. This was not a bad scene for snow and cold. As long as she stayed inside, she'd be fine. All she had to do was find Max's thief, aka hacker, then she could go home. For now, she'd make the best of it.

"Very hot, William," she said. "I'll just take a look around while you tend to my bath." She laughed. If Camden heard her now, she'd crack up. If her employees heard her now, they would bust a gut.

"Yes, ma'am," he said before heading down a long hallway to what she assumed was the bathroom.

The entire wall of the living area was glass, which was the big wow factor. Across from the window was a floor-to-ceiling rock fireplace. Plush sofas in soft beiges faced one another. Several tables were scattered throughout with books and magazines. Brightly colored pillows were placed invitingly throughout the area, just begging for one to curl up with a good book or simply enjoy the view of the mountains. She found the kitchen to be just as perfect, with a small dining-room table for six, stainless-steel appliances, and a black-bear theme throughout: bear canisters, salt-and-pepper shakers, a paper-towel holder, plus place mats and matching curtains. Hannah liked the idea of the bears as long as they were just a decoration. Anything more . . . well, she wasn't sure how she'd react if she were to encounter a real live bear.

The condo, at least as much as she'd seen so far, was eminently, completely suitable for her. As soon as William left, she planned to soak in the tub and call Camden. She wanted to check on Leanne, and to tell her about Liam McConnell.

William chose that moment to appear. "If you need anything else, please call the number on the card and I will see to your every need."

"Thanks, William, I'm good for now," Hannah said, hoping he was finished. She wanted that bath and a strong cup of coffee. She wondered if she asked William for a cup of coffee, exactly how many seconds it would be before a steaming mug was in her hand. That was something she didn't care to find out at the moment. Or anytime soon, for that matter. No use getting spoiled rotten when she would be leaving sooner rather than later.

"Then I'll be waiting for you at eight o'clock promptly."

She must have had a strange look come over her face because William looked quite shocked at whatever her expression was. "Mr. Jorgenson has arranged for you to join him for dinner tonight at Eagles Nest."

And here we go again, she thought. *More Max.* "I wasn't told, but if it's on the agenda, then I'll be ready at eight." And not a moment sooner, she wanted to add. It was just after five. That gave her three hours to relax in the tub, talk to Camden, and prepare a list of questions for Mr. Max Jorgenson. And make herself presentable, just in case Liam was invited to this dinner, too. Something told her that he would most certainly be there as well.

"Then I'll see you at eight o'clock," William said before nodding and quietly leaving the room.

She wanted to run behind him and lock the door, not because she felt unsafe but because she feared he would return and offer some other service.

"This is the life," she said out loud. "No, it's not. I have the perfect life in Naples; close to perfect, anyway. I come and go as I please, I have a very successful business, I love my work, I love my friends. And if I wanted to live like this, I could. I certainly have much more than enough to support this sort of lifestyle.

"Yes, Hannah, you are talking to yourself. Now go make the coffee."

She rummaged through the cupboards, finding them fully stocked. "Did I expect anything less?" she asked herself as she found a bag of Elevation Coffee. "Never heard of it," she said, then read the label: *Join the mile-high club.*

"Okay, let's see if this merits joining the mile-high club."

Hannah made fast work of preparing the coffee. While she waited for it to brew, she found her cell phone in her bag and turned it on. She had a few voice mails, but nothing urgent. She punched in Camden's cell-phone number. Her friend answered on the first ring.

"I was starting to worry. You said you'd call when you landed in Denver and, according to my schedule, you're about three hours and four minutes behind. What gives?"

Camden was the most organized person on the planet. Hannah loved those skills in their professional relationship, but as her friend, she wasn't so sure she cared for them. But she had promised to call. She'd been sidetracked. Big-time.

"I'm in a condo in Telluride. I have a manservant, and Liam McConnell flew me here in his private jet," Hannah explained as she made her way back to the kitchen. She found a dark green mug with black bears on it and filled it to the brim. She took a sip. Good stuff. She might consider joining the mile-high club, at the least the one that served such good coffee.

"Slow down and start from the beginning. I thought you had a long ride ahead of you. Explain," Camden said.

For the next twenty minutes, Hannah told her about meeting Liam, and how Max seemed to have arranged everything so the two of them would be thrown together. "I'm having dinner with Max tonight at eight o'clock. William plans to escort me to dinner."

"And you're wondering if Liam McConnell received the same invitation?"

"I'm pretty sure he did. I would guess we're going to discuss whatever it is that Max brought us here for."

"Makes sense," Camden said, but she didn't sound 100 percent convinced.

"Is there something you're not telling me?" Hannah asked. "Because if you're up to no good, I will find out."

"Good grief, Hannah! What would I be up to? I have no clue what's going on, at least no more than you do. From what you've said, it sounds like you're attracted to Liam, and maybe you're trying to read more into the situation than what's really there. It has been a while since you were in a relationship."

"Coming from Miss Hot Lips herself, please!"

"For your information, and not that it's any of your business, but I just so happen to have a date tomorrow night with someone," Camden singsonged.

"Someone? That could be a bird in your case," Hannah teased. Camden truly didn't get the meaning of the word *date,* at least not in the sense that she was using it now. She used the word as it suited her needs.

"Well, it's not. Remember Art Greenfield?"

Hannah tried to recall the name. "No, I don't remember him. Should I?"

"Remember the guy who was caught stealing catalytic converters from the Lincoln dealership in Cape Coral last year?"

Hannah almost dropped her mug of coffee. "You're going out with a thief? Please tell me I heard you wrong."

"Not him. Art was his assigned counsel. He defended the guy," Camden explained.

Hannah gave a sigh of relief. "That's good news. So, how did this come about?"

"I was at the grocery store earlier, he was buying lox

or something, and we started talking. He invited me over to his family's house tomorrow evening to celebrate the first night of Hanukkah. It starts at sundown."

Camden would make sure to bone up on any and all Jewish traditions before her date, of that Hannah was certain. Which was good. Camden needed a little bit of romance in her life, too. They both did. They worked too hard and too much. And neither was getting any younger. They'd discussed having families, and both wanted children and all the traditional things that went along with raising them. Camden was also an only child.

"Good. I'm happy. I wouldn't want you spending the holiday alone."

"Oh, stop it! You don't give a hoot about holidays. Never have. Unless Liam has suddenly changed your mind," Camden retorted.

"No, he has not. And I've never said I didn't like the holidays, I just think it's silly to . . . it's okay when you're a kid."

"Sure, whatever you say, Ms. Scrooge," Camden teased.

Odd, since Hannah had referred to herself as Ms. Scrooge just a few hours ago. "Listen, I need to ask about Leanne, then I have to go. Did you see her at the hospital today? Was that brute of a husband skulking around?"

"Leanne is okay. She's still in a lot of pain, and no, that bastard was nowhere to be found. I think I've finally convinced her to take out an order of protection against him, but she's really afraid of him and his family. I feel so bad for her."

"Keep trying to convince her, Camden. Do whatever it takes. Get ugly if you have to. It just might save her life."

"I can do ugly. I'll stop by first thing in the morning to check on her."

"Thanks. Keep me posted."

"I will. And let me know how dinner goes with Liam tonight," Camden added, then said good-bye before Hannah could respond.

She poured another mug of coffee and headed for the master suite.

A giant tub was filled with steamy, scented water. An array of bath products had been placed in a basket next to the tub. "Perfect," she said before stripping down and sliding into the warm water.

"Decadent, if I do say so myself. Colorado might be cold, but right now I'm loving it," Hannah said as she succumbed to the amenities.

Chapter 9

The ride up the mountain to Eagles Nest was quite unique to the area, Hannah learned. She and William traveled in an enclosed snow coach, which he explained to her was an MPV, a multiple-passenger-vehicle type of sleigh with skis. They were pulled by a small, tractorlike contraption, and Hannah was delighted when she learned that the snow coach had heat. What she didn't know, and William had neglected to tell her, was that Eagles Nest was one of the highest fine-dining restaurants in North America, at almost twelve thousand feet. She'd never been so high on a mountain in her life and wasn't sure if she was a wee bit frightened or just a little bit excited at the thought that she *might* see Liam at dinner.

Inside, she was greeted by a young man dressed in an elegant black suit, though he wore a Stetson on his head, which kind of ruined the image for her. But she remembered what part of the country she was in and knew this was accepted as normal. She tried not to laugh.

The restaurant itself was beautifully decorated for the holiday. Several giant spruce trees were placed throughout the rooms, all decorated with bright-colored lights and western ornaments that blended perfectly with the western decor. Hand-hewn beams and what appeared to be furniture made from wine barrels gave the place a rustic ambience. Eagles Nest was inviting, to say the least. Several wood-burning fireplaces throughout made it comfortably warm, and the stone floors and exposed wood beams added to the frontier flavor. Sheepskin throws were tossed casually over the backs of sofas and chairs. Hannah found herself wanting to curl up and get comfy, but maybe another time. Tonight's dinner was all about business. She'd dressed with that and warmth in mind.

She wore her black tights and boots with a dark green wool skirt and matching sweater. Her burgundy coat, along with a matching scarf and gloves, completed her ensemble. She'd need a warmer coat if she lived here, but this would do since she only planned on running in and out of the cold; she certainly had no plans to frolic in the snow. Though she had to admit, it might be fun. It was the cold she didn't like. If only you could have snow without the cold.

The dressed-up cowboy, as she thought of him, led her to a small room that overlooked the mountain. A table for six was set, yet there was no sign of Max or anyone else. The cowboy must've seen her look of surprise. "They're outside at the wine bar. Would you care to join them?"

An outdoor wine bar? In these temperatures? Of course she wanted to join them.

"No thank you; I'll stay inside if that's all right," she said politely.

"Of course. What may I bring you to drink?" the cowboy asked.

Hannah had a brief flash of dipping beer from a trough and offering her horse the first sip but tried to erase the image from her mind as quickly as it came. Maybe she *was* suffering from a bit of altitude sickness. It wasn't like her to have such bizarre thoughts. She did have a quick wit, but this wasn't witty. This was nuts!

"Your drink, ma'am?" Cowboy repeated.

"I'll have a glass of white wine," she said, and gave him her sweetest smile. "Is that proper here?" she asked, exaggerating her Southern accent a bit.

Cowboy smiled. "It's mighty proper, ma'am. Now, if you will excuse me."

He'd gotten her joke or dig or whatever one wanted to call it.

Hannah sat down at the table, not caring if it was rude. She was tired, and hungry, and really thought this dinner might be a quick bite, business discussed, then she could call it a night. Max Jorgenson was going to get a piece of her mind. She'd no more had the thought when the man himself walked through the doors that led to the outdoor wine bar.

"Hannah, I'm sorry I wasn't here to greet you. A couple of ski bums caught me and I couldn't get away."

She stood up and offered her hand. This was a business dinner, not a social gathering. "That's perfectly fine. It gave me a few minutes to admire the view."

"Please, sit down." Max pointed to the chair she'd just vacated. "I know you're tired, and with the time difference, I apologize, but I wanted to give you the heads-up as soon as you arrived."

Max sat in the chair across from her. Apparently, it was just going to be the two of them for dinner. Her heart sunk a bit when she realized the large table must be part of this semiprivate room. He wore dark slacks, a turtleneck, and a ski jacket with his name sewn on the breast pocket. She had to remind herself he was a world-famous Olympian. Of course people would want to pull him aside and talk to him about his gold medals. Which reminded her of a promise she'd made.

"I know this isn't the right time, but is it ever the right time?" she asked but didn't wait for him to answer. "Today, the young man in the limo, Terrence. He was so kind, and sweet. He mentioned he'd lost his mother, though I do not recall if he mentioned how recently. He has a younger sister, Tasha."

"Of course I know Terrence and Tasha. He works for the limo service at the resort. Though I was unaware that his mother had passed away."

"Apparently, Tasha has high hopes for the Winter Olympics," Hannah explained. "Terrence wants to find a good coach for her. He said she was extremely talented. Though I know absolutely nothing about the sport, I am a good judge of character. If Terrence says his sister has talent, I am inclined to believe that she does."

The cowboy brought her wine and placed it on a napkin in front of her. She took a sip, then continued with her story. "He's working here in hopes . . . he didn't say this, but I believe he's hoping you'll see Tasha ski and possibly coach her. If not, is there someone you would recommend? I'll take care of the costs personally." Hannah took a deep breath, then another sip of wine.

"You remind me of Grace," Max said. "A soft heart."

"I'll take that as a compliment," Hannah replied.

"As it was meant."

"Thanks," she said. "Do you have someone in mind? I would love to be able to help those two kids, especially this time of year." She couldn't believe she had just said that.

Especially this time of year. Whatever happened to Ms. Scrooge?

Camden might be onto something with this holiday stuff. Maybe Hannah was getting a bit soft in her old age. Of course she wasn't *that* old, but still.

"I will personally invite Terrence and Tasha to the party we're having Sunday evening. I'm lighting up a couple of the trails. Ella's all excited this year. She's at that age where everything is fascinating to her."

"I can only imagine," Hannah said for lack of a better response. She knew that Ella was around three or four, and that was about it. "I really am serious, Max. If Tasha shows signs of talent, I want to . . . sponsor her, or whatever they do these days. In addition to all the stock Dad left me, I've got millions in the bank just sitting there earning a paltry bit of interest. I'd much rather see some of that money used to help Tasha's career if she's anywhere near as good as Terrence says."

"I will take care of your request, I promise. If Tasha really wants to ski, I'll train her myself. Ella's not interested yet. Patrick's stepdaughters, Amanda and Ashley, love to ski, but I don't think they're interested in a career. I need something else to do besides run this crazy resort. Speaking of that, I want to give you some of the details, but Liam is late. Seems he got stuck in the Hummer, and I had to send Patrick to pick him up. That's why I'm running behind. I should have told you. If you want to call it a night, I'll certainly understand. I know Liam would, too."

"No," she practically shouted. She lowered her voice. She didn't want Max to see how excited she'd gotten at the mention of Liam's name. "This is important. We need to get started as soon as possible. I'm not here to play," she added.

"I take it you didn't open the box Mandy gave you?"

The box! She'd forgotten all about it when she'd arrived at the condo. After having her coffee and talking to Camden, she'd taken a long bath, then had to rush to make sure she was ready promptly at eight o'clock. She hadn't wanted to keep William waiting outside her door.

"No. I'm sorry I didn't get around to it. I was a bit rushed," she explained.

"No worries. You can open it later."

The cowboy returned to the table just in time to greet Liam and another man. When she saw him, her entire being filled with happiness. "Ms. Ray, Max, sorry I'm late. I couldn't get that damned Hummer to move."

"Patrick is the resident Hummer expert. I'm sure he can take care of whatever it needs," Max said.

"Now that we're here, let me introduce Patrick to you, Hannah."

She stood and held out her hand. "Nice to meet you."

"Likewise," he said, then they all sat down. Liam sat next to her, while Max and Patrick sat across from them. Perfect arrangement, she thought excitedly.

"Patrick is the one who discovered the money missing from The Snow Zone. That's our biggest ski shop. Stephanie, his wife, is the manager, but since they've had little Shannon, she hasn't wanted to work too much, and I can't say that I blame her. Candy Lee, her assistant, has taken over Stephanie's position until she goes back to college after the New Year. She's worked for me since she was in high school. I trust her implicitly, so we can rule her out."

Liam wore a dark gray sweater over a chambray shirt. She saw that he still wore the jeans he'd had on earlier, but he'd added socks and boots. And she'd seen him remove a heavy-duty black parka when he came inside. He wasn't really dressed for this kind of weather, either. She liked that about him, too. He wasn't a wuss. She'd dated a few of those and had vowed never to do so again.

"And where do I come in? You said you're being hacked. How do you know this, and what's being messed with?" Liam asked.

"All of the bank accounts associated with The Snow Zone. Every other day there is a wireless transfer. And apparently, the bank believes it to be legitimate. I've contacted the fraud unit, so they're aware of what I suspect, but at this point they're telling me there isn't anything they can do since the transfers appear legit," Patrick explained. "Max, Grace, Stephanie, and I are the only ones with access to the bank accounts. And I know for a fact that we're not ripping Max off."

Did Hannah detect a trace of defensiveness in Patrick's attitude, or was he simply at a complete loss, just as Max appeared to be? She watched him as Liam continued with his questions.

"Of course you're not, don't even go there," Max said, shaking his head.

"When did the first transfer take place?" Liam asked. He pulled out the iPad he'd tucked inside the back of his jeans. His fingers moved across the touch screen so fast, Hannah could see why he was so skilled. He didn't waste a second. "And how much was taken?"

"Exactly one month ago today," Patrick said.

"And it was twenty-five thousand dollars," Max said.

"Whew! That's a pretty hefty sum," Liam said, as his finger continued to fly across the touch screen.

"What about new employees? Do you perform background checks? Anyone you've hired who might have a bit of computer knowledge they forgot to mention on their job application?" Hannah asked. Though she'd left her laptop in the condo, she did have a small pad and pen in her purse. She removed it and started taking notes. When she saw Liam smile, she said, "I'm a pen-and-paper kind of girl." As soon as she said it, she wished she could take it back. She wasn't a girl at all. She was a grown woman and didn't want to come off as some sappy, lovestruck kid. But he didn't know that, so she felt she was safe for now.

Lovestruck?

She would definitely have to think about that word, but not now. Later. When she had time to truly contemplate what was going on in her head. It had to be altitude-related, didn't it?

"We hire dozens of people. Almost daily. Most of them are seasonal, here to work and ski for free. It's the skiers' way. They come from all over the world. We do a basic background check, drug testing, but that's it. People come and go so often, I sometimes wonder why I even bother," Patrick said.

"Because you're the general manager and it's part of your job. And you're damned good at it, so don't start blaming yourself," Max insisted. "This could happen to any business, especially one the size of this one."

"How much do you take in daily? Just at The Snow Zone," Hannah asked.

Patrick looked at Max. "You really want me to give her the figures?"

"Of course I do. We can trust Hannah and Liam, and it's not like I'm cheating the IRS, for crying out loud!" Max seemed a bit ticked that Patrick wouldn't want to give them the financial figures.

Patrick removed a pen from his pocket, scribbled something on his cocktail napkin, then slid it across the table for both Hannah and Liam to see.

"Okay, so we are talking big, big bucks. Whoever is doing this knows that, compared to this"—Hannah tapped her index finger on the cocktail napkin—"twenty-five thousand dollars is pocket change. To the resort. To them, most likely, it's a small fortune."

"So what can we do to catch whoever is doing this?" Max asked.

Liam spoke first. "I'll need to get into your system, which should be pretty simple since we're not talking about an entire floor of servers or anything like it. It shouldn't be hard to track. I'll want to set up in The Snow

Zone, if possible, since that's where the shop's main computer is located. If not, I can access it by other means."

"I can work as extra holiday help," Hannah said. "The sad part is, I know absolutely nothing about ski equipment, or skiing, for that matter."

"We could send you in as a live model," Liam suggested. "You've certainly got the looks and build for it. You could wear a new ski suit every day, entice the customers to purchase whatever you're wearing."

Hannah was glad the lighting in the room was dim because she could feel the heat rising to her face. A model? And he thought she had the looks *and* the body for such a job? She didn't know whether to laugh or call him a sexist for eyeing her up. Though she'd certainly had her eyes on him.

"Hannah," Max asked, "would you be willing to do that? I agree with Liam. It's actually a fantastic marketing idea. If sales increase, I'll make sure to do this again. So, what do you say?"

"That's fine, but I have one favor to ask." She knew she was about to come off as silly, but what the hell, she was about to become a model, and she was a blonde. "If anyone, and I mean anyone, lays a hand on me, I want your permission to knock the shit out of him."

All three men looked at her as though she'd lost her mind, then they all started laughing. Softly at first, then it got a bit louder, and a bit louder still. So loud, in fact, that Cowboy returned to the table with another man whom Hannah guessed to be the manager.

"I take it that means yes," Hannah said, then stood up, letting them know she was truly ready to leave.

They all nodded and watched her as she stormed out of the room.

Liam was the first to get up and follow her. "Hannah," he called out when he saw her enter the ladies' room. "Wait."

She stood at the sink and splashed her face with cold water. The door creaked open slowly. She didn't look to see who it was because she was too pissed to care. She tossed another handful of cold water on her face. What the hell had she gotten herself into? Was she supposed to prance around in some stupid ski costume and let the customers cop a feel just because they could?

"Hannah?" Liam came up behind her, and she practically jumped out of her skin.

"This is the ladies' room, you idiot! Get out!"

"Calm down, Hannah. You've mistaken the guys' reaction. Trust me, I know what I'm talking about."

She grabbed several paper towels and rubbed them against her face. "Then fill me in. I have never felt so degraded in my life! I am a professional, a freaking attorney, not some, some . . . hot-looking chick who needs perverts pawing all over her."

"And we all agree with you. You're not that kind of woman; I mean, you're hot, but not in that way." He stopped, as though trying to piece together what he really wanted to say, and it wasn't coming out right. "Look, no one meant to offend you. And I certainly didn't mean to imply anything . . . bimbo-ish." He raised his eyes to meet hers. "God knows you're anything but that, Hannah. Trust me, you're . . ." He couldn't say what he really wanted to say. Not now. Way, way too soon to be having the kind of thoughts he was having.

"I'm what? Go on, I can take it."

"Okay, but remember this is coming from me as a man, and not a professional. You are gorgeous, Hannah

Ray, you're built better than most models, and, yes, I looked, and, no, I am not sorry."

Well, she didn't have a snappy comeback for any of that, so she said what came naturally. "Thank you. I think," she said. "I'd better get back to the table. I am so hungry I could eat a bear."

"Me, too," Liam said, and opened the door for her. He stood beside the door. "Ladies first."

Chapter 10

Hannah wanted to open the box, but she was too tired. As soon as William escorted her back to the condo, all she could think about was sleep. Tomorrow. The box would keep another few hours. She was on Florida time still, and even though there was only a two-hour time difference, she felt it in seconds. She tossed her wool skirt and sweater on the floor, grabbed a pair of Miss Piggy pajamas from the luggage she'd yet to unpack, then found the closest bedroom and practically fell on top of the bed. After pulling the heavy covers over her, it was only minutes before she drifted off into a deep, heavy sleep.

The xylophone tone of her cell phone woke her. She opened her eyes and tried to familiarize herself with her surroundings. Then she remembered she was in Colorado, and why she was here. And then she remembered last night.

Her cell phone continued to ring in that annoying tone. "Okay, okay," she muttered as she threw the covers aside. Her cell phone was lying on the bathroom counter, where she'd left it last night. She slid her finger across the phone to answer the call. "Hello," she said in a dry voice.

"I take it you just woke up," Liam said in his sexy, slightly accented voice.

"You'd be right. What do you want?" she asked, none too kindly.

"Did you forget we start our new jobs today?"

Dang! She'd overslept. "Uh, no. I just overslept. Tell me what the plans are." She needed William right now. She'd bet anything he could make a mean pot of coffee. She saw his card and was tempted to pick it up and call, but since she was already on the phone, it would make no sense whatsoever to have Liam hold on while she called William over to make her coffee. Instead, she went to the kitchen and proceeded to prepare a pot for herself. As soon as she hit the BREW button, she wandered into the great room, saw that the fire was still slightly ablaze, tossed a log on top of the red embers, then plopped on the sofa to admire the view. She was still waiting for Liam to tell her the plans when she heard a knock on the door. "I'll call you back," she said, then hit the END button and tossed the phone on the chair.

Another knock. "Be right there," she said, wondering if anyone had any patience this morning. Or manners.

She yanked the door open without bothering to look through the peephole.

"Good morning to you," came Liam McConnell's cheerful voice.

She instantly became wide-awake. She instantly looked down at her Miss Piggy pajamas. "Oh shit. Come on in."

He roared with laughter. "There is nothing pretentious about you, is there?" he asked as he followed her into the kitchen.

"If there was, it's gone now," she muttered as she filled two mugs with coffee. "Sit. And don't speak until I finish my coffee."

He did as instructed, but he didn't let her command distract him from gazing at her. His blue eyes were the color of the sky at night, his smile as white and clear as a perfect pearl. Hannah quickly finished her coffee and got up to pour herself a second cup. "You want more?" she asked.

"No, I'm fine. I had a pot of coffee at the restaurant this morning."

"What time is it, anyway?" she asked.

"Ten after twelve," he said, looking at his watch.

"What? I never sleep this late!" Embarrassed, Hannah tried to come up with a possible reason why she'd slept so long. It had to be the altitude. "Do I look sick to you?" she asked him.

"No. Do you feel bad?"

Did she? She wasn't sure. "I don't know."

"Why don't you take a hot shower? I'll whip up something to eat and then we can get down to business."

She nodded. "Sure, I'll be just a few minutes." She warmed her coffee and took it with her. She glanced at the clock on the opposite side of the table. Unless it was wrong . . . no, Liam had said it was after twelve. She ran back into the great room to get her cell phone. She knew the time automatically changed when she entered a different time zone. She found it lying in the chair she'd vacated earlier. She looked at the clear white numbers. It was ten after seven. Seven in the morning.

"Liam McConnell, you ass!" she shouted before heading back to her room. She was going to give him a piece of her mind as soon as she showered and dressed. *Noon, my ass,* she thought as she turned on the water and took a scalding-hot shower.

Ten minutes later, she returned to the kitchen, where Liam had made himself at home. Not that she cared. The smell of frying bacon and toast made her realize just how hungry she was. She'd ordered a bowl of soup for dinner last night, and it hadn't been enough, but at the time she hadn't wanted to linger at Eagles Nest any longer than she had to. She'd been too tired to think straight. Now, she was clearheaded and starving.

"So you can cook, too," she said as she poured herself a third cup of coffee.

"I can do many things," he assured her, keeping his back to her.

"And I can only imagine what they are," she tossed back.

He filled a plate with a dollop of scrambled eggs and two slices of thick bacon and gave it to her.

"Toast and jam are on the table. And you don't have to imagine anything if you'd rather not."

"Thanks, but imagination is good. Seriously, though, you didn't have to do this. But then again, you didn't have to call me and wake me up this early. So maybe you did have to do this. If I remember correctly, The Snow Zone doesn't open until nine."

"And you were going to sleep until what, eight thirty?"

"You're here, I'm awake, it doesn't matter now. So"—she forked up a bit of egg—"how are we going to work this today?"

"Max wanted you to wear the ski suit that's in the box

you probably still haven't opened. Said it's the spiffiest—his words not mine—ski suit on the market. You'll be representing the manufacturer. Max will give you a new suit each day, and you'll just walk around. Kind of like the casino girls do out in Vegas."

He laughed and held up his hand. "I'm teasing. Seriously, I would ask Candy Lee. Max said she knows what the customers want, so let's wait until we're there before we get all bent out of shape."

"I'm not 'all bent out of shape,' Liam, trust me. I just don't like being lied to, that's all."

"I'm sorry. I don't require much sleep. I assume the rest of the world doesn't either. I promise not to wake you again."

Hannah nodded and chewed her food. "Apology accepted. What about you? Are you going to be able to work at The Snow Zone or not?"

"Max wants me to set up in his office. I can connect from there. This isn't a complicated system, so there shouldn't be a problem."

As ticked as she was that he'd awakened her and seen her at her worst, she felt a tiny bit sad at the thought that they weren't going to be working together. In the same building. Lovestruck, isn't that what she'd thought last night before she'd responded to the guys' reaction to her when she'd asked if it was okay if she kicked butt if she were touched in a way she wasn't comfortable with? Yes, it was, and she was not going to go there. Not now.

"Good. I'll want to take a look at the applications for the past three months to start."

"Done. Though they're electronic. You've a computer with you?"

"Yes." She went to the bedroom and grabbed her laptop and cord, bringing both to the kitchen table. "I guess this will work as an office," she said, indicating the kitchen with a bob of her head. She booted up her laptop, then hit a few keys. "Send me the applications to this address." She turned the computer around so he could read the e-mail address. He touched the iPad screen a few times, then Hannah heard the familiar ring letting her know she had mail. She opened the files and started reading through them. Nothing stood out, nothing unusual, but she knew that finding something unusual was the exception, not the rule. It was the things that didn't stand out that were often overlooked.

"I sent you the ones I haven't looked at, just so we're not doing double the work," Liam explained as he continued to read the applicants' information.

Hannah finished her toast, rinsed her plate, and placed it in the dishwasher. "You want more coffee? I can make another pot," she said, just to be nice. He *had* made her breakfast.

"No, I'm good."

Hannah quickly cleaned up the breakfast dishes, then headed back to her room, where she'd left the box. Knowing what was inside kind of ruined the excitement for her. She and her father rarely exchanged gifts at Christmas, so the only time she really had had presents as a child was on her birthday, and since that was on Christmas Eve, they were always wrapped in Christmas wrap. She didn't know why, but as a child, it had always made her sad to have her gifts wrapped that way. It was as though her birthday was just too close to the holidays to bother with anything extra. Maybe this was behind her reason for not bothering with the holidays? Her father had tried to be both a mother and a father to her, but there were some things a child needed. Specially wrapped birthday gifts were one of those things. If she ever had children, she would make such a big deal over their birthdays that they would remember them forever as being the best days of their lives.

Crap! She was going off track again. It had to be this altitude. She was going to down about ten gallons of water. Isn't that what Pierce had told her to do? Without another thought, she removed the bows and carefully unwrapped the pretty paper.

She removed a shiny red jacket with matching ski pants from the box. "Nice." A matching hat, gloves, and scarf followed. A pair of red UGGs. "Nice again," she said out loud. How did Max know that red was her favorite color, or was it just a coincidence? No matter, she liked what she saw. She read the size, and it was also correct. Grace must've taken a good guess. Women were talented at that sort of thing. There were no tags to remove, and she wasn't sure what she should put on first, then she saw the handwritten list.

The red-hot chilis and the matching top. The red wool ski socks, the ski pants, the red-and-gray shirt, then the jacket. The handwriting looked to be that of a young girl. She'd bet this came from Candy Lee, the young college student who was managing the ski shop while Stephanie was away on an indeterminate maternity leave.

She needed to look the part, so she went into the bathroom, braided her long hair in a French braid, then proceeded to apply her makeup as though she truly were a fashion model. She had good skin, so she added a bit of tinted moisturizer. She needed to look like an outdoorsy type. She was, but in a beachy way. She applied bronzer, then a dusting of rose-tinted blush across her cheeks.

Using black liquid eyeliner, she lined both eyes, flicking the edge up to give her a bit of a cat's-eye look. Two coats of mascara and a swipe of Dr Pepper–flavored lip balm. She checked her reflection in the mirror. Not bad for thirty-three, she thought. The beginnings of crow's-feet were starting to form around her eyes. She'd have to be much more diligent with the sunscreen. She was a Floridian, and Floridians used sunscreen as if it were hand lotion. She certainly did, and so had her father, which was probably one of the reasons he had aged so well. She grabbed her purse and her ski jacket. She felt a swirl of excitement as she headed back to the kitchen. Hannah couldn't wait to see Liam's reaction when he saw her.

She found him still seated at the kitchen table. When he realized she was standing there, he looked away from his iPad.

He simply stared at her. There were no words needed. Hannah could tell he thought she was hot. Very hot.

She gave him a sexy grin, then twirled around. "So, think I'll pass as a model?"

"I'd hire you in a heartbeat," he said, then stood. "Let's get this show on the road."

Chapter 11

They rode to The Snow Zone together in the yellow Hummer. "I take it this thing isn't going to leave us stranded," she quipped as they wound over the winding road that led to the main area of Maximum Glide and The Snow Zone.

"There wasn't anything wrong with it last night. Patrick said it didn't move because I left the emergency brake on."

Hannah laughed. "That's a good thing, then."

"Well, I felt pretty stupid."

"You're not stupid, just in an unfamiliar car. I always mess something up when I'm in a rental. Give me my little red Thunderbird any day."

"You look like you'd own a red car," Liam said.

"Red's my favorite color. Isn't it odd that these ski clothes just so happen to be red? Don't you find that the least little bit strange?" She needed to know if someone had checked up on her. Maybe Max had contacted Camden, or maybe Grace had. For some silly reason, it mattered to her that whoever put this outfit together knew it would be perfect for her. Had it come from anyone else other than Max, she would have thought the coincidence a bit on the creepy side.

"Wait until you see the skiers on the slopes," Liam said as they pulled into The Snow Zone's parking lot. There was only a smattering of trucks and SUVs so early. The slopes didn't open until nine, so Hannah had a good half hour for Candy Lee to train her on what to do and what not to do. They'd agreed last night that when the shop was empty, Hannah would use the time to continue reading over the applications. Liam had sent her forty-seven, and she'd gone through three of them already. At this rate, she'd be reading them every spare minute she had. She wanted to find out who was stealing from Max and why. She did not like thieves and enjoyed catching them when she had the opportunity.

Liam parked the Hummer next to a black one. "Patrick's here." Liam pointed to the Hummer. "Max says he's the king of Hummers."

"Good to know," Hannah replied.

"Yep, it is."

"As you said, let's get this show on the road. We've got a thief to catch."

"Hannah, wait a minute," Liam said. "I know we're here as professionals, and there isn't time to . . . play around, but if we have an extra hour or so, would you ski with me? I haven't skied in years, and I can't imagine enjoying it with anyone else but you."

She hated cold weather. Hadn't she made that clear?

She *was not* cold now. The ski clothes kept her extremely warm. She did not know how to ski, but right now, she was willing to learn. "You know what, Liam McConnell? I detest cold weather and snow, but I'm so warm right now, I am going to have to take you up on your offer. Just to see if this ski stuff really does keep me warm all day." She was grinning from ear to ear when she spoke, so she was sure Liam knew that she was fine with skiing. "But you need to know: I have no clue how to ski."

"Listen, I was taught by the best. I'll show you a couple of moves. If you don't catch on, we'll have a hot toddy. Sound reasonable enough to you?"

She wanted to tell him it was the best offer she'd had in years but didn't want to come off as hard up and desperate. She was just picky, that's all.

"It sounds like a plan. Now, let's go introduce ourselves to Candy Lee."

They were greeted at the main entrance by Patrick. They still had half an hour before the shop opened to the public. "That suit looks great on you," Patrick said as soon as he saw her.

"I like it. And red is my favorite color," Hannah said. She was so excited, she just couldn't keep it out of her voice. She probably sounded like a teenager, but she was happier than she'd been in a very, *very* long time. And it had something to do with Liam, of that she was sure. Not lust. Well, yes, lust, just not full-fledged, knock-you-down, drag-you-to-bed lust. She didn't know him *that* well, and she had never been a bed hopper.

Inside the shop, they were greeted by the pleasant scent of pine mixed with cinnamon and chocolate. Christmas music was playing in the background. A giant spruce was centered in the middle of the store. Hannah walked over to the tree and touched a delicate glass ornament in the shape of a mitten. And it was red, too. She laughed. "This tree is beautiful."

"I decorated it myself. I do it every year. Or at least every year since I've worked here. You must be Hannah, the fashion model. That suit fits you like a glove. You'll have the guys crawling over you like spit on snow."

"Candy! For crying out loud, do you always have to be so gross?" Patrick asked.

Hannah and Liam laughed.

"It's okay, Candy. In my business, I've heard much worse," Hannah informed her.

"And you'll hear more today, trust me. The ski bums cuss like sailors and the snow bunnies eat it up. Disgusting, don't you think?"

Again, Hannah laughed. "I promise I won't be offended and yes, it is disgusting. Now, why don't you tell me a bit about this ski suit I have on, just in case one of the bums or bunnies asks."

"Okay, listen up. This particular jacket you're wearing is one of the latest styles. Made for a woman, girl, whatever, the cut is slim. Some girls really want to show off their figures when they're skiing or snowboarding. The jacket is lightweight; the insulation is synthetic. It has a great warmth-to-weight ratio, meaning it'll keep you nice and toasty without all the bulk. You'll appreciate this when you have to pee, too. Easy to get into and out of. The pants, I meant. They have thigh vents that help to release excess heat." Candy Lee stopped and smiled at Patrick.

He rolled his eyes. "Knock it off, Candy."

"That's what it says on the label, trust me. I have it

memorized. Basically, all you need to do is shake your booty a bit, smile, and leave all the details to me."

Hannah let out a deep sigh. "It's been a while since I've flirted, but I'll do my best. Now, is there someplace I can set up my laptop so I can do a little brain work when I'm not shaking my booty?" Hannah asked.

"In the office; I cleaned the desk for you. It was covered with empty donut boxes and *People* magazines. I can't imagine what Stephanie would say if she saw how messy her office was." Patrick narrowed his gaze at Candy Lee.

"I've been too busy to clean up. By the way, some man keeps calling here for Stephanie. He's rude, too. I told him she was away on maternity leave, but he keeps calling anyway."

Patrick, Liam, and Hannah instantly became alert.

"Why didn't you tell me this?" Patrick asked.

"Men call here for Stephanie all the time, Patrick, you should know that by now. Just because she married you doesn't mean other men don't find her attractive. I'm still trying to figure out what she saw in you."

"Enough, Candy, and I mean it. This isn't the time or the place. You know we've had some serious theft going on here. If Max hadn't vouched for your character and honesty, Hannah and Liam would probably be running a background check on you right now."

Candy's mouth dropped open like a treasure chest. "Do *you* think *I* have something to do with all this theft, Patrick? Because if you do, I am quitting right this very second. You really are an asshole, you know that!"

"Candy, wait!" Patrick called out, but she was already heading for the back of the store.

"I shouldn't have said that. Candy Lee is one of the best employees we have. Excuse me while I go to apologize."

"Don't bother, I heard you," Candy Lee called out from the back of the store. "I'm telling Max, too, just so you know," she said as she made her way back to the front of the store.

"Seriously, Candy Lee, tell me about this man you said was calling Stephanie."

"Yes, you should. It might be something, or not," Hannah said as kindly as possible. The young girl's feelings had been hurt. She felt bad for her and would try to make it up to her later. Patrick was a bit of an asshole, but she knew he was good at his job. His relationship with Candy Lee was rough, but one could tell that they really did like each other. At least that was Hannah's current assessment of the situation.

Liam whipped out his ever-present iPad. "Can you remember how long ago this particular man began calling?"

Candy Lee took a deep breath, then slowly let it out. It was a calming technique Hannah recognized.

"About a month ago. I remember because he called like three times in one day. He was rude, but then I got rude back, and he started acting all ass-kissy with me. I tried to explain to him that I didn't know when Stephanie was coming back to work. She'd just had a son, I told him. She wants to spend as much time with her baby and the girls as possible. He hung up on me that time."

"I'll get the phone records, though I doubt it will do any good," Hannah said. "Unless you can be as specific as possible with dates and times."

"He usually calls in the morning, that much I know. Right after we open. I think he's probably some perv who saw Stephanie in the shop and is getting his kicks by calling all the time."

"Okay, it's time to open up. Candy Lee, you make sure to show Hannah the ropes. If anyone, and I mean anyone, lays a finger on her while she's prancing around, she has Max's and my permission to knock the shit out of him." Patrick grinned at Candy Lee, and she grinned back.

"Can I add a punch, too?" she asked eagerly.

"If you have to. What I need from you more than anything is to monitor the phone. If this guy calls, I want you to write down the exact time he called, and look at the caller ID. Shit, why didn't I think of that?" Patrick asked.

"I already did. It comes up as a private number," Candy informed them.

"Then I'll need you to record the exact time. Try to remember exactly what he says. Get a feel for him; ask him a question. Come on to him if you have to, or say something to piss the guy off. His tongue might loosen a bit," Patrick indicated.

"He's right, Candy," Hannah said. "Try to get friendly with him, see what he says. Now, I'm going to set up in the back office. Patrick, you want to show me around?"

Hannah hated walking out of the room without telling Liam 'bye, or see you later, but the doors opened, and a crowd of skiers piled in.

And they were all wearing red ski suits.

Chapter 12

Hannah managed to get through twelve of the applications in between strutting her stuff and acting like an airhead. Candy Lee sold six of the ski suits at fifteen hundred bucks a pop. No wonder Max's sales receipts were off the charts. Maybe she should invest in a ski resort herself. It was almost four o'clock by the time Candy Lee told her the doors were locked. "That guy didn't call today. I wish he would. I want to help catch him. I wish I'd paid more attention."

"That's okay; you didn't know. I sent my associate a printout of the phone bills for the past three months. She'll find something. She's good." Max had e-mailed her copies of all the bills and she'd sent them to Camden, explaining about the modeling job that kept her out on the floor. Camden said she wanted overtime pay. Hannah agreed, and remembered to ask her to call as soon as she returned from her Hanukkah date with Art.

Hannah had hoped Liam would stop by, but he hadn't. They were here to work, and she had to remember that. If time permitted, maybe she'd invite him for a drink tonight. In her condo. She'd invite him for a working dinner. She would cook. She loved to cook. While she made dinner, he could go through the files.

No! No! No!

She had to forget about spending time with Liam, at least until they finished this job. She was ashamed at her own thoughts.

"That dude is out back in the yellow Hummer waiting for you," Candy Lee said. "He's been there for about thirty minutes."

"Let me get my laptop," she said, hurrying to the back office and grabbing her purse and computer.

She was about to leave through the back door when Candy Lee stopped her. "Wait! You need tomorrow's ski suit. I've spent quite some time looking you over today. I think we need to put you in something tighter, not so warm. So, this is what I want you to wear tomorrow." She handed her two large shopping bags. "Don't worry, I've got all the right sizes. You'll like this outfit, too. It's partially red. Now, go on so I can lock up."

Hannah gave the girl a hug. She really liked Candy Lee in spite of the tough exterior she showed the world. "I'll see you tomorrow at nine o'clock sharp," Hannah said before hurrying out the door.

Liam waited in the Hummer. Hannah knocked on the window before opening the passenger-side door. "Didn't mean to startle you. Candy Lee said you'd been out here for a while. You should've come inside. The kid makes a mean hot chocolate." She put the bags on the backseat, then fastened her seat belt. She looked at Liam. He wasn't wearing his seat belt.

"Buckle up," she said as he backed out of the parking place.

"Yes, ma'am. Bad habit, I know."

"So, did you work on the system? Any chance you found the thief who's stealing Max's money?"

"I have a couple of hits, but nothing is one hundred percent yet. All the hits were at one of the five or six local Internet cafés. That doesn't make it easy, but it's not so difficult that I won't catch them. They were all in the late afternoon, so whoever is doing this is probably a local. Goes to one of the cafés when he knows most of the locals are either working or on the slopes. There is no obvious pattern as to which of the cafés they go to on a given day. With only fifteen transfers so far, it could take months before an outsider could find the pattern. And it could be a function of the traffic at the cafés.

"It's not much, but it's something. I called Max. Told him what I'd found. I also told him about the calls Candy Lee's been getting. His antennae went up immediately. Did you get anything back on the phone records?"

"I haven't checked my e-mail yet. If there was something significant, Camden would've called. So I guess that means no." And her heart leapt with joy. She'd get to work another day at The Snow Zone, prancing and probing. Never in a million years had she ever had even the slightest thought that she would enjoy spending time at a ski resort, much less modeling for an appreciative audience. Never say never, her dad had always said. And damned if he wasn't right.

"So we spend the rest of the night going over more of the applications," Hannah said.

"Actually, Max gave me the night off," Liam said.

"Lucky you," Hannah replied sullenly, like a pouting child.

"And lucky you, too, if you accept my invitation."

"Okay, where and what time?" Hannah said a bit too quickly.

Liam chuckled. "Anxious for a night out on the town? Even though it's supposed to drop way below zero tonight?"

"I'll wear this jacket. I kid you not, I haven't been cold at all today. Whatever this stuff is made of really does work."

"I can guarantee that if it didn't, there wouldn't be as many skiers out in this crazy weather."

"I believe you."

"A friend of Max's wife is directing a Christmas play tonight at the local high school. He asked us to join him. Said to tell you Grace and Ella would be there, and Stephanie and her girls, plus a few others he wanted you and me to meet. Are you game?"

She'd never been to a Christmas play in her life. Of course she was game. She'd spend the night out in the cold if Liam McConnell were beside her.

"Sure, it'll be a fun way to kill some time. When should I be ready?"

"The play starts at seven, so say, six thirty?"

"Six thirty it is," Hannah said.

Thirty minutes later, she was soaking in the tub and singing at the top of her lungs.

"'Jolly old Saint Nicholas, lean your ear this way . . .'"

Chapter 13

The school gymnasium was packed as it was opening night for *A Christmas Carol*. The play was being directed by Angelica Shepard, a former Broadway star who'd recently married Dr. Parker North, a trauma doctor from Denver. This information was included in the program they received as they made their way to the front row, where Max had reserved two seats for them. They'd made a few wrong turns trying to find Telluride High, which had cost them precious time. They'd planned to meet Max's other guests before the start of the show, and they still would, but not until afterward.

Hannah wore a pair of slim-fitting black wool slacks with her black boots. She wore the purple, red, and black ski top Candy Lee had given her for tomorrow and its matching jacket, hat, scarf, and gloves. Her legs were a bit cold, but her upper body was warm and toasty, just as Candy Lee had explained.

They settled into their seats. The crowded gymnasium was completely silent except for the sound of a baby with the hiccups. A few soft laughs could be heard, then all went silent as the deep maroon curtains were opened.

Hannah watched in fascination as the young actors and actresses performed the story of Ebenezer Scrooge. The stage was set to resemble an old house in need of repair. The young student in the starring role performed as though Charles Dickens's tale of Scrooge had been written for him exclusively. When Scrooge was later visited by the ghost of his former business partner, Jacob Marley, the audience oohed and ahhed. A couple of small children cried and were taken out of the gymnasium.

Hannah couldn't take her eyes away from the stage. She was so caught up in the action, she didn't realize that Liam had taken her hand in his until he gave her a squeeze when the Ghost of Christmas Present took Scrooge to visit the impoverished Bob Cratchit, where he was introduced to a very ill Tiny Tim, who might die because Scrooge was too cheap to pay Bob Cratchit a decent wage. In Act Two, when the Ghost of Christmas Yet to Come frightens Scrooge with visions of his own death, and former associates will only attend his funeral if lunch is served, Hannah gave Liam a return squeeze. In the final scene, when Scrooge was transformed on Christmas morning, with love and joy filling his heart, Hannah's eyes filled with tears. This was her during Christmas, minus all the mean stuff.

The audience gave the kids a standing ovation, and the clapping lasted so long that Hannah's hands were beginning to sting. She'd never been so touched by something so simple. Though she knew the story, she'd never really connected its true meaning to herself, but this was so her. She'd even referred to herself as Ms. Scrooge. No more. She wiped the free-flowing tears from her face and sat down when the director, Angelica, came out onto the stage. She thanked her students, the parents, the volunteers, and the art department at the local community college. And once again, there was a standing ovation.

When all the excitement had simmered down a bit, Max said he wanted to introduce Hannah and Liam to the guests they were supposed to have met before the play.

"They're serving cookies and punch in the cafeteria. Let's meet up there; we'll be able to hear better."

Liam and Hannah followed Max through the crowded gymnasium down a long hall that was decorated with Christmas trees cut from green construction paper. Bells and angels and snowflakes had been placed neatly on bulletin boards. Hannah couldn't get enough of the cheery scene. How had she missed this as a child? It wasn't as though she'd had a bad childhood. Her father had been wonderful, but sadly, he hadn't bothered to share the joy one should share with a child and their loved ones during this festive time of year. Like the fictitious character created by Charles Dickens, Hannah had experienced a life-changing moment, only hers wasn't nearly as dramatic as the story of Scrooge. But it was far more of an eye-opener. She would not let another minute pass without being forever thankful to Angelica Shepard and the students at Telluride High. As a matter of fact, she had all those millions at home just sitting in the bank. She would find something charitable that she could be a part of, maybe something to help children from abusive homes.

Yes! That was it. She would talk to Grace later and see what she thought of the idea.

Cheered by her newly discovered love for Christmas and the joy it brought to so many, Hannah couldn't wait to call Camden and tell her about her experience.

In the cafeteria, Max had gathered a large group of people, and one by one, he introduced Hannah and Liam.

"This is Stephanie, Patrick's wife. And this"—Max fluffed the blond curls on the head of a little baby boy—"is Shannon Patrick Edward O'Brien, future Olympian."

"You don't know that," said a young girl with dark brown hair and large brown eyes. She appeared to be around ten or so.

"Amanda, mind your manners," Stephanie said. "This is my daughter, Amanda. And this"—Stephanie motioned for another girl, who had been talking with a group of kids her age and was the spitting image of Amanda to come over—"is Ashley, who is thirteen."

Both girls shook hands with Hannah and Liam.

Next they were introduced to Ella, Max and Grace's daughter. "I'm three," she said, and held up three pudgy fingers.

"It's nice to meet you, Ella. I am three, too, but twice," Hannah explained to the little girl with dark hair and green eyes just like her mother's.

The little girl didn't have a clue what Hannah was referring to, but since everyone else laughed, she laughed right along with them.

"This is Bryce, Grace's brother, and his beautiful wife, Melanie."

More handshaking and nice-to-meet-yous. Hannah knew she wouldn't remember everyone's name, but at least when Max spoke of them, she would be able to recall their faces. Faces she always remembered; names . . . well, not so much. That was Camden's job.

Patrick kept looking around, then spied a couple, raced across the room, and practically dragged them across the cafeteria. "This is my sister Claire and her fiancé, Quinn Connor. They're attorneys, too. Quinn is from Ireland."

Liam stepped forward to shake his hand. "Nice to meet ya," he said with an overly exaggerated Irish accent.

"And ya, too," Quinn said in a genuine Irish accent. "We'll have to talk shop another time."

"Nice meeting you both," Hannah said. There were so many people, she was a bit overwhelmed by it all. In a good way.

"Okay, I think you've met most of the clan. We're all going to Eagles Nest for a late dinner, minus the kiddies, of course, if you want to join us. We'll take the gondola up, though. No snow coach this time." Max searched the group, stopping when his eyes found Grace. They were a handsome couple, Hannah thought. Though she didn't think Max could hold a candle to Liam, but now wasn't the time or place for those kinds of thoughts.

"Do you want to go?" Liam asked her.

"I'm game if you are," Hannah said excitedly. "I am hungry, come to think of it. I don't think I've eaten since breakfast."

"Then I'll take that as a yes." To Max, he said, "We'll meet up in say"—Liam looked at his watch—"half an hour?"

"Perfect. Grace's mother, Juanita, is in town tonight, so she'll handle the kiddies. She's got some help, I think." Max looked at Grace.

"Yes, her *beau,* as she calls him, is hanging around tonight," Grace said. "Mom is a widow, but I think that might change soon."

"How nice," Hannah said. "I guess we'll see you at dinner."

Finally, they were able to make their escape. When they were inside the Hummer, Hannah leaned back against the headrest. "I think this has been the best evening of my life. And to think what I've missed all these years. I am going to make up for it, I promise."

"What have you missed?" Liam asked as he carefully maneuvered through the parking lot.

"Christmas. I've missed Christmas."

On the drive to the gondola, Hannah gave him the condensed version of her life and her distaste for the holidays.

"I've never been big on celebrations, but I never had anyone to celebrate with. But now I think that's changed for me as well."

Hannah said nothing. She let the silence of the night envelop her and wrap her in the best gift of all.

The future and all its possibilities.

Chapter 14

The next day, nothing happened at The Snow Zone. No calls, no weirdos wanting to poke her. And when Camden called, there was no news on the phone records. She'd stayed out too late last night and enjoyed every single moment, but today she was truly tuckered out. And to think she'd agreed to ski with Liam after they'd finished up for the day.

Max met up with them long enough to tell them the slopes were theirs for as long as they wanted and insisted on keeping two of the bunny-hill lifts open just for them.

"This is employee time, too. Don't forget, these people live to ski. Tasha and Terrence are skiing, too. Don't say anything to either of them. I want to watch her first. If I see she's got a bit of talent, I'll pop up on the slopes. I need to loosen the old bones anyway. Haven't had time to ski."

Hannah and Candy Lee went to the rental shop, where she was fitted with ski boots, beginner skis, and poles. "Oh. My. Gosh. My feet feel like they weigh a ton," Hannah said as she slowly walked out of the rental shop.

"You'll feel as light as a feather once you start gliding through the snow. We have four inches of fresh powder. It'll be perfect for you. Have fun." Candy Lee waved and headed for her car. She had a date tonight, and she had told Hannah that while she could ski anytime she wanted, she didn't always have a date. Hannah told her that she completely understood.

Liam waited for her at the bottom of the bunny hill. She carried her skis over her shoulder as she'd been instructed. She dropped them on the snow-covered ground next to Liam's. "I'm a bit nervous. Are you?"

"A little, but you're with me. I won't let anything happen to you." He looked in her eyes, and Hannah knew what was going to happen next.

His lips were warm when they touched hers. He tasted like peppermint and chocolate. She kissed him back, softly, her lips gently touching his. The slight kiss sent butterflies to her stomach, and she was sure they were dancing. Liam raised his mouth from hers and gazed into her eyes. "This is okay?" he asked.

She didn't bother to answer with words. She stood on her tiptoes in the uncomfortable ski boots and pressed her mouth against his. Waves of desire burned in the center of her, unlike any she'd ever experienced. Liam took that as a sign and deepened the kiss. He parted her lips with his tongue, and she allowed him free rein over her lips, her tongue, her teeth. He continued to explore her mouth until the sound of a snowmobile blasting past them brought them back to earth.

They broke away from one another, and each felt a bit shy, different, as though their first kiss had changed the status of their relationship. And it had, for both of them.

Terrence and Tasha came flying through the snow once again, stopping this time when they saw that the couple was no longer in a lip-lock.

"I knew you two were a couple; don't ask me how, but I did," Terrence said as soon as he removed his helmet. "This is Tasha."

"I've heard a lot of good things about you. Your brother told me about your dream of becoming an Olympic skier. I think it's fantastic."

"Thanks," Tasha said shyly. She was petite but muscular. Her honey-colored skin was flushed from the cold, but Hannah knew the girl could have cared less. She saw two sets of skis hooked on the back of the snowmobile. "I'd love to see you ski a bit before I give it a try. Maybe I can learn something from you," Hannah said, then looked at Liam and winked. He knew what she was up to. He gave her a slight nod.

Tasha put her skis on first, then her helmet and gloves, along with a pair of goggles. "You're not supposed to go on the mountain without goggles unless it's sunny. Right, Terrence?" She looked to her brother for approval.

"Right, but Miss Ray and Mr. McConnell are guests of Mr. Jorgenson. I think he'll let them get by without them just this once."

At the mention of Max's name, Tasha's eyes lit up like a Christmas tree. "He's the best, you know. Ever."

"So I hear. Go ahead, show us your stuff. We'll be waiting here."

Tasha didn't need to be told twice. She and Terrence took the lift up to the top of the mountain. Somewhere out there, Max would watch her, and she'd either get her hopes and dreams crushed, or—and for some reason, Hannah was almost sure this would be the case—Max might've found another gold-medal winner.

Twenty minutes later, Tasha came flying down to the bottom of the mountain like a speed demon, but graceful as ever. Terrence was several hundred feet behind her, but both Hannah and Liam saw Max in the distance as he slowed down, waiting for Terrence to join his sister at the bottom of the run.

When they'd taken off their helmets and poled their way over to where Hannah and Liam waited, Max zoomed down the rest of the run, then stopped beside them, sending snow flying through the air.

"Max Jorgenson!" Tasha shouted. "I. Can't. Believe. This."

Terrence appeared to be truly shocked. Neither was expecting to see Max. Hannah was thrilled to be here to share in the moment. She knew just by the look on Max's face that he'd seen something special in Tasha, just as Terrence had said.

"How would you like to have me as your new coach?" Max asked the young girl.

There were no words. Just happy tears and hugs.

All those present knew that they would never forget this moment: the birth of a new Olympic-class skier.

Chapter 15

Hannah and Liam had spent the better part of the next day locating the culprit who'd hacked into The Snow Zone's computer system. The result had come as a shock to everyone, except for Stephanie.

Glenn Marshall, her abusive ex-husband, who'd recently gotten out of prison early for good behavior, had been behind the entire plot. While serving time in the state penitentiary in Cañon City, Colorado, he'd become best buds with his cellmate, a young guy who happened to be serving the tail end of a five-year sentence for credit-card fraud and identity theft. He was smart and computer savvy, and Glenn saw him as a way to grab some heavy-duty cash, as well as to spy on his ex-wife and daughters.

Philip, the computer expert, had been out of prison for

three months before Glenn was released and had used the time to case the joint, so to speak. With what he had learned, they'd plotted to steal as much money as they could from The Snow Zone. The next part of their plan was to travel to Mexico, where they would open a strip club with the money they had stolen.

When her ex was identified as one of the perpetrators, Stephanie was shocked, humiliated, and mortified. Grace and Max knew this was in no way her fault, and, to be on the safe side until things settled down, both insisted that she and Patrick take the girls to Hawaii for the rest of the year. Not wanting to put his family in harm's way, Patrick agreed immediately and was now training Terrence to act as his temporary replacement. Max would be there, too, but this also provided an opportunity to help out Terrence and Tasha. They were good kids with a bright future ahead of them. They needed a break, and it seemed that this year Santa was in a very giving mood.

Tonight was the big ski party, when the main trails would be lit up just like a real Christmas tree, and Tasha would get to show her stuff to the locals and the media. Max had dropped a few hints, and before he knew it, the lighting party had become the big event of the Christmas season at Maximum Glide.

The biggest surprise of all: Hannah absolutely loved to ski! She'd picked it up instantly that first evening on the slopes, and in a matter of two days was skiing the blue runs like an old pro. She and Liam were both having the time of their lives. She hated to go home, but she knew that while this was a special time for both her and Liam, their relationship would deepen when they returned to Florida. Her heart felt light, and she knew that was because she was falling madly in love with Liam McConnell.

And he felt the same way; he'd hinted as much when he'd kissed her a second time.

Lovestruck? Yes! Snow? Yes!

Cold? Absolutely!

Epilogue

The ski runs were as bright as the stars as several hundred people waited to see the girl who was being touted as the next Lindsey Vonn.

Tasha Alexander was sixteen years old, and after tonight, her life would change forever.

The announcer called for Tasha to take her mark at the top of the mountain. Crowds were gathered at the base of the mountain, all hoping to catch a glimpse of the new Olympic hopeful. Though she had obviously missed the February 2014 Winter Olympics in Sochi, the sixteen-year-old Tasha would be ready for the Winter Olympics in PyeongChang, South Korea, come 2018.

All watched in silence as the petite girl wearing a hot-pink ski suit flew down the mountain, weaved in and out of the flags without touching a single one, and came to a perfect stop at the end of the run, where the crowd cheered her on, beginning to chant, "Tasha, Tasha, Tasha."

She bowed and waved her hot-pink helmet in the cold night air.

"You know that we're watching history tonight," Hannah said as she and Liam stood with Max and Grace in a special stand set up for the media.

"I know. And we're going to share our own history, too. You okay with that?" Liam whispered in her ear, sending goose bumps down her spine.

"I'm very definitely okay with it."

"Then let's go home to Florida tonight. Pierce can be here in a matter of hours."

Hannah didn't want to ruin the moment, but right now she didn't want to return to Florida. And she had to tell him why.

"I don't think I've ever told this to anyone, but I'm going to tell you. On Christmas Eve, I'll turn thirty-four. I have never had a birthday present that wasn't wrapped in Christmas paper. I would love to have a real, bona fide birthday party at Eagles Nest. Does that sound childish or what?"

"Wow! I had no clue. You should have told me."

"Well, it isn't something a grown woman goes around telling. It's silly, but I remember when I was little, I always felt slighted, cheated in a way. Dad was great, but never once did he bother to wrap any of my birthday gifts in anything except Christmas paper. I always felt like my birthdays were too much trouble since they were on Christmas Eve."

"Well, Ms. Ray, I will make you a promise. From now on, you are going to have the biggest and the best birthday party money and I can plan and buy. But right now, how would you feel about taking a midnight stroll through the snow?"

"I never thought I'd hear myself say this, but I would love to." Hannah stopped. "I forgot something. I need to make a phone call. I know this is bad timing, but I promised Camden I would call and check on Leanne and Art."

"Okay. I'll just step aside and give you some privacy," Liam said, then turned to walk away.

"No! I want you beside me. In case I get too cold. You'll have to wrap me in your arms to keep me warm."

"Now there's an idea for some birthday-party wrap. Me and you," Liam said. He kissed her, then pulled her next to him.

"Now make that phone call and be quick about it. I can't wait to take that walk and smooch in the snow."

Hannah laughed loudly. This was almost too good to be true. But it is what it is, and she was going with it. All of her reservations about the holidays and men were going to be a thing of the past, just like the Ghost of Christmas Past in *A Christmas Carol*.

She dialed Camden's number. Camden answered on the first ring.

"You're late; you realize that, don't you?"

"Yes, I do, but I have a good excuse. Now, first of all, tell me about Leanne."

"She's still in the hospital, but I convinced her to get an order of protection. She's agreed, and I've taken care of all the paperwork. All I'm waiting for is Judge Sturgis to sign the papers. The cowardly hubby has skipped town, but that was to be expected. With all that family money behind him, I'm sure they'll keep him hidden for a very long time. Leanne said she wants to return to Hope

House when she gets out of the hospital. I told her we would make all the necessary arrangements. You think your friend Grace will let her go back?"

"Of course she will. I'll call her tomorrow and explain the situation. Grace will help her, I'm sure. Now, we haven't talked about your date with Art. How was it? Is he a keeper? Did you like his family? Do they like you?"

"Good grief, Hannah, you sound exactly like my mother! I swear, if I didn't know better, I'd think she had been reincarnated and come back as you. I mean that in a funny way, so don't say anything. Art. Okay. Art is absolutely the nicest guy I've met in a very long time. His mom and dad are two adorable little Jewish people with white hair and sparkly blue eyes. They sort of reminded me of a miniature Mr. and Mrs. Claus, but I didn't want to tell them that, them being Jewish and all. Seriously, they're adorable. I can't wait for you to meet them. You should taste her potato latkes. They're to die for. So, now that you've caught that lousy thief, when are you coming home? I just bought Stephen King's latest book for our beach staycation. I hate lying out alone."

"I'm not sure when I'll be home. I know for a fact that I'll be staying here long enough to celebrate my birthday."

"Okay, there is something you're not telling me. Spit it out."

"What makes you think that?" Hannah asked, her voice radiating the joy that suffused her entire being.

"Come on, Hannah. How long have we known each other?"

"I can't remember. Long enough."

"Well, if you really want to know, it's been seven years, three months, and two days. That is how long we've known one another. Long enough for me to know you're keeping something from me. Now spit it out."

Hannah took a deep breath, wrapped her free arm around Liam's waist, and whispered into the phone, "I think I've met the man of my dreams."

She looked up at Liam. He whispered in her ear, "And I know I've met the woman of *my* dreams."

"I can't hear you, speak a little louder," Camden said.

"I am only going to say this once more, then I am going to hang up because I have been invited for a midnight stroll through the snow with *the man of my dreams*!"

"You're kidding me, right?"

"No, Camden. I have never been this serious in my life. One more time. Liam McConnell, the security dude I told you about, the one with the Learjet. He is the man of my dreams, and I am going to hang up now so I can go on that stroll. Good night, Camden."

" 'Night, Hannah. And hey, congratulations."

Hannah pushed the END button on her phone, then turned to the man of her dreams.

"Are you ready to take that stroll now? I think I've got everything that needs to be under control controlled."

"Let's go, Hannah Ray. I've waited for this moment for a lifetime," Liam said, his voice filled with love.

"Ditto, Liam. Ditto."

Together, hand in hand, they strolled down the snowy path, knowing that this was just the beginning.

Connect with Us

Visit us online at
KensingtonBooks.com
to read more from your favorite authors, see books
by series, view reading group guides, and more.

 Join us on social media

for sneak peeks, chances to win books and prize packs,
and to share your thoughts with other readers.

facebook.com/kensingtonpublishing
twitter.com/kensingtonbooks

Tell us what you think!

To share your thoughts, submit a review,
or sign up for our eNewsletters, please visit:
KensingtonBooks.com/TellUs.

Books by Bestselling Author
Fern Michaels

___ **The Jury**	0-8217-7878-1	$6.99US/$9.99CAN
___ **Sweet Revenge**	0-8217-7879-X	$6.99US/$9.99CAN
___ **Lethal Justice**	0-8217-7880-3	$6.99US/$9.99CAN
___ **Free Fall**	0-8217-7881-1	$6.99US/$9.99CAN
___ **Fool Me Once**	0-8217-8071-9	$7.99US/$10.99CAN
___ **Vegas Rich**	0-8217-8112-X	$7.99US/$10.99CAN
___ **Hide and Seek**	1-4201-0184-6	$6.99US/$9.99CAN
___ **Hokus Pokus**	1-4201-0185-4	$6.99US/$9.99CAN
___ **Fast Track**	1-4201-0186-2	$6.99US/$9.99CAN
___ **Collateral Damage**	1-4201-0187-0	$6.99US/$9.99CAN
___ **Final Justice**	1-4201-0188-9	$6.99US/$9.99CAN
___ **Up Close and Personal**	0-8217-7956-7	$7.99US/$9.99CAN
___ **Under the Radar**	1-4201-0683-X	$6.99US/$9.99CAN
___ **Razor Sharp**	1-4201-0684-8	$7.99US/$10.99CAN
___ **Yesterday**	1-4201-1494-8	$5.99US/$6.99CAN
___ **Vanishing Act**	1-4201-0685-6	$7.99US/$10.99CAN
___ **Sara's Song**	1-4201-1493-X	$5.99US/$6.99CAN
___ **Deadly Deals**	1-4201-0686-4	$7.99US/$10.99CAN
___ **Game Over**	1-4201-0687-2	$7.99US/$10.99CAN
___ **Sins of Omission**	1-4201-1153-1	$7.99US/$10.99CAN
___ **Sins of the Flesh**	1-4201-1154-X	$7.99US/$10.99CAN
___ **Cross Roads**	1-4201-1192-2	$7.99US/$10.99CAN

Available Wherever Books Are Sold!
Check out our website at **www.kensingtonbooks.com**

More by Bestselling Author
Hannah Howell

__Highland Angel	978-1-4201-0864-4	$6.99US/$8.99CAN
__If He's Sinful	978-1-4201-0461-5	$6.99US/$8.99CAN
__Wild Conquest	978-1-4201-0464-6	$6.99US/$8.99CAN
__If He's Wicked	978-1-4201-0460-8	$6.99US/$8.49CAN
__My Lady Captor	978-0-8217-7430-4	$6.99US/$8.49CAN
__Highland Sinner	978-0-8217-8001-5	$6.99US/$8.49CAN
__Highland Captive	978-0-8217-8003-9	$6.99US/$8.49CAN
__Nature of the Beast	978-1-4201-0435-6	$6.99US/$8.49CAN
__Highland Fire	978-0-8217-7429-8	$6.99US/$8.49CAN
__Silver Flame	978-1-4201-0107-2	$6.99US/$8.49CAN
__Highland Wolf	978-0-8217-8000-8	$6.99US/$9.99CAN
__Highland Wedding	978-0-8217-8002-2	$4.99US/$6.99CAN
__Highland Destiny	978-1-4201-0259-8	$4.99US/$6.99CAN
__Only for You	978-0-8217-8151-7	$6.99US/$8.99CAN
__Highland Promise	978-1-4201-0261-1	$4.99US/$6.99CAN
__Highland Vow	978-1-4201-0260-4	$4.99US/$6.99CAN
__Highland Savage	978-0-8217-7999-6	$6.99US/$9.99CAN
__Beauty and the Beast	978-0-8217-8004-6	$4.99US/$6.99CAN
__Unconquered	978-0-8217-8088-6	$4.99US/$6.99CAN
__Highland Barbarian	978-0-8217-7998-9	$6.99US/$9.99CAN
__Highland Conqueror	978-0-8217-8148-7	$6.99US/$9.99CAN
__Conqueror's Kiss	978-0-8217-8005-3	$4.99US/$6.99CAN
__A Stockingful of Joy	978-1-4201-0018-1	$4.99US/$6.99CAN
__Highland Bride	978-0-8217-7995-8	$4.99US/$6.99CAN
__Highland Lover	978-0-8217-7759-6	$6.99US/$9.99CAN

Available Wherever Books Are Sold!

Check out our website at
http://www.kensingtonbooks.com